all the perils of this night

other works by
Elizabeth Cunningham

Novels

The Return of the Goddess

The Wild Mother

How to Spin Gold

THE MAEVE CHRONICLES:

Magdalen Rising
The Passion of Mary Magdalen
Bright Dark Madonna
Red-Robed Priestess

Murder at the Rummage Sale

Poetry

Small Bird

Wild Mercy

So Ecstasy Can Find You

Tell Me the Story Again

Graphic Novels

The Book of Madge (Her Book)

Musical Work

MaevenSong: A Musical Odyssey Through The Maeve Chronicles

all
the
perils
of
this
night

Elizabeth
Cunningham

IMAGINATION FURY ARTS
Nashville, TN

Printed in the United States of America
Book and cover design by Ray Curenton

LIBRARY OF CONGRESS CATALOGING-IN-PUBLICATION DATA
Names: Cunningham, Elizabeth, 1953- author.
Title: All the perils of this night / Elizabeth Cunningham.
Description: First edition. | Nashville, TN : Imagination Fury Arts, [2020]
Identifiers: LCCN 2020027730 (print) | LCCN 2020027731 (ebook) | ISBN 9781944190149 (hardcover) | ISBN 9781944190156 (paperback) | ISBN 9781944190163 (ebook)
Classification: LCC PS3553.U473 (print) | LCC PS3553.U473 (ebook) | DDC 813/.54--dc23
LC record available at https://lccn.loc.gov/2020027730
LC ebook record available at https://lccn.loc.gov/2020027731

First Edition

First Impression

Imagination Fury Arts
imaginationfuryarts.com

prologue
Perilous Night

July 1968

Hold me, Katherine wants to say, but she doesn't want to hear him say no. Instead she takes off her shirt, and then her bra. Surely he will touch her. She needs him to touch her everywhere, to erase that other....

"Am I too ugly?" she asks, and the tears spill over.

"No," Frankie says.

"Then touch me, just touch me. You don't have to be my boyfriend or anything, I just need you to touch me."

And he does. It feels like the sun is touching her. The tears keep coming without sound, and he touches those, too. Then he holds her.

"Who hurt you? Tell me, Katherine, tell me. I'll beat them up for you. I'm your brother."

She wants to stay here, in this dream. She will not open her eyes, she will not—

Katherine woke up.

Where was she?

Streetlight came in through a barred window. Outside someone kicked a garbage can and cursed. There was a bed and sheets that didn't feel clean. She didn't feel clean. She had to go to the bathroom, badly. When she got out of bed, she felt stiff. Everything hurt. Her head hurt; she might have to throw up. She moved slowly across the room, feeling for a door. Why was she naked? She couldn't go out of the room without anything on. She went back and wrapped herself in the sheet. She just had to get to the bathroom; then she'd figure out where she was.

In a bar of light, a doorknob. She turned it, but nothing happened. She turned it the other way. It was broken. She shook it and turned it some more.

It was locked.

She began pounding on the door, and finally she cried out, "Help! The door's locked, help!"

(Was someone screaming? He paused on the threshold of the stairs. One of his little girls? That's right. A new one had been brought in today. They did take on so. At first. He hesitated a moment, then looked at his poised foot, large yet elegant in a velvet Prince Albert slipper. More pounding. A nuisance, but he would not hear it for long. He mounted the staircase, the heavy door closing behind him.)

Lucy Way sat bolt upright in bed. For a moment she hardly knew where she was, it was that dark. But someone had been screaming for help.

"Katherine?" she called out loud.

And then she swung her legs out of bed, orienting herself by the crack of light under her bedroom door. Of course, she was at home, of course. At home alone. But she couldn't help herself. She went down the hall to the room she now called Katherine's and opened the door, hall light spilling onto the empty sleigh bed, neatly made, the satin quilts Katherine loved folded at the foot.

"Shirrup with that filfy racket!" someone shouted, a woman's voice.

"The door's locked!" Katherine called. "Help me, please! I have to go to the bathroom."

"Wot! Wot's she on about, a bath in the middle of the bloody night?"

The woman was English. Now she remembered. She was in England. They said "loo."

"I have to go to the loo!" Katherine was almost sobbing now.

"You got a pot under yer bed, ain't you? Shut your gob and let decent folk sleep."

"Where am I?" she said, this time in a whisper.

"Katherine!" Lucy called her name again, though of course the child wasn't there; she was an ocean away.

Still, Lucy left the door to the room open, as if to hear her if she cried out again, and went back to her own room. Pulling a thin cushion from under her bed, her only concession to her years, Lucy knelt.

"Defend, O Lord, this thy child from all the perils of this night."

No other words came to her, so she prayed them over and over, aloud, then silently, till she laid her head down on the bed and, without meaning to, fell into a fitful sleep.

(Inside his rooms, he took off his evening jacket and dress pants. He set his top hat on its stand, but his slippers stayed on as he wrapped his majestic bulk in his silk dressing gown. Ah. He closed the brocade curtains. The world outside wasn't real. He lumbered into his sumptuous bed. He would have a look at the new girl tomorrow, see what role might suit her best.)

Where was she? How did she get here? Back on the bed, Katherine searched her memory, terrifyingly blank, for some clue.

Her aunt had been in the hospital for minor surgery, so her uncle had sent her out with a map to explore London. Katherine had been wearing a hat, purple, flowered, she'd bought for a quarter at the rummage sale. A man sat down next to her on a park bench.

"What's your name, luv, if you don't mind my asking."

That's when it happened.

"Eliza. Eliza Doolittle."

Full out cockney.

"Well, Liza, if I may call you that, I know a quiet little pub nor far from 'ere. 'ow 'bout I stand you to a pint or two?"

"Don't mind if I do, I'm sure," said Eliza Doolittle.

"You're a funny little bird, ain't you?" the man said, standing up. "Come on, then."

She couldn't remember anything more. The room started to spin, and Katherine felt herself falling asleep. Of course she wasn't awake. It was just a dream, a bad dream.

(He is having that hideous dream again. All the dolls on the shelf, sitting still where he'd put them, looking perfect, each one in her own costume. Then they start to move, their faces contort. They are singing a horrible song, like cats all yowling at once. They won't stop. Why won't they stop!)

In her dream, Lucy feels her neck begin to cramp, but she doesn't move, she mustn't move. She is kneeling beside a bed where Katherine lies huddled, alone and frightened.

Defend, O Lord, this thy child from all the perils of this night, defend, O Lord....

Lucy woke suddenly. The phone was ringing, though it was barely light.

Katherine, Katherine.

She struggled to her feet and ran to answer.

part one

What Happened Before

Chapter One

Katherine Bradley got out at the bus station at the corner of Market and Main Street in Riverton. She had never been in the city alone before, only with her mother when she took them clothes shopping at Lucky Platts or to buy shoes at a small store on a side street. She couldn't see any of those familiar sights. She had never been in this part of the city. It was ugly and beautiful at the same time, ugly with no trees, litter in the gutters, buildings without color, some boarded up, beautiful because the morning light made the sidewalks shine. Pigeons stirred the air with their sudden flight. Anything might happen. She was scared and glad at the same time.

Her father had won. Or maybe she had.

"But why can't you at least drive her to the place on your way to work?" her mother had pleaded after dinner last night.

Her parents were still in the dining room having cigarettes and coffee. The twins had gone outside to play Frisbee with the dog, Bear, who would tease them by stealing it and running away until they gave up in frustration. Katherine was in the living room, looking at a coffee table book of photographs of England. Her awful uncle Bob had gone there to work for a year, and her less awful aunt Pat had sent the book. Katherine wanted to see pictures of where the Beatles had grown up, but there wasn't much about Liverpool. She flipped to London instead, to Buckingham Palace, searching in vain for pictures of Prince Charles. Really she wasn't paying much attention to the book. It took too much concentration to eavesdrop.

"I told you. I have an early meeting on the other side of town. I'll pick her up in the afternoon. She can take the bus to Riverton."

"But tomorrow is her first day!" her mother protested.

"She's been to the daycare center before. She's met everyone. They're expecting her."

"Why can't someone come and meet her at the bus station. She's only fourteen!"

Her father made a sound, not unlike the one he made if he stubbed his toe or stumbled in the bathroom.

"She's starting high school in the fall," he argued. "You don't understand. The teachers are dealing with dozens of kids, with whole families in crisis, families who can't stretch the welfare check far enough to feed everyone. They can't spare someone to babysit Katherine. She's supposed to be there as a volunteer. To help."

"Fine then, I'll drive her. For God's sake, Gerald. You're the one who's glued to the nightly news. Every week there's another riot in another city. It's not safe."

There was a pause. Katherine could hear a cigarette lighter being flicked.

"What you really mean is it's not white," said her father, exhaling. She wondered if he were blowing smoke rings.

And Katherine knew her mother would have to back down. Or else it would prove that she was prejudiced. Maybe she was. Her mother had never approved of her best friend Aramantha Green. But then she didn't like Frankie Lomangino, either, and he was white, though lately he claimed he was really an Indian or part Indian.

"Listen, Anne. Riverton isn't Atlanta or Boston or even Buffalo. It's just an overgrown town. The daycare center is only five blocks from the bus station. You do enough chauffeuring of those kids."

Since her father had stopped being the minister at the church in the village and they'd moved five miles out into the country, they couldn't go anywhere without their mother driving them. Her father worked in Riverton, fifteen miles away, doing whatever he did, fighting the war on poverty, so why hadn't they moved there? Then no one would have to drive her.

"Don't the twins have swimming lessons or something in the mornings?" he went on. "You can drop her off at the bus on the way to the club. It's time Katherine learned to take care of herself. She lives too much in a fantasy world. You've told me yourself you worry about her."

Really, her mother worried about her? Katherine hadn't known that.

"It's time she got a glimpse of reality."

Reality was her father's favorite word. It usually had the adjective "grim" in front of it. It was almost synonymous (a word she had recently learned) with poverty and injustice. A few times at the dinner table, she had tried to argue that reality could be beautiful, too. Weren't beautiful things like trees or music just as real? Her father's voice was much louder than hers; his face turned red. His forefinger mashed her argument as if it were a cigarette to be stubbed out. She didn't know anything. She couldn't know anything. She was too young; she had always had it easy. She was (one of the dreaded words that started with S, like selfish and sin) spoiled.

Katherine's mother always came to comfort her after her father yelled at her. "I wish he were a better father to you," she'd say, but she would never take Katherine's side in an argument.

Now the dining room was still silent. Her mother had given up. In a moment, she'd clear the table, and the rattling dishes and silverware would speak for her. Katherine got up, leaving the book open on the floor. Her legs felt hot and shaky, like they might not hold her up, but she walked into the dining room with her head held high—as if she were Joan of Arc going to the stake.

"I'll take the bus to Riverton," she told her parents. "I want to take the bus."

She was gratified to see her father look startled—and, she thought, impressed. What a fearless daughter I have, she imagined him thinking. And it was true. It was reality. Hadn't she caught a murderer when she was only seven years old? How could she be afraid of taking a bus by herself?

"See, dear?" he said to her mother with the little smile that turned down instead of up.

Then he lit another cigarette.

Her mother cast her one glance, so swift Katherine couldn't tell if it was angry or worried, and she retreated to the kitchen.

And now, here she was. Turn left when you leave the bus station, her father had said. Turn right on Lower Main Street. Market Street was deserted except for an old lady with a cane, walking slowly on the other side of the street. She had so many clothes on, and her face was shadowed by a hat, Katherine couldn't tell if she was Negro or white. Even though there were no cars coming, she waited for the light to change at the corner of Market and Main. Then she started down the street. Here, there was not only paper trash, but broken glass, sharp and bright in the sunlight. Men sat on stoops, some of them drinking out of dark bottles. Women leaned out of upstairs windows.

She was the only white person on the street.

She thought of Aramantha, how so often she was the only Black person in a class. Did it bother her? Aramantha thought it was stupid for Katherine to do a volunteer job at a daycare center. "You're old enough now; you could make money babysitting." At sixteen, Aramantha had what she called a real job, as a file clerk at a law office, a job Katherine's father had helped her get. She wished Aramantha were with her now.

Katherine felt even more awkward wearing the khaki slacks her mother had insisted on, when she would have preferred jeans, and a striped, tailored, button-down shirt instead of a T-shirt, and loafers with tassels and white socks. (She would have liked to wear no socks.) Hardly anyone else walked on the street, just sat or leaned.

No one called out to her or asked her why she was there; they just let her pass, walk on. And on.

She was not afraid, she told herself. She was not afraid.

But, she realized, she had not kept count of the blocks. She hoped she would know the daycare center when she saw it. She crossed one more street, and then almost stopped. Music came from an upstairs window. The rhythm rolled over her, a harmonica wailed, and then a voice, sweet and gritty all at once. Out on the sidewalk on the other side of the street, a little girl, in a pink summer dress over diapers, danced in perfect time to the music.

In that moment, between one step and the next, everything changed.

Some part of her she hadn't known existed remembered something she could not possibly have known. Though she had no claim to it, somehow this music was hers, was her. She walked on, the music following her and changing how she moved.

In another block the music was lost in the din coming from a narrow black-topped playground wedged between two buildings behind a chain link fence. This was the daycare center, she was almost sure, but she couldn't remember how to get in the building. She stood uncertainly, watching the chaotic milling of children, some playing hopscotch, the squares drawn in chalk, some caught up in a wild game of tag.

"Who that white girl standing out there?" she heard someone say.

"Oh, my goodness!" A large woman answered. Mrs. Simmons, Katherine remembered. "That's Mr. Bradley's girl. She our volunteer. Kathy? Kathy?" she called.

It took Katherine a moment to know who she meant.

"Door's in the alley on the right. I'll come meet you."

By the time Katherine got there, the door was open, and Mrs. Simmons was gathering her in with one hand while holding on to a small boy with the other. The boy's hair was cropped so short she could see his scalp. His shorts were too big for him, and his bony knees made his legs look even thinner.

"I am so glad you're here," said Mrs. Simmons. "Stuart here is having a rough morning. He needs some extra attention."

Katherine found her hand transferred from Mrs. Simmons' to Stuart's.

"Stuart, this here is Kathy. Show her the playground."

He grunted and began to pull her along with surprising strength.

"He doesn't speak much," Mrs. Simmons called after her.

Katherine followed Stuart outside where he led her with great insistence to a sandbox, not quite as full as it could have been with tired-looking sand. As soon they sat down, he threw a handful of sand in her face.

This was reality.

She brushed off her face, not sure what to do. She didn't want to do what grownups did, tell him in a fake nice voice that it wasn't nice to throw sand. She couldn't do what another child might do, throw sand back at him. Instead she looked around, and spying a shovel, she started to dig a hole.

In a moment, Stuart made a squeaky sound and said a word that might have been "me."

"You want to dig?" she asked.

She remembered how Frankie had told her he'd pretend his altar boy beanie was a beatnik beret. He'd snap his fingers to some imaginary music and say "dig it." He even did it once in the middle of Mass. He wasn't allowed to be an altar boy after that, which he said had been his plan all along.

She handed Stuart the shovel.

"Dig it," she said, "dig it, daddy-o."

Suddenly both of them were laughing.

"Me!" Stuart shouted, as he plunged the shovel into the sand. "Dig!"

Katherine found another shovel and they dug together all the way down to the bottom of their tiny world.

Chapter Two

By the end of June, even the most carefully tended gardens burgeoned out of control, Lucy thought, as she waded into her perennial beds, pulling up our lady's bedstraw (she loved the name and even the weed that wrapped everything in a light, exuberant embrace, but it had to come out). People who did not garden thought of spring as a beginning and autumn as the end, but really the cycles of flowering and decay went on all season in waves. Of course there were distinct stages. First the early spring garden, the thrill of raking and finding snowdrops and crocuses, delicate and fresh, the ground to be prepared for planting, so full of promise. The garden's childhood. Early summer might be compared to adolescence, plants and weeds sprouting up overnight, wantonly, some getting crowded and bullied, some taking over in their ecstatic response to the sun's full strength. Then there came a time in later summer when the weeds slowed and the flowering and fruiting plants almost took care of themselves, a brief adulthood before autumn, when she'd put the garden tenderly and ruthlessly to bed, carting away the dead, saving seeds for the next season.

Lucy straightened up and took an unwieldy armful of bedstraw to the wheelbarrow. Gardening kept her back limber, her arms and legs strong, gave her the illusion at times that she was young and, at others, confirmed that she was not. She ached more often and tired more easily. The wheelbarrow was overflowing now, her signal to take a rest, so she wheeled it to the wood at the edge of her yard and added the bedstraw to a pile. Until the last few years she used to prune the shrubs and fruit trees herself and had mowed her own lawn with an old-fashioned push mower that had no motor, just blades that she took to be sharpened at the hardware store once or twice a summer. Now Frank Lomangino would not hear of her doing any heavy work. He helped her with the pruning, and his son Frankie Jr. had taken over mowing her lawn with his father's machine. Over Frank Sr.'s objections, she insisted on paying Frankie. He had saved her life, after all, he and Katherine Bradley, when they were mere children.

Lucy set the wheelbarrow on its end next to the garden shed in case it rained and went to sit in a weathered Adirondack chair under an old oak tree, its leaves still new, not summer dark and dusty yet. From one spreading limb hung a wooden swing where Katherine still liked to sit and daydream when she visited. Katherine and Frankie were both teenagers now, as young people were called these days, though traces of the children lingered, especially in Katherine, who was a year younger than Frankie. It was not just the roundness of her cheeks, it was her dreaminess. She still lived half in this world and half in another, where Frankie, Lucy sensed, no longer wanted to linger. Frankie had grown his hair long, as was the fashion, and he had taught himself to play guitar, rather well. He had proudly informed Lucy that he was going to start his own band.

Out of the corner of her eye, Lucy glimpsed the half-grown kittens, Lennon and McCartney, crouched in the beebalm ready to spring for a butterfly or stalk a bird, she hoped without success. If they became proficient at birding, she would have to get them belled collars. Katherine and Frankie had surprised her with the kittens a few months ago, not long after her old cat Tabitha Twitchit had died at the venerable age of twenty. Lucy hadn't planned on having more cats at her age, but she hadn't had the heart to refuse the kittens or to change the names the children had chosen. Katherine had confided privately that she had wanted to name them John and Paul, but Frankie (as was his wont) had decreed that to call them by first names was "dumb." As it turned out McCartney, a calico, was female, so perhaps it was just as well. Lennon was a classic tuxedo cat.

Watching the alert stillness and stealthy movements of Lennon and McCartney, it struck Lucy that felines had a lifelong ease with their forms, kittens growing seamlessly into cats. Human children were less predictable, disappearing into awkward or beautiful bodies, sometimes one becoming another, a transformation that could be almost as profound as caterpillar to butterfly. She knew it was foolish to wish that Katherine and Frankie would remain fast friends, perhaps become sweethearts and, in due season, marry and live happily ever after. Fairy godmothers, as Katherine still insisted Lucy was, were no more wise or powerful than any parents who wished their children to be spared whatever they themselves had suffered and to enjoy fulfillment that had passed them by. As true love and marriage had passed Lucy by. At least, by extraordinary circumstance or grace, Lucy had a chance to love these two no-longer-quite children. And love them she would, no matter what happened to them or between them.

The afternoon was warm. Lucy began to feel comfortably drowsy, but she didn't close her eyes. Falling asleep in a chair too often led to a stiff neck. She looked down the length of her garden. She could just see her statue of Saint Fiacre. Wild thyme grew between his toes, and his head was a favorite perch for birds. (Now and then she had to give the saint a shampoo.) As she gazed, something strange happened, not for the first time. It felt as though she were dreaming, but she knew she was awake. And the dream was not hers. It was as if a window opened on another time or place or a curtain lifted on the wind. Now she glimpsed a slender figure, Lucy could not tell if it was male or female, standing alone in another garden. No, not only a garden, a cemetery. Lucy could see the headstones. The figure hid its face in its hands one moment, then in the next, lifted the hands and wrung them as if to yank down the sky. Lucy had the impression of overwhelming grief and something less comfortable. An emotion Lucy herself avoided.

Rage.

Now the figure stiffened. Whoever he or she was sensed danger or intrusion. Lucy half rose from her own chair, wanting somehow to intervene. Then the scene vanished as if it had never been. Lucy stood, dazed and a little dizzy. Was she going mad? She ought to speak to her doctor. But the person who came to her mind was not Dr. Haydock, the old curmudgeon she had seen for years and who had missed the signs of foul play when Charlotte Crowley was murdered. She recognized with some consternation that she wished she could confide in Father James, Gerald Bradley's successor. There was something about his quiet demeanor that she found reassuring. But unlike Mildred Thomson, who had availed herself of Father James' counsel almost before his moving van was unloaded, Lucy had never been the sort to burden priests with her personal problems.

Problems. She did not like to think of herself as having problems. It sounded so modern. Troubles perhaps, troubles that she had always kept to herself. In this case, the trouble was, Lucy could hardly remember what had just happened. Perhaps she had fallen asleep, after all. It must have been a dream. If so, what a queer one....

Good heavens! Was that the telephone?

Yes, it was. She'd better get a grip on herself. Dismissing her vague maunderings, she turned and ran for the house to answer before whoever was calling hung up.

Chapter Three

Anne felt that subtle lifting of her heart as she turned onto the country road that would wind uphill, past a field of corn here, a herd of Black Angus there, then a wood sloping down to a streambed, to her house (her own yellow house) on the left across from a field gone to wildflower and milkweed, no other houses in sight. It had been a year since Gerald had resigned as rector of the Church of Regeneration to join President Johnson's War on Poverty (just before Johnson got the country disastrously mired in the other war). Already Anne realized that the jerry-built old farmhouse she'd fallen in love with had been a mistake. It was five miles out of the village. The children could no longer walk to school but had to ride a school bus on a long torturous route, torturous because of the social complications—older children who bullied younger ones, cliques that Katherine was sure excluded her, though she had plenty of friends at school, friends who lived ten miles from their new home, friends Anne had to drive her to see. The twins, now going into sixth grade, had their own separate sets of friends, male and female, like them. Anne spent much of her time in the car. Yet still when she came home to the first house she had ever owned, she knew a moment's happiness, even if it disappeared as soon as she walked in the door and began picking up after everyone, especially Gerald, and even if only she ever brushed and fed the longhaired Samoyed dog everyone else had wanted. At least Katherine walked the animal, though the term walk hardly described their hours-long rambles from which the dog returned covered in burrs and Katherine more often than not with rips in her pants from scrambling over barbed wire. Yet with all the complications and inconvenience, Anne loved the place.

She pulled into the driveway and parked near the kitchen. Janie and Peter tumbled out of the car and then raced for the door, still young enough that being the first one mattered. Bear barked and jumped up on them, bad behavior the twins did nothing to discourage.

"Bear and I are dancing," shrieked Janie. "Dance with me, Bear, dance."

Excited Bear began humping Janie's leg, a habit that persisted even though he had been neutered several months ago.

"That's not dancing, stupid," Peter told his twin. "He's mating. He wants to have puppies with you."

"Down, Bear!" called Anne. "Peter and Janie, come back and help carry in the groceries."

Gerald and Gerald's mother were always criticizing her for not getting the children to do more chores. They claimed she spoiled them. Her mother-in-law had a nerve. Gerald didn't even take out the trash, traditionally the husband's job, and he had no more idea than Peter that dirty socks belonged in the laundry hamper. Lately Gerald had decided it was hip (was that the correct slang?) to bake his own honey-sweetened sour-dough bread. It was delicious, but she was the one who cleaned the mixer and the pans and wiped up the crumbs. She found it was just easier to do most household chores herself. The path of least resistance, it was called, a well-trodden path she could walk in her sleep.

Janie and Peter did take a bag of groceries each. Bear still jumping excitedly, knocked the bag out of Peter's arms and made off with a box of frozen pizza.

"Peter, take it away from him before he eats the whole thing, plastic and all!"

Anne picked up the remnants of the torn bag and balanced it on her hip, while Janie dropped her bag just inside the door (where Anne would have to pick it off the floor) and went to join the chase. Yes, it would have been simpler to carry the groceries herself. She stepped inside, grateful to have the house to herself for a minute. Gerald and Katherine weren't back from Riverton yet. She hoped he had stopped on the way home to take his daughter out for a soda or an ice cream to celebrate her first day at the daycare center. That she would get to spend more time with her father was the main reason Anne had agreed to the idea of Katherine being a volunteer. Anne had foolishly allowed herself to believe that when Gerald left the church and was not on call twenty-four hours a day, he would be more available to the family. But if anything, they saw less of him. His office, which used to be down the driveway, was now fifteen miles away. And the poor (which Jesus said would always be with you) tended to have more urgent crises than his former parishioners—though so far, thank heavens, none of his current clients had been murdered.

As Anne put away the groceries, she felt a prickle of uneasiness, thinking of Katherine walking alone in, well, a ghetto. Lower Main Street Riverton could not be described any other way. And Gerald had no problem calling it a ghetto when he was holding forth on the insidious racism of the North, less blatant than Jim Crow, but all the more difficult to combat. Really, she shouldn't have allowed Katherine to go on the bus. Acquiescing to keep the peace was her besetting sin, she knew. But Katherine must have arrived safely or someone would have called her—though of course she hadn't been home most of the day. Or surely they would have called Gerald's office.

He had gone into the office early this morning. He was supposed to leave early to pick up Katherine at three. What time was it now? Anne made herself finish putting away the frozen foods (minus the pizza, which she'd just seen whirling past the kitchen window, in Bear's unregenerate jaws). It was nearly five, the sacred hour of the martini. Even if Gerald had taken Katherine out for ice cream, they should be back by now. She felt the familiar tightening of her stomach. Really, it was mothers, not business executives, who should develop ulcers. She hated this place she found herself trapped in so often, some dark narrow crevice between fear and rage. She left the canned goods in the bag by the door and went to the wall phone to call Gerald's office, though she doubted anyone would still be there.

And what was the number of the daycare center? Had Gerald even given it to her?

Just then, she heard the sound of wheels on the gravel driveway and relief flooded her, making her almost dizzy. Really, it was true what Gerald said. She overreacted, always fearing the worst. They were only a few minutes late, and they were home now; she could safely put the lid back on. Anne lit a cigarette and went back to putting away groceries. A moment later, Katherine came through the back door into the kitchen.

"Hello, dear," she greeted her daughter. "How was your first day?"

"Fine," she answered, as Anne knew she would. You had to wait to find out what really happened, especially with Katherine. "Lucy Way brought me home. Can she stay and have supper with us?"

"Lucy brought you home?" Anne queried. "But where's your father?"

Katherine gave a minimal shrug and opened a cabinet to look for a snack just as Lucy came to the door, knocking politely even though it was ajar.

"Lucy? I am so sorry you had to drive all that way to Riverton and back. I suppose Gerald tried to call me, but I was out. If you're free, please join us for supper."

Lucy, to Anne the epitome of grace and calm, looked flustered and concerned.

"He didn't call her," Katherine explained; she never used the word Dad or Daddy. "I did. I didn't know what else to do."

"You did perfectly right, Katherine," Lucy assured her.

"But where's your father? He was supposed to pick you up."

Katherine shrugged again and quickly turned away.

"Please come in, Lucy," said Anne.

Just then the phone rang. Lucy waved and made motions to leave.

"Don't go, Lucy," said Anne as she picked up the phone. "Stay for supper. Please!"

"Anne?" Gerald's voice. "Anne?"

Because if Lucy didn't, Anne couldn't answer for what she might do.

Chapter Four

Gerald hung up the phone and looked around the dingy little basement office at the daycare center. A spider plant precariously perched on the sill of a barred window struggled for light. Gerald went and felt the dirt in the pot. Dry. Without thinking, he went to the kitchenette, found a coffee cup, filled it and watered the plant.

What he hadn't told Anne was that he'd been half way home before he remembered that he was supposed to pick up Katherine. Anne didn't need to know that, and even if he had been stupid enough to say it, she'd already hung up on him. But he knew it. He'd gotten caught up in a crisis, the Combs family being illegally evicted, all ten of them last count, and Sally Combs pregnant. He had gotten a call from their social worker a little after lunch. By making calls (and calling in favors) he managed to get a temporary court injunction against the eviction. Some of the community leaders called an impromptu meeting to begin organizing a rent strike against James Macken, a notorious slumlord, who owned most of Lower Main Street. They had wanted Gerald at the meeting. All in all, it was a good day's work, or would have been if he hadn't forgotten to pick up his daughter.

When he got to the daycare center, it was locked up, but he had a key. He went in hoping to find a reassuring note from Loretta Simmons, the director. Something like, "Your office called to say you were busy with the Combs family's case, so I phoned your wife, and she came to pick up Katherine, who did just fine today, by the way." The unwritten text of this fantasy note was even better: "We all know you are a good man, who works hard for the community. We appreciate how you always go the extra mile. We hope your family understands and is behind you one hundred percent."

But of course there was no note. Mrs. Simmons might possibly harbor such warm and generous sentiments (you never could tell; he worried sometimes that the people he worked with saw him as just another white man, more well-meaning than most, but still to be met with generic smiles that hid their real feelings). He could not fool himself about Anne. As glad as she had been to leave the rectory (the fishbowl, as she called it) the world of a small-town Episcopal Church was at least one she understood, was part of. (She still sang in the choir at the Church of Regeneration instead of attending services with him wherever he had supply work.) When he found the parish ministry too constraining, she had encouraged him to follow his calling to more direct social action. Though she had made a visit to his new office and met some of his co-workers, she did not share in his passion.

That's too much to ask, son, he imagined his father saying, his father the perfect parish priest, whose poor and hungry had come to the door of his city church during the Depression. *Go home now and face the music.*

Gerald put the coffee mug in the small dish drainer and locked up. Out on the street, he greeted some men sitting on the next-door stoop. He knew a few by name, and they all knew who he was. He waved as he got into his beat-up old VW bug. It was not a fancy car, not worth stripping for parts. Still, it was a car in a place where few people had bus fare, and it was taking him to a world these men would likely never visit. It bothered Gerald. He could come into a poor neighborhood, visit homes where people more often than not would insist on giving him something to eat, but he couldn't invite them home. To his huge (compared to a slum apartment) house in the country. That he owned. Private property. Unlike the church, the parish house, even the rectory where he could always welcome the stranger, where he was morally obligated to do so.

Preoccupied with the inconsistencies, you could even say hypocrisies, of his life, Gerald forgot about Katherine and the wrath of Anne till he came to the same bend in the road where he'd turned around to go back to the daycare center. As he drove on, his stomach balled up tight as a fist and sweat broke out on his temples. He rolled down the window all the way, but he still felt like he couldn't breathe. He was going to need a good stiff drink when he got home, but if he drank enough to ease his tension, Anne would be even angrier, which is to say more silent, colder.

He had done the unforgivable in Anne's eyes. He had failed a child.

Poor kid, he thought of Katherine for a moment. He hoped she hadn't been upset. But it had all worked out. She'd gotten home safely. No one was hurt. No one had to worry about spending the night on the street or missing a meal. That's why he had wanted Katherine to work at the daycare center, so that she could see what life was like, real life, for so many people. He had been proud of her for taking the bus on her own.

And then he'd forgotten her. He'd have to make it up to her somehow. He'd have to make it up to Anne.

He didn't know how.

As the scenery turned lush and green, he let his mind go back to the Combs family out on the street in the afternoon heat, the younger kids without shoes. Sally Combs sat on the stoop, so large in her pregnancy, so Black. It was a terrible comparison (probably racist) but she made him think of the Black Angus in the fields near his house, belligerent and patient at the same time. When he arrived with the court injunction, his co-worker Jeremiah Blake had placed himself between a growing crowd of angry men and the landlord, who had called the police. Jeremiah was relieved to see him, but Gerald felt badly swooping in to save the day, wearing his priest's dog collar for emphasis.

"By any means necessary, Ger," said Jeremiah when they walked back to the office together. "And you know it's not over. I asked Big Mike, Lucius, and May to gather some folks for an emergency meeting at the office in about an hour. Hope that's okay by you."

"By any means necessary, Jer," Gerald said back to him.

No one else called either of them by the first syllable of their names. It was their personal joke.

In the year that Gerald had worked for the OEO, Jeremiah had become a friend, one he *had* invited home to dinner. In some ways Jeremiah was more of an outsider in the ghetto than Gerald, even though he was Black. A minister's son, which gave them some things in common, Jeremiah had gotten a scholarship to Yale where he could have gone on to law school (and should have, Jeremiah sometimes sighed). Instead he went to theological school. He was working on a doctoral degree when he dropped out to take a job with the Southern Christian Leadership Conference as a community organizer, which had eventually led him to his job in Riverton, a temporary job to help get the program on its feet. That's what Jeremiah traveled the country doing. Despite his credentials (he had worked with Dr. King on the Montgomery bus boycott) it had taken the community a while to accept this educated, light-skinned, somewhat shy Black man, not given to grandstanding. But he had gradually won people over with his dedication. He also had an uncanny ability to listen so profoundly that people found themselves changed; their entrenched positions shifted without his ever saying a word.

Gerald imagined himself talking to Jeremiah now, maybe sitting in May's kitchen over coffee or taking a walk in the drug-infested park by the river.

"I blew it, Jer, I blew it again."

And Jeremiah would just nod, without excusing him or judging him, the way light fell on dirty streets and grass pushed up through cracks in the pavement.

Then something Anne said came back to him. She so rarely offered an opinion about anything, it was hard to forget when she did.

"I like Jeremiah," she had said, the evening after he'd come to dinner. "Very much. But don't...I hope you won't...make a hero of him."

The way he had Rick Foster, she did not say. Rick Foster, the golden Democratic congressional candidate...but how could she even mention (or not mention) those two men in the same breath?

He wanted to get indignant, but she had gotten up from the table too quickly.

And really it wasn't Jeremiah she was warning him about.

Gerald turned onto the dirt road, the last mile home. As the road climbed, his spirits sank. He should build a doghouse, a real one, in the back yard, so that he could sleep there, alone with his shame, or with his shame and Bear. He envied Jeremiah his single rented room.

When he pulled into the driveway he recognized Lucy Way's car. He hoped she was staying for dinner. A brief reprieve, a temporary grace.

Spring 1968

Chapter Five

It was still mud season, Katherine's mother insisted. The mud-room was full of winter coats that no one wanted to wear anymore and boots and shoes that her mother was constantly wiping clean and setting straight on mats underneath the bench. Bear no longer resembled a polar bear or even a dog. Unless he was kept indoors, his belly was matted and wet and brown. Her mother only let him in as far as the kitchen, which she could mop. Her father, who always forgot to change out of his own muddy shoes and carelessly tracked mud in, sympathized with the dog.

"You are *canis non grata*," he would tell the dog as he whimpered at the threshold of the dining room, and then, smirking, her father would disappear with his drink into his den without explaining the joke.

Right now Bear was jumping up and down outside the mudroom window, making muddy paw prints on the glass because he knew that Katherine was getting ready to go outside and that could only mean that she would be taking him for a walk.

Because there was nothing else to do here. Nothing. Her mother was driving the twins somewhere, and her father was working even though it was Saturday. Her father always said, sure he would take her with him sometime, but he always had some reason not to. Her job (she liked to call it a job) at the daycare center had ended when she went back to school, and she hadn't been to Riverton since then, at least not to Lower Main Street. Unless her mother would drive her to a friend's house, she was stuck here. She couldn't even bike to her friends' houses. They lived too far away, and even if they didn't, her mother would not allow her to bike on the main road, which meant she could not go anywhere.

But outside. Out into the woods and fields. It was a warm day. She would not wear a coat, but she would wear boots that she could wade in and walk through mud up to the ankles.

"Down, Bear, down," she said after he jumped on her and muddied her old pink sweatshirt that was too ugly and uncool to wear except at home. She was embarrassed to think she had once liked it.

She and Bear set off down the driveway. The crocuses along the edge of the house were blooming, and the buds on the tips of the trees were red and swollen. A strong wind lashed them against a blue sky. Everything about to become something else it wasn't yet. It made Katherine feel adventurous. Maybe she would find a path that would lead somewhere, to something unexpected. She would meet someone, something would happen.

She crossed the dirt road and climbed over the barbed wire fence without catching the rusty iron on her jeans. (Her mother complained of so much mending.) Then she held the bottom rung as Bear wriggled through, leaving a tuft of fur behind. The birds would use it for their nests, she knew. Lucy Way had once found a nest lined with her own soft white hair. Katherine did not know if the birds would want her hair, too short, too brown, too boring.

She began striding across a field.

"Don't eat that!" she scolded Bear who had found an ancient cow pat.

He paid her no attention. And if he found a woodchuck, he would not hesitate to break its neck by tossing it into the air. Any dog would do that, but Bear also came of reindeer-herding stock, something he remembered when they came across a herd of Black Angus. She had been scared the first time she encountered the huge black cows. They would not back away from her and when she turned her back on them, they followed, getting closer and closer. Then Bear, who had been off chasing a rabbit, came to her rescue. Barking and nipping at the heels of the huge animals, he skillfully moved the whole herd from one field to another. Since then, he had repeated this feat many times. She wished they would come upon a herd today, but it was still probably too early in the year for the cows to be out to pasture.

At the bottom of the field, she followed a stream, loud and full with snowmelt. She picked up a stick and amused herself by balancing on the rocks in the stream, even though it didn't matter if her feet got wet. Bear, of course, was getting as wet as he could.

At a bend in the stream, Katherine left the water to walk through an old apple orchard where all but a few trees had died. She decided to continue through another field, past a wood that ran along a ridge to a rocky field with a pond, for watering cattle, her father said, but somehow the configuration of the rocks, the openness of the sky reflected in the water, made Katherine imagine she was in another country, ancient Greece maybe, or…Narnia.

"You're always pretending," Frankie's voice intruded in her mind. "Like a kid."

Katherine sat down on a rock, looking at the wind feather the water, wishing she had brought a jacket as a cloud passed over the sun.

Frankie used to pretend with her. They used to pretend all the time, sneaking off to the woods by the church where she used to live. Frankie had believed in fairies then, too. Something he would never admit now, though somehow it was still cool to believe in aliens. Aliens were real; they came from other planets or galaxies you could see with a telescope. They had already landed on earth, Frankie informed her; the government didn't want people to know. It was a conspiracy of secrecy. Katherine still preferred fairies who lived in a realm you could only get to by chance or magic, right here in the world of wood and water but just out of sight. Why shouldn't that world be real, too? Who decided what was real and what wasn't? When they were kids together, pretending to be Indians, Katherine and Frankie had become blood brother and sister by cutting themselves with a real knife. And even when they believed in fairies (and their own fairy blood) they had caught a real murderer. They had saved Lucy Way's life. Katherine had thought they would be best friends for life. But now she hardly ever spent time with Frankie.

"I don't know why you worry yourself about that juvenile delinquent." Aramantha was unsympathetic. "I know for a fact he's smoking dope in the woods beyond the playing fields. I just hope he's not dealing. He could end up in jail, just like his daddy did. Plus, in case you hadn't noticed, he likes his girls dumb—and stacked." She looked Katherine over critically. "And I hate to break it to you, you ain't neither."

It had been better for Katherine when Frankie still went to Catholic School with the nuns he called penguins, who had always been so mean to him. He spent most of his time during grade school plotting revenge. Glue on their chairs, snakes in their desks, loading the rulers they liked to bang with ammunition from cap guns. He used to boast to her about his tricks, his favorite being when he locked Sister Mary Immaculata in a supply closet and threw away the key. He seemed to be proud that he hadn't learned much at all. There was no way he could go on to the Catholic high school in Riverton. His grades were terrible, and he was always in trouble. The penguins predicted reform school in his future, but unless he was arrested and sent away, the public high school had to accept him.

Before this year they had known each other only outside of school. They would go for walks in the woods, find trees to climb, look for snapping turtles. Best of all, they would visit Lucy Way together and cook fancy dinners with her. A few times, she had taken them to visit museums in New York City. Their time together had nothing to do with school or with other kids. No one could make fun of them for liking each other. At first she thought it would be great to have Frankie in public high school with her. And because Frankie had repeated a grade, they would both be freshman. But being in the same school had ruined everything.

Something had ruined everything, anyway.

Frankie would nod at her if he saw her in the hall, but he wouldn't talk to her or have lunch with her. When he started his rock and roll band with a bunch of older guys, some not even in school any more, he stopped going to Lucy's house with Katherine for dinner. He said he was too busy practicing.

One day, when Katherine didn't have to take the bus, because her mother was picking her up after choir practice later in the afternoon, she followed Frankie as he walked home. (He still lived in the village, and she wished she did, too.) For once, he was alone. His buddies had football practice, and Frankie had gotten thrown off the team for bad grades—and for goofing off. He took a short cut through the woods, the same woods where Frankie and Katherine used to play, the woods where they had set a trap that caught the murderer. Frankie might make fun of her for pretending, but because of their games, she did know how to walk through the woods without snapping twigs. She knew how to slip from tree to tree to keep from being seen. It was harder in a skirt (her mother made her wear her skirts two inches longer than anyone else!) and with a book bag, but so far Frankie seemed oblivious to her presence.

Stupid boy, Katherine thought. If he were a real Indian (as he sometimes claimed he was) he should know she was tracking him. Of course maybe he was just ignoring her, even here. And she had no idea what she would do if he did turn around or what she hoped to gain by sneaking up on him. Just that something, something had to happen. She couldn't stand things the way they were anymore.

Frankie stopped when he came to the steep hill near the stream where a few years ago he had shimmied up a tree and tied a rope to a thick branch. If you grabbed the rope and walked to the top of the hill, you could swing out over the stream bed. After hesitating a moment, Frankie took the rope and began to climb the hill.

In an instant Katherine knew what she would do. Grabbing some small stones from the path, she went and crouched in the undergrowth by the stream, hidden by the time Frankie reached the top of the hill. He positioned himself on the rope and let go.

"Geronimo!" he yelled as he flew out over the stream.

Her aim and timing exact, Katherine sprayed him with pebbles. Startled, Frankie dropped from the rope before he meant to and got his feet wet in the stream.

"What the fuck, man?"

Katherine rose up from the brush, and she couldn't help it. She laughed.

"It's not funny, Katherine!"

"It is," she insisted.

"I coulda broken my leg," he said, but she could tell he wanted to laugh, too. "What the hell were you doing?"

She didn't know what to say. She felt embarrassed now.

"I was just sneaking up on you, like an Indian."

Like we used to do all the time, she did not say.

Frankie made a derisive sound, not quite a raspberry, and shook his head.

"You're still such a kid, Katherine. Don't you think you're a little old for that? Besides you didn't sneak up on me. I knew you were there the whole time."

"Liar!" Katherine was starting to feel angry now. "And who are you to call anyone a kid!"

"What's that supposed to mean?"

She looked him straight in the eye.

"Geronimo?" she said. "*Geronimo!*"

Now he looked embarrassed and began kicking at dirt, like he always had when he was the sullen little boy hanging around the church yard where his father worked as sexton. She knew even then her mother didn't approve of Frankie. She had called him an imposition, which Katherine had thought meant a large imp.

"Why were you following me?" he demanded.

How could she admit: I wanted to see you. You never talk to me anymore. She would sound whiney, pathetic.

"Who says I was following you? These aren't your woods. I have as much a right here as you. I was just taking a short cut to the church."

"Oh, right." Frankie rolled his eyes. "I forgot. You still sing in the choir."

"So?" she said defiantly. "What's wrong with that? Miss Ebersbach helped you learn guitar chords. And so did Miss Barker."

Miss Barker, Miss Eberbach's...girlfriend?...had gone to the hospital with Frankie's mother when she gave birth to his little brother. So they were practically like Frankie's aunts, or something.

"Nothing?" Frankie's eyes rolled up all the way to the treetops. "I mean nothing against Miss Ebersbach. But I'm just not into that churchy music."

Why are you so mean? she wanted to scream at him. When did you become such a mean boy, when you started going out with that dumb blonde junior Sheryl Anderson? Her cup size is bigger than her IQ, she'd heard boys snickering. But Frankie didn't just go out with Sheryl. He went out with someone different every week. All the girls had crushes on him. He was tall and broad-shouldered, which was why the football coach had wanted him on the team. He had dark hair and a Beatle haircut. Girls argued over which Beatle he looked like most. But to tell the truth, he looked more like Elvis Presley but without the pompadour. And here was another truth she would never tell. To her, he looked like the comic strip hero Prince Valiant. She used to dream that Prince Valiant would crash through the school window on his horse and rescue her from fourth grade. Then she would be his faithful squire, which was how Frankie used to treat her. Until recently.

"Ave Ma—ree—ee—a." Frankie sang in a stagey falsetto.

"We don't sing things like that," Katherine said.

"Like what?"

"Schmaltzy crap like they sing in your church. Miss Ebersbach has better taste."

"It's not *my* church," Frankie corrected her. He had gotten kicked out of being an altar boy and had refused to go to church after that. Not even his mother (who was much stricter than his father) could make him. "I forgot how pissy you E-*piss*-copalians are. You only sing Johann Sebastian *Botch*."

Katherine glared at him for a moment, then her heart started beating wildly and her hands trembled as a daring idea came to her.

"That's not all I can sing," she said, so nervous she had to swallow a couple of times.

"Oh, yeah?" Frankie said, brushing off his pants and turning away. "Well, that's nice. I gotta go. I got a rehearsal, too. Like the Beatles told old Beet-oven, roll over for rhythm and blues."

"Chuck Berry wrote that song," she couldn't help correcting him.

And you misquoted it, she did not add. Katherine knew way more about rhythm and blues than Frankie did.

"I could sing in your band," she said.

Geronimo! she screamed silently.

"Say, what?" Frankie turned around.

Katherine took a deep breath.

"*What you want, baby, I got it, what you need, you know I got it....*"

And it happened, the magic happened right there in the middle of the woods, she conjured Aretha, she was Aretha. Her voice, her body. She wasn't white anymore; she wasn't Katherine. She forgot about Frankie until she stopped singing. He was standing there, staring, looking almost scared. Maybe she really had disappeared and Aretha had stood in the wood instead, shiny, Black, and glamorous.

"Yeah," he said at last. "Yeah, you can sing."

And in an instant, Katherine forgave him all his meanness.

"I could sing in your band," she said again.

Frankie looked at her like as if she had broken out in spots, as if she were a one-eyed purple people eater.

"No girls," Frankie shook his head. "Rock n' roll bands don't have girls. Hey, I'm gonna be late. Gotta run."

And he turned and did just that. Ran. Away from her.

"Grace Slick," Katherine called after him. "Jefferson Airplane!"

But he didn't look back.

"Who cares about that stupid old white boy music anyway!" she shouted. "You can't dance to it."

Over his shoulder he waved as he bounded up the steps. She started to lift her hand, but decided not to wave back. He wasn't looking anyway.

Even in the chill of the cloud passing over the sun, the memory of that day made Katherine feel hot and sticky. She had shown Frankie something, something of her secret self, something that she hadn't even known about herself till last summer. But he didn't want her or her secrets. She stood up on a rocky outcropping above the pond. No one was watching, so she pretended, yes pretended, she held a microphone in her hand.

"*R-E-S-P-E-C-T! Find out what it means to me!*"

The open air swallowed her voice, and she fell silent as the sky, as the movement of high clouds that you could see but not hear. The song didn't seem to belong out here in a meadow full of old cow pats. The same way she hadn't belonged on Lower Main Street, but something had woken up in her then, even if it wasn't hers, exactly. The truth was, she didn't know anymore who she was or where she belonged. Frankie kept saying she was a kid, but she wasn't. Not anymore. Not really. When she was a kid, she had never felt this uncertain.

"I am a woman." She tried the words out loud, but they didn't sound true, even though she'd had her period for three years, and her breasts had grown (would they ever get bigger?) valiantly swelling to fill (almost) an A cup (as distinct from the double A she started with when she snuck off to the department store with her allowance to buy the bra her mother said she didn't need).

"A natural woman," she added, like the title of one of her favorite songs on Aretha's new album. But she had no one to sing to. She did not have a boyfriend. She hadn't even kissed anyone except Billy Abel at a spin-the-bottle party. (Did kissing have to involve so much saliva?) Frankie wasn't her man; he wasn't even her friend. But he had been her more-than-brother for seven and a half years. Half her life, half her life.

The sun came out again, and the wind turned warm. She could smell the earth coming back to life, grass and mud and wild onion. Who cared about Frankie? She would find her own way without him. Who knew where she might go?

"*By yon bonnie banks and by yon bonnie braes,*' she sang in her folksinger voice.

She could sing in almost anyone's voice, Joan Baez, Judy Collins, Joni Mitchell, Laura Nyro, Aretha Franklin, Diana Ross....

"*Where the sun shines bright on Loch Lomond.*"

Good old Bear came bounding back from some excursion of his own and howled along tunefully.

Katherine started to walk again.

"*Where me and my true love were ever wont to gae.*"

A true love far worthier than Frankie. Prince Charles or Paul McCartney....

"*On the bonnie bonnie banks of Loch Lomond.*"

Yes, this voice was best for open air. It rang out over the meadow. Maybe someone, somewhere was hearing her, wondering who sang so strongly, so beautifully. Then, for a moment, Katherine listened to herself and forgot everyone else.

Chapter Six

(He watched from his window, seeing but unseen. He'd had the glass treated. Not only could he see out and no one could see in, but the window appeared from the outside to be cracked, a window in a derelict warehouse. How he loved the illusion, the dreary outside, the exotic opulence within. He watched his old school chum, if he could be called that, walk down the dreary alley littered with overturned bins and broken glass.

None of them had been his friends, not really. But they had to pretend. They still did. He had a gift, a sixth sense for what was hidden behind closed doors, concealed inside expensive trousers, pushed to the back of small, conventional minds. He knew what they wanted, and he knew how to get it for them. He still did. And so they did him favors before he even had to think of calling them in.

The man below (far below) was a bad man, a stupid man. Not that he cared. The man had enriched him immeasurably, all while solving a little waste disposal problem for him. Now he turned the corner and disappeared back into his contrived little life, built precariously on lies, on envy, perhaps crude and needless violence.

Whereas his world was far more ingenious, far more lasting, its strength the weakness of others.

As he turned from the window, something caught his eye. A shadow against the wall? What had cast it? It wasn't moving. Had it always been there? Why hadn't he ever noticed it before? Just as

he reached for the binoculars he always kept close by, the shadowy
shape disappeared, as if some spotlight had moved on.)

She has to keep this man in sight without being seen. She does
not know who he is, come to that, she does not know who she is. But
somehow it is vitally important. She moves silently, sticking close to
the wall, hiding behind wheelie bins. Now and then, he stops to look
at a map, then he keeps on through this warren of dingy streets until
he stops at a door, number 26, she thinks. The steps up to it are at
least swept clean, and there is a pot of geraniums that looks cared for.
She crouches down while he knocks, then pounds on the door.

"Open up, you slut!" he shouts; perhaps he's had a few more
than is good for him. "I'll teach you to interfere in my life. I'll show
you who matters and who doesn't."

Then suddenly she stands up.

"Who are you looking for?"

It isn't her own voice. It's deep, commanding.

The man stops pounding on the door and whirls around.

"I beg your pardon, sir," he says. "Don't mean to make a row.
Looking for my stepdaughter. Can you imagine? After everything
that's been done for her, public school, Oxford, she chucks it all to
live an unnatural life in a slum."

She feels her hackles rising. If she were a dog, she would growl.

"You must be mistaken. You have no stepdaughter."

The man looks wary, affronted.

"The devil, I don't!" he says. "And how would you presume to
know? Are you a friend of—"

The man stops abruptly. He looks as though he is seeing a ghost
or some other horror. Then without warning he lunges for her throat.
Before she knows what is happening, she has broken the man's hold,
pinned him against the door, her fingers in his throat, (long, slender
fingers, with a man's heavy insignia ring. Who is she?) But there is no
time to wonder. This is survival. She brings a knee to his groin and
stops just short of grinding it into him.

"That's right. You know who I am," whoever she is says. "And I
know who you are. I know what you are. And I know what you did."

He chokes and splutters.

"It was your bullet."

"Hunting accident," he wheezes. "Inquest. Case closed—"

She tightens her grip.

"I can get that case reopened, and I will if you don't tell me now. Where is Pippa! Where are all the others!"

She loosens her hold enough to let him speak.

"How should I know. I had nothing to do with your slut girlfriend disappearing or any of the others. She brought it on herself, snooping, threatening, blackmailing. But if you miss her so much, I can help you find her again. You can be together again. Forever."

She feels stunned. She has no idea who Pippa is but there is a sudden roaring in her ears and in her heart, a grief that threatens to break over the whole world and drown it. She feels her arms flailing, swept with the current. And in that moment the man grabs her, twists her arms behind her and catches her neck in a choke hold. The man starts to say things, terrible things that she cannot comprehend. He is grinding the truth into her like glass, because...because he is going to kill her.

As the air seeps from her lungs, the world turns red, and a surge of rage gives her the strength to use her weight to topple him backwards down the steps. Before he can recover she is on him, her hands on his neck, her heavy ring digging into the man's flesh, the sound of his head cracking against pavement....

Lucy woke drenched in sweat and gasping for breath.

She had killed someone.

No, she couldn't have. She was at home. Awake in her bedroom.

It was a dream, a nightmare. Not real. She hadn't killed anyone. But in the dream someone had. She'd had her hands on someone's throat. She had dreamed of killing someone. She had killed someone in a dream.

It was a dream, only a dream.

Her breath began to slow, but she still clutched her hands together to keep them from shaking. She had never been that full of rage, not in life. Not in this life. Then a memory she couldn't place came back to her, or was it another dream? Someone standing alone in a grave-yard...who was it? Could she have murdered someone in another life? Could your sins carry over in your dreams?

She got up and pulled back the damp covers. She'd have to change the sheets tomorrow.

It was a dream, she told herself again. She hadn't murdered anyone.

Not in this life. Not here where she was safe at home.

It was only a dream, thank God. Thank God.

"Defend, O Lord, this thy child from all the perils of this night." The familiar prayer rose to Lucy's lips.

Who was she praying for?

Herself.

"Are you all right, Miss Way?"

Lucy opened her eyes and her head jerked upright. She felt disoriented for a moment, then she remembered, it was Saturday afternoon, she'd come to prepare the altar for Sunday services. After she'd finished, she had thought she'd sit quietly for a few moments in her favorite pew. She'd hoped the peace of the church would help dispel the horror of last night's dream. Its impression had lingered far longer than usual. She had soothed herself by gazing at the afternoon light shining through the stained-glass lost sheep held in Jesus' arms....

Now here was Father James looking at her with such kindness. He was a tall, angular man with hair that could be grey or could be blonde, hair like wet sand on a beach. There was something about his presence that calmed her, the way walking along the shore would have.

She did hope her mouth had not been hanging open.

"I'm fine," she answered. "I'm afraid I must have nodded off. I didn't sleep well last night."

She almost bit her tongue. She didn't want to be one of those women of a certain age (or past a certain age) who maundered on about their health.

"I was just about to make myself a cup of tea," Father James informed her. "Can I persuade you to join me?"

It was so deeply ingrained in Lucy never to impose that she almost excused herself pleading errands to run. On the other hand, she did not want to appear rude or dismissive, in case his invitation had been sincere. After all, he had found her sleeping in a pew. How pressing could her errands be?

"Thank you, Father James. I would love a cup of tea."

She rose from her seat. He waited in the aisle and gestured for her to go ahead. Then they walked together to the rectory, where he held open the door for her. "Sally is out doing the marketing," said Father James, almost apologetically. "So, I'm on my own. Won't be a minute. Make yourself comfortable."

He led her into the living room and gestured for her to take a seat on the couch. She was glad he did not expect her to follow him into the kitchen. She needed a moment to recover herself. Lucy busied her mind with looking around the room. She'd only been inside the rectory a couple of times since the James' had moved in a year or so ago. She had been a frequent visitor in the latter years of the Bradleys' tenancy. She and Anne had gone from acquaintances to allies and friends as they stumbled onto the truth about Charlotte Crowley's murderer. And, of course, since that time Katherine had become Lucy's unofficial Godchild.

The rectory had a different feeling to it now. Anne had had an appreciation of art, so above the level of children's sticky fingers, one could see Chagall or Cezanne prints as well as some authentic Chinese scrolls, while closer to the floor toys abounded, blocks and doll houses tucked into corners. Sally James was a school teacher and liked to do crafts in her spare time. She had made the gingham curtains that hung in the window and the large braid rug on the floor. Mrs. James struck Lucy as cheerful, content even, far less complicated and conflicted than Anne. The James' were a little older than the Bradleys. They had a daughter in college, who had been home for the Christmas holidays, and a son serving overseas in the armed forces. She did not know much more than that. Father James did not illustrate his sermons with personal anecdotes. Unlike Gerald Bradley, he did not insist on tying the Gospels to the latest news headlines. He was not showy in any way, which was not to say that he was dull either. He did not explicate the scriptures, so much as illuminate them, like light through stained glass.

Lucy felt a bit disloyal to Gerald, but she did like Father James' less insistent approach to parish ministry. Happily, Gerald also liked Father James, who volunteered as a draft counselor and made no secret about his opposition to the Vietnam War, despite or maybe because of having a son in harm's way. And no one, not even Anne, could help liking the good-natured Sally.

"Here we are!"

Father James returned and set down not a cup of tea, but a tea tray complete with a teapot in a cozy, no doubt crocheted by Sally, and a bowl with lumps of sugar and tongs and a small earthenware cream pitcher as well as a plate with slices of lemon, in case she preferred her tea that way.

"Will you be mother or shall I?" he asked.

Lucy was not quite able to hide her wonder that a man knew all the formal niceties of serving tea. She bet he had even warmed the pot first and that no modern tea bags desecrated it.

"My mother was English," he explained. "She scandalized her family by joining the Voluntary Aid Detachment in the First War. That's how she met my father. They were both stationed in France. She was an ambulance driver, of all things, and he was a doctor with the American army."

"Oh!" Lucy could not help exclaiming, "My parents met in France, too. Before the war, of course, quite a bit. My mother was a young American lady on her Parisian tour. She stayed at my paternal grandmother's very respectable pension. My father's father ran away from England to Paris to be a painter. Young men did things like that in those days. His family disinherited him when he married his landlady's daughter. But they thought better of it when he had a son."

Lucy stopped, embarrassed to be talking about herself so much.

"Did you grow up in Paris?" Father James asked before she could return the subject safely to him.

"I spent my early childhood there, yes. Until I was what was then considered the proper age to be sent away to school in England. Then of course, there was the war. My father insisted my mother remove to

England. She refused to go back to the States while he was in danger. He was in the army of course, killed in action at the First Battle of the Marne."

"I am so sorry," Father James said, as if she were newly bereaved.

"It was long ago," she said. "Another world, really."

And yet she could remember herself at nine years old, far away from the war in the drab ordinariness of her British school, waking suddenly before dawn, to the flashing of gunfire, the sound of screams. She remembered feeling a huge hole in her side, seeing daylight through it.

"Yes, it was another world," he agreed. "Not that I remember directly. I was born a year after the war ended. If it ever did end," he added. "All wars are supposed to end all wars, aren't they? Yet somehow each one leads to the next one. What is that wise French saying?"

He looked at her, smiling to cover his seriousness, she thought.

"*Tous ca change, toujours le meme chose? Ah. Oui.*"

She smiled back at him, the same way. His eyes were grey, she thought, as some Northern sea, but with flecks of light. The conversation lightened for a time as they spoke of places they both knew in England. Then there came a lull, not a silence, more like a rest note in music, a patch of blue in a drift of clouds.

Then, out of that blue, he asked, "Do you often have trouble sleeping, Miss Way?"

"Not often," she said. "Do you, Father James?"

Lucy was taken aback by her boldness.

"Sometimes," he said. "I have nightmares from time to time. I suppose everyone does. It may be presumptuous of me to say so, Miss Way. You always look so serene, as though you have wrestled your demons and won."

Lucy hoped that the warmth that rushed to her face did not show in her cheeks. She did not think blushing became an older woman with white hair. She was quite taken aback that Father James had taken any notice of her at all, let alone come to such a conclusion.

"If only that were true!" she said. "I do live a very quiet life. I was a nurse in the second war. I saw my share of horrors. But that was more than twenty years ago."

He took a sip of his tea, then rested his cup and saucer on his knee.

"I don't think time is quite chronological, do you? Or not only chronological. The past can be very present sometimes."

She glanced at him, wondering if he had served in the war. If he had memories that haunted him. But to ask such a question struck her as overly familiar.

"I believe you are quite right about that," she ventured. "But the dream I had last night was not about the past, at least not my past. Not in this life, I mean...."

She stopped herself. She was blithering. She'd be going Mildred Thomson one better if she started going on about her dreams. What could be more tedious?

"Please go on, Miss Way. That is, if you'd like to. I find it sometimes helps to talk about bad dreams out loud."

She looked at him, his cup poised in his hand. There was something about his interest that was both sincere and at the same time not intrusive. To refuse to respond might seem coy or curt.

"In this dream," she began, "the person I was, was not myself. Not the self I know. That's not unusual. As I grow older, I am often not the subject of my dreams. But in this one, I was *someone*, someone I didn't know. I don't even know if the person was male or female. But I felt everything the person felt. I felt," she paused for a moment, and without meaning to, closed her eyes, seeing again that red. "I felt murderous rage. I had my hands on someone's neck. I believe, I believe, I, whoever I was in the dream, killed a man."

Father James had set down his cup. He sat with his pointer fingers pressed together so that they made a triangle.

"I did wonder," she went on, "if I might be remembering another life. And if there is such a thing, do sins carry over? Is it possible to atone?" She stopped herself, embarrassed. "But I don't imagine you believe in such things, Father James."

He half rose and picked up the pot.

"More tea, Miss Way?"

"Thank you," she said.

He appeared to be overlooking her eccentric speculations. Then he sat down again and turned to her, looking her directly in the eye, and she found she could not look away even if she wanted to.

"As you know, the church has no specific teaching on reincarnation. But personally, I don't rule it out. If there is such a thing, I suppose you could say that in each life, in each moment, we have a chance to make amends. Though how is not always clear. Some wrongs from the merely human point of view seem impossible to right."

He looked away from her now and seemed for a moment to have forgotten her.

"But with God all things are possible?" she ventured so softly she half-hoped he hadn't heard her.

"Just so," he said, and he turned to her again. "But your dream, if I may be so bold as to speculate...."

"Please," she murmured.

"I suppose a Freudian might say you have repressed anger or desires or some such rubbish. But I am more inclined to believe that since the dream was so vivid, so tactile, so removed from your own life and yet so upsetting, that you might have dreamed something that happened, or something that will happen."

Lucy was taken aback. Was this mild-mannered, reticent, comforting priest talking about....

"Do you mean I might have had a clairvoyant dream?"

"Perhaps you are a skeptic about such things. Forgive me, I don't mean to shock. I can assure you I am not an occultist."

Lucy thought of her childhood friend Rowena Trebilcock who had annoyed and terrorized their classmates with her psychic pronouncements. They had met again during the war. In addition to driving an ambulance, Rowena had participated in an esoteric more or less Christian circle that fought the war on a psychic plane. Lucy had gone with her to several meetings. Did that mean Lucy herself had dabbled in the occult?

"I'm not shocked in the least, Father James. But I can't recall ever having such dreams. Why would I dream about people I don't know? And if the dream is clairvoyant, well, I witnessed a crime. And I haven't the first idea what to do about it."

Father James reached for his almost empty cup and took a last sip.

"If it was only a nightmare, it will fade. If it is something more, no doubt its purpose will become clear. In the meantime, again I don't mean to be presumptuous, you can pray for clarity and peace. You might even pray for the people in the dream."

What an extraordinary and extraordinarily sensible suggestion.

"Yes," Lucy nodded. "Yes I can. I will."

Their eyes met again, his the color of that northern sea, calming but not altogether calm. There was something hidden in those depths.

You look as though you have wrestled your demons and won, he had said of her.

Was he wrestling some demons of his own?

She would pray for him, too, Lucy decided. Yes, she would pray.

Chapter Seven

Anne was alone in the kitchen, except for Bear who looked at her lovingly and woefully every time she glanced at him, and never failed to thump his bedraggled tail. Katherine had been walking him out in the muddy fields as usual. Anne was ostensibly getting dinner ready, though really there was nothing much more to do. Now that the children were older, the family ate together more frequently, which was as it should be. In some ways it had been easier when she fed them hamburgers at the kitchen table at five and didn't have to mediate between their needs and Gerald's in terms of menu and conversation. Tonight they were having beef stew, something (amazingly) everyone liked, one of the few things she made from scratch. She wished she still had something to chop. Perhaps, though she had never been interested in cooking, resented in fact having to come up with ideas for meals day after day, just perhaps she would take a class, maybe in Chinese or Japanese cuisine, something that involved the use of sharp knives and swift precise motions.

With nothing else to do, Anne wiped the clean counters one more time. Gerald was drinking his martini and watching the news, the main item being Robert Kennedy's announcement that he would run for president, after all. Or more precisely, after Eugene McCarthy had proved in New Hampshire that an anti-war candidacy might succeed. She had already watched Gerald tear up when the announcement first came through. She knew just the line that got to him, the one about closing the gap between Black and white, rich and poor. It was laudable, of course it was laudable, Gerald's passion for social justice. Intellectually she shared it. But she hated his tears, tears that never fell when she needed them, when they might have softened her towards him.

Anne rinsed and squeezed out the sponge, then got the ready-made biscuit dough out of the refrigerator. Both her best friend Rosalie and Lucy Way had offered to show her how to make biscuits from scratch when she'd admired the ones they made. It was easy, they said. Anne didn't care. She didn't bake from scratch. It was almost a matter of principle, even if it was absurd to have such principles. She got out a baking sheet (on which her children sometimes baked cookies from pre-mixed dough, which they ate raw whenever her back was turned.) Unlike the cookie dough, these raw biscuits were actually pre-formed. She just had to lob them onto the sheet. She would bake them at the last minute as they needed a higher temperature than the stew. No need to put them in yet.

Anne sat down at the kitchen table, picked up her half cup of cold coffee and lit a cigarette. She considered getting up again to set the table, but Gerald might fuss if she didn't make one of the girls do it. What, she wondered, would Gerald think if she said out loud (at the dinner table?) Robert Kennedy is a spoiler. Actually, it surprised her even to think it in her own mind. She did not usually have political opinions, not strong ones. Gerald had enough for both of them, and she, as a rule, agreed with him. She did object to his vehemence on occasion. He had threatened repeatedly that if Goldwater won against Johnson, he would move the family to New Zealand. Anne had come upon Katherine poring over details of New Zealand's geography and climate with Peter and Janie in the *World Book Encyclopedia*, explaining to them they would have Christmas in summer. Janie was just young enough then to be seriously worried about how Santa's sleigh would travel without snow. Katherine, with her vivid imagination, had spun a story of how Santa's sleigh had pontoons as well as sled runners. And the reindeer would be equipped with water skis. Santa would ride in on a big wave and land on the beach. When Goldwater lost, the children were quite disappointed.

Anne had not taken an active role in McCarthy's campaign, but she had followed it, and even sent a donation. She kept the checkbook and paid all the bills. Gerald was hopeless at such tasks, so there had been no need to discuss her contribution, which she had made the day after Gerald had said, dismissively, "McCarthy can't win. He's a one-issue candidate and even when he has the advantage, he doesn't know what to do with it." Anne disagreed. She thought Eugene McCarthy knew the rules of the game perfectly well. He had a pronounced distaste for demagoguery that Anne found she shared. Of course she was against the war in Vietnam; but McCarthy appealed to her not just as an anti-war candidate, but as the underdog in the race. She was always on the side of the underdog. Not in the way Gerald was, with his championship of Civil Rights and social justice. In a specific, idiosyncratic way; the reason why she always rooted for whatever team played against the Yankees. Even with the tragedies that had befallen them, she could not help but view the Kennedys in a similar light to the famous baseball team. McCarthy had deferred to Robert Kennedy from the beginning, and Kennedy had repeatedly and emphatically declined to run. Now that McCarthy had done all the grunt work, he was essentially saying, "Thanks, Gene. I'll take it from here. Because we both know, I can win and you can't—or you cahn't," as he would say with his Boston accent.

There wasn't much she could do about it. Anne stubbed out her cigarette and went to start the biscuits. If New York State had a primary, she might have volunteered to distribute leaflets or what not. How shocked Gerald would be! Would he admire her acting on her principles? Or find a way to belittle her for political naiveté? Probably both. She wondered if she might voice her opinion at the dinner table. Would it be good for the children to know that their parents could have a respectful disagreement? The problem was, with two martinis (at least) in him, Gerald was likely to hold forth. He might anyway, but she did not want to be the direct object of a political tirade. And besides, she had a long-ingrained habit of keeping things to herself; she didn't know if she wanted to break that habit or even if she could.

"You can't teach an old dog new tricks," she remarked to Bear.

He smiled agreeably (he really did smile) and whined at the smell of meat as she took the stew out of the oven.

"You'll have scraps in a little while," she reassured him. "If you're good."

She turned up the heat and slid the biscuits into the oven and went to look for Katherine or Janie to set the table. A girl's job. Peter would take out the garbage if she insisted, not that he had learned the traditional manly chore from his father. But really, why shouldn't Peter set the table or wash the dishes? She had never read *The Feminine Mystique* when it was all the rage a few years ago; she never liked to jump on a band wagon. But maybe she would look for it next time she went to the library. Maybe she would even join the National Organization of Women, go on a march of her own. What would Gerald think of that? She could already predict. Women's Libbers (as he called them) were a bunch of spoiled middle-class white women, complaining about conditions the welfare mothers he worked with couldn't even dream of.

Anne paused in the doorway to the living room. She saw Walter Cronkite's face as usual at this time of day, and she had to admit that news, especially bad news, was better delivered by Walter than anyone else. Gerald was in his easy chair watching and sipping his drink. The surprise in this scene was Katherine curled at one end of the couch, a book in her lap, but Anne could see she was not reading. She watched Katherine's almost surreptitious glances at her father, as if she were trying to learn something he would not tell her directly, as if she did and did not want him to know she was there.

Anne walked quietly through the living room. Neither one of them noticed her.

"Janie?" she called up the stairs. "Janie. Janie *and* Peter!" she straightened her spine. "Dinner is almost ready. Please come set the table!"

"No," Gerald mashed his finger into the table, as if it were a cigarette stub that had to be snuffed out. "If you think that most people have any choices available to them at all, you're just naïve."

She's only *fifteen*, Anne wanted to say. She could feel the words. They were stuck, not in her throat but some place further down, a sick place, below her stomach, darker and more primitive. Peter started to get up from the table, and Janie followed suit.

"Did you ask to be excused?" Anne managed to speak to her youngest children.

"May we be excused," they said together. "Please," Janie added, then appealed to Katherine. "*Mary Poppins* is on tonight,"

"Supercalifragilisticexpialidocious," said Katherine, not unkindly, but she didn't move. "Yes, you may be excused," answered Anne, though they were already leaving the room.

"Come back and take your plates to the sink!" yelled Gerald after the twins. "Your mother is not your slave!"

But she was their slave. A slave was someone who was not paid for her work. She would never say that to Gerald. That would be disrespectful to the suffering of people who had really been slaves, who were not privileged, over-privileged as Gerald had just accused Katherine of being.

"I'll clear the table," Katherine said. "Don't get up, Mum."

Anne ached for her. She knew Katherine wanted her father to notice, notice and admire her for doing a chore without being asked, proving that she was not spoiled. But Gerald appeared to have forgotten Katherine. He sat wreathed in cigarette smoke, his empty dish of sherbet pushed aside as he picked up his drink and rattled the ice cubes.

"I'll just make some coffee," Anne said, more to Katherine than to Gerald. "Thanks for clearing. I'll do the dishes. Go watch *Mary Poppins* with Peter and Janie."

"Don't you want to watch it, too?" Katherine asked.

"I'll be there in a little while." Anne tried to smile.

Anne felt the familiar tension in the room before Katherine even spoke. She turned back and saw her daughter standing, facing her father, her hands trembling. Her face working as if fighting back tears. Why did this have to happen almost every night?

Don't, she wanted to cry out to Katherine, not knowing what she meant. Don't expose yourself, not to him, not to the world. Look at yourself. Your cheek, still soft and round as a baby's but not a baby's. Anne didn't want to see it, but she had to. Katherine was not a child anymore. Her long heavy-lidded grey eyes smoldered, looking out from under her long bangs. Her lips were full. She was such a tomboy still, but she had rounded breasts, a new swell of hips. Danger, danger. Don't! Anne wanted to place herself between them or at least push Katherine from the room, the way she might have pushed her out of the way of an oncoming car. But she was frozen, like a rabbit, frozen.

"You're wrong!" said Katherine, her voice sounding louder than it was.

Anne felt the sick below her stomach rise and spread out into her limbs. Why must Katherine antagonize him? Deliberately. Fear and anger got all tangled up in Anne's nerve endings. She did not know where to direct either.

"People do have choices. They're not just products of their environment. If they are, then there is no point in doing anything. There's no point in what you do. Those are people in the ghetto, they don't just suffer, they make music, they dance, they—"

"Now don't go romanticizing poverty," Gerald cut her off. "That's just a cheap, easy way to make white people feel good about themselves—"

"You don't even know what I'm talking about!" Katherine shouted. "I bet you don't even know who Stevie Wonder is or Aretha Franklin or Taj Mahal or Nina Simone or B.B. King or even Muddy Waters!"

Before Gerald could answer she rushed from the room as she had so many nights before after shouting matches with her father. Anne would find her crying and do her best to comfort her. She supposed it was just her age, teenaged girls were notoriously sensitive, but she worried about Katherine. Her emotions were so extreme. She wished Gerald could be more understanding. Her hands shook as she measured out the coffee, dry grounds spilling on the counter. She wiped them up and then went back to dining room doorway.

"Gerald, why can't you, why can't you...."

He did not look up at her, but mumbled something that sounded like, "I'm sorry, dear. I just...."

Then he got up and made his way somewhat unsteadily out of the room.

"You should go...talk to her." Anne said to his back.

But she knew he wouldn't. (And maybe that was just as well.) When she brought him his coffee, she would find him nodding in his easy chair in his study, one of D.H. Lawrence's horrible novels splayed open on his lap.

She wished her children were still little, all of them. Hal. Hal. She wished she could go back and do it all again. She wished Gerald could, too.

Chapter Eight

When Gerald walked into the OEO office on the first day of April, Jeremiah was already there. Gerald was used to finding him with a phone on one ear, pad and pen in one hand, while another phone rang. The office didn't have an official secretary, so everyone used the typewriter. The immediate vicinity was usually surrounded by balled up drafts that somehow missed the wastebasket. Today Jeremiah, still wearing his coat, was actually just sitting, his feet up on the windowsill vying for space with a peaked African Violet. The plant leaned into the sliver of light that found its way to the alley for a few minutes every day. Mrs. Allen, across the way, took the opportunity to hang out her wash. On the desk, a cigarette was burning itself out in an overfull ashtray next to a cup of coffee (black with two sugars) that Gerald guessed was already cold.

"I find myself speechless," Jeremiah said, letting his long legs fall easily to the floor as he turned to greet Gerald.

"You speechless? That's got to be an April Fool's joke."

"April Fools? Oh, yeah, that's right. I forgot."

"No chance of forgetting at my house," Gerald said. "Green scrambled eggs this morning, and sugar in the saltcellar."

Jeremiah laughed that easy generous laugh that put Gerald, and everyone else, at ease.

"Oh, the paternal joys I'm missing out on," Jeremiah said. "But seriously, last night was no joke. You heard the speech, right? On and on and on about our righteous sacrifices in Vietnam and bam at the end, three sentences, maybe four. '*I have concluded that I should not permit the Presidency to become involved in partisan decisions.*'"

Jeremiah did his show-stopping imitation of President Johnson, his smooth dark face suddenly suggesting jowls, his lively voice, ponderous.

"Did you see it coming, Ger?" he asked.

"I don't think anyone did, not even his closest aides, from the commentary last night," said Gerald. "It's hard to say yet what it's going to mean, or even if he means it. You're too much of a whipper-snapper to remember, but Roosevelt did pretty much the same thing in 1940. The party drafted him to run anyway, and he won. Johnson is wily enough, he could be angling for something like that."

"You mean a Brer Rabbit 'Please don't throw me in the briar patch!' maneuver? Well, of course I wasn't hardly born yet," Jeremiah deadpanned, 'but as I recollect from the dusty old history books, FDR didn't have a crown prince like Bobby Kennedy breathing down his neck. This is a wild card, man. Anything could happen now. One thing I know, we got to be the ones to play it."

We. Gerald felt a surge of something he didn't dare call happiness but couldn't deny.

"What do you say we go out and get the papers," said Jeremiah, unfolding his lanky height from the chair, "then we grab a coffee at the Lunch Encounter," their nickname for the local diner, "find out the word on the street."

"Part of our job description," agreed Gerald.

His and Jeremiah's.

The Lunch Counter was named for the lunch counter sit-ins all over the South, and it was one of the few Black-owned and operated businesses in Riverton. The first time Gerald went in with Jeremiah a year ago, Mabel Harris, high proprietress (as he'd come to think of her) gave him a stony look from behind the counter (which might as well have been a communion rail where Gerald would gladly have knelt if asked). Raising one elegant eyebrow, she addressed herself to Jeremiah.

"We don't serve his kind here."

Everyone in the place froze as if they were playing a children's game of statue, forks suspended in the air, coffee cups hovering over saucers. Gerald could feel himself turning red. How the hell did a race of people who visibly blushed ever get away with any kind of supremacy? He opened his mouth and began to mumble what would have been an apology, had he been capable of coherence, preparatory to turning tail.

"Ma'am," said Jeremiah. "This is a sit-in. It is time for this establishment to end discrimination and to serve all people regardless of color, class or—"

"Creed!" someone shouted from a back table.

"Shut your Black Muslim trap, Ali!" Jonny Harris, one of the largest, Blackest men Gerald had ever seen lumbered out of the kitchen. "Ima discriminate against your ass."

Suddenly the room exploded into laughter and the sound of palms slapping together as people high-fived each other.

"Okay, that's enough!" ruled Mabel, a sly grin overtaking her scowl. "Sit down, you two."

Gerald looked at Jeremiah bewildered.

"I'm sorry, man. I set you up. Just think of it as a kind of primitive Negro initiation rite."

Gerald, still the shade of a ripe tomato, joined in the laughter.

Since then Gerald had gotten used to being one of the few white people "to brighten the door of the place," as Jeremiah joked. The regulars had gotten used to him, and the flow of conversation no longer slowed or shifted when he walked in. People greeted him as 'Rev' and they called Jeremiah 'Prof,' because he was, as an old drunk known as Methuselah pronounced, "a educated nigger." For which Mabel always cuffed the man, threatening to throw him out on the street "where you belong" and reminding him and everyone else with some regularity that Dr. King had a Ph.D.

Today there were no private conversations; even people in booths sat at the edges of the seats or stood up to make themselves heard.

"It's a conspiracy!" Ali shouted as he usually did. "A white man's conspiracy."

"You know any other kind?" Methuselah called back. "Ain't that a, uh, redundification?"

"FBI sure think there is," said Ali. "Probably got an infiltrator in here, right now."

"Coffee?" Without waiting for an answer Mabel poured Jeremiah and Gerald each a cup. "'Bout time you two showed up."

"You trying to tell us something, Ali?" called Jonny from the grill.

As Gerald and Jeremiah swiveled their stools to join in the conversation, Mabel slapped down two pieces of pie on the counter.

"Sweet potato. Baked this *morning*," she said in menacing tone, which Gerald had come to understand meant: ignore my cooking at your peril. He turned back to give the pie due reverence, while Jeremiah remained tuned to the talk.

"How am I ever going find that man a wife, he don't appreciate homemade pie," Mabel grumbled to Gerald, fortunately moving off to make more coffee before Gerald had to answer.

Gerald had had this conversation with almost every married woman in Riverton. Jeremiah remained a frustrating mystery. Women of all ages took his single status as a personal affront and challenge.

"What you mean by a conspiracy?" Bobby Green challenged, one of the few steadily employed men, who had found new pride in his occupation because of Dr. King's solidarity with the sanitation workers' strike in Memphis. He always took his break at the Lunch Counter. "How is the man saying he ain't gonna run again a conspiracy?"

"Depends on who's behind that decision," Ali insisted. "Who's holding a gun to the man's head? When did you ever see a white man volunteer to give up power?"

Gerald had the sense not to mention Jesus' refusal to be king. Jesus' color was a sensitive point. Gerald had always despised sickly sweet blonde Sunday School Jesus, anyway. Terence Wilson, one of the Elders from First Baptist was here. Let him weigh in.

"The real conspiracy is the war in Vietnam," Elias Abel spoke up, a Vietnam Vet who'd lost both legs in Vietnam; whatever he said carried weight. "Johnson's the one who dragged us into that. Did someone hold a gun to his head and force him? Maybe they did. And maybe that why he stepping down. He know he screwed up."

"You got that right, Elias," Methuselah said. "First, he declare war on poverty, and the next thing you know we're dropping bombs on some other poor people. What happened to his Great Society? What great society?"

"Them two still got jobs," Ali jerked his head in the direction of Gerald and Jeremiah. "But nobody else does."

"Speak for yourself, man," countered Bobby.

"I'm just saying, war on poverty supposed to end poverty," Ali went on. "Am I right? What gonna do that? Not some school lunch program. Ain't no free lunch. Everybody know that. What we need is jobs, man, real jobs! Back in the Depression time, Roosevelt at least had the public works. What jobs did Johnson create? I tell you what, frontline in the infantry. Ain't that so, Elias? That's where the Black man gonna find a job today!"

"And the poor white man," Jeremiah finally spoke up. "And the poor brown man."

"And the red man," someone called out catching Jeremiah's rhythm.

"That's why Dr. King is calling for a poor people's campaign," Jeremiah went on. "How many of you are signed up to go to Washington? How many of you are gonna be at the fundraiser at First Baptist Wednesday night?"

"Depends on who's preaching and who's frying the chicken."

"I'm frying the chicken!" Jonny called out. "Your asses better be there or y'all can fry in hell."

"Poor people's campaign," Ali shook his head. "I believe that when I see it. Shoot, poor white trash can have a dirt floor, eat dirt, shit in a hole—"

"Ali!" warned Mabel. "I told you before—"

"—and as long as they's a ni—"

"Ali!"

"—excuse me a person of African descent anywhere in the vicinity, they think they superior. They ain't gonna march and unite with no—"

"And that's why Dr. King is leading this campaign and not you," Elder Wilson finally spoke up. "Even Malcolm X, God rest his Black soul, was coming to see the need for unifying across racial lines. God don't discriminate."

Ali was quiet for a moment. It was a sensitive subject.

"Say that's true," Ali recovered himself, "say Dr. King succeed in the impossible."

"With God all things are possible," put in Elder Wilson.

"You think the white man gonna let him get away with that? Overthrowing the rich, the whole damn economic system. They'll say he's a communist. They'll string him up for treason."

"They're already calling him a communist," put in Gerald. "He's taking a risk. He knows it. But he's not taking it alone. That's why we have to stand with him, stand together."

"Excuse me, Rev, I don't mean no disrespect, but, first of all, Black people got to stand together. No one's gonna give us anything. We sick of handouts. It's time we learned to take what's ours, it's time we fight—"

"We done heard enough out of you, Ali," pronounced Mabel. "Let the Reverend have his say. Speak, Rev. What you think about all this mess, the president refusing to run again. What's it gonna mean, for us?"

No one could put you on the spot like Mabel Harris. This was a command performance, and he better make it good.

"If Johnson means it, I think it's a chance, a chance to get out of the quagmire of Vietnam and get back on course. Like my good friend and colleague said to me," he lightly touched Jeremiah's back, "it's a wild card. We've got to play it."

"We?" Ali could not help himself.

"Yes, we. White and Black together, Black and white together," he quickly amended. "With Johnson out of the race, Bobby Kennedy has a real chance to win. Whatever mistakes he's made in the past—"

"Like FBI taps," put in Elias.

"Like FBI taps that the Kennedys ordered," Gerald acknowledged. "Bobby Kennedy is with us now, with Dr. King. I'm sure you all know he sent a message to Dr. King last summer and said bring the poor to Washington. Confront the president."

"Like Dr. King needed a white man's permission." Ali stopped just short of spitting.

"Not permission," Gerald went on. "Backing. Solidarity. This is the real world. Politics and politicians aren't going away. That's why the poor people's campaign is going to Washington. But just imagine, if we had a president willing to listen, willing to work with a leader like Dr. King, a leader of a mass movement across racial lines, think, just think what might be accomplished…. The great society, it might actually—"

To his horror Gerald found himself choking up, his face turning red as he fought tears. It did and didn't help that Jeremiah put his hand on his back.

"Amen, Rev, Amen," said Elder Wilson. "I'm with you there, we all with you, and we appreciate that you with us. We pray for Mr. Kennedy that his heart will stay in the right place, that it won't never harden like Pharaoh's. We all know that power can corrupt a good man, and sometimes a bad man can see the light and work for good. But a man is just a man—"

"A white man—" began Ali.

"White, Black, a man *is* just a man, let me tell you, I seen 'em all."

Serena Evans surprised everyone by moving into the center aisle from where she'd been standing in the corner by the jukebox. Today, even in a beige raincoat that had seen better days, with a fresh bruise on her cheek, she managed to look disdainful and beautiful. Everyone knew she was a prostitute, hooked on junk, but for some reason unknown to Gerald, she had Mabel's protection while on her premises. "Politicians nothing but pimps. Sometime they give you a little of your own damn money. Most of the time they put it in they own pocket after they beat you up. Don't be naïve!"

Here she swayed toward Gerald. Was she calling him naïve? Some vague memory stirred. He had said those words to someone else. Who?

"Naïve," she said again standing in front of Gerald, then she almost whispered, "You mean well, I know you mean well. Robert Kennedy," she lifted her voice again, "he a man. Even Dr. King, he a man. You know what I mean? They men, not God."

"Serena, that's enough now," Mabel spoke to her as if she were a child. "Sit down. I get you some gumbo. You know you like my gumbo."

Suddenly docile, Serena sat down next to Jeremiah.

"How you doing?" he turned toward her.

"I be doing better if you marry me, sugar," she said to him, as she always did. "You know, if you was running for president, I'd vote for you."

"Hey, everybody." Mrs. Simmons from the daycare walked in. "How come it's so quiet in here all of a sudden? Who died? Or is my wig crooked?"

She reached up to adjust her hair, and the tension eased and everybody laughed and went back to talking.

"Ima do you all a favor before I go back to work," said Bobby getting to his feet and flipping a dime in the air as he stopped at the jukebox.

"F6, Bobby," Serena called out.

"Not 'Ain't No Way' again. How 'bout something with a little more backbeat?"

"Pretty please with my long-lost cherry on top."

The jukebox whirred, and the record dropped; the song started, full of yearning and sorrow. Gerald recognized the voice. He had heard it coming from Katherine's room.

"Sit down for a minute, Loretta," said Mabel to Mrs. Simmons. "Jonny will load up your car."

Gerald and Jeremiah had long since given up making any argument with Mrs. Simmons about Mabel's private subsidy of the lunches the government issued to the daycare program.

"No offense," said Mrs. Simmons. "We take it, but the children need something hot to go along with boiled eggs and government issue peanut butter. Mabel and me, we got it worked out."

Nor would Mabel go along with their efforts to get funding for what she supplied.

"We have our ways of looking out for each other," was all Mabel would say. "We always have. Everything could change tomorrow. Children still need to eat."

"It's good to see you, Mr. Bradley." Mrs. Simmons was one of the few who called him that. "How's my girl doing?"

For a moment Gerald did not know who she meant. Was she expressing concern for Serena, who was beginning to nod over her gumbo?

"She did such a good job with Stuart. He hardly spoke before that summer. Sometimes he still talks about her. Calls her Kat. At first, I didn't know what he meant. Kept looking to see was there a cat around somewhere. Then I figured out that's how he say her name."

Kat, Katherine. A confusing mix of shame and pride stirred in him. It was like waking up from some important dream he couldn't quite remember.

"Katherine's fine," Gerald said. She was, wasn't she? "Doing very well in school."

"Good. That's good," said Mrs. Simmons. "Bring her by sometime, if you can."

Gerald remembered that Katherine had asked to visit a couple of times last fall, but of course she was in school during daycare hours.

"Maybe I can bring her to the fundraiser on Wednesday night," Gerald said. "Will you be there?"

"Course I'll be there. That would be a treat. Maybe I can get Stuart's mama to come on out with some of her younger ones. You know I have been meaning to talk to you about that family. You have a minute?"

"Of course," said Gerald. "That's why I'm here."

And he bent his head closer to listen over the song the jukebox was wailing now with a sorrow Gerald dimly knew was his own.

Chapter Nine

"No!"

Katherine had never heard her mother shout at her father before, or shout at anyone.

"You are not driving to Riverton in your condition!"

Katherine did not know what her mother meant by condition. That he'd had too many martinis, that he was crying? She wanted to cry, too, but she couldn't. Her parents were too upset, so upset they didn't notice her and the twins, sitting on the couch, huddled close to each other, while the reporters kept talking about how Martin Luther King had been shot. He had just been pronounced dead.

"I have to!" her father shouted back. "I have to go *now*. I have to open the office. People need to know we're there."

"I said no! You are not driving, like this, into the midst of a riot—"

"You don't understand. That's why I have to go. I have to be there with Jeremiah. I have to help him keep things calm!"

Her father was on his way to the door, fumbling in his pocket for car keys, when the phone rang.

"Katherine, answer it," called her mother.

The nearest phone was across the front hall in her father's office. She had to duck past her parents to get it. Out of the corner of her eye, she saw her mother snatch the car keys from her father's hand.

"Hello," she said. Her voice sounded scared. Her hands were shaking.

"Katherine?" a man said her name.

"This is she," she answered, just as Lucy Way did.

"Hi, sweetie, it's Jeremiah Blake. Is your father there?"

"Just a moment. It's Mr. Blake."

Katherine held out the phone to her father, but her mother grabbed it first.

"Mr. Blake, this is Anne. Yes, Gerald is here. I'm sorry I don't think he should—"

Katherine was still standing in the doorway to her father's office when her father yanked her mother's arm with one hand, so hard that she lost her balance and stumbled backwards against the door. With the other hand, he took the phone.

"Jer?" he said. "What's happening? I can be there in half an hour."

Pushing Katherine aside, he slammed the door to his office.

Katherine turned to her mother, who stood holding her arm where Katherine's father had grabbed it. In her right hand she had the car keys.

"Everyone in Riverton knows my father," Katherine said to her mother. "I was just there with him last night at the fundraiser for the Poor People's March. No one would ever hurt him. No one."

Her mother turned to stare at her in a way that frightened Katherine, as if her mother didn't know who Katherine was. Then she shook her head and went upstairs. Katherine returned to the living room where Peter and Janie had changed to one of the only channels that didn't have news and were watching old boring cartoons. She changed the channel back to CBS.

"We have to watch. It's important. Martin Luther King was just killed."

She felt very grownup, knowing how important it was.

"But it made Daddy cry," Janie protested.

"Mum doesn't want us to watch," objected Peter.

"She's just upset," said Katherine, sitting down again, putting a restraining hand on Peter. "Everyone's upset. There might be riots in Riverton."

Katherine heard her mother coming down the stairs, just as her father came out of his study. Before either of them could speak, Katherine called out to them.

"Look. It's Robert Kennedy!"

Both her parents stood behind the couch watching silently as Robert Kennedy, standing somewhere in the night, lights and cameras flashing, spoke to a crowd. The crowd wailed when he told them Martin Luther King was dead, a sound Katherine had never heard before, except in Church when the congregation acted the part of the crowd at the crucifixion. The crowd hadn't known Martin Luther King was dead. They'd been standing outside waiting for the speech. When the wail quieted, Robert Kennedy went on speaking. Her whole family listened, even Janie and Peter. Then Robert Kennedy recited his favorite poem:

> Even in our sleep, pain which cannot forget,
> falls drop by drop upon the heart,
> until, in our own despair,
> against our will,
> comes wisdom
> through the awful grace of God.

Katherine could hear by the catch in her father's breath that he was crying. Even more silently, her own tears came.

"I have to go, Anne," her father said when the speech was over.

"Robert Kennedy told the people to go home, go home and pray," her mother's voice broke; she was crying, too.

"But people need to know that white people care. There's a prayer meeting at First Baptist. That's what Jeremiah called to tell me. I can drive. The shock sobered me up."

Before her mother could answer, Katherine slipped from the room unnoticed and ran upstairs to her mother's roller desk. In one of the cubbies where she kept bills, Katherine found the car keys. She had seen her mother hide them there before. She raced back down.

"Here!" she said, putting the keys in her father's hand. "I want to go, too. Take me with you!"

Her father looked at her in bewilderment, and then looked at her mother.

Her mother's face was a high, smooth cement wall no one could get over. A cement wall with barbed wire on top.

"Absolutely not," she said.

"I won't be late," her father mumbled, and he turned away.

"Go to bed now, Katherine," said her mother much later.

Katherine had kept watching the news while her mother read to Janie and Peter upstairs. Riots had broken out in Washington, DC, right near the White House. Everyone thought New York would be next, but Mayor Lindsay had gone to Harlem where he was walking the streets and talking to people, showing people he cared, just like her father.

"I want to stay up till my father gets home," she said.

She couldn't call him Daddy, the way Janie did. That wasn't who her father was. Her father who everyone in Riverton loved.

"There's no knowing when he'll be back," her mother said. "It's after ten. I'm turning it off. Get ready for bed."

"He said he wouldn't be late," Katherine argued. "There won't be any school tomorrow. I heard it on the news."

Her mother was quiet for a moment. Katherine didn't look at her; she kept her eyes on the television, buildings on fire, people running in the streets.

Then her mother turned the television off.

"I know you're upset, Katherine," she used her reasonable voice, but Katherine could hear something underneath it. "I know you care about the people in Riverton, too," she paused. "Like your father. I understand, but—"

Katherine didn't want to talk, not to her mother.

"But you don't," she said, getting up from the couch.

"That's not true, Katherine. I just didn't want your father to risk his life—"

Katherine paused in the doorway. "Like Robert Kennedy? Like Mayor Lindsay?"

Her mother sighed. She wanted to say something more, but Katherine didn't want to hear it.

Katherine woke up in the dark not knowing what time it was. The house had the feeling houses have when no one is awake, when something in the house itself or in the dark wakes up and watches, not over the people asleep, just watches. It was an eerie feeling, almost scary but not quite. Had her father come home? If he hadn't, would her mother be up waiting for him?

Katherine had to know.

She got up and opened her door slowly. She had learned how and when to put her weight on the handle, so the hinges wouldn't squeak. The only light in the hall was the nightlight. Her parents' door was closed, and no light came from under the crack. Would her mother just go to sleep if her father was still out in Riverton, where a broken bottle might hit his head, or someone might bash in his car windows with a baseball bat? She had seen these things on television. Or what if someone set fire to the church, the church she'd been in only last night? Or bombed it like the bomb that had killed those four girls in Birmingham?

She thought of opening her parents' door and looking to see if they were both there. But somehow this thought was scarier than being awake alone at night, scarier than opening the door and seeing if her father's car was in the driveway.

And if it wasn't?

She would have to wake her mother, she would have to.

Katherine held onto the banister as she tiptoed down the dark stairs. The living room door was closed but dim light slid underneath the crack. As she stood with her hand on the doorknob, she could hear the blurry crackle of static. Someone had left the television on after the station went off the air. Katherine opened the door.

There was her father, sitting on the couch, leaning forward, his head in his hands, on the coffee table, a gin bottle, almost empty, and a tumbler, half full. She tiptoed over to the television, wondering if she should turn it off, but then the room would be all dark, and maybe her father would not know where he was. Why she thought that, she did not know, but she did. She could turn on a light, but that also seemed wrong, somehow harsh, something her mother would do to make her father see how bad he was. So she just turned the sound down all the way and left the TV to light the room with its dull grey light, its sad light.

Her father hadn't moved or spoken. She didn't know if he was asleep or awake. She didn't know if she should just leave him there or if she should help him in some way. Then he reached for his glass and took another drink.

"Are you all right?" she asked, taking a few steps closer to the couch.

He looked up at her bleary-eyed.

"Katherine?" he said as if he wasn't quite sure.

She took another step.

"Are the people all right? The people in Riverton? Mrs. Simmons and Mrs. Harris and Stuart and his brothers and mother and Mr. Blake—"

"All right, all right," he said, or she thought that's what he said. It sounded more like are, arrrr, are, arrrt.

Then he started to sob, not just cry, but sob, only he didn't cover his face, he just looked at her and sobbed.

"Katherine," he said, still weeping, "you care, you care about people, Black people, you care, don you, Katherine, you care. You undershtand. Like me, you're jush like me."

She nodded slowly.

"Come mere, Katherine, come mere. We care about Black people, you and me. Someone hash to care. Your mother doeshn't undershtand. Someone hash to care. Martin Luther King ish dead. I was with him in Mongomry. You knew that din you? I was there, with Dr. King in Mongomry. I shaw him with my own eyesh. I heard him speak."

And he wept again, this time silently with his face all twisted.

Katherine sat down on the edge of the couch. She didn't usually get close to him. She didn't know how. But she had to do something, he was so sad. She put her hand on his arm and all of a sudden he fell against her, head buried in her chest, arms wrapped around her, pulling her closer and closer.

"I love you, I love you sho much," he whimpered.

Katherine held her breath until she had to gasp for air and then she held her breath again. He kept pulling and crying until she was underneath him, and he was on top of her. She couldn't breathe; she couldn't see. He kept holding her and crying. She felt like she was buried in a tunnel, a dark dirty tunnel like the crawl space under the church she and Frankie had broken into once. Then his hands started moving all over her, like bugs, like small animals, squirming hairless things just born, blind, trying to find something. They went everywhere, up her legs and under her night gown.

She couldn't breathe, she couldn't breathe.

Then his tongue fell into her mouth.

The walls crumbled, the roof caved in. She couldn't breathe.

Everything went black. Somehow she had gotten outside, into the cool night, stars and fire sirens and search lights. Someone was chasing her, but suddenly, she remembered: she could fly. Even if she could only skim a little above the ground, she could fly. She could get away. She had to get away.

Then everything was still and dark, warm and heavy. Her father was snoring.

She had to go to the bathroom, she had to.

She moved her head and found the air.

"I have to go to the bathroom," she whispered, and then she said louder. "Let me up."

Her father grunted and sat up.

"What are you doing up this late?" he asked her. "Where's your mother?"

"I have to go to the bathroom," she said again.

She got off the couch. Why was she on the couch? She stopped at the living room door and looked back. Her father was just sitting there. Then he picked up the bottle, poured the rest of the gin into his glass and drank.

Katherine tiptoed upstairs to the bathroom. She had to go, but for a long time she couldn't. When she finally did, it stung and burned. She wiped herself.

Blood. But she had finished her period last week.

Blood.

Chapter Ten

"Have another drink, *liebling*," Elsa Ebersbach urged Lucy.

Lucy was sitting with Elsa on the screen porch of Elsa's little cottage in the woods. The May evening was mild, and it was that lovely, fleeting moment in spring just before the leaves burst into full leaf. The porch faced southwest and Elsa's small yard, dark in the summer, was a wash in light that seemed almost to come from the iridescent flowerets in the trees. Lucy had been sipping vodka infused with violets and sweetened with St-Germain, part of Elsa's campaign to persuade Lucy that hard liquor could transcend the vulgarity of the modern American cocktail and rival wine in beauty.

"Elsa, you know I am not accustomed to taking strong spirits," protested Lucy.

"And you know I have roast pork in the oven and the potatoes like fingers and fresh asparagus with butter. And Viennese coffee and strudel for dessert. This little bit of vodka will lose itself.

"You spoil me, Elsa," Lucy sighed, handing over her glass.

"And why not?" Elsa said lightly, retreating into the house.

Lucy had long ago forbidden any further expressions of Elsa's gratitude for saving Elsa from being tried—and possibly convicted—for the murder of Charlotte Crowley.

"But I didn't!" Lucy would always insist. "If it hadn't been for Katherine and Frankie, I would have been as dead as Charlotte."

"Ah, but you see, since I was in jail at the time, I would have had an iron-clothed alibi for your murder, and the police would have had to open up the investigation. I would have had to be eternally grateful to you anyway. And I would have had to feel remorseful for your death, because you did figure out who did it, Lucy. So clever of you and yet so stupid, going into the woods like that with a murderer."

Almost eight years had passed since Charlotte's death. Some good had come of Charlotte's poking her nose into Elsa and Clara's affairs, an intrusion that had caused Elsa to drunkenly (and with unfortunate witnesses) declare that Charlotte should be executed at dawn.

Since then Clara had been reconciled with the children and grandchildren of the fearsome patriarch who had disinherited Clara when Elsa had "stolen her away" from the mental institution where Elsa had been a teacher and Clara a patient.

"Yah, so much *sturm* and *drang*," Elsa would acknowledge.

Right now Clara was away for the weekend visiting a great niece and her new baby. (Strange, socially awkward Clara had developed a passion for newborns ever since she had accompanied Teresa Lomangino to the maternity ward.) Lucy, at loose ends because Katherine had cancelled their Friday overnight, had gladly accepted her old friend's dinner invitation.

Elsa returned carrying a tray with their drinks and a plate of crackers and cheese. Lucy took a moment to admire the fresh violet adorning her drink, touched by the uncharacteristic care Elsa had taken. German-born, Heidelberg-trained Elsa played Bach with passion and absolute precision, but domestic niceties had never much interested her, and she rarely entertained. She was making a special effort for Lucy tonight, and Lucy was grateful.

"*Prost!*" said Elsa, lifting her glass to Lucy's.

"*Sante!*" Lucy answered, touching her glass to Elsa's.

The two friends sipped in silence for a time, a contented silence, Lucy thought, like sheep grazing on a hillside or cows ruminating, somehow solitary yet part of the herd at the same time. Goodness, the vodka must be affecting her, mellowing her to an absurd degree. She might as well be mindlessly chewing cud. Not a bad way to spend a life, really. It could be argued that cows and sheep came to a useful end, becoming someone's food. More useful than her own inevitable, unknown end.

Stop it! She interrupted her own thoughts, their mindless grazing, that kept them wandering to the same old fence where they'd leave tufts of wool if they tried to get to the grass on the other side. Katherine was all right, Lucy told herself. She was growing up, that was all. Even if Katherine had been the daughter of Lucy's flesh as well as her heart, the girl would need to kick up her heels, try her wings. Lucy couldn't expect a young girl to want to spend so many evenings reading aloud with an old spinster. Lucy could understand the restless longings of youth, not only understand but summon up the memory of her own youth. That was one of the secrets of age that youth couldn't fathom. Older people remembered being young, but young people could not easily imagine being old. Katherine was all right, she reminded herself again, and yet Lucy was aware of an undertow of something else, some concern she could not name.

"Did you ever wish you could turn time back?" Katherine had asked the last time she visited Lucy.

They'd been washing dishes, Katherine at the sink and Lucy drying. Katherine had not turned to her when Lucy paused, dish in hand, between the dish drainer and the table. She kept on washing the dishes, not looking up.

"I suppose I have," Lucy answered carefully.

Turn time back to before her father was killed, turn time back to before she lost her baby, before she conceived the baby, turn time back, rewinding it, setting it on another course altogether. And that was just her own life, part of a vast complex of lives. Human history was full of tragic "what ifs?"

"What do you want to undo, Katherine?" she'd asked.

Anne had told Lucy that Katherine had taken the death of Martin Luther King very hard. She'd been unusually quiet and listless. Anne was thinking of taking Katherine to see a psychiatrist. Katherine's reaction to the national tragedy struck Anne as extreme. Lucy wondered if what ailed Katherine was as simple or complicated as excessive grief.

"I don't know," Katherine spoke, her head bent so that Lucy could hardly hear. "I just, I just want to start over again. I want to go back to before."

Lucy waited a moment. She was no psychiatrist. But she knew there was something Katherine needed to say. The words were struggling, like something trying to hatch. No, more like something trapped, not getting the air it needed or the light. How could Lucy help her without disturbing something delicate and fragile?

"Before what, dear?"

Katherine shook her head and reached for the roasting pan. Lucy waited while Katherine scrubbed fiercely in small tight circles.

"I can't, I can't see anymore," she said. "I used to be able to see things, see magic, at the edges of things, just out of sight, but there, real. Remember how you used to talk to Frankie and me about fairies? You said we had fairy blood. And I believed it. I believed *you*."

Lucy stood accused, perhaps justly. She began putting away the dried dishes. It was not time for the defense to make a case. Let the prosecution speak.

"But there are no fairies, or if there were, they're gone. I don't have fairy blood. There's just, I just have...blood."

Katherine stopped abruptly. She turned on the faucet full blast and started to rinse the pan, soaking the front of her shirt and spattering water on the floor. Lucy kept walking to the cabinets and back, an internal litany matching her steps, the blood of sacrifice, the blood of life. Could Katherine be having difficulty with her menstrual periods? Ought Lucy to inquire? She was a nurse, after all. But Lucy wasn't sure what Katherine had meant.

"It is like death," Lucy began, not sure what she meant to say, "when your childhood ends. And there is blood. For women. And for men, too, if they face battle. As for magic, the magic changes. Perhaps it has to die before it comes back."

Katherine turned off the faucet and turned to face Lucy.

"How can it come back, if it's dead? Martin Luther King is not coming back. My brother is not coming back. The Bible says Christ rose from the dead. But how do I know that's true? Why should I just...take it on faith?"

She was as ferocious as a young lion, facing Lucy down in her kitchen, but under the fierceness, the young rebel's challenge, Lucy sensed anguish.

"'Faith is the substance of things hoped for, the evidence of things not seen,'" Lucy quoted.

Katherine stared at her. Lucy could see that the child was trembling. She wasn't merely defying Lucy.

"I used to believe that Aslan in the Narnia books was real. I used to dream of him. But I don't anymore."

Then she had burst into tears. When Lucy put her arms around Katherine, she'd held herself stiff and apart.

"How much do you want for them?" Elsa asked, recalling Lucy to the present.

"Pardon me?" said Lucy.

"Your thoughts," said Elsa. "I want to be sure to give you a fair price. They must be worth more than a penny."

"Doubtful." Lucy smiled. "If you haven't got a penny, a ha'penny will do."

"I have no such absurd, archaic English coinage."

"In that case, I won't charge you," said Lucy. "I was just thinking about Katherine, Katherine Bradley. How hard it is to be young."

"Ah, yes," said Elsa, leaning back precariously in her wicker chair and taking what could only be described as a swig of her drink. "Youth. I suppose we were all young once, but not the way these children are young. With their long hair and their rocking and rolling and their disrespect for the older generation. We did not have such liberties. We had war. Children barely out of short pants becoming soldiers. At least in Europe."

"There is a war now, too," said Lucy, a trifle sharply. Father James' son was risking his life in Vietnam. How he had come to be drafted with student deferments available and with his father a draft counselor Lucy did not know, but it explained the pain she had sensed in him.

"True," conceded Elsa. "Somehow Americans always seem to manage to fight on someone else's soil. And this war, look at all the protest in universities, and the streets, the draft card burning, the running away to Canada. Only today the draft records burned, burned with napalm. *Gott in Himmel!* Imagine doing a thing like that in Hitler's Germany! You would not live to see the light of another day. Only here can you be so dramatic, only here where you are so secure in your freedoms. You take them for granted."

Elsa only talked about Hitler when she was well into her cups.

"Not that you are so very American, Lucy," she amended, "with your so strange mix of Parisian worldliness and your prim English school girl ways."

Lucy laughed to hear herself described so.

"My mother was from Pittsburg, don't forget," Lucy said. "And I don't believe freedom is ever secure in any nation. People who stand up for what they believe are always at risk. Sometimes they are killed. It is not such an easy time to be young, seeing your heroes shot."

They were silent for a moment, each taking another drink.

"Yah," Elsa sighed. "Yah, this is true. And the *schwarze*," Elsa used the German, Lucy suspected, to avoid having to choose between Black, negro, or colored, "I know they live in fear, like the Jews did. You know little Katherine, she is a strong alto, and her sight reading is very good. But she tells me, she wants to sing gospel music, like, what is her name, Urethra. She brings me some of her records. What that woman does with her voice, well, it is amazing, truly, but it is… outside of my training."

It was outside of Lucy's ken, too. She could not hear what Katherine heard or understand how the music moved her. It was emotional, even sexual, but Lucy knew she could not judge how others knew God.

"Perhaps you could talk to Father James about Katherine's idea," suggested Lucy. "See what he thinks."

Was it the vodka? Lucy felt herself blushing a little when she spoke his name. She had seen him only in passing since the day he had given her tea, and they, or at least she, had talked so personally. But it must have done her good. She'd had no nightmares since then. Well, really, who had time for nightmares when the waking world was so full of trouble?

"Ah, dear good kind Father James," said Elsa. "He does not know any more about popular music than I do. He is like me, classically trained all the way."

"It must be wonderful for you," ventured Lucy, "to work with a rector who is a musician."

"Oh, yah," agreed Elsa, "it is, it is. But you know I miss old Gerald. He did not know that much about music. Anne is the one Katherine gets her talent from. But Gerald cared about how the hymns and the sermon go together. And we could have arguments, good arguments. He could raise a raucous." Lucy supposed she meant ruckus, but did not bother to correct her. "I miss that about Gerald. I hope it goes well for him now. Terrible, terrible for him this death of this King man."

It is terrible for us all, Lucy almost said, but she realized that Elsa was right. It was especially terrible for Gerald. She still remembered the sermon Gerald had given after he marched in Montgomery with Dr. King, how his voice broke when he described a battered boy scout canteen as the chalice, passed from black lips to white in the land of segregated drinking fountains.

"Excuse me for a moment, Lucy," said Elsa.

"Is there anything I can do to help?" Lucy asked, supposing Elsa had gone to put the last-minute touches on dinner. "Shall I set the table?"

"No, no," said Elsa. "You just sit, what is the expression, sit tight."

In fact, Lucy was a little tight, as the slang expression went. That she was even thinking in slang was an indication of the vodka's effect. But it was not an unpleasant sensation, in moderation. She felt a big sigh summoning itself up from some unsuspected depth and releasing on the shimmering air, mingling with the pollen. Katherine would be all right....

What was happening? Lucy's heart was suddenly pounding; her lungs felt raw. Then through the young spring green of Elsa's yard, she glimpsed another forest, more ancient, darker. Someone was running, running through the trees, following something that was hardly a path....

Then Elsa returned, the half-spent Vodka bottle in hand. Without asking, she poured herself and Lucy another shot.

She must have been dreaming awake.

"No more!" Lucy protested. "I do believe I just dozed off. I won't be able to walk!"

But she had just been running. No, it was not she. Someone else, dark and tall. Slender as a sapling.

"Surely we've both had enough!"

But Lucy found herself picking up the drink, her hands shaking.

"We have not." Elsa downed her drink in one swallow. "Lucy, I am just going to spit it. I have *krebs*, both breasts. They will have to go. *Sofortig*. Before it spreads to the lungs."

Was she still dreaming? No, there was Elsa beside her, staring into the yard where the afternoon glow was beginning to seep away.

"Oh, Elsa," Lucy said. Tears sprang to her eyes too quickly. Elsa did not need to contend with Lucy's emotions right now. She took another drink. "Does Clara know?"

"Not yet. If she knew, she would be here hoovering over me and wringing her hands. I wanted her to have a few more days of happiness. There have not been so many days like that in Clara's life, you know."

Lucy did know or had some idea. Clara had been a beautiful, fragile young woman, a brilliant pianist, so tightly wound almost anything could snap her. And she had snapped—or someone had made her snap, locked her away in an institution until Elsa found her and poured all her own lost love, and some of her grief and madness, into restoring Clara to some semblance of life. Elsa had always been protective of Clara, even overly protective.

"You can't keep it from her for long," Lucy cautioned. "You can't keep major surgery a secret, *cherie*."

"I know," Elsa said. "I know. Lucy, we will need your help. Both of us. I hate to ask it but—"

"You have no need to ask, dear friend." Lucy reached for Elsa's hand, and Elsa grabbed onto her with a desperate strength. "I will be with you. I will come and nurse you while you recover."

"Thank you, Lucy," said Elsa. "*Mein lieber freund*."

Elsa let go of Lucy's hand and reached for the bottle again.

"No more for me. Surely dinner must be ready?"

"Yah, you are right," sighed Elsa. "We must eat before we are falling down drunk."

"Speak for yourself," said Lucy getting to her feet a little unsteadily.

And they both laughed till they wept, holding onto each other to keep from falling over.

The sun slipping behind a cloud shot its rays up, turning the sky and the tips of the trees red. The ground started to cool, and a little breeze stirred. *It's starting*, a voice inside her said, *the season is starting for you*. Not spring, the season of parting.

No, she silently answered the voice, *she can recover. I will help her*.

"Let's go in," said Lucy, "and rescue that roast."

She slipped her arm through her friend's arm. Warm, alive, warm.

(They had found him. Dead, dead and beginning to molder in the bottom of a wheelie bin. How tasteless. How uncouth. How it proved that underneath all privilege and pretense was flesh, putrid flesh.

Unbidden the image came. His mother's flesh, under her maid's apron. His father lifting her skirts while she stood hanging out linens—fine linens whose filthy stains, blood and sex, she had scrubbed out time and again—he lifted her skirts, concealed by the billowing sheets, he took her from behind.

He reached for himself. He couldn't help it. It was over quickly.

He had to think of other things. Whoever had killed the imbecile might know something or suspect something. That person must be found.)

Chapter Eleven

It was terrible, monstrously selfish, but when Gerald had burst into the bathroom early Wednesday morning to tell her Robert Kennedy had been shot, Anne's first thought had been: he'd better not die. She could not cope, she simply could not cope with another national tragedy. But he had died, twenty-six harrowing hours later. And her family was in disarray again, or maybe she was just looking for something, anything to blame. An assassinated leader would do.

It was just before noon. She'd done her chores and run her errands. The house was quiet. Anne poured herself another cup of coffee; she didn't feel like having lunch yet. The kids had gone back to school this morning, after a day of national mourning. Gerald had gone to New York with Jeremiah Blake to swell the crowds at St Patrick's Cathedral where Robert Kennedy lay in state. Before she'd sat down with her coffee, she opened the back door and shooed Bear out.

"No, I am not going to take you for a walk." She ignored his whining appeal. "You'll have to wait for Katherine."

At least Katherine still took the dog for walks, about the only reason she would leave her room, where she stayed with the door locked and music turned up as loud as Anne would permit. She had not even come out to watch the coverage of the shooting, which surprised Anne as she'd had to drag Katherine away from the television when Martin Luther King was killed. Gerald, on the other hand, had not allowed any disruption to the coverage of the fresh tragedy. Their

TV shows pre-empted, Peter and Janie had retreated upstairs for a long and rancorous game of Monopoly (or Monotony, as Katherine called it, refusing to join in).

Anne sat down at the kitchen table with her coffee and lit a cigarette. Her lighter snapping closed sounded loud in the silence. She was aware of her own breath as she drew on the cigarette, then let out the smoke in a long sigh. Only she knew the house this way, in its stillness, and (now she was being fanciful) only the house knew *her*, as she was, alone, not tending to anyone's needs. Of course, she had her routines when everyone left for the day. Dishes washed and put away, counters cleaned, floors swept, beds made, marketing two or three times a week. And then this moment of release, when she sat down with her coffee and cigarette, and, if she were honest, loneliness laced with anxiety. Free-floating anxiety, awful Dr. Aiken used to call it, though these days the anxiety usually fastened on Katherine or anyway hovered nearby, a brooding maternal cloud.

Anne loved this house and its seclusion on a back country road. She had hated living in the rectory where there was no privacy. People coming and going all day, peering into her backyard when she hung out the laundry, finding some excuse to ring her doorbell, even when it was clear Gerald wasn't at home. Charlotte Crowley had even snooped in her bedroom, rifling through her bureau drawers. Anne had always felt like a fraud as a minister's wife, but, she realized now, the role had given her something to resent. Something definite and understandable, rational. Now there was nothing concrete to come up against, except perhaps Gerald himself. And where was he? Same places as always: at work or in his cups. If she pushed against him, he might well fall over.

But that wasn't fair, she told herself wearily. For all his domestic faults, Gerald had a place in the world, a sense of purpose. If she didn't, it was her own fault. She thought of Gerald now, on the train with Jeremiah, both of them reading their newspapers, but feeling free to interrupt each other to talk about the terrible state of the world. When they got to the cathedral or as near to it as they could, they would stand together shoulder to shoulder and silently grieve. Really, Jeremiah was the one Gerald had turned to for comfort during both tragedies, not Anne, and who could blame him? Jeremiah shared Gerald's most passionate convictions. And so had Rick Foster, she could not help remembering. It wasn't that Rick and Jeremiah were alike (they were as different as, well, black and white.) It was something about Gerald that bothered Anne. He was still so eager for approval. Despite being in his forties, he sometimes seemed like a child to Anne. But not *her* child, not a child she wanted to love and protect.

What she wanted, she realized all at once, was someone to protect her. And there was no one, not since her father had died. Not since her son died. Because no one could protect you from things that ought not to happen. Murder, accident, complications of childhood pneumonia. No one could protect you from life—or death. So she trusted neither. That's what faith was for, she supposed, a faith like Lucy Way's that transcended tragedy or transmuted it somehow. Anne sensed that faith in Lucy, but she could find it nowhere in herself.

The phone rang. Anne startled and spilled some of her coffee on her blouse. She stubbed her cigarette out and went to answer.

"Hello," she said and stretched the cord as she walked to the sink.

"Mrs. Bradley?"

"Yes?"

She turned the tap on to a trickle so her caller wouldn't hear the water running, wet a paper towel and dabbed at the stain.

"This is Mr. Myers at the high school."

The guidance counselor. Anne's knees literally buckled under her and she grabbed the side of the sink.

"Is Katherine all right?" She could barely breathe.

Why else would they call?

"She's fine," said Mr. Myers. "I'm sorry, Mrs. Bradley, I didn't mean to alarm you."

Was it that obvious?

"I was wondering if you might be free to come in for a parent conference. Would two o'clock today be convenient?"

"Yes?" she said as if it were a test and she was guessing at an answer she didn't know.

"I know it's short notice, but I wonder if Mr. Bradley might be able to join us."

They wanted the *father*? It must be serious.

"He's in New York today," she said.

"Then I'll see you at two. Goodbye, Mrs. Bradley."

He hung up, leaving her holding the phone, her shirt front damp, as she stared out the window. Bastard, she thought, a word that was not part of her vocabulary, not something she would ever say out loud. Anne crossed the kitchen, hung up the phone, then immediately picked it up again and dialed a number she could have dialed in her sleep.

"Hello?"

"Rosalie?" Her breath was still short; her heart racing. "Can I stop by?"

"You come right over, honey," Rosalie answered, hearing everything she hadn't said. "I'm putting a fresh pot of coffee on now."

It would be a simpler world, Anne thought as she sat in Rosalie's tiny, sunny kitchen, with her latest avocado pit attempting to grow into a tree on the windowsill, if women would band together and take care of the children while men stayed out in the woods sharpening their antlers or whatever it was male deer did. Procreation, that's what they were good for, and they ought to drop off a paycheck to support their children. Women were so much more sensible and available. She did not need to translate herself to Rosalie or shout to make herself heard over the newspaper. She looked at her friend, short, plump, with a face that must once have been sweet and dimpled and was weathering into lines of kindness and good nature. She wore a kerchief over hair that had suffered from too many home permanents, because Rosalie couldn't afford a beauty parlor. Just the sight of Rosalie was comforting.

"Katherine's a good kid," Rosalie was saying. "She's never been in trouble before. She's always on the honor roll. If she's kicked up her heels a little, maybe that's a good sign."

Rosalie always tried to see the best in people, never judged anyone, and for some reason Anne didn't resent her for it, though she lacked such charitable qualities herself. She relied on Rosalie's floating relaxation to balance her own tendency to anticipate the worst, though, Anne noted with some concern, Rosalie had taken to having sweet sherry with her lunch. A recent development. She sipped it now while Anne nibbled at the tuna fish sandwiches Rosalie had made for them.

"I hope you're right, Rosalie. I don't know what to think. Katherine's been so withdrawn lately, so secretive. She put a hook and eye lock on her door, even though Peter and Janie would never dare go in her room without permission."

Rosalie reached for the coffee pot and warmed up Anne's cup. Then she topped off her sherry and lit another cigarette.

"Katherine's always been imaginative," Rosalie observed. "I remember when she was a little girl, it seemed like she had one foot in another world. I love that about her. It wouldn't surprise me if she was holed up in her room writing stories. I wish Lisa had an interest, besides boys."

"Lisa's still at the top of the class," Anne said. Katherine had been a few points behind Lisa all their lives, and she never seemed to mind. Anne figured Katherine took it for granted, Lisa getting the best grades, like a fact of nature. "She's good at all her subjects. Has she ever had less than 100 average in math? Lisa's going to be Valedictorian, you know. She'll get a scholarship to any college she wants to attend."

Anne reminded Rosalie of Lisa's unlimited possibilities almost every time they spoke. It was a sore point with Rosalie's husband, who insisted he could not afford to pay for college. Lisa should take secretarial courses at the community college and be grateful.

"He can't stop her," Anne added.

Rosalie shook her head and took another sip.

"Dave doesn't mean any harm."

Anne doubted that. She almost wished Rosalie would get tipsy enough to say what she really felt about her husband, who always beat Gerald by a mile in the Most Horrible Husband of the Year awards.

"It's just, I think he's afraid of losing her. He worships Lisa. He, well, it's like, he almost flirts with her. They used to rough house and wrestle when she was little, and he still wants to do it. He tries to provoke her. He snaps at her bottom with a towel, and he pinches her. I think, I'm not positive, but I think he even pinched her breast once."

Gerald was a terrible father, absent and neglectful and he could be bombastic and even cruel when he was drinking, but at least Anne didn't have to worry about that…sort of thing. Unless he was haranguing her at the dinner table, Gerald barely noticed Katherine; certainly he had never wrestled or flirted with her.

"Has Lisa said anything to you about it?" asked Anne.

"You know Lisa. She's not one for complaining or confiding. I can tell she doesn't like it, but she's always been his favorite. He's treated her more like a buddy than a daughter. Taught her everything about auto mechanics. She can change a tire, change the oil, take an engine apart. He's always been so proud of her. I think neither of them knows what to do now that she's turning into a woman."

Anne noticed the word woman, a word that seemed to have nothing to do with Katherine, who was still more a tomboy than a girl. But Lisa had become voluptuous a couple of years ago. The clichés of the smart girl who had to dumb herself down for boys or who didn't know how to attract them did not apply to Lisa. A little on the heavier side, she was dark and almost bovine in her serenity and effortlessly sultry. She knew Rosalie worried that Lisa might go too far too soon in the back of some boy's car.

"I tried to talk about it to Dave once, about how he is with her." Rosalie stopped abruptly.

"What did he say?" Anne prompted.

Rosalie took a deep drag and let out a cloud of smoke on a long sigh.

"'Mind your own business, woman. Do I have to remind you who brings home the bacon around here? And while you're at it, try being a better wife.' And we know what that means."

Rosalie had confided in her once: every night. To keep the peace.

"I'm sorry, Anne," Rosalie said. "Here I am telling you my troubles, and you're the one who has to go meet with Mr. Myers. I'm sure it's nothing. Maybe he wants to put her in some special program for talented students."

Rosalie strained for the bright side.

"He asked if Gerald could come, too," countered Anne.

"Oh."

There was nothing positive Rosalie could say to that. She put out her cigarette and reached for Anne's hand. Anne surprised herself by holding on to Rosalie's hand. Tight.

"No," said Anne as Katherine reached to turn on the car radio. "Not now."

Usually Anne was tolerant of Katherine's desire—or was it need?—for the pop music station. She even liked some of the Beatles' music. ("Yesterday" was her favorite.) But today she intended to cut off Katherine's escape routes. Katherine didn't argue, which would have given Anne an opening. She just shrugged and looked out the window.

We need to talk, Anne did not say, what is going on with you? All things that Katherine would meet with that awful silence. How much easier it would be if Katherine were given to histrionics, fits of weeping. Anne could not let the silence be. Now was their chance to talk in the car alone, without the twins popping in and out (she decided to let them take the bus home as usual), without Bear jumping up and yipping with joy. Without Gerald and his cloud of pipe smoke and oblivion. Just the two of them, the June countryside, the green still so fresh and lush, flying past them, the grey road with its yellow lines to guide them, to beckon them on. Maybe she should just keep driving, past the turn to their back road, on to Connecticut, beyond into some unknown place that would allow them to be their secret selves, not just anxious mother and sullen daughter.

"Katherine," she finally spoke. "I'm worried about you."

Katherine did not speak for a moment.

"Katherine?"

"Why?" Katherine said at last.

"Why am I worried about you?"

After she had just learned that Katherine had stopped turning in assignments, except in English? And that was only the beginning of what Mr. Myers had told her.

"Of course it is not unusual," Mr. Myers had informed Anne before Katherine was called in to the conference, "for students to slack off in June, especially seniors. But Katherine is a freshman, an honor student...until this quarter. There is no question that she is college material. If she has one bad grading period, it won't count against her too much, but she needs to pull her grades back up and keep them there if she wants to be admitted to a good college."

He had gone on for a bit in this vein with Anne nodding and murmuring, "of course."

"Is there anything wrong at home?" Mr. Myers had asked, it seemed to Anne, rather abruptly.

Anne must have appeared flustered.

"I am sorry to have to ask. You know our talk here is strictly confidential."

"No," Anne said; she wasn't about to confide in a high school guidance counselor who fancied himself a psychologist.

"Any changes?" he persisted.

"Well," Anne decided this was a safe topic, "as you may remember, we moved out of the village recently. Mr. Bradley changed jobs. He works in Riverton now."

"So he isn't home as much?" Mr. Myers prompted.

Anne found herself focusing on a large pimple on the left side of Mr. Myers' nose; surely some of his students could have given him guidance on how to clear his complexion.

"I wouldn't say there's been much of a change in his hours," Anne said. Feeling she ought to offer something, she tossed in, "Katherine might miss being in the village, closer to her friends."

Mr. Myers, who did in fact have skin on the oily side and not enough hair slicked over a central balding spot, took time to sigh and then fix Anne with what felt like an overly familiar gaze from behind thick glasses.

"Friends like Frank Lomangino Jr.?"

What was the man insinuating?

"Frankie and Katherine were childhood friends," said Anne. "I don't know if you lived in White Hart at the time." Anne vaguely remembered that Mr. Myers was a new hire last year. "They solved the Crowley murder case when Katherine was seven years old. I'm afraid they've grown apart since then."

If she were truthful, Anne had been relieved. There was something about Frankie that both touched her and disturbed her. He had parents who loved him; she knew that, and Lucy Way had taken Frankie as well as Katherine under her genteel wing. Yet Frankie seemed intent on failing at school and fulfilling everyone's worst expectations of him.

"I am sorry to have to be the one to inform you, Mrs. Bradley. I didn't just call you in to discuss Katherine's academic performance. Today Katherine and Frank Lomangino left the school premises together."

"Left?" Anne could not hide her alarm. "Then where are they now?"

"They're in the principal's office. Mr. Banning suggested I have a word with you before they are sent home to see if you have any insight into Katherine's behavior."

"Her behavior?" Anne repeated. "What do you mean?"

"Miss Flaxon, the girls' gym teacher, saw them sneaking off into the woods beyond the playing fields. She has complained before that Katherine has left her position on the outfield to slip into the woods, which by the way is private property—"

"If you mean Rosewood," Anne interrupted, "Katherine has been going for walks there since she was a child. She has permission. It's the next door property to the church. No doubt those woods feel like home to her. If she was upset about something...."

Mr. Myers took off his glasses and wiped them off, as if to give her time to stop to finish her sentence, but she didn't know what else to say. What must he think of how little she knew? She'd had no idea, till now, that Katherine had stopped doing her school work. Unlike the twins, she never needed any help with homework or even any reminding.

"Miss Flaxon saw them running off into the woods." He put his glasses back on and peered at her through them. "Miss Flaxon was outside with the seventh graders in the volley ball court. When the period was over, she went to look for them. We are aware that some students in the high school and even the junior high are abusing cannabis. We have reason to suspect that Frank Lomangino Jr. may be a dealer."

"Why?" For some unaccountable reason Anne bristled. "Because he's a rock musician?"

Because his father has a criminal record, she did not say.

"Mrs. Bradley, please, we are discussing your daughter's welfare. She is a good student, an exceptional student, whose grades have dropped alarmingly, who has violated a school rule in the company of someone who is a bad influence at the very least."

Anne felt hot and cold all over. Frankie and Katherine were minors, but drug use was against the law.

"And were they caught taking drugs?"

"Not so far as we know," he said slowly.

Then what was all the fuss about? So they cut a class? They snuck off to their childhood haunts. Really, it sounded almost…innocent.

"Mrs. Bradley, I'd better just come right out and say it."

"I wish you would."

"Your daughter was found in a compromising position."

"What do you mean?" Anne said sharply.

"She was not wearing a blouse. Frank Lomangino appeared to be fondling her. We don't know how far they went."

Did he mean? Katherine and Frankie? How could that be? They'd known each other since they were children. They were practically brother and sister. Or had been. Katherine's chief complaint was that Frankie ignored her in school. How had they ended up half naked in the woods together?

"We do know that they cut Algebra class, which they are both in danger of failing, and left the school premises during hours when they are required by law to be present unless they have a written excuse from a parent for a legitimate purpose like a doctor's appointment."

Anne fought a sudden, inappropriate urge to yawn.

"I'm afraid Mr. Banning intends to take disciplinary action. Frank Lomangino, who is already on probation, will be suspended for two weeks, subject to expulsion as he is already sixteen. Since this is Katherine's first serious offense, she will be placed on probation and report to detention for the next two weeks. Unless you have something more to say to me in confidence, perhaps it's time to call Katherine in."

"Whatever anyone has to say about my daughter ought to be said in her presence," Anne said. "She ought to have a chance to speak for herself."

When Katherine entered the room, she looked flushed and wild, almost exhilarated, better than Anne had her seen for weeks.

"Katherine," said Mr. Myers, "is there anything you would like to tell your mother or me, something that would help us understand your behavior today."

"I am pleading the fifth."

"Excuse me?" Mr. Myers opened his eyes so wide, his glasses slid down his nose, stopped only by the pimple.

"We learned about the bill of rights in social studies. We had to memorize them, like the Ten Commandments. I have a fifth amendment right not to answer any question on grounds that it may tend to incriminate me."

Perversely, Anne felt proud of her daughter.

"We are not in a court of law, Katherine. I assure you what you say to me here will be kept in confidence. We only want what's best for you."

A sentence, Anne thought, that perhaps should be struck from the English and any other language.

Katherine just shook her head.

There was not much to say after that. When Anne and Katherine left the office, they saw Frankie sitting beside his uncle, Joe Petrone, staring into the middle distance. Once the deputy to the village constable, now Joe was going to night school to earn his RN. Anne guessed Frankie's parents were at work, so Joe had come in their stead. She and Joe looked at each other and shook their heads.

"I pled the fifth, Frankie," Katherine called over her shoulder as Mr. Myers hurried them out. "If they ask you anything, just say, I plead the fifth."

"Katherine," Anne said again, as they neared the turn. She had only a few minutes left. "I need to ask questions. And remember, you can't plead the fifth with your mother."

Katherine's quiet had a different quality.

"Who says?" she asked.

"I do," said Anne firmly.

"So," Katherine shrugged, "ask."

All the questions she should have asked—what's wrong? why don't you care about school anymore?—turned tail, leaving Anne with only one.

"What were you doing with Frankie? I thought you and Frankie were barely speaking."

She could not bring herself to say. Why did you have your shirt off? Maybe Miss Flaxon had been wrong. She had to give Katherine a chance to confide.

"I wanted to find out."

"Find out about what?"

"Sex."

Anne said nothing till she made the turn onto the dirt road, then she pulled off to the side, braking so hard, loose gravel sprayed into the air. Katherine kept looking out the window.

"Katherine, you have to tell me." She took a deep breath. "How far did you and Frankie go? Did you...did you have sexual intercourse? Katherine, you do know what I mean by that? You must tell me, you could...you do know about the risk of pregnancy?"

No answer.

"We are going to sit here till you tell me."

Katherine opened the car door.

"I'll walk the rest of the way."

Before she got out, Anne got a glimpse of Katherine's face. She was crying.

Chapter Twelve

Gerald found himself pulling into the driveway at the Church of Regeneration not quite sure how he had gotten there. He had been on his way home from Riverton, but without even realizing it, he must have taken the turn for the village. Now here he was in his old driveway. He would have parked in his old parking place, but someone else's car was there. Ralph James' old Renault. Of course, this was James' church now.

Then what was Gerald doing here? He wasn't in the habit of dropping by his former home. He was friendly enough with his successor, but he had been careful not to intrude. Should he drive on out the other end of the driveway? Or should he get out and pretend he had some reason to be here, in case someone had seen him stop and recognized his car?

You need a priest.

The thought came so suddenly, seemed so not his own, he hardly registered it. He was tired, over-tired. Work in the wake of the assassinations was tense, demanding. And home, home was worse. Maybe he would just get out and stretch his legs for a moment. Too bad Elsa didn't seem to be here. He would have enjoyed saying hello and catching hell for interrupting her practice. He wondered if she still kept a fifth of vodka secreted among the organ pedals.

"Hey, Rev!" Amos McCready knocked on his window and leaned over to peer in. "I thought that was your wee wreck of a beetle."

"Amos." He rolled down his window. "Haven't you been fired yet? I hoped the new broom might make a clean sweep."

Always good to have a running joke. The antique Scot was supposed to have retired as sexton under Gerald's watch after he broke a hip falling off a ladder.

You need to see a priest.

"Not so easy to fire such an exemplary Christian lambie as myself," Amos was saying.

A lamb who kept a flask of single malt Sheep Dip in his overall pocket, fired off ethnic slurs and told scandalous stories about the prophets by way of teaching Sunday School.

"I was just here helping out the wop. Christian charity, Rev, purely Christian charity. The vines were wreaking havoc with the stucco on the north side of the church. The lad wanted the benefit of my superior wisdom and experience, not to mention a steady hand on the ladder. Say Rev, I'm just on my way to the Corner."

Corner was short for the Corner Bar & Grill where local blue collar workers congregated. Despite his dog collar, Gerald was always welcome there, because he had served in the fire department. In fact, Gerald was legendary for drinking beer with the best of them at firehouse clambakes and refusing to take the hint and excuse himself when it was time for the porno flicks. "The dago said he might meet me there after he stops in at home. Care to join us for a wee dram?"

The dago being Amos' other fond epithet for Frank Lomangino Sr., former bookie, exonerated murder suspect, and the father of Frank Lomangino Jr., with whom Gerald's daughter had been caught AWOL from school premises. And not just AWOL, Gerald knew, but he didn't want to think about what else they had been doing, and he didn't want to raise a glass with the man who had spawned Frankie Jr. even if the boy-hero turned juvenile delinquent had saved Lucy Way's life.

"Thanks, Amos," he said. "I'm on my way home myself."

A priest. You need a priest.

"Well, don't be a stranger, Rev. Take a rest now and then from toiling amongst the benighted big city heathen and visit us rustic folk."

"You bet, you old reprobate!" said Gerald, as Amos patted the hood of his car and shambled down the driveway, weaving a bit from side to side, no doubt from dipping into the Sheep Dip.

Gerald saw men walk like that every day on Lower Main Street, homeless, jobless, listing, listless, each one to be cared for as Christ himself, the least of his brethren, Gerald's brethren. If he admitted the truth, Gerald found all those least brethren so much easier to understand than a wife—or a daughter.

They'd had a terrible time with Katherine when she found out Frankie had been suspended from school, and she had only been given detention. The first day of Frankie's enforced absence, Katherine had refused to go to school. She had accused Gerald of being a hypocrite for trying to make her go.

"You know, you *know* the only reason I'm not being suspended is because I am white and middle class, the minister's daughter, who has always been such a fucking goody-two-shoes."

"Katherine!" said Anne, who rarely defended him. "You will not use that language to your father."

After she missed the bus, Gerald had grabbed Katherine and dragged her to her room, just like the Fox throwing Brer Rabbit into the briar patch. Then he had called the truant officer, another mistake, one that gave her a chance to call him a fascist pig.

He should go home. Gerald put his hand to the ignition key. Anne was at her wit's end with Katherine, who was just scraping by with her grades, Gerald suspected, so she wouldn't have to go to summer school. But what she was going to do all summer, besides hide in her room or walk the dog, they didn't know. Gerald had assumed she would volunteer at the daycare center in Riverton again. He knew she liked Mrs. Simmons. But when Anne insisted Gerald have a talk with her about the job, Katherine mutely (and resolutely) shook her head.

"You need to stop contemplating your navel," he had yelled at her, exasperated. "Stop thinking only of yourself. There are people suffering hardships you can't even imagine. You are privileged. Over-privileged." By which he meant spoiled rotten. "You have an obligation to help others. If you were older, I'd ship you down South to register voters."

As if Anne would ever agree to such a thing.

Katherine turned and looked at him for the first time in what seemed like weeks, months, forever.

"Send me South. Send me to the most dangerous place there is," she said. "I would gladly be murdered."

He wanted to hit her when she said that, knock her across the room. Her eyes stopped him. Those eyes, they held the same expression as the photo of her as a child that he'd had on his desk, clear, piercing, yet distant, looking up at him, looking through him. Those serious child's eyes in a face no longer a child's, a young woman's face, provocative, sensual, insolent. He turned and left the room. Fled, if he were honest. Later he'd put the photo in the bottom of a desk drawer, under a pile of old sermon notes. He couldn't look at it anymore, he couldn't look at her.

A priest.

Without knowing what he meant to do, Gerald took the key from the ignition and slipped it into his pocket. Then he got out of the car and stood in the driveway. The late June air was balmy. It was balm. It smelled like the color green; as if the air itself were green. The roses should be blooming. Gerald didn't have roses at the new house yet. He hadn't had time to plant much. Just a few hanging plants in the entryway, some morning glories getting ready to climb a trellis. He missed the church garden, an old-fashioned garden, planted more than half a century ago. He and Jeremiah were working on getting funding for a community garden in Riverton. Mrs. Simmons and Mrs. Harris weren't waiting (and might very well require legal defense for the vacant lot they had summarily taken over. Community organizing at its finest, Jeremiah had shrugged). They'd already planted lettuce, peas, beans, collards, tomatoes and conned the old men and little kids into weeding. Gerald had spent a couple of hours staking tomatoes that afternoon.

"Go on home, Ger," Jeremiah had said when he'd come back to the office. "You look like you're about to have sunstroke. White folks! Mad dogs and Englishmen. That's you. But seriously, you haven't been yourself lately. Go home. Get some rest."

He didn't want to go home.

Gerald found himself walking down the driveway to the garden where peonies past their first bloom dropped petals and sweet peas tangled as they climbed the garden twine Amos staked each year. The roses were indeed blooming, blousy careless-looking roses scenting the air with a spicy sweetness.

"Hello, Gerald."

Startled, he looked up to find Lucy Way standing beside him. He hadn't noticed her approach.

"I've always loved sweet peas," she said. "They remind me of my school days in England, such a Victorian flower."

So like Lucy not to remark on his presence here. He was grateful.

"I've always liked them, too," said Gerald. "The garden is doing well. I hope the James' are enjoying it."

And he hoped he struck the right tone, generous, not judgmental.

"Oh, I know they are. That is, I mean...."

And Lucy stopped herself, as if she were embarrassed. Was she afraid to sound too enthusiastic about his replacement?

"It's all right," he mumbled.

"What is?" she surprised him by asking.

What was all right? He wished he could tell her. Nothing, nothing is all right. But this was Lucy, his former parishioner, his wife's friend, his daughter's—

"Lucy," he hesitated, then plunged on, "has Anne talked to you about Katherine?"

"Yes." Lucy hesitated in turn. "Gerald, I wish...I wish I could take Katherine with me, on a trip somewhere, get her away from everything...and everyone."

What a brilliant solution! Anne would agree. Relief flooded Gerald's body and he felt dizzy with it.

A priest, the voice came again, unbidden.

"Lucy." He turned to her ready to offer his thanks and blessing when he saw he'd made a mistake.

"Gerald, I think it's all right for you to know now. I think she'd want you to know. Elsa has breast cancer. She will be having surgery and then chemotherapy. I have promised to help care for her."

"Of course," said Gerald, ashamed that his dismay was not just for Elsa, "of course, she'll need you. Poor Elsa, she'll hate being ill."

But his mind was still on Katherine. He had not known until Lucy said it how much he wanted Katherine to go away, somewhere, anywhere. Now it was too late to get her a job as a junior counselor at a summer camp, even if she would have cooperated, which was doubtful. And Anne would never allow him to force her to do anything.

Force her?

"I don't mean to intrude or be presumptuous," Lucy said. "But Anne tells me your brother-in-law's company has posted him to England for a couple of years. I think, well, I think Katherine would love England. I wonder, is it possible she might visit her aunt and uncle for a few weeks?"

At the possibility of a reprieve, Gerald broke out in a fine sweat. A breeze stirred and he felt almost chilled.

"That's a good idea, Lucy. I'll talk to Anne. And, Lucy, I am so sorry about Elsa. If there's anything I can do...."

"Visit her," said Lucy, promptly. "Let her rail at you and curse. She needs a chance to behave badly, and she won't mind doing it in front of you."

Gerald was taken aback, but he had to admit Lucy was an astute judge of character.

"Maybe I'll just stop in and have a word with Ralph on my way out," said Gerald. He could not bring himself to refer to his successor as Father James, even though using the British pronunciation of Ralph, Rafe, as the rector preferred, was almost as awkward. "I assume he knows about Elsa? I wouldn't want him to think I'm presuming if I visit her in the hospital. He's her priest now."

You need a priest yourself.

"Oh, I'm sure he wouldn't, of course I shouldn't speak for him. It's just that I'm sure he'd understand that you and Elsa are old friends."

Gerald vaguely wondered why Lucy was so flustered.

"Since I'm here, I'll just stop in briefly."

Grace Jones, the church secretary was gone for the day, so he couldn't ask her about James' schedule.

"Yes, do," said Lucy earnestly.

She knows you need a priest, the voice said, as he watched Lucy hurry—it seemed as if she hurried—to her car. To get away from him? Did she know or suspect something about him that he did not know himself?

Gerald walked slowly up the driveway. His legs felt so heavy they ached. Maybe he was coming down with something. Maybe he had a fever. Ralph James received his parishioners' personal confessions, something Mildred Thomson had always been pestering Gerald to do. He didn't believe in it, considered it a high church affectation. The general confession should suffice: *We have done those things we ought not to have done and we have left undone those things we ought to have done and there is no health in us.*

What if he didn't know what he had done or left undone?

Father forgive them, for they not what they do.

You let Hal die, an old voice.

He hadn't really. But no one had ever absolved him. *And Katherine, something about Katherine.* He had forgotten her. How could you forget her, Anne had accused, on her first day at the job?

Gerald stepped onto the front porch where his children used to park their tricycles. He stopped in front of the heavy oak door that kept the front hall so dark and cool. He remembered finding Katherine sobbing in front of it. She had run downstairs on her fifth birthday sure that now she'd be able to open it, and the door hadn't budged.

Behold, I stand at the door and knock.

Gerald knocked, but he knew the door was too thick for a knock to be heard unless you hammered on it. So he rang the doorbell.

A moment later Ralph James opened it. He was tall, a little bony. His hair looked like faded sunlight. It was a little on the long side. He was in shirt sleeves, no dog collar. He looked...he looked at ease.

"Gerald, how nice to see you. I was just about to make some tea. Will you join me?"

Tea? How had this man managed to be ordained in the Episcopal Church?

"Oh, no thanks. Listen, I just heard about Elsa Ebersbach and I wanted to touch base with you—"

"Come in for a moment, if you can. I'd appreciate your thoughts on Elsa's situation. You know her much better than I do. She can be a bit—"

"Prickly?" Gerald suggested.

"Just so. Good heavens, it's after five. Perhaps something stronger than tea?"

A priest, said the voice, *you need a—*

He needed a drink. "Sure, maybe. Just a quick one."

And Gerald stepped into the cool, dark absolution of the front hall.

part
two

Captivity

part
two

Captivity

("Mummy, mummy," he tried to call her, but no sound came out. "Make them stop."

Then without opening his eyes, he was awake. It was quiet and dark behind his eyelids, no dancing, howling dolls. But his mother wasn't here. He was in that place where it was always winter and always cold, but also where it was hot and horrible and stifling with hands doing things to him under the covers.

No!

He opened his eyes.

Relief washed over him, for a moment he was a baby again. Innocent, safe.

He was in his own place, his own dream, his own dollhouse where the dolls did as they were told. Lesser men might have had to use cruder methods, drugs, petty acts of violence. But he was a master of, no, he did not want to name his genius. Suffice it to say, he had survived his own cruel initiations. He had lived to triumph. Now....

Everything he saw was his, everything he touched.

And everyone.)

Chapter Thirteen

"I need to call my uncle," Katherine said again, louder this time, in case the woman was hard of hearing.

The woman wore some kind of dress that looked like a uniform, like a maid or a nurse—or a prison matron. She had taken Katherine to some open showers and "hosed her down" as the woman called it, then tossed her some clothes that were not her own, a generic shift that was too big for her. When Katherine was dressed, she'd taken her to a basement kitchen and without asking Katherine what she wanted she'd given her a cup of sweet milky tea and spooned something grey and tasteless into a bowl and handed it to her to eat with a bent spoon.

Gruel, Katherine thought, what Oliver Twist ate in the workhouse. (Where was her bag with her book? Where were her things?) Unlike Oliver Twist, she would not ask for more gruel.

"I said I need to call my uncle."

"Why Bob's-yer-uncle, dearie," the woman responded at last. "We all got uncles, 'aven't we?"

Katherine felt confused for a moment. How did the woman know her uncle's name? Then she remembered, Bob's-your-uncle was an expression. She had no idea what it meant.

"Oh, I daresay, we know all about uncles 'ere."

The woman winked at Katherine and laughed a horrible laugh, leaning towards her across the table, bringing her ugly, made-up face too close, so that her features were unnaturally large. Katherine could smell stale cigarette smoke on the woman's breath. She felt like Jill in the Narnia books at the giants' castle at Harfang. Only it had been nicer at the giants' castle, cleaner and with better food, hot water for baths and fires in the enormous hearths. Of course, Jill didn't know until she saw the open recipe book that the giants were fattening them up to be made into pie for the autumn feast. Then Jill, Eustace, and Puddleglum had managed to escape. Katherine would escape, too…if she were a prisoner. She had to find out. Now.

"My uncle will be worrying about me."

Would he? It occurred to Katherine to wonder. He didn't like her, but still he must feel responsible for her. When he found her (or she found him), he would be furious. He would call her parents and tell them what she had done. What *had* she done?

"Oh, I wouldn't trouble myself too much about that, if I were you. Most uncles are of no account. Only uncle matters around 'ere is Uncle Toby, that's Mister Tobias to you."

Katherine felt as though she were in the sort of book that just plunged you in and didn't introduce you to any of the characters. Things just started happening willy-nilly and somehow you were supposed to know who everyone was. She desperately needed to make sense of something.

"Is Mister Tobias that man who, that man who…."

There was a word for what the man had done, but she couldn't remember it. Her brain felt fuzzy, far away.

"Kidnapped me!" she suddenly blurted out.

The woman squinted her already squinty eyes at Katherine and made a sort of hissing sound.

"That won't do at all, dearie, that sort of talk, not at all."

"Why?" Katherine demanded. "What will 'appen?"

More than had already happened? What had happened to her? Her mind blanked again, but she noticed her dropped h. Some instinct was prompting her to imitate the woman's accent.

"I couldn't say, I'm sure." The woman sniffed and went to a cabinet where she found a bottle and added something to her tea. Katherine knew that smell: gin. "Be a good girl now and I'll give you a nip.

Roughed you up a bit, did 'e? No doubt you deserved it. Still, Uncle Toby don't like it when he leaves marks."

"Uncle Toby," Katherine repeated, "'e wasn't the man who—"

"Lord love you, no! That wasn't never Uncle Toby. That were Tom. Said you two was having a right nice time together, when all of sudden, well, let's just put it that you forgot your manners, didn't you?"

Katherine just stared at the woman who was filling her teacup to the brim. The woman must be crazy and soon she would be drunk. Maybe she would doze off like the giantess cook at Harfang, and Katherine could escape. She began looking around the room; there were several doors, but only one high window where occasionally someone's feet passed by. The door to the outside must be on the same wall.

"Don't even think about it, lovey. There's a good girl. I'll give you this last bit."

And she poured a couple of drops into Katherine's tea cup.

"Thank you," Katherine said, and she pretended to drink, hoping her meekness would put the woman off guard.

"Now then, bottoms up and finish yer porridge if you know what's good for you. I got no more time to waste on you. Got the whole gaggle to get up and ready. Lazy sluts. You'd think they was all the Queen of Sheba."

There were others?

She started to ask a question when the woman pulled her none too gently to her feet and smacked her bottom.

"Where am I going?"

"Now what kind of a question is that? Back to your room, you silly little sheep, till Mister Tobias has had a look at you."

"Please," she pleaded. "Please just let me use the telephone."

"Please," the woman mimicked her, "please just let me use the telephone. What kind of hoity-toity talk is that? Tom says you's from the East End tossed out in the street by your dad and stepmum. Won't do to put on airs around 'ere."

Katherine felt dizzy, as if she had downed the gin.

"But I'm not, I'm—please just let me use the phone."

"Do you see a bleedin' telephone anywhere around 'ere?"

Katherine hadn't seen one, but there must be one somewhere. Not that she knew her uncle's number. But she could call the operator, ask for his work. It had the same name as a gas station. Petrol, she told herself. They called it petrol. Or she could call her mother, the operator would help her.

"Take me to a pay phone," she pleaded. There must be one not far, on some street corner somewhere, red like the double-decker busses. She had no coins, but surely someone would help her.

All at once, she twisted out of the woman's grip and bolted. The first door she came to opened onto a broom closet, but the second one led to a hall. She ran till she came to a door. Locked. Katherine was cornered. She could hear the nurse-jailor laughing and wheezing as she made her way down the hall.

She grabbed Katherine by the shoulders, turned her around and smacked her hard across the face.

"No more of that," she said. "Or I'll 'ave to set Tom on you again."

Chapter Fourteen

"Hello?"

Lucy heard the clock strike seven, later than she usually slept, but then she'd had a bad night. Still early for a phone call. Her heart pounded from being woken from a sound sleep and running for the phone. The person at the other end of the phone seemed breathless too.

"Lucy?"

"This is she."

"Lucy, it's Gerald. Bradley."

She already knew that. She recognized his voice. But Gerald never called her. It was always Anne who called to see how she was or to make arrangements for Katherine, or, more recently, Katherine herself who called.

"What's wrong, Gerald. Where's Anne?"

"Nothing," said Gerald too quickly. "I mean Anne's fine, I mean, no, she's not fine. She asked me to call you. I told her we shouldn't worry you, but she insisted. It's probably just a misunderstanding. I am sure everything is all right."

"Gerald." Lucy took a breath and sensibly sat down on the window seat beside the hall phone, something Gerald should have told her to do, but never mind. He was clearly in a state. "Please tell me what has happened."

"Katherine, Katherine is...we got a call from my brother-in-law, Bob. Katherine is missing. I'm sure it's a mistake."

Gerald blithered for a minute, but Lucy hardly heard what he was saying.

"How long?" She cut him off.

"Just over twenty-four hours."

"So, the police have been alerted," Lucy stated.

"Yes," said Gerald, silent for a moment.

She could feel it hitting him.

"She went into London for the day with her uncle. My sister's in the hospital recovering from surgery. Bob says she had his phone number, address, and a map. She was supposed to meet him back at his office at five...."

Gerald was off and running again, attempting to reassure himself and her that of course Katherine was all right.

"Gerald, listen," Lucy said when he repeated himself for the third time. "I think we had better clear your phone line. Please let me know if there is anything I can do."

There was a silence. Lucy could hear Gerald struggle to speak now that she'd cut him off from the refuge of empty words.

"Pray," he finally said.

He might as well have told her to breathe.

"Of course," she said, then added, "Is Anne, does Anne need—"

"I don't know," he said, suddenly sounding far more desperate than he had before. "But yes, please come, Lucy. Please come as soon as you can. I don't know, I don't know how to—"

"I'll be right over, Gerald," she said, and she hung up the phone.

When Lucy arrived at the Bradley's house, Gerald's car was gone from the driveway. How could he? was her first thought. How could he leave Anne alone at a time like this? Don't judge, came the immediate response, don't judge.

The white dog Bear bounded from the backyard to greet her, ceasing his barking as soon as he recognized her voice. The Bradleys had never quite managed to break the exuberant dog of jumping up to lick the faces of guests. He liked it all the better if they fell over and he could continue his ministrations with them on the ground. She braced herself to meet his embrace, but Bear seemed unusually subdued and came forward whining softly, placing his muzzle in her hand.

He knew, Lucy thought, he knew something was wrong. Animals always did. As she bent to comfort the dog, her own panic and grief threatened to overwhelm her. She must stay calm, for Anne.

"It's all right, old boy," Lucy murmured. "She'll be all right."

Lucy went to the front door. Beside it, morning glory vines climbed a trellis. In July they were not yet in bloom, but their leaves, heart-shaped, had unfurled. Gerald was the one who planted and tended flowers, Anne had told her so more than once, not so much in admiration but in exasperation for all he did not tend. Anne did not spell out her husband's failings, she did not complain, exactly, but Lucy knew, more than she wanted to. She was, and wasn't, part of this family whose unhappiness she sensed but did not fully comprehend.

No one answered her ring or knock, so after a moment, Lucy tried the door and found it unlocked.

"Anne?" she called from the front hall. "Anne, it's Lucy."

Before she could decide whether or not to look for her in the kitchen, Anne called to her from the top of the stairs.

"I'm here, Lucy! Come up. I'm packing."

Lucy had seen Katherine's room, of course, and Peter's and Janie's who each had a room of their own in this sprawling house, which had been built onto in a haphazard way. She had never been in the master bedroom, but her reticence had no place here. She climbed the stairs and found Anne in her room where she had resumed her packing. There was nothing remarkable about the room; it was tidy, as Anne's house always was, with some good prints on the wall, Durer, Cezanne. Only the top of Gerald's bureau hinted at any disorder, loose change and pipe tobacco, a couple of envelopes opened but not filed.

Anne cleared what must have been Gerald's chair, dropping the clothes she found there into a laundry basket. Gesturing for Lucy to sit, she turned to her own dresser, its surface spare. Where other people might have been helpless or distraught in a crisis, Anne became more efficient. Someone who didn't know Anne might have thought her cold, but Lucy knew Anne was terrified. Counting out underwear and folding it neatly into her suitcase on the bed was all that stood between Anne and the howling abyss. Lucy knew better than to push her over the edge with sympathy that could mean nothing in this moment. So she sat quietly and waited.

"Gerald told you," Anne stated, rummaging around in another drawer of her bureau and finding a toiletry bag.

"Yes," Lucy said, biting her tongue to keep from asking if they had heard anything more.

"Did he ask you to come and babysit me?" She sounded angry.

Lucy hesitated for a moment.

"He said you asked him to call me," she felt obliged to say. "I offered to come."

Anne said nothing for a moment, her face disturbingly blank as she moved back and forth between the bureau and the suitcase. Clearly she was still in shock.

"I told him to go away," said Anne after a moment. "I made him take the twins to their lessons. I couldn't...Lucy, I couldn't stand the sight of him. I know it's wrong. She's his daughter, too, and I suppose he must love her. I know couples are supposed to cling together in a crisis, but I couldn't, I can't...."

Anne disappeared into the bathroom and began going through the medicine cabinet. Lucy got up and went to sit on the edge of the bed, so that she could hear Anne if she wanted to say more. Lucy knew Anne and Gerald's son had died, more than a decade ago now, before they had come to the Church of Regeneration—the real reason, Lucy suspected, they had moved to a small town from the city where Gerald had been curate at a fashionable church. Anne had never spoken much about her son, but Lucy guessed his death had not brought Anne and Gerald closer. Grief was like that sometimes, people stumbled around in it, blind, alone.

"We haven't told the twins yet," Anne said. "I don't know what to tell them. I don't even know what's happened.... I wish I still had those tranquilizers horrible Dr. Aiken prescribed. I need something to get me through the flight. If I drink, I'll just be sick."

Anne had told Lucy more than once that she had no intention of flying, ever. The very thought of air travel filled her with horror. She'd seen Europe in her youth before the war, crossing the Atlantic on the Queen Mary. She'd had no desire to go back or not enough to make her consider boarding a scrap of metal where she'd be trapped miles above earth.

"Take Dramamine. It will make you sleepy," Lucy advised, glad for a chance to offer something practical. "When is your flight?"

"Tonight at seven. I'll be in London in the morning."

Lucy noticed the singular pronoun.

"Is Gerald not going with you?"

Anne's back stiffened, and she dropped something, almost hitting her head on the sink as she bent to pick it up. A small leather manicure case.

"The twins could stay with me, you know," Lucy added gently.

Anne put the manicure case in a separate zippered pocket.

"I think it is best for one of us to stay here with them. And Gerald has his work. He'll be better off with something to occupy his mind."

He would not be able to concentrate. Lucy knew that. Anne must know it, too.

"I could at least stay with them while Gerald takes you to the airport."

Lucy saw Anne hesitate, a lipstick in her hand. Reaching into the toilet article bag, she found a smaller zipper bag and put the lipstick and a pot of rouge inside that.

"I've hired Joe Petrone to drive me."

It was probably for the best, Lucy considered. Gerald would be beside himself. Joe Petrone, Frank Lomangino's brother-in-law, who was putting himself through nursing school by providing limo service, would be a calm presence.

"Oh, what a good idea," Lucy said, and then, oddly enough, she wondered if it was.

"Yes," said Anne, as if she had doubts of her own. "We have to agree on what to tell the twins before I go. We could say I am just visiting Katherine. But I don't know if I can count on Gerald to...."

Stick to the story when he's had a few drinks? Lucy guessed the rest of the sentence.

"Forgive me for saying so, Anne," she said. "But they will know something is wrong."

Anne snapped closed her toiletry bag, put it down and held onto the sink. Then she looked into the mirror, and Lucy caught a glimpse of Anne's reflection, saw her register how stricken she looked and how the sight of her own face suddenly made the horror of what was happening more real. She turned abruptly from the mirror and met Lucy's eyes for the first time.

"But what can I tell them?" Anne's voice rose now, her rigid control giving way. "Lucy, I can't bear not knowing. Is she lost or…did she, did she run away? She wasn't happy with her aunt and uncle. They weren't happy with her. Katherine said so in a letter, and they… they actually suggested Katherine might be, there might be something wrong with Katherine. Fey, my sister-in-law called her. I'm afraid it was a terrible mistake to send her there."

Lucy's mistake, Lucy did not say aloud. It was not for Anne to comfort her.

"Do you think Katherine would run away?" Anne went on. "Just a few months ago, I would never have dreamed she would do such a thing. But now I don't, I don't know anything. You know her. You know her better than I do right now. Better than anyone."

Did she? Lucy wondered. Did she? Katherine had withdrawn from her, too. Fey. What an odd word to choose. Did Katherine's aunt know that the fairies were called the fey? Lately it had seemed that some part of Katherine had gone away, been stolen away. She did not want to worry Anne any further. Anne needed her help.

Help, Lucy heard the voice in her dream again, Katherine's voice, *help*.

"She's not dead, Anne," Lucy heard herself saying, and she heard also the note of conviction in her voice, as if she were not merely saying what Anne longed to hear.

"How do you know, Lucy?" Anne almost whispered. "*What* do you know?"

"Oh, Anne," said Lucy, and she stood up and went to her. Anne was not someone who welcomed touch, Lucy knew. Not someone you could comfort that way, but Lucy took her hand. Maybe it was her own need, a need to be anchored somewhere, not lost in the terrible places between one world and another. The waterless country where demons wandered. "Oh, Anne, I don't know."

"But you do know, Lucy Way," Anne was suddenly fierce. "You *do*, tell me!"

Lucy took a breath.

"It's just...I thought I heard her calling me last night," Lucy said. "In my dreams. I even got up to look in her room."

Her room.

All at once Anne put her arms around Lucy. "I'm sorry. She's your child, too."

They held each other for a moment. Lucy did not know if the tears on her cheek were Anne's or her own.

"She's alive, Anne," Lucy said again when they let go. And in terrible trouble, she did not say aloud. "I don't think she meant to run away, but—"

Lucy suddenly felt confused, as if she were talking in her sleep and then woke up enough to know she was not making sense.

"But?" repeated Anne.

"I don't know, Anne, I truly don't know. Sometimes a flash of something comes, and then it goes. I'm sorry."

Anne put the toiletry bag in the suitcase.

"I suppose God knows where she is?" Anne appealed to Lucy.

Lucy knew Anne struggled with faith, did not have what she considered to be the gift of faith, a talent, like musical ability. She envied and sometimes resented those who did. She needed Lucy to have it now. Though in this moment, it was Anne who was reminding Lucy of something, something she had forgotten.

"Yes," said Lucy. "Yes, indeed, God does know where she is."

And he will keep her safe, Lucy longed to say. But hadn't God known about all the people in the death camps, hadn't he seen all the people trapped alive under rubble during the Blitz. Hadn't he seen the gunmen when Dr. King stepped out on the balcony and Mr. Kennedy left the podium....

Lucy, said a voice inside her, chiding, loving. The voice she loved best in the world.

I don't understand, she answered the voice.

You don't have to.

Be with her, Lucy prayed. *Let us find her. In your name, I pray.*

Aloud she said, "I am going to make us some coffee and sandwiches, Anne."

"Please don't say you must keep your strength up," said Anne.

"All right," said Lucy. "I won't. "

"I'm going to tell the twins she's gotten lost," Anne decided. "But I'll find her. I will find her."

Anne took a breath and let it out. For a moment she had convinced herself, found her own faith, far better than relying on Lucy's.

"I'll be down in a minute," Anne said. "I just have to pack an extra pair of shoes and some galoshes."

"I'll be in the kitchen," said Lucy.

And she turned. And fled.

Chapter Fifteen

"*Precious Lord, take my hand,*" Katherine sang, softly at first, then almost wailing it. It did not matter who heard, maybe someone would hear. "*Lead me on to the light! Precious Lord, please, please take my hand.*"

She did not know what time it was, though it appeared to be daytime still, the indirect light cast a grey pall first on one wall, then another. A while ago, someone had unlocked her door, shoved a tray through, closed and locked it again before she could even see who it was.

"Come back," she shouted a few times, though she guessed it wouldn't do any good.

She was a prisoner. She didn't know why, but that's what she was. The door was locked; the windows barred. She supposed she ought to be grateful—and oddly enough she found she was—that someone had emptied her chamber pot and cleaned up the vomit in the sink while she was out at the shower and eating gruel in the kitchen. Maybe her attempt to make a run for it accounted for the tray being shoved through the door.

She had been hungry, and there was nothing else to do, so she'd picked up the sandwich, white bread and some thin spread of greyish, brownish paste. There was a cup of tea, or she supposed it was tea. It looked and tasted like watery milk. She'd sniffed at the sandwich and almost gagged. Liverwurst. Worst liver, as she and the twins called it when their grandmother once tried, unsuccessfully, to make them eat it.

The twins. Her little sister and brother. If she closed her eyes and concentrated, she could picture them in the yard outside the house, the yellow house. Where they lived. Where she had lived. It seemed long ago. Not quite real. Before. Eat your sandwich, her grandmother had ordered, don't waste good food. You don't know what it's like to be hungry, to not know where your next meal is coming from. When her back was turned, they'd slipped the sandwiches to Bear who was conveniently located under the table.

Girl, you better eat, no matter how bad it tastes. A voice spoke in Katherine's mind; it sounded like Aramantha. *You don't know when your next meal might be.*

Maybe she was going crazy, hearing voices. But even imagining Aramantha's voice made her feel braver, less terrified and alone. She managed a few bites before she gagged. The same with the tea. Thank God, there was a sink in the room. She dumped out the contents of the cup and had a drink of water, a long cool drink of water. And then she lay down on the bed and went to sleep.

She woke up before she opened her eyes. She knew she did not want to open them. So she lay awake with them shut for as long as she could. A distant toilet flushed. Someone ran water, old plumbing groaned, pipes rattled, traffic sounded louder, more insistent though still distant. A pigeon whirred and cooed, and she opened her eyes and sat up in time to see a flutter of wings. Grey wings with a tiny bit of green and purple iridescence.

She was still in the room, her cell. She wanted to weep. She would if she thought of her mother or Lucy Way or Frankie. No, not Frankie. Thinking of Frankie might help. How many times had she and Frankie played games of danger (and once they had really been in danger). Being taken aboard spaceships or being pirates fighting on ship deck. They saw the movie "The Great Escape" every Saturday afternoon for weeks. After that, they pretended they were prisoners of war, outwitting the Nazis. The crawl space under the church was a tunnel they'd dug. These were only imaginary games. But even as children they knew: terrible things really did happen. A few years ago, Katherine had read *The Diary of Anne Frank* over and over. Anne Frank had been a prisoner, hiding in that attic space with her family, never able to go outside. Having to keep quiet. And later she had died in a concentration camp. Being brave did not always mean you survived, Lucy had said when she asked her about the war. And still somehow being brave mattered.

Was she brave? She didn't know. She wanted to find out.

At least she did not have to hide or be quiet. Her captors, whoever they were, knew she was here. That man had brought her to whatever this place was, that man who had...(She could see him from outside, as if she hovered in a basement window looking down at him holding her down on the bed, heaving himself into her. Only she wasn't there. How else could she see his bottom, so much whiter than the rest of him, pumping up and down?). And that ogress with the squinty eyes and the huge nostrils had locked her in here. She had told her to shut up. Well, she wouldn't. She would show her. She would show them.

And she began to sing all the Aretha songs she knew. Aretha made her feel braver than Joni Mitchell or Judy Collins, even braver than Laura Nyro. She sang her way through *Lady Soul* and then she found herself singing "Precious Lord" again. She didn't know it that well. She had only heard it a few times on the radio and seen Aretha singing it on television for Martin Luther King, Jr's funeral. She didn't know all the words, but she found it didn't matter. She could just keep singing the song without knowing where it was going. Words came to her. The song sang itself in her. And while she was singing, there was nothing else.

"*Through the storm, through the night, lead me on to the light,*" she sang over and over. "*Please, ple—ee –ee—ee—ee—ee—ze, lead me on.*"

Katherine paused for breath and heard tittering and whispering outside her door, muffled giggles. Suddenly she became embarrassed. Much as she might have wanted someone to hear, someone passing by who might come and rescue her, the audience had been imaginary. She didn't want people laughing at her. She held her breath, listening hard, to the scuffles and whispers.

"Go on," someone said at last, a young voice, "sing more. You're a right a Maria Callas, you are."

Katherine wasn't sure if the girl was making fun of her or not. She didn't know much about opera, her mother wasn't a fan, but she thought Maria Callas was a famous opera singer. Opera was something people her age usually made fun of. And a far cry from Aretha.

"Not really," Katherine answered, cautiously.

"Cor," said the girl, thrilling Katherine for a second by sounding just like the real Eliza Doolittle. "Don't gimme that. You got a pair a lungs on you."

"A regular songbird," someone else put in.

"Yeah, like a canary in a coalmine."

More giggles.

"Good thing the Angel of Death is down for the count."

It was hard to talk to people you couldn't see. She didn't even know how many of them were out there, but she didn't want to miss a chance to find out where she was, and maybe how to get out.

"Who's the Angel of Death?" she asked.

Laughter.

"You must have seen 'er. Bitch dressed like a bleedin' nurse. If you 'aven't, you will all too soon."

"You mean the one who drinks gin out of a teacup?" Katherine ventured.

"That's 'er. She passes out round this time of day. Only break we get."

"But then we pays for it," someone put it.

"Wakes up meaner 'an a snake, she does."

"You'll see."

Katherine did not see much yet.

"We better get back to our rooms before she wakes up or we'll all catch it."

"Wait!" Katherine said. "Are you prisoners, too?"

A burst of laughter subsided into a silence Katherine found unnerving.

"What is this place, anyway?"

More silence followed by a whispered conference.

"That's a lotta questions for someone 'ose face we ain't even seen yet."

"Nor name we don't even know."

"And you talk funny."

"I talk funny?" repeated Katherine.

"Yeah, almost like you was an American or somefink. Tom Cat said you was from Stepney, but you don't talk like nobody I know."

Katherine wanted to say, I *am* an American. There's been a terrible mistake. I am not supposed to be here. If they didn't trust her, how could she trust them?

"There's something doesn't add up about you, and if Uncle Toby gets wind of what you might call a fishy smell, it'll be the worse for you."

"You might end up like Sephie, as we knew her."

"Who's Sephie?" asked Katherine. "What happened to her?"

There was a silence on the other side of the door that was full of things unsaid. She could almost hear glances being exchanged, heads being shaken, fingers held to lips.

"Short for Persephone," someone finally spoke.

"Queen of the Underworld. That were her beat."

Katherine felt even more confused.

"No one's took her place yet, not as we know of. Maybe you'll be the one."

"Long as it's not me," said someone else.

"There's other empty cribs, too. It weren't just Sephie—"

"No, it were anyone wot listened to 'er daft schemes. Me I'm keepin' me 'ead down."

"Listen," Katherine felt desperate. "I have, I mean I 'ave no idea wot you're on about. Where in the bleedin' 'ell are we?"

There was another silence.

"Cor, will the real you please stand up!" someone whistled.

But what if there *was* no real her?

Before she could think of an answer, someone hissed, "Sharp's the word, ladies. I just 'eard the trumpet sound."

Soft titters.

"She means the trumpet at the Angel of Death's back end, luv. You'll learn to 'arken for that sound. Toora then."

Katherine heard sound of scampering feet. She didn't dare call after them. Then she became aware of someone still lingering at the door.

"Word to the wise," someone whispered. "The less anyone knows about you, the better. Specially Uncle Toby. Good luck, then."

That's right, agreed Aramantha. *Forget about brave, what you need to be is smart.*

"Thank you," Katherine whispered back.

Chapter Sixteen

Anne waved her last to Gerald, the twins, and Bear, as the sedan pulled out of the driveway, every muscle in her body so tense, she was not sure she could ever move again. Then almost against her will, she leaned back against the seat. She did not want to relax. She did not want to rest. But for the first time since the call had come, there was nothing else to do. If Gerald had been driving, she could not have let go. She would have been sitting bolt upright beside him, map at the ready, annoying him by warning him too far in advance of a turn or exit, which often as not he missed, cursing, until he—or more likely she—could figure out how to get back on course. He was an erratic, distracted driver, always adjusting himself in the seat, taking off his coat, fumbling for cigarettes and lighter, fiddling with the radio dial, annoyed when he found it tuned to Katherine's pop music station.

Katherine, oh, Katherine.

If Anne wept in the back seat, Joe Petrone would not know, or if he did, he would not comment. She moved over to the middle of the seat where he would not be able to meet her eyes in the rearview mirror. Thank God for the man, if there was a God, thank him. She had wondered if she ought to sit in the front seat. She and Joe were acquaintances, family friends, sort of. They had both helped to catch a murderer. Gerald would have sat in the front seat with Joe, to prove he was not an upper middle class snob. But Joe had resolved any question of where she should sit by opening the door of the back seat, and helping her in, his hand under her elbow. He would make a good nurse, she thought, his touch firm and kind at once, impersonal but... personable. Caring but not demanding that she care. What a relief to be the sick person, she thought, no, not the sick person, the passenger.

As Joe turned seamlessly onto the entrance ramp to the parkway, Anne fell asleep.

When she came to she felt disoriented, almost drugged. It took a moment for what had happened to catch up with her, for the sick weight to plunge to the pit of her stomach. She remembered that from when Hal died; every waking was like that, the terrible knowledge breaking over her again. Hal. Dead. Katherine. Missing.

Without even knowing she did it, she bent over and put her face in her hands as if she could burrow back into forgetfulness. It was dark behind her hands, but the late afternoon light blared all around like the traffic noise. She dropped her hands and looked out the window at the hideous wastelands you had to pass on the way to any airport. The last time she had been to this part of the world had been the 1964 World's Fair. Of course it had been hot, and the lines had been long. She remembered Katherine and Frankie, whom they'd taken along at Katherine's insistence, annoying everyone by calling out "sit-down strike!" and sitting cross-legged on the filthy pavement while they waited to get into some exhibit or another. She'd had to speak sharply to both of them for making fun of Pepsi's Small World exhibit, which had entranced Janie. Katherine and Frankie had been eleven and twelve then, still like brother and sister, just before their, what could you call it, estrangement? Teenaged awkward phase?

Which had somehow ended in the woods with Katherine half-naked. Anne still did not know how far they had gone that day. Despite Katherine's brazen admission of sexual curiosity, she would not tell her mother what had happened. What it meant. She and Frankie did not seem to be dating in the usual sense, not that they would have been allowed to after being caught off in the woods and getting hauled into the principal's office.

Now it occurred to her wonder: Would Frankie know? Would he know what had been going on with Katherine, why she'd been so withdrawn, even hostile? If he did, would he talk? Would he admit it if they had gone all the way.... Dear God, what if Katherine ran away because she was pregnant! Without knowing it, she had sat up straight at the edge of her seat, as if straining to see out of the front window.

"All right back there, Mrs. Bradley?"

Of course she was not all right, she didn't say. She would not be all right anywhere in the world until she found Katherine.

"I mean are you comfortable?" he added as if he read her thought. "Need any more air?"

"I'm fine," she said. "I was, I was just looking to see where we are. Have we passed the World's Fairgrounds yet?"

They were still there, a ghostly monument to a more hopeful time, the Unisphere a beacon of the small friendly world, where costumed dolls whirled to music sung by children.

"Coming up pretty soon," said Joe. "We're making good time. Not too much traffic, considering it's almost rush hour."

Anne knew Joe had factored in time for possible delays, so there would be no need for added worry. She might end up with a lot of time at the airport. Alone. When was the last time she had been alone? Apart from in her house, doing housework. How would she get through the awful waiting in the ugly, sterile building with all the strangers who would not know that her child was missing (the second child she had lost, but Katherine was not dead. Lucy had said so). And then the hours and hours in the air, in the dark, over the dark ocean, and the landing after a sleepless night. What is the purpose of your trip? Would they ask that at customs? Business or pleasure?

Sorrow, terror.

Then the ruin—it felt like a ruin—of the World's Fair come into view.

"Did you know Frankie came with us to the fair?" she asked. "It seems so long ago now."

She saw him nod. Did he sense there was more she wanted to say?

"Joe, I mean Mr. Petrone."

"Joe," he corrected her softly.

"You probably know…that's right you were there. Frankie and Katherine got into trouble towards the end of school."

"Yeah, I remember. All too well."

"Do you think," she began not quite sure what she wanted to ask, "do you think Frankie knows what's going on with Katherine? I mean, sometimes kids tell each other things they won't say to their parents. Do you think, more happened between them than we, well, than I know?"

Joe waited so long to answer, she thought he hadn't heard or maybe had chosen not to. It was an awkward, intimate thing to talk about.

"I know Frankie's shook up. I could talk to him. If it makes you feel any better, that day they went AWOL, I know it looked bad, but I don't think they did anything much. A lot of people think Frankie's trouble, but he's a decent kid. Hides it pretty good, but he is. If he can tell me anything more, I'll let you know right away."

Before Anne could say anything, he signaled to change lanes so he could pass a noisy truck. Then briefly—she must have moved closer to the window when she was asleep—their eyes met as he checked the rear view mirror before switching lanes again. There was something so reassuring about him, she found herself wishing he could come into the airport with her, wait with her, stay with her till she landed.

"Is someone meeting you in London?" he asked, again almost as if he could hear her thoughts.

"My brother-in-law, at least I think he is."

Gerald had made those arrangements. Pat was Gerald's sister. She had never been close to either of Gerald's sisters, who, like Gerald's mother, always implied they knew better than she did how to run a household and raise children. They were all handier and thriftier and did not tolerate laziness or what her mother-in-law called woolgathering in children. They thought she spoiled her children and didn't let Gerald have enough say in their upbringing. For all that, Anne was fond of her peppery little mother-in-law (not quite five feet tall) and fended off her criticism of her housekeeping by saying, "I have saved this closet or drawer for you to clean out." As long as she had a task, her mother-in-law was generally cheerful.

"But my mother would come and stay with the twins," Gerald had protested when she told him she wanted to go alone. "Or Ellen would." His other sister. "I can't let you go alone."

But, she noted, he had. And his family would blame her. Maybe she was to blame. For everything.

"I think, I hope we will go straight to the police in London. I want to know what they know, what they are doing. I don't know what I can tell them, but maybe something...."

Anything. Her aunt and uncle didn't really know Katherine. But what could she tell the police? She is imaginative. Kind. Brave. Angry. And I don't know why.

"Joe, have you ever, I mean, when you were with the police, did you ever find a missing person?"

"We never had a missing person case when I was on the force," he said.

And then he hesitated. She wondered if he knew of some case, something so awful he didn't want to tell her. Don't spare me, she almost said. But maybe she didn't want to know.

"It's not the same situation at all," he began, "but my wife and son, well, they went missing. In Korea."

Anne felt a jolt to her whole body, like waking suddenly from a dream of falling.

"Oh, Joe. I'm so sorry. I didn't know."

Who did know, she wondered? His family, surely. But no one had ever mentioned it to her. She had vaguely wondered why he wasn't married. Then when he had quit the police force to go to nursing school, she was sure she wasn't the only one who had thought (without really thinking about it) that he might be homosexual.

"And they never, I mean the army never—?"

She looked in the rearview mirror, but he didn't meet her eyes.

"I shouldn't have mentioned it, Mrs. Bradley. You've got enough on your plate."

"Anne," she said. "Please call me Anne."

Chapter Seventeen

"I know it's none of my business," Jeremiah was saying.

Gerald took another large gulp of his drink, gin and club soda; the nameless bar on lower Main Street did not have tonic, and the gin was not his usual brand. It didn't matter as long as it dulled his pain and confusion. But he knew when people said, "it's none of my business" they meant they were going to tell you something you didn't want to hear. So he fortified himself.

"Give it to me straight up, Jer."

Was that the expression? Or was that what you said when you ordered a drink? Was he drunk already? On just a few swallows? Maybe he was. He didn't think he had eaten that day. Anne had kept him busy and away from the house driving the twins places, and then doing what seemed like six months' worth of grocery shopping, which took him forever, because Anne was the one who did the shopping, so he didn't know how to find anything and was too stunned to ask. His mother had arrived, unannounced, moments after Anne had left in Joe Petrone's sedan, bringing with her a whole turkey, thrusting it into the oven before she greeted anyone. It wasn't as easy to escape to the office as it had been when he lived at the rectory and his office was just down the driveway. But that was the excuse he'd made to her. He had to get away somewhere or he felt his head would burst, his skin would explode, or he would tear it off.

"You be back here at six for dinner," she had shouted after him, shaking the turkey baster she had clutched in her fist like a weapon.

She was staying with them, she had announced, whether he liked it or not, for as long as she deemed necessary. Staying, cooking, cleaning, laundering, driving the twins wherever they needed to go, driving him crazy.

"Okay, Ger, listen up. You have to go."

Gerald did not immediately understand. Have to go? Leave his job? Was he that ineffectual? Was Jeremiah firing him? But wait. Jeremiah wasn't his boss. He wasn't Jeremiah's boss. They both worked for the OEO. Colleagues, more than colleagues, friends.

"Why? What have I done?"

What had he done? *You have done those things you ought not to have done, and left undone those things you ought to have done. And there was no health in him.*

"You haven't done anything, Ger," Jeremiah went on. "That's the point. Even if there's nothing you *can* do, you got to go. You got to be over there with Anne. You got to look for your daughter."

Gerald didn't answer. He stared into his drink. He was drinking it faster than the ice cubes were melting. The sea level was sinking, the ice cubes rising like an arctic mountain range. He lifted the glass and the ice cubes collided with his nose. Icebergs crashing into the Titanic. And he was sunk.

"No one expects you to be at work, Ger. Everyone feels for you. They would care even if they didn't know Katherine. But they all remember her from last summer. They love her, and they love you. Did you know they already got a prayer chain going? Somebody will be praying for that little girl 'round the clock. Now your mother is here with the twins. You got sick days, vacation days, whatever. Go! If you need money for airfare, just say the word. We'll take up a collection. The community's got your back, man."

As if to illustrate the point, the bartender showed up at their shadowy back booth and set another gin and soda down in front of Gerald and a beer in front of Jeremiah.

"This round on the house," he said, and then he disappeared.

Nobody wants to see a grown man crying into his drink, and that's what Gerald was doing as quietly as he could. He didn't deserve it, to be cared for this way. He didn't deserve it. Under the table, Jeremiah put his hand on Gerald's knee and let it rest there warm and sure as a patch of sun on a cold day in hell.

Gerald took a long drink and got a hold of himself enough to speak.

"Anne didn't want me to go with her," he almost whispered it. "She insisted on going alone. She said, she said the twins needed a parent with them. I don't...I don't think that's the real reason, but that's what she said."

Jeremiah didn't answer. His hand kept resting on Gerald's knee. Jeremiah's hand didn't judge him.

"I'm a lousy father, Jeremiah," he said. "That's the truth. That's why Anne doesn't want me near her now, because I—"

Because he what? Confusion overcame him again. Why can't you spend more time with them, he could hear Anne saying. How could you forget to pick her up and on her first day of work? After you insisted she take the bus! How could you forget? Why are you so hard on her? Why were you so hard on him? She's only a child, he's only a child, they're only children.... But there was something more, and he didn't know what it was. He couldn't ask Anne. He couldn't ask Jeremiah. Only God knew. Oh hell, God knew. Gerald did not believe he could ever be forgiven.

"That don't make no never mind," said Jeremiah softly.

Gerald had noticed Jeremiah's speech became more Black when he wanted to make a point.

"We all sinners, Ger, you know that. We all stumble and fall." Jeremiah who, unlike Gerald, had refused to follow in his preacher father's footsteps, could still preach. "The question is, will you get up? Do what you got to do to be a man? Anne is crazy out of her mind with worry. We know this. And maybe she's mad as hell at you for who knows what. The question is, what do you need to do now? I told you what I think, now I'm asking you, my brother."

Gerald looked up at Jeremiah and realized he'd been avoiding his eyes till now. It was the same as not looking directly into the sun. Too much fire and truth. Too much....

Love.

"You're right, Jer," he said. "I don't need to be here. The twins don't need me. You know we had them after...after my son died. We never talked about it, but I think we were both glad there were two of them, not just one. Made it less like, well we couldn't replace Hal anyway. The twins always had each other."

He looked back at Jeremiah who continued to hold Gerald steadily in his gaze.

"And Katherine?" Jeremiah asked. "Where did she fit in?"

Gerald took a ragged breath, downed the rest of his drink, and signaled for another. Jeremiah wasn't accusing him, he told himself. This was his chance. This was his chance to...what?

Confess.

"I don't know, Jer. I think she kind of got lost."

She is lost, he remembered, and the panic and grief rose up and hit him like a rogue wave. He couldn't breathe. He didn't think he could make it.

"Go on," prompted Jeremiah.

"She used to follow me around when she was a baby. Anne remembers it better than I do. I think I must have favored her, favored her over Hal. He would have these tantrums, but Anne worshipped him like he was the only begotten son of God. She, well, I always thought she spoiled him, indulged him too much."

Gerald paused. His head was reeling or the room was spinning. He put his head in his hands to try to hold it still. Or he would be sick. Sick right here in front of God and everyone. In front of Jeremiah.

Get it out.

He didn't know if Jeremiah spoke or God or his own mind.

"I beat him. Not spanked him. Anne doesn't believe in spanking. I beat the shit out of him, Jer. But that's not why he died. I didn't, oh my God, that wasn't why he died. It was the pneumonia—"

"I know, Ger, I know."

Jeremiah held his hand now. It was dark inside the bar, but Jeremiah's hand was light, pure light. *Precious Lord, take my hand*, someone had sung that when Martin Luther King died. *Lead me on, lead me on.*

"But after Hal died, she would look at me, just look at me...not Anne. Anne hardly ever looks at me, even now. Katherine. Thosh eyes." He could hear himself starting to slur, but Jeremiah wouldn't judge. "Have you seen Katherine's eyes? They just look, they just look through you, like she can shee everything, like she knows everything. I couldn't look at her anymore. I couldn't love her anymore, so...so I, I didn't. Now she hates me, I know she hates me. But she's so much like me. I think she understands me better than Anne. I think, I think she loves me more than Anne, and I, I can't bear it. I told her one night. It was the night Dr. King died. I told her—"

What had he told her? He told her he loved her, hadn't he? He told her, and then. And then everything went blurry; there were two Jeremiahs looking down at him like Jesus on the cross. Father forgive him. The floor was where the ceiling should be, and his stomach was in his mouth. Jeremiah's hand was the only thing, the only sure thing.

"I think I'm going to be sick."

Someone's arms were around him, lifting him, holding him, guiding him.

Lead me on, lead me on.

Chapter Eighteen

A huge man in evening dress is walking down a dim hallway. His top hat barely clears the ceiling. Then he pauses before a door and takes keys from a waistcoat pocket. As soon as the door is open, he steps into its frame, removing his hat, so he can fit. Lucy cannot see past him inside the room. He is as wide as the opening. There is something monstrous, even predatory about the man's bulk and presence, a large animal forcing its way into a smaller animal's warren. She wouldn't have been surprised to hear snuffling and digging. Though she cannot see who it is the man has cornered inside the room, she can sense the fear of his prey, the stilled, flattened down trembling, the widened eyes.

"Hullo, hullo, hullo," the great mass speaks, "what have we here? There's no need for fear, my dear, none at all. I am delighted, quite delighted to extend to you the shelter of my humble abode. That's what we do here, you see, offer aid and comfort to the lost and lorn."

It's as if she is inside a Dickens novel. How did she get here and who is she in the story? Whoever the man addresses does not answer. The fear still prickles at the back of Lucy's neck, but now it is mixed with something else. Desperation? Hope?

"Cat got your tongue, has it?" He pauses a moment. "That's not what I've heard about you, my lovely. Yes, oh yes. You've got quite a reputation already, and it precedes you. You're a little songbird, my sources tell me. And you are perhaps not quite what you seem, what?"

Lucy can hear the menace in the man's voice, faint and strangely seductive, even hypnotic.

"Stand up, then, and let us have a look at you. It doesn't do to be cowering in the bedclothes. That's not how a lady of quality greets her benefactor. That would be me, my dear."

In the silence, Lucy hears the creak of bedsprings as the girl, Lucy is certain it must be a girl, complies.

"Well, well, well, now."

Holding onto his hat, the man takes a step into the room but still blocks Lucy's view of what must be a much smaller figure. He extends an arm and begins to make an examination that appears to involve stroking and caressing.

"Most regrettable, most regrettable," he murmurs. "May I extend to you my deepest, my sincerest apologies for any unnecessary rudeness or barbarity towards your lovely person. I hasten to assure you that the party responsible will be called to account. Most rigorously and severely. But you are young and I daresay in good health. You'll be right as rain in a day or two, with some care and feeding, right as rain.

"Now my dear, I must, with all due respect and tenderness, yes, no one has more tenderness for the lone and lorn than I, I really must insist that you tell me your name and provenance, which is to say the circumstances that have brought you here to my care."

Lucy wonders for a moment if his victim, as she began to think of the invisible girl, will resist. Lucy can feel her own resistance rising along her spine, sap in a tree, a wave that could overtake terror.

"My name is Eliza," she answers.

"Eliza? Such a pretty name. Eliza who?" the man says, his voice a hair sharper, like a blade that he could draw at any moment.

The girl hesitates a moment too long. "Doolit-tle."

Eliza Doolittle! Holy mother of God. The girl is Katherine!

Lucy strains to take form, to have some way to push past that monster to snatch Katherine into her arms and run.

She strained so hard, she woke breathless, not sure for a moment where she was. Then, in the late slanting light, she recognized the contours of her own parlor, her desk by the window, her house plants spiraling toward the western light shining through the French doors. It took her a moment to remember. She had come back from the Bradley's house, exhausted. She had thought she would just close her eyes for a few minutes, but she must have slept for hours.

And she had dreamed. Lucy closed her eyes again, trying to get it clear in her mind, to see if she could recall any detail that she might have missed. But that horrid man's back was all she could see, and she had an impression of starkness, the light in the room a naked lightbulb, the walls, colorless. How she wished she'd seen his face. But that voice, that oily, unctuous voice, she would recognize his voice if she heard it again. If only the police had records of voice as well as face and fingerprints.

The police. Someone should call the police. And say...what? Katherine Bradley is being held by a portly man in top hat and tails who sounds like a character from a Dickens novel? I know because I dreamed it?

She should call Anne, at least. Anne would want to know, and she could decide what to do. Lucy was halfway to the phone when the clock struck half past six. Anne would be at the airport now, getting ready to board the plane for London. Gerald then. She should call Gerald. It wouldn't be as easy to talk to him as to Anne, but she must do her best. He could leave a message for Anne with his brother-in-law, though it would be, Lucy calculated, eleven thirty at night in England. She couldn't imagine Gerald making a late night call to relay what could be easily dismissed as an overwrought woman's anxiety dream. She only wished she had dreamed something more useful.

But wait. If her dream was clairvoyant (dare she think so?) the information might be useful. The police ought to know that Katherine could be passing herself off as cockney girl named Eliza Doolittle. Lucy hardly needed to identify her source as a dream.

Because it was exactly the sort of thing Katherine would do.

Resolved, Lucy went to the phone and dialed.

"Bradley residence," a woman answered the phone.

Lucy recognized the voice of Gerald's mother whom she had met many times when Gerald was rector of the Church of Regeneration.

"Mrs. Bradley?" Lucy ventured.

"Yes, Mrs. Bradley, senior," she clarified. "My daughter-in-law has been called away on a family emergency."

"Yes, I know, and I am so very sorry, Mrs. Bradley. This is Lucy Way. We've met before—"

"Lucy? Oh, Lucy! Of course I know who you are, and I know how fond Katherine is of you. I'm afraid we still have no news, if that's why you're calling."

"I am so sorry," said Lucy again. "I don't want to tie up the phone line. There is something I need to tell Gerald. May I speak with him?"

There was a silence on the other end, long enough to make Lucy wonder if they'd been disconnected.

"Mrs. Bradley?" she ventured after a moment.

"Call me Julia," she said. "It's less confusing when there are two Mrs. Bradleys. I am afraid Gerald isn't here."

Before Lucy could decide whether to leave a message, Gerald's mother went on.

"After Anne left, he said he had to go to the office. I know they couldn't have been expecting him. It was just an excuse to get away. Why do men always think their mothers are stupid?"

Lucy sensed that no more than an ambiguous but sympathetic murmur was required.

"That colored gentleman he works with, what's his name, Isaiah, Zechariah, Jeremiah, Amos, one of those Old Testament prophets."

Lucy recalled that the elder Mrs. Bradley had a habit of running through all the given names of her children and grandchildren before she got the right one. The same with the extended family's long line of dogs and cats.

"He called to say Gerald was too sick to drive, a sick headache. Poor Gerald's suffered from those since he was a child. He's keeping Gerald overnight with him. Now that's a good Samaritan."

Lucy had met the man she believed was called Jeremiah at the Bradley's once before. It was easy to imagine him in the role of rescuer. She hoped it was not too uncharitable of her to suspect that Gerald's sick headache might have something to do with a large measure of gin. Poor man, she couldn't blame him. She usually avoided hard liquor but found herself contemplating the brandy she kept on hand for emergencies.

"Gerald will be back in the morning to pack," his mother went on. "I gather he's decided to go London, too, on the evening flight tomorrow. If they had listened to me in the first place, he'd be on the plane with Anne now. But better late than never—"

She stopped abruptly and there was another pause Lucy felt helpless to fill.

"You don't think it's too late, do you, Lucy? Oh, I could wring my worthless son-in-law's neck (I will admit to you, Lucy, that I never liked Bob. He is a pompous ass.) Imagine letting that foolish child go off on her own. In London. And with my daughter in the hospital! I knew I should have gone over there for the surgery. If I had, this never would have happened."

Lucy could hear that Gerald's mother was close to tears, and that she did not believe in crying. And would be furious with herself if she gave way.

"Well, my place is here, now. I won't hear any nonsense about that."

"I'm sure it's a great comfort to the twins to have you there, Mrs. Bradley." Lucy forgot to call her Julia. It was strangely comforting to have someone older than herself to defer to. "And to Anne and Gerald. And no, I don't think it's too late. Not at all."

If only Lucy hadn't...but self-reproach could wait; it would be always with her. Lucy could hear the elder Mrs. Bradley take a ragged breath, resuming her iron grip on herself.

"Did you want to leave a message for Gerald?"

I had a dream that Katherine has been captured by a human ogre. No, she did not think that was the sort of message to leave with a grieving grandmother.

"If you could just tell Gerald to call me in the morning, I would appreciate it."

"I certainly will, Lucy. Goodbye, my dear. Pray for us."

"I will, Julia, of course I will. Do call me if you need anything."

She gave Mrs. Bradley her phone number.

As soon as she hung up, Lucy remembered she was going with Elsa to the hospital in the morning and would be with her all day. Elsa had chosen to undergo the chemotherapy, considered experimental and extreme for breast cancer patients. She was horribly ill for days afterwards. Lucy thought if she had cancer, she might let nature take its equally dreadful if more certain course. But Elsa was terrified of dying and leaving Clara behind to cope on her own. While Lucy had no one, no one who needed her.

That is not true, a voice spoke inside her. *Not anymore.*

She could call Gerald from the hospital. She would just keep calling until she got through.

(He tried not to have favorites; after all, they all belonged to him. Each one had her special place and purpose created by him. But sometimes a new one was so shiny, so untouched. Of course that brute he kept about the place, that dull, senseless drone, couldn't see it, but surely the harm could be undone. He would undo it. He would restore her to perfection, polish her, make her innocence a flawless mirror of his own lost innocence. Through her, he would find it again. Of course, he would have to let the others play with her, but only up to a point. Enough for them to envy him. Because she belonged to him, his precious little girl....)

Chapter Nineteen

Anne stared out the window at the dreary landscape that surrounded all airports everywhere. She thought perhaps the green was greener here, the result of the famed British rain and fog, but her overwhelming impression was of grey. Was the day overcast or was it so early the sun hadn't yet risen? She had lost track of time. She'd knocked herself out with Dramamine on the plane. She was still so woozy that her knees had almost buckled when she stepped onto the tarmac. She was here. In England. Katherine was somewhere on this same soil, this same ordinary, pedestrian ground. It gave her strange comfort, absurd hope. It had been all she could do to stop herself from calling Katherine's name.

Anne's brother-in-law appeared to be concentrating hard on the route, with its endless series of roundabouts that made driving on the left all that much more challenging. He had greeted her awkwardly, a handshake and a kiss on the cheek. They were not especially close, only related by marriage to a brother and sister. They saw each other at Thanksgiving dinners at one household or another. Gerald could never travel at Christmas or Easter and Anne drew the line at having to entertain out-of-town family on these holidays. But she and Bob had formed a sort of alliance as in-laws and outsiders in a clan firmly ruled by their mother-in-law. When he was younger, Anne remembered, Bob had been dark-haired and quite handsome, if always a bit pompous and opinionated. He could be gracious and charming and seemed to have a flattering appreciation of Anne. Time had thrust his belly forward and his hair backwards along with the chin that was disappearing into a wattle. His nose had grown and made him resemble a turkey vulture. But he had not realized the loss of his looks and still tried to flirt with her on family occasions. He made her uncomfortable by praising her for her quiet, ladylike demeanor. Here he would always cast a sly glance at his wife to see if she had heard, but Pat was usually talking too loudly to hear anything but her own adenoidal voice. Would her voice be changed by the operation, Anne wondered?

She would find out soon enough. Pat was due to come home from the hospital later that day. That was about all her brother-in-law had said apart from a hurried mumble that she supposed meant: I am sorry I lost your daughter. I had no idea she had so little common sense or home training. No, he hadn't said that. He wouldn't. He probably didn't even think it. Why did she feel so defensive?

She blamed herself. How could she not? She was Katherine's mother.

Bob signaled and appeared to be taking an exit. She hadn't taken much note of their route, but now it seemed that they were leaving the main road that led to London.

"Aren't we going straight to the police station?" Anne asked.

"I thought you might like to stop at the house, freshen up a bit, rest a little," said Bob, without taking his eyes off the road.

Are you out of your mind? She wanted to scream. My daughter is lost. There is no time to spare.

"Thank you," she said. "That won't be necessary."

He turned off on the exit for whatever drab little suburban town they lived in. Had he not heard her?

"Your appointment with Detective Smith-Jones is not until eleven," Bob explained. "We can drive in. The traffic won't be bad by then. Afterwards we'll have lunch, and then we'll pick up Pat on the way home."

It all sounded so ordinary, so well-planned. What had Anne thought she would be doing?

Walking the streets, trying to retrace Katherine's route.

"Maybe," Anne heard herself saying, "maybe after we meet with the detective I'll take a hotel room in London, I don't mean to be rude or ungrateful. But with Pat just home, she'll want to rest, and I...."

Anne felt her words petering out, a few spatters of rain from a leaden, withholding sky. Bob didn't answer right away, but she could sense his disapproval. It filled the car as if it were made of some kind of gas, invisible, without a detectable scent but deadly. This atmosphere would have suffocated Katherine. She would not have been able to tolerate it.

Had she run away, had she?

"Pat is expecting you," he said. "She'll need a little help till she gets her strength back."

What? Could she be hearing him correctly?

"I've taken several days leave from work, and of course I'll be glad to meet Gerald's flight, but then...."

"Gerald's flight?" she repeated.

"Oh, didn't you know?" Bob made it sound as though it were moral laxity or gross inefficiency on her part that she did not. "Julia called last night, very late UK time, to let me know he would be arriving on the same flight tomorrow."

"Julia?"

"Our mutual mother-in-law," Bob said with a nod to their old camaraderie. "I imagine she has taken charge of your household and is packing Gerald off. I gather you have not been informed or consulted?"

Anne shook her head, suddenly so overwhelmed with exhaustion that she could not find the strength to form words. The edges of her vision blurred.

"Take it easy now, Annie," he said.

No one but Bob called her Annie. No one else would presume.

"This is rough on all of us."

He reached over and patted her knee. Anne rolled down the window a little, afraid she might be sick.

"But take it from an old scoutmaster, we'll find her."

Chapter Twenty

"Right then, doll face, you're the lucky one today."

The ogress known as the Angel of Death unlocked Katherine's door.

It was her second morning as a prisoner. Although she had not lost track of time, Katherine knew from books and movies that captives often did. She had to devise some way of counting the days. She had no knife to make notches with but there was a chunk of wall where the paint had peeled away that she found she could mark with her thumbnail. Little thumbnail moons of time.

"After breakfast you're 'avin' a complete beauty treatment, courtesy of Mister Tobias."

So that man who called himself her benefactor, that huge man who took up practically the whole room, had been Mister Tobias. He looked like an over-sized Toad of Toad Hall, dressed up, puffed up, with small gleaming eyes. But Toad, however reckless on the road, had been friends with Ratty and Mole. She did not know if Mister Tobias could be counted on to fight against the evil weasels. He hadn't hurt her, not physically. He had touched her bruises gently. He had even apologized for what the other man had done to her. Still, the thought of him made her skin crawl.

"New wardrobe, too, picked out by Mister Tobias hisself. Put on your old dress for now."

It's not *my* dress, Katherine wanted to say, but she had decided her best chance was to pretend, like Jill at the giants' castle, to be delighted by everything and to simper mindlessly.

"Loverly," she tried it out.

"What's that?" the Angel of Death snapped. "None of your cheek now."

"No'm," Katherine said for the first time in her life.

"Ma-*dame* Angelique is 'ow you are to address me from now on."

Katherine wanted badly to laugh at the ill-fitting title, but she had to stay in character. She was in a play. If she put her mind to it, she could watch everything from the outside. She saw the stout, hard woman, who looked not in the least bit French or angelic, watching the young girl slip off the night gown over her head. Katherine imagined the girl looked slender, the bruises on her arms still dark. She thought she might have lost weight. Her hair was longer than she remembered and matted in back. Angelique of Death had yanked at it with a brush after the hosing down yesterday, but she had no comb or brush of her own.

"Undergarments," muttered Angelique of Death. "We'll have to burn the ones she's got on."

They had been her favorite pair once, pale pink with roses, but now they were stained and the elastic had come loose. The lace on her bra looked grey.

"'urry up. I 'aven't got all day."

"Excuse me, Madame Angelique. But I 'aven't any shoes? If we're going to a beauty parlor…?"

"Won't be needin' 'em. Not yet. Come along, Liza Jane or whosoever you might be. If I was you, I'd answer to whatever Mister Tobias wanted to call me. You're the lucky one," she said again. "So far, that is."

Her second warning against revealing who she was. For now, Katherine decided, she'd better heed those warnings.

You got that right, said the Aramantha in her head. *These people are like something out of Psycho.*

Katherine had hoped she might see the other girls, the ones who'd spoken to her through the locked door. The same ones, she guessed, that Angelique of Death excoriated as fancying themselves queens of Sheba. But it seemed she was still in a sort of solitary confinement. At least her breakfast hadn't been shoved through the door like her lunch and dinner, if you could call that piece of unidentified meat and the chalky mashed potatoes dinner. Madame Angelique sat her down at the table. Then she went to the stove and shoveled some cold, watery scrambled eggs onto her plate, extracted some burnt toast from a toaster and plopped it down in front of Katherine.

"'ere, 'ave some marmite with it."

And the ogress fetched a crusty-looking jar from a cabinet and slapped it down on the table. Katherine had no idea what marmite might be other than a small Australian animal. But then she could still remember Lucy Way's gales of laughter over Katherine's confusion of aspic with asp. ("No, *cherie*! Cleopatra did not clasp a tomato aspic to her bosom!") So perhaps marmite was not made of animal parts. Katherine did not want to betray her ignorance, so she reached for the spread gingerly, not sure whether it was meant to go on the eggs or the toast.

"Right then," said Madame Angelique. "I'm just going to fetch the morning paper. Back in a 'alf a mo' if you know what's good for you, you won't get up to anything while I'm gone."

At least she could find out what marmite was. With some effort, she unscrewed the top. Then seeing that she had no knife or even fork (of course, she realized, they could be used for weapons) she stuck her spoon into the dark sticky mess, brought it tentatively to her mouth, then gagged at the salty, foul-smelling paste. When she had recovered, she quickly spooned up her eggs and mopped the plate with her toast so that Angelique of Death would not know she had spurned her treat (if marmite was a treat and not some sort of punishment or test).

Katherine pushed away her clean plate just before she heard the Angel of Death coming back down the hall. She sat back in her chair, hands folded in her lap, wondering if she might dare ask for coffee instead of tea and a bit of gin in either. But it wasn't Madame Angelique who came into the room.

"'ello, luv."

She turned and there he was leaning against the counter, arms folded in front of his chest, the man with the gold tooth, the man who had tricked her into captivity, who had.... She felt herself beginning to shake. The awful eggs rose in her gorge. The marmite hung heavy on her breath.

"And 'ow are we this fine morning?"

Weather, she recalled someone advising Eliza Doolittle to confine herself to remarks about the weather. Colonel Pickering or maybe Henry Higgins' mother.

"The rain in Spain stays mainly in the plain."

There. That was better. She was Eliza Doolittle studying to be a lady.

"Wot's that? Wot you on about then?" demanded the man.

His surface friendliness peeled away like old paint or old wallpaper to reveal the rough menace she had already encountered.

"In Hartford, Harringford, and Hampshire, hurricanes hardly ever happen." She huffed her H's and avoided looking at him.

She heard the flick of his lighter. He must be lighting a cigarette. Then she heard him loudly blowing out his smoke, aiming it in her direction. She wondered if she should ask for a cigarette (a fag, they called them. Can you spare a fag?). Maybe it would distract him, give her something to hold, like a weapon. She pictured driving the lit end into one of his eyes....

"Don't you go putting on any la di da manners wiv me, like you was some 'oity-toity society lady."

A lady is a lady, because of how she is treated, Katherine searched for Eliza's line. Under her breath, she muttered:

"To Colonel Pickering I will always be a lady, to you, never."

She heard his steps crossing the room; still she did not look at him. Then he yanked her head back by the hair and brought his face too close to hers. Close enough to see the tobacco stains on his teeth and the dark hairs in his nose.

"You got somefink to say to me, you say it to me face."

All right then, she thought, she would.

"Mister Tobias," she ventured, "Mister Tobias. He, 'e," she corrected herself. "'e apologized for what you done to me. Most regrettable, 'e called it. 'e said you was to be called to account."

The man stood back again and regarded her. She thought he would be angry; she hoped he would be afraid. Instead a slow, awful smile spread over his face, and he took another long drag on his cigarette.

"Did 'e now? 'e said 'e were going to call 'is old friend Tom, 'is trusty right 'and to account?"

"The party responsible, 'e said," Katherine answered. "That's you. You made the marks on my arms and face. You," say it, she ordered herself, say it, "you raped me."

As soon as she said the word, she wished she could unsay it. She felt like a mouse or rabbit in an open field, no thicket to hide in, no story to hide behind. His searing blue eyes narrowed. He had her in his sights.

"Now you listen 'ere, Miss 'igh and mighty. Mister Tobias, 'e knows me and 'e knows what kind of a man I am. That's why 'e keeps me about. And I know you. I knows what kind of girl you are." He leaned in again. "You're a bad girl. A bad, bad girl."

Katherine found she could not take her eyes from his. He held her fixed in his gaze. He eyes bored into her, as if he could see things in her she didn't know about herself, didn't want to know. He was, she thought, faintly, helplessly, while she could think at all, he was hypnotizing her.

Don't look at him! warned Aramantha. But it was too late.

"You're worse than a bad girl. You're the kind of girl 'oo wants it, begs for it, then says she never, tries to get a man wot never did no 'arm to 'er in trouble. I didn't do noffink to you, noffink you didn't ask for."

She hated it, hated that she suddenly felt hot and swollen between her legs. He was forcing her all over again.

"Now Mister Tobias, 'e got a tender spot in his black 'eart for virgins. Likes to make them flowery speeches, like the one you no doubt fink you 'eard last night. But you and me both knows wot you are."

What was she? What was she? Not a virgin, not a virgin. But how, she thought wildly, seeing as I know no man. She closed her eyes, to shut out the sight of him. The dark was hot and sweaty. A man was telling her he loved her so much, weeping, gasping, suffocating her. And it hurt and bled.

"No worries, my pretty little bird. I set Mister Tobias straight about you. Count yourself lucky if 'e don't call *you* to account."

For not being a virgin? For pretending to be one? She opened her eyes again. He was moving away from her, turning his back on her. And then—whoever thought she'd be glad to see her?—the Angel of Death bustled in.

"Wot you 'angin' about 'ere for, you old drone. You know Mister Tobias don't like you to bother the new girls. 'ow bout fixin' that broken winder like you said you was a week ago."

He was a handyman, Katherine told herself, not Mister Tobias' right hand, a handyman.

"Bossy old cow." Tom stopped just short of spitting in the ogress' direction.

He cast one more glance at Katherine, gave her a curt nod, which Katherine took to mean, you haven't seen the last of me, and he skulked out the door. The Angel of Death put the kettle on to boil and Katherine reached surreptitiously for the paper, scanning for a headline. Girl missing. American Girl Missing.

"Get your filthy mitts off my paper." Angelique whirled around. "And wash your dishes. I'm not the maid around 'ere."

Katherine did as she was told while Madame Angelique made a pot of tea, then settled down at the table with her gin bottle and the paper, seeming to forget all about Katherine. She hadn't offered Katherine anything to drink at all. Quietly, Katherine got up, found a glass, drank some water.

"Please, Madame Angelique," said Katherine, sitting back down again, "please may I 'ave some gin."

She lowered her paper and stared at Katherine as if she were a newly discovered and loathsome form of infestation.

"I'd quite forgotten about you," she sighed. "No, you may not 'ave some gin," she mimicked Katherine, "and don't even think about trying to sneak it. Come on, then. Time for your beauty treatment."

Chapter Twenty-One

Anne was very relieved that Bob had not accompanied her to her interview with the detective. He was stopping in at his office and would meet her afterwards to take her to lunch as threatened. She had been ushered into Detective Smith-Jones' small, plain office, decorated in grey on grey on grey, file cabinets, blinds shielding a window that couldn't have had much of a view, a tidy desk. Mr. Smith-Jones himself was a nondescript man of no particular height or weight, sandy grey hair, hard to say how old he was, but he seemed kind. He offered her tea, then got her coffee on her request, with a plate of nondescript cookies he offered as biscuits.

Anne lost no time in getting out her envelope of photographs and spreading them out on the detective's desk. Unfortunately, she did not have many pictures from the last couple of months. Katherine had become camera shy, if you could describe surliness and belligerence as shyness. But there was quite a good photograph of Katherine in her bit part in *My Fair Lady* wearing Anne's old skirt and a purple flowered hat. She also included slightly younger pictures of Katherine from just after they moved from the rectory to the house in the country. Katherine with her arms around Bear as a puppy; Katherine standing between the twins, and one with Katherine and Lucy in Lucy's garden where Kathrine still had that sweet and grave expression Anne thought of as particularly hers.

"A lovely girl," Detective Smith-Jones remarked, whether politely or sincerely, she didn't know. "These photographs will be helpful. I am afraid your brother—"

"Brother-in-law," Anne corrected.

"Well, I am afraid he was rather vague. Typical of men. Couldn't remember her eye color, height, or much of anything, except that her hair was always in her eyes."

"That much is true," said Anne. "Her hair is longer all the way around than in any of these pictures. Shoulder length, apart from the bangs. And in case you can't tell from the pictures, her hair is dark brown and her eyes are grey-blue. When she's tired or ill, the fold over her right eyelid droops—"

A flash flood of tears threatened at the thought of that lid, how without even thinking, she had always known whether Katherine was sick at a glance.

"Thank you, Mrs. Bradley." He looked up from the notes he was taking. "Just the sort of information we need. Keep going when you're ready."

Anne took a breath, closed her eyes, trying to see every detail of Katherine before her. She had tried to sculpt Katherine's head once, but she had never finished, and now Katherine was older, but the structure of her face was largely unchanged.

"She has her father's jaw," Anne began.

"Oh, yes?" encouraged the detective.

"A strong lower jaw, with a chin that juts out. She had an under bite, too, but it's been corrected."

"Had orthodontic work."

She wasn't sure if he was asking or making a note.

"Much more common among you Yanks. Good to know there are dental records available."

Anne must have blanched.

"I'm terribly sorry, Mrs. Bradley. I didn't mean that the way it must have sounded."

What other meaning could there be? Anne did not ask.

"It's just that anything you can tell us, anything at all might be helpful. Any identifying marks or traits, that sort of thing."

Anne was silent for a moment, seeing the childlike roundness of Katherine's cheeks just beginning to give way to cheekbones Katherine so wished were higher, even as her sturdy tomboy's body began to round to breasts Katherine thought too small and hips she worried were too big.

"She's about average height, five three," Anne began, "and weighs somewhere between 110 and 115 pounds, that is. I don't know weight in stone. She is somewhat big-boned for her age. She was a bit of a tomboy, still likes to walk for miles and miles, but doesn't care for sports."

He made notes, which he did not read aloud.

"How was she getting on at school?" he hesitated, then added, "And at home?"

Were there problems, he was asking. Was Katherine a problem? Well, there were, she was, and there was no point in pretending otherwise.

"Until recently, she did very well, exceptionally well, at school. She had, she has friends. No boyfriends, yet, not really. Well, there was one boy she's been friends with since she was a little girl, but he—"

She was making a mess of it. There was too much to say and somehow not enough. Her older brother died when she was three. Katherine and the boy who is not her boyfriend, or maybe he is now, prevented a murder when she was seven. Was that relevant? Katherine has a fairy godmother, a real one, but somehow she is still lost.

"When did you notice a change in her, Mrs. Bradley?" Detective Smith-Jones prompted her to focus.

Anne thought for a moment and surprised herself by being able to pinpoint it, the moment Katherine changed from being an ordinary teenaged girl, obsessed with pop music, occasionally moody, to someone who seemed like a human fortress under siege.

"This spring, a couple of months before the end of school. She stopped doing her homework, her grades dropped, and she was caught, caught with that boy, that friend of hers, well, I don't know if they had sex or not."

"I see," said the detective.

How could he see when she did not, what did he see? Was he judging Katherine? Was he judging her? Well, why shouldn't he? She was the mother. She had failed to protect her child.

"A sudden change, then," said the detective. "Forgive my asking, but was there any particular event that might have brought on the change? A death in the family, parent losing a job, anything that might have happened at school—"

All at once Anne knew.

"Martin Luther King. Right after his death."

How had she not made that connection before? And what did it mean?

"Was he a particular hero of hers?" the detective asked.

"Her father's," Anne said slowly. "He was her father's hero. Her father works in the OEO, the Office of Economic Opportunity, that is, with, well, with negroes in a small city nearby, trying to help them organize to…improve their lives."

"I see," said the detective again.

What *do* you see? she almost demanded. What do you see that I don't?

"And are she and her father very close?" He seemed to be making a note.

"No," Anne said abruptly. "I mean, I don't know."

Again she felt at a loss to explain. Her father never paid Katherine much attention. He wouldn't drive her to her job at a daycare in a ghetto. He forgot to pick her up on her first day. He shouts her down at the dinner table when she ventures an opinion. And yet, he had been Katherine's preferred parent when she was small, before Hal died.

"Sometimes fathers and daughters have difficulties when the daughter begins to grow up," the detective suggested.

He was more understanding and helpful than Dr. Aiken had ever been. But she did not need a stranger's sympathy, his excuses for how wrong things had gone in her family. She needed her daughter back.

"He tried, her father tries," Anne began. "He got her a volunteer job in a daycare with his program last summer. She did very well. She believes in his cause, Civil Rights, that is. But she refused to go back to the job this summer. She refused to do anything. It was her father's idea to send her to England to visit her aunt and uncle."

"She didn't want to go?" the detective asked.

He was asking did they force her.

"She did," Anne defended them against the implied charge. "She has a special friend, an older woman who grew up in England. They read books together, Dickens, Shakespeare. Then, of course, like all girls, she loves the Beatles. I think she thought England would be… like a fairytale."

"Ah," said the detective, as though he had seen it many times before. "And the reality disappointed her."

"She was unhappy with her aunt and uncle," Anne said. "And they were unhappy with her. I am sure my brother-in-law told you, his wife had to have surgery. She's just coming home today. Katherine was left alone with him…."

Katherine alone with that man, who had patted Anne's knee in the car. Alone in the house with him. What if, what if he had tried to touch her. She could not believe she was even thinking such a thing. Bob might be a bit judgmental, but he wouldn't….

"You think she might have run away," the detective said.

Anne heard the sound coming out of her, as if it was someone else. A horrible sound, an animal sound. The detective handed her a clean handkerchief, a real one. She hid her face in it.

"Mrs. Bradley," he said when she had quieted again, "we are going to do everything we can to find your daughter. Your help is invaluable. As I said, your brother-in-law seemed not to have noticed her much at all, except with vague disapproval. He said she was dressed eccentrically the day she disappeared, wore an odd sort of hat. That was about all he remembered. It would be helpful to have more to go on."

Anne sat up and then leaned over the desk, pointing to the picture of Katherine on stage.

"It has to be that hat," she said. "She bought it at our church rummage sale. She loved it. She insisted on bringing it with her, wore it on the plane."

"This is the sort of detail we need, Mrs. Bradley," he said. "With your kind permission, I'd like to keep this photograph and a couple of the others, make a composite picture."

"Of course," said Anne.

The detective was getting to his feet, and helping her to hers. She felt panicky. The interview was over? What was she to do?

"We will blanket the area with flyers and make inquiries in all the bus and train and tube stations, all the youth hostels...."

Why couldn't she just stay here in the grey haven of this office, with a man who seemed to care about her daughter, who had never harmed her. Why couldn't she go with him everywhere?

"I assume we can reach you at your brother-in-law's home?" he was saying. "And here is my card. You must let me know if you think of anything, anything at all, that might help us find your daughter."

But she had only just begun, only begun to tell him about Katherine. She needed him to tell her what to do, how to draw one breath and the next. But this kind man, this bland man was seeing her to the door. He would do his job, nothing more. She wished he were Joe Petrone. It was terrible to think it, but she wished Joe was arriving tomorrow instead of Gerald.

Chapter Twenty-Two

"Behold," Mister Tobias said, leading her towards a full-length antique mirror. "You are perfection, confection, innocence in its most delectable form."

The girl in the mirror had nothing to do with her. Katherine had vanished as completely as a dove or rabbit pulled from a hat then banished into thin air. Someone with blond ringlets stared back at her.

I have naturally curly blond hair, she remembered another child once taunting her, and she had asked her mother why she didn't, why she couldn't. Her mother had put her hair up in curlers, but the curls had wilted into straightness by lunchtime.

Now curls rolled out around her head, like sausages or worms. They were hideous. Perched in them like a moth was a black and white polka-dotted bow. Lashes had been painted onto her face around her eyes. Two rosy circles marked her cheeks, and her mouth—was that her mouth?—that horrible red blotch, shaped to look like she wanted a kiss and would pout till she got one? Below her neck was just as bad, maybe worse. She wore a short (very short, the length of baby doll pajamas) what was the word for it? Pinafore? Black and white to match the bow. She had something lacy—could they be bloomers?—peeking out underneath, white stockings attached to red garters (hadn't Mister Tobias ever heard of tights?) and shiny patent leather shoes, the kind she had worn when she was in kindergarten.

All at once she knew who she looked like, who she was supposed to look like: Shirley Temple. At a funeral.

"I see you have been rendered speechless, my dear."

Mister Tobias came to stand behind her, resting his hands lightly on her shoulders, his huge form taking up the whole mirror. In front of him, she did look small, like the child he'd dressed her up to be. Where had her real self gone? Even as a child she had never looked like the apparition in the mirror. She had worn blue jeans every chance she got. She had climbed trees. She had carried a jackknife. She wished to God she had that knife now.

"Many girls are stunned when they see themselves through the eyes of a master, someone whose genius is to draw out the exquisite, the hidden essence."

His words were horrifying and mesmerizing. He commanded her gaze, so that she could not look around the room, as she wished to do, for the nearest door.

"In time you'll come to thank me, my dear, for lifting you up, rescuing you from slavery to trivial, fleeting trends, from the banality of convention...."

The only good thing about his sickening self-congratulations was that she didn't have to say anything. Then even the refuge of silence was denied her.

"Just give me one word, one word to describe the magnitude of the transformation you see before you."

There was a word. She and her friends used it jokingly some-times. She saw now that none of them had known what it meant.

"Perverted," she said in a voice quieter than a whisper.

"Eh, what's that, my dear?"

Hide, Katherine, hide, hissed Aramantha in her mind. *Don't let him see you. Disappear.*

"Noffink, Mister Tobias." She went back into one of her standby characters (Jill babbling to the giants at Harfang; Eliza Doolittle would not simper) not sure of what the creature in the mirror was supposed to say. "It's all very fancy, but wot...wot's it for? Am I to go to a party?"

She'd got it right. He was melting like a giant ice cream cone.

"Adorable, just adorable. No doubt about it, none at all," he murmured to himself, and then to her, he said, "Yes, my dear. Yes, little Liza Jane. Yes, indeed. You shall be going to a party. I dare say, a great many parties. And if you are a good girl and do exactly as I tell you, you may call me Uncle Toby."

And if she wasn't and didn't?

Chapter Twenty-Three

Lucy and Clara sat with their handiwork on either side of Elsa while the chemicals dripped through the IV. Lucy had taught Clara how to crochet. Because she was a pianist, Clara's fingers should have been quite agile, and she was used to using both hands in complex ways, but knitting had proved to be beyond her; the mayhem resulting from a dropped stitch provoked in her unbearable anxiety. Crocheting was a much more forgiving craft, especially with a large needle and thick yarn. It seemed to soothe Clara. She had even learned to be unruffled by Elsa's favorite bad joke.

"How's my shroud coming along, *liebling*? Do you think you could make it a little gaudier?"

"It's not for you, Elsa," Clara would answer every time with absolute seriousness and severity. "You know very well it's a scarf for little Joey."

Little Joey, Frankie Lomangino's not-so-baby brother, was now a strapping eight-year-old with huge feet like a puppy who is going to grow up to be a large dog. "What does he need with a scarf in the middle of the summer?" Elsa would tease.

"It's for school. In the fall. It's his football team's colors."

"Orange and puke?"

"Puce," corrected Clara. "How many times do I have to tell you? Puce."

"I think you should make me a shawl, a lovely, light blue shawl."

"I will, darling, I will," Clara would promise earnestly. "When I am done with Joey's scarf. Lucy is going to show me a pattern."

Elsa was too exhausted today for even this ritual exchange. Lucy had not told them yet about Katherine's going missing. It would upset them terribly, and there was nothing they could do. But there was something she had to do. She still hadn't gotten through to Gerald. He hadn't come home when she called at eight this morning. Surely he would be back by now. He had to pack. He'd be leaving for the airport in the early afternoon. She had hoped she might dream something more useful last night than that fragment that had come to her yesterday afternoon, but her dreams had been inchoate, impossible to grasp. She glanced at Elsa, whose face was drawn, almost grey, but she appeared to be asleep. Really, Lucy wasn't terribly useful at the hospital. It was at home that Clara and Elsa needed her most.

"Go, Lucy." Elsa spoke without opening her eyes.

"I beg your pardon?" said Lucy.

"You heard me. Go make your phone call. I am not as *bewusstlos* as you think. I feel you over there. You are sitting on ants. Maybe the chemicals are making me psychic as well as seasick. Go on."

"I'll be right back." Lucy got up.

"And when you come back, you will tell me what is the matter."

"So imperious," Lucy retorted. "I take that as a good sign."

Elsa had always been direct to a fault. Blunt or tactless were words the less tolerant might use to describe her, but she had never been prone to mindreading. Was Lucy's agitation that obvious? She did not like to think so, but the other possibility was worse, that the veil between one person and other, between life and death was growing thinner for Elsa. Lucy attempted a reassuring smile and left the room, hurrying towards the pay phone outside the main entrance.

"You bet, Lucy," Gerald said. "I'll tell Anne. 'Bye."

Lucy held onto the phone for a while after Gerald hung up, as if the instrument itself could call him back, make him take her seriously. Slowly, she replaced receiver and gathered up the extra dimes she had laid out to make sure she wasn't cut off before she finished what she had to say. She hadn't needed them.

"What's that?" he'd said after she had told him she believed Katherine might be calling herself Eliza Doolittle.

He sounded distracted. Well, who could blame him? He must be beside himself.

"I had a dream, Gerald," she decided to admit her source. "I know not everyone believes in clairvoyant dreams. But sometimes I do have dreams that are not like dreams at all. In this one I heard Katherine's voice. She called herself Eliza Doolittle. I had the impression that she was trying to protect herself from a man who frightened her. A very large man in formal evening dress."

She did sound deranged, even to herself.

"I know it's not much, if anything, to go on," Lucy pleaded. "But Katherine is such an imaginative child. It is the sort of thing she might do."

Gerald didn't answer. She thought she heard the sound of a lighter, and then nothing.

"Gerald? Are you still there?"

"Sure, sure." She heard him exhale loudly.

"I won't keep you," she said. "I know you've got a plane to catch. Please do tell Anne and tell—"

And that was all she had managed to say before he hung up.

Lucy stepped out of the phone booth into the humid July morning, the air heavy and green as the dense foliage everywhere. There was so much pressure behind her eyes, she could hardly see, and such a lump in her throat, she could hardly breathe. If she were dreaming now, she would not be able to speak or move, flee whatever monstrous thing pursued her.

Her own grief. Her own terror.

She was in no condition to return to Elsa's cubicle right now. If Elsa pumped her for information, Lucy might break down. She needed a few moments to collect herself. She would go to the hospital chapel, the plain little chapel of no denomination but anguished hope and fearful loss.

"Miss Way," someone called out to her as she opened the main door.

She turned and saw Father James walking towards her. He quickened his pace and held the door for her, gesturing for her to pass through first.

"Are you coming to visit Miss Ebersbach? I am, too. I understand she is having another treatment today?"

"I've been sitting with her and Clara," said Lucy. "I just stepped out to use the phone. If you are going to see her, could you tell her I will be back shortly. I just, I just need to...."

She looked up, suddenly disoriented, trying to remember which turn would take her to the chapel. How stupid of her to forget. Then she felt Father James' hand on her arm.

"Are you all right, Miss Way?"

Then to her horror, Lucy burst into tears.

A little while later, hardly knowing how it had happened, Lucy found herself on a bench in a small courtyard, with a cup of tea in her hand and Father James sitting beside her patiently. How many men, how many human beings, knew how to wait?

"Thank you, Father James," she said. "I'll be all right now. You ought to go see Elsa."

"I stuck my head in before I got your tea to give her your message, and Elsa pretty much ordered me to go see to you. Is there more news of Elsa's case?"

Lucy shook her head. "Not that I know of. I believe they are waiting until the treatment is complete to do more tests."

Neither spoke for a moment. The silence was so restful and comfortable, she felt her eyes half closing. She hadn't realized till now how tired she was.

"Have you been having more dreams, Miss Way?"

"Yes," she said softly. "Yes, I have."

She opened her eyes to find him looking at her. His gaze felt like a calm sea that reminded you of how small you were. Small as that little fleck of gold in his eyes that looked like a tiny bird, wings caught in light. She felt that she could tell this man everything, and it would be absorbed into some vastness or depth beyond them both. And she did, starting with Katherine's disappearance, which no one had told him about yet, and the sharply vivid dream. Then she also confided the dramatic change she had noticed in the spring, Katherine's anguished question: *Do you ever wish you could go back to before?* Clearly something had gone seriously wrong and Lucy had missed her chance to get to the bottom of it.

"So you see, I can't help feeling I am to blame," she said. "Foolishly I had talked to Katherine about taking her to England one day. Then Elsa became ill. I knew I couldn't go this summer. So I suggested Katherine visit her aunt and uncle there. I knew she didn't know them well, perhaps didn't care for them much, but I thought she needed a change, so I, I meddled, to make up for letting her down this summer. If I hadn't, none of this would have happened. Katherine wouldn't be lost or in danger."

Lucy almost wished she could weep again, see the plain truth through a softening blur of tears, but she couldn't. She waited for Father James to say, "don't blame yourself." She braced herself against his comfort.

"Miss Way," he said at length. Their tea had grown cold, but they both held onto their cups. "I would like to reason with you. I could, but I know it wouldn't do any good."

Was it the long breath she let out that finally stirred the still air, lifting the upper reaches of the leaves?

"It might help for a moment, but then the part of you that feels at fault would argue back and it would be all the worse."

He had described her condition so exactly. How did he know? How did he come to have the language to explain it?

"I know from experience," he said as if in answer to her question. "Before my son Luke enlisted, yes, enlisted; not many people know that—we had an argument, what you and my English mother might call a row, a terrible row. I wanted to save him. I wanted him to do what I wanted, for his own good, because I thought I knew best. I told him he must do the honorable thing, apply for status as a conscientious objector or go to prison if need be. He felt I was judging him, for wanting to run away to Canada, for dropping out of college. He accused me of caring more about my moral code, my outdated ideas of honor than I did about him. He left that night in a fury. The next we heard from him, or Sally heard from him, was a postcard to say he was in basic training at Fort Dix. It was his way of saying, pardon my language, to hell with you, to hell with you and all your moral scruples. How his mother ever forgave me I don't pretend to understand."

Oh, how dreadful for them all, Lucy thought. And yes, he was right. There was no use in reasoning away self-blame. That argument always led you right back to the beginning.

"Where is your son stationed?" she asked after a moment.

"Da Nang," he said. "As an enlisted man, he could have avoided combat, perhaps avoided Vietnam altogether. But he chose to train as a medic. He goes out on a chopper picking up the wounded."

Lucy knew that meant he was in the line of fire and could be killed at any moment.

"I dream of him almost every night," Father James went on. "No, I don't just dream of him. Sometimes I am him. I see what he sees, feel what he feels. Sometimes I am one of the wounded, and sometimes...sometimes, I'm an enemy sniper. Sometimes it's all a jumble, and sometimes it's as vivid, more vivid than my own memories of Iwo Jima...."

No wonder he became a pacifist.

"Please forgive me, Miss Way. I have no business burdening you with my troubles. All of this was just to say, I believe dreams can tell us things we can't know in waking life."

"Not at all," she said quietly. "Thank you for telling me. And if you don't mind, please call me Lucy."

"Very well, Lucy, if you will call me Ralph."

"Thank you, Ralph." Of course, he pronounced it Rafe, like the English composer Vaughan Williams.

"All right then, Lucy," he said. "Back to your dream. If it is clairvoyant, your dream indicates that Katherine is alive, which means there is hope, great hope of finding her. I have little doubt that you will keep dreaming, and the information you receive may prove invaluable."

Lucy paused for a moment, finding the courage to speak.

"And there is great hope for your son, Ralph. You must be proud that he chose to save lives instead of take them."

He looked away abruptly and Lucy was afraid she had spoken too boldly.

"Yes, he did," he turned toward her. "And yes, I am."

Chapter Twenty-Four

"Put the seat back and rest, Gerald," said Jeremiah. "You might not sleep much on the plane."

Jeremiah was driving Gerald to the airport in what he called the Jesus Christ-ler, (for the frequent expletives that doubled as prayers) a piece of rust held together by grace and spare parts. The seat didn't adjust much but Gerald leaned back, though he did not think he would ever sleep again. Still, it was easier than looking at Jeremiah, better than trying to talk, or trying not to talk. But when Gerald closed his eyes, all he could see was the dawn light in Jeremiah's tiny bedroom that doubled as his home office, books and papers everywhere, soft worn sheets, a forgiving mattress.

And Jeremiah's arms around him, his back to Jeremiah's front.

Spooning it was called. They had fallen asleep spooned. Gerald didn't know how it had happened. The last thing he remembered was being sick in the men's room at the bar, and Jeremiah guiding him down the street to his apartment.

Why hadn't Gerald rolled away when he woke up, why hadn't he leapt out of bed? Jeremiah was still sleeping. He told himself he hadn't wanted to disturb him. So he lay still, keenly aware of Jeremiah's warmth yet also lulled by it. The truth was, he didn't want to move. He must have dozed again. When he woke, Jeremiah was out of bed, fully dressed, bringing him a cup of black coffee and a stack of toast. Had Gerald dreamed that earlier waking? Why would he have a dream like that?

And if it wasn't a dream?

"How's the head this morning, Ger?" was all Jeremiah had said.

Gerald had registered that his head had the precarious lightness that came after a migraine. The absence of pain and nausea, such a strong sensation, was more like the presence of something else. Peace. The peace that passeth all understanding. Peace he did not deserve to know but could not deny. Such a profound peace, the pain that went before it almost seemed worth it.

"Fine," Gerald said. "I feel fine."

"Good. Your mother just called."

"Is there any news?"

Katherine, let her be found, God. Let none of this ever have happened. None of it.

"Your mother says Anne arrived safely," said Jeremiah. "And one of your old parishioners has been trying to reach you." He hesitated a moment. "Your flight is arranged. I could pick you up later and take you to the airport, if you're all right to drive yourself home now."

"I'm fine," Gerald said again. "Thanks for—"

"Clothes are on the chair," Jeremiah said and left the room.

Gerald saw that he was wearing only his boxer shorts and an undershirt. Jeremiah must have undressed him. Undressed him and gotten into bed with him.

And held him.

Too restless even to pretend to rest, Gerald sat up and searched his pockets for his cigarettes and lighter.

"Want one?" he asked Jeremiah.

Jeremiah nodded, and Gerald placed a cigarette between his lips. Why had he done that? Why the hell had he done that? Because Jeremiah was shifting gears on the entrance ramp to the parkway. Gerald's hands shook as he flicked the lighter and lit Jeremiah's cigarette and then his own.

"Did your old parishioner ever reach you?" asked Jeremiah.

Old. Parishioner. Gerald drew a blank. He could hardly remember the last few hours. His mother hovering around him as he tried to pack, finding things like fresh handkerchiefs, extra dog collars. She seemed to have some idea that everyone would take him more seriously and search more diligently for Katherine if it was clear that he was a clergyman, like his forefathers before him, his own grandfather born in England. A succession of balding clergy emerging from the womb already collared. Finding him hopeless at packing, his mother had shooed him out of the house to take that "infernal creature," as she called the dog, for a walk. Then for a brief, blessed moment, he'd had the house to himself while she picked up the twins from some lesson. He'd poured himself a drink, just a small one, and smothered the gin in V-8 juice. Then—now he remembered—Lucy Way had called. What had she wanted?

"Yes," he said. "Katherine's unofficial Godmother called."

"I think I met her," said Jeremiah. "Miss Way. Lady with snow white hair and a hint of British accent?"

"That's the one," said Gerald.

It was all right. He and Jeremiah could still talk, just like they always had, about anything. Everything. No, not everything.

"Nice lady," Jeremiah said. "A real lady who treats everyone like they matter, am I right about that?"

"You bet," Gerald said.

You bet. That's what he had said to Lucy when he hung up, not really taking in what she'd told him. Of course Gerald admired Lucy Way, everyone did. She had taken Katherine under her wing, the Lomangino boy, too. But the truth was, Gerald had never been entirely at ease around her. He suspected she found him lacking as a priest and, well, maybe as a husband and father. Lucy and Anne had become friends during the murder investigation. Did Anne confide in Lucy about their marriage? He didn't think Lucy would encourage anyone to be indiscreet. Besides, she was a spinster. What could she know about marriage anyway?

"How's she doing?" Jeremiah asked. "I know Katherine is close to her heart."

Gerald felt a wave of shame break over him, hot, unpleasant. How could he keep, well, not forgetting, exactly, but losing his focus. On Katherine. Lucy had wanted him to tell Anne something, something she thought was important. What was it? He couldn't remember. He recalled the sound of Lucy's voice, but he knew he hadn't listened. Instead he'd kept seeing that dawn light, remembering the warmth and weight of a man's arms. Damn it. *Damn* it! His daughter was missing. What if Lucy had said something important? Well, of course she had. She wouldn't have called otherwise.

Jeremiah finished his cigarette in silence and kept his eyes on the road. He must have taken Gerald's lack of response as an indication that he didn't want to talk. But he did want to talk. He needed words to hold on to. Like a rope. Help me, he said to someone. Jesus? Jeremiah? Help me!

"Jer, I think I might be losing my mind," Gerald said at last.

No, it was already lost. "I can't remember what Lucy Way said."

"You got a lot on your mind," Jeremiah said.

Did he mean last night? Had anything…happened between them, any more than…. Gerald had wondered before if Jeremiah might have…tendencies. He could not recall Jeremiah ever mentioning a girlfriend. What if….

"It'll come back to you," Jeremiah tried to reassure him. "Maybe she called to see if you'd heard anything. Or to tell you she'd be praying. I bet that lady's prayers are powerful. A lot of people praying for Katherine, Ger."

Another hot wave hit Gerald, then receded, leaving a hint of relief. Maybe nothing had happened between them last night, nothing at all. Jeremiah was just his friend, caring for him the way any friend would, nothing more. Greater love hath no man than that he would…hold his friends in his arms all night. Stop, Gerald ordered himself. Stop.

"You still believe in prayer, Jer?"

That's what they were talking about, prayer. Gerald knew Jeremiah had had some sort of crisis of faith, had been estranged from his Baptist minister father, had refused to follow in his footsteps. He'd had more guts than Gerald.

"I believe in sun, rain, wind," said Jeremiah at length. "Prayer is a force. I don't pretend to know how it works."

Gerald's prayers had always been bound in a book, a prayer for almost every occasion. What were those prayers but detailed instructions to God in ornate language to save them, please, though they were not worthy. Suddenly he saw prayers scattered on the wind, falling like rain.

"Me neither," said Gerald. Who else could he admit that to?

Anne, Gerald reminded himself, Anne. But come to think of it, he never had. Anne had her own private lack of faith that she guarded fiercely. She had never been curious about his faith—or faithlessness.

"Don't matter," said Jeremiah. "Pray anyway. One thing I do know, it can't hurt. It might help, especially when you feel helpless."

Helpless, help for the helpless.

Jeremiah began humming softly and then he sang, *"He's a mother to the motherless, a father to the fatherless."*

All at once the image of Katherine smote Gerald. Katherine walking down a street alone, Katherine left waiting for him to pick her up. Katherine running away from the dinner table. Katherine frightened by some man, some unknown man. Lucy Way had said that, how did she know, how did she…?

Gerald began to weep, soundlessly at first, then in gulping sobs. When Jeremiah reached out and took his hand, Gerald held onto it.

Black and white together, Black and white together. He had held black hands before, marching in Montgomery with Dr. King. Dr. King. That night that Dr. King had been killed. Katherine had been there with him. If only Dr. King hadn't been killed….

Just then a truck they'd passed on the way up a hill accelerated and began to gain on them, still in the right lane. When the truck was neck and neck with them, the driver rolled down his window.

"Nigger lover! Faggot!" he shouted and a gob of spit landed on Gerald's window.

Jeremiah let go of Gerald's hand so abruptly it felt like he was pushing him away, almost pushing him out of the car. Slowly, excruciatingly slowly, the truck moved past, and Jeremiah slowed and moved into the right lane behind the truck, out of sight. He decelerated till several more cars passed and placed themselves between the Christler and the truck.

"I'm sorry, Ger. I didn't mean to get us almost killed."

Jeremiah's voice sounded far away, flat. More than anything Gerald wanted to take Jeremiah's hand again. But he didn't.

"You got a plane to catch."

Chapter Twenty-Five

Katherine did not know where she was or why she was there, but disorientation was becoming such a familiar state, she hardly felt any fear. It was quite possible that she dreaming. As often happened in dreams, she was and was not Katherine. The dream story seemed to be about some other person called Liza Jane. This Liza Jane character had been whisked away from the dreary room with peeling wallpaper (to which she had been briefly returned after what Madame Angelique called her makeover) into something like the stage set of a nursery. There were dolls with china heads in period costume (which did not match her own costume) seated at a doll-sized tea table with a doll-sized tea set. There were old-fashioned picture books on a shelf, a puzzle with pieces beginning to cohere into an image of Queen Victoria spread out on a child-sized table. Since the chair in front of the table was uncomfortably low, Katherine perched at the end of a small four-poster bed. She had never really liked *Alice in Wonderland* or *Through the Looking Glass*, but it felt like she had fallen or been forced into a world like that where things changed shape and size and had no purpose she could understand.

Like this nursery that wasn't really a room, more like a diorama in the Natural History Museum in New York where you looked through a window into a scene of life-sized figures of primitive peoples cooking or hunting. Her nursery set was not behind glass, but it was open on one side framed with heavy brocade drapes, drawn back with a gold rope.

There was corridor after corridor of these sets. At last, the Angel of Death had turned down one of these halls, hurrying her along so quickly she hadn't seen much, just enough to retain an impression of dark temple walls carved with contorted figures. Out of the corner of her eyes, she saw one of the figures move. Another set appeared to be a barn stall with an assortment of riding crops arranged on the wall. She thought she'd seen a throne on a raised dais in one room and in another an altar before a stained-glass window. Directly across the hall from her nursery was a rather dark room with a fireplace and a fake fire, a small round table with a decanter full of some amber liquid and a single glass next to a wingback chair. On two walls were bookshelves full of leather books with gilt titles.

Katherine was considering disobeying Madame Angelique's strict admonition not to move from her place when she saw a girl, maybe a little older than herself, enter the library diorama. She was wearing a short, tight-fitting black dress, and a ruffled white apron. Her dark hair was tucked up under a frilly white cap with a tendril escaping down the back of her neck. She carried a feather duster. After she entered the set, she peered down the hallway to the right and the left, and then slumped down in the chair, resting her face in one hand while the feather duster dangled from the other. She hadn't even glanced in Katherine's direction. But she was the first person close to her own age Katherine had actually seen since she'd been imprisoned. She tiptoed to the edge of her nursery set and summoned her nerve to speak.

"Hello," she said too softly and too much, she realized, in her own accent. "Might I 'ave a word?" she said more loudly, carefully dropping the h. "See, I'm new 'ere and—"

The girl looked up, not startled, not particularly interested.

"Won't be new for long," she said. "Not after a night or two. You'll be as wore out as the rest of us."

Katherine hesitated, not sure if it was a good idea to admit how much she didn't know. But she might not get another chance like this one.

"Would you mind telling me what, well, what exactly it is we do?"

The girl looked at her for a moment and shook her head, with pity or contempt, Katherine couldn't tell.

"Oh, Lor'," the girl sighed. "Or as I, Fifi the French Maid, might say, *Bon Dieu* or *oo la la*. I reckon I'm not supposed to tell you noffink. They like the ones playing Babe in the Woods to be bloody babies for real. Uncle Toby's orders no doubt." The girl in the black dress had called him uncle. "The Angel of Death does whatever 'e says. I don't want to get in no trouble. Last Little Girl in Knickers didn't last long. Screamed 'er bloody 'ead off. We didn't 'ear no more from 'er after that."

Katherine's informant drew her finger across her throat and rolled her eyes up into her head.

"Say, you're the warbler, ain't you?" The girl looked at her with slightly more interest.

"I was singing the other day," Katherine acknowledged.

"Word is Uncle Toby's quite taken wiv you. Lucky you while it lasts." She snickered, and Katherine didn't know whether the girl was being sarcastic or not. "Maybe 'e'll go easy on you, your first night and all."

First night of what? Just then a bell rang, a harsh sound like the hall bell at school.

"Places, everyone!" barked the Angel of Death from somewhere down the hall, her voice booming in what Katherine realized now was a vast space, though each set was quite small, like a stall on a huge market place.

The girl in the black dress sprang from the chair and began to dust the bookshelves.

"Please," Katherine whispered as loud as she dared. "Are we in a play? Or a museum?"

The girl didn't answer, just kept dusting, her reach higher, so that her—Katherine suddenly saw—naked bottom peeked out from under her dress. She was wearing only stockings and garters underneath. For the first time Katherine was grateful for her absurd bloomers or knickers, whatever they were.

"Please," Katherine pleaded again. "Tell me what's 'appening."

The girl turned for a moment, glanced quickly down the hall and then hissed to Katherine.

"Shut yer gob and pretend to pour your dollies some pretend tea."

Chapter Twenty-Six

Fog. The kind of fog you see in dreams or in London, making a misty halo around a street light, swirling at your feet, now and again turning into rain. This is not a part of London that she knows. Alley cats and rusty prams left by the steps because the flat is too crowded. Grimy pubs, their signs too worn and dull to decipher, drunken songs and the occasional brawl overflowing into the street.

What are these gentlemen doing here, in fancy dress, skirting the odd broken bottle or refuse heap, as they speak in the crisp, clipped tones of Eton and Oxford.

"I tell you, you've never seen anything like it. It is…phantasmagorical. A veritable medina of smut and camp."

"Why hide it away here? In a place one hardly likes to walk down the street for fear of rats and contagion?"

"Why, that's half the fun, don't you see? You feel as though you're slumming and then…well, I don't want to spoil it. Wait and see. We're almost there."

The men turn down an alley between two buildings that look like abandoned warehouses or factories, complete with fallen bricks and open windows. They climb up some side stairs with a metal railing and one of the men gives a sharp rap on the metal door and steps back. A small window hidden in the door is cracked open.

"Little Jack Horner," says the man who knocked, and the door opens just wide enough for the men to disappear inside.

There was a loud whistle, and Lucy woke with a jerk, righting herself as she leaned forward almost slipping from the rocking chair. Elsa lay dozing on the day bed in the small living room, most of it taken up by a grand piano.

"The kettle is boiling, Lucy," Clara poked her head out of the kitchen. "And I am afraid I burnt the toast. I didn't want to disturb you—"

"That's quite all right, Clara. I will see to the tea. That's why I am here. Perhaps you could wake Elsa gently and see if she needs the commode before we eat."

Clara went to Elsa, and Lucy retired to the kitchen where she turned off the flame under the kettle, hotted the tea pot and poured, the steam swirling up into her face, a momentary fog.

Fog. She had just had a vision of fog, a dreary street. In London. It had to be London.

Lucy put down the kettle and held onto the kitchen table.

She must have had another dream.

"Elsa says she'd rather have vodka and tonic," Clara called to Lucy as if Elsa did not make this outrageous request every day.

"I've no doubt she would," answered Lucy as she always did.

She wondered if Elsa had some vodka hidden away somewhere. It was strictly *verboten* to mix strong drink with her pain medication, but Lucy wouldn't put it past her to try. And Lucy wouldn't have minded a drink herself after all the emotional upheaval of this day, weeping in front of Father James, hearing his anguish over his son. Ralph, he had told her to call him Ralph. When was the last time she had wept in front of anyone? It was one of the benefits of being a spinster. Private sorrow.

Lucy set the tea cups on a tray, tossed out the hopelessly burned toast and started another batch, doing everything by rote as she tried to call up and memorize every detail of her puzzling dream. Puzzling indeed. For each dream must be a piece of the puzzle. And if she kept dreaming, surely she would be able to put all the pieces together. They must be real.

Ralph James believed in her dreams.

Chapter Twenty-Seven

Anne was almost glad to see Gerald, except there was no gladness in anything now. Maybe relieved would be a more exact word.

It had been awkward to be alone with Pat and Bob. Everything they said was wrong, and everything they didn't say. Pat's voice was so loud, even after the strain of the operation. And when she didn't speak, Pat would sigh, sighs you could hear across the room.

"You must rest," Anne insisted desperately when Pat tried to join her in the kitchen. "No, really. I don't mind cooking in the least. Keeps my mind occupied."

"You poor thing!" her sister-in-law said. "You don't know how terrible I feel, if only—"

"Please sit down, Pat. I'll bring you some tea."

"Coffee please. Anne, I've had so much tea since I came to this country, I'd like to dump it all in the Boston Harbor again. And the British simply don't know how to make real coffee. I've always loved your coffee, Anne...."

And her voice would go on and on from the other room. After a while, Anne didn't hear the words, and she knew Pat wasn't waiting for an answer.

And Bob was worse. She had just given up trying to conjure a package of peas or beans from the tiny freezer to go with the meat-loaf she managed to throw together. Before she had her surgery, Pat had left carefully labeled casseroles for Bob to heat for himself and

Katherine, but the last of these was gone. Pat prided herself on never using frozen veg (as she called vegetables). She even mashed her own potatoes by hand, scorning the instant mixes Anne relied on. Anne was bending over, gingerly opening a bin where a cabbage of uncertain vintage confronted her when Bob came up behind her. She picked up the cabbage, shoved the drawer closed and stood up. Bob remained standing close, too close, so that she could smell the scotch on his breath.

"Is there anything I can do for you, my dear?"

She whirled around, clutching the cabbage. Had he done that to Katherine? Crept up behind her, pressed himself on her. Her fingernails dug into the cabbage to keep her from smashing it into his face.

"Please," she pleaded, "go watch the evening news with Pat. Dinner will be ready soon."

As soon as I figure out what to do with this repulsive vegetable, she did not say.

In the end she boiled it more or less whole, then hacked it into pieces and divided it among their plates. Her desecration of the cabbage must have rendered Pat uncharacteristically speechless. Dinner was a silent meal that she might have found humiliating if she were not so exhausted. Anne excused herself after a few bites, washed the dishes over Pat's protest and fled to bed.

When she saw Gerald, walking towards her from baggage claim, scanning the crowd but not yet spotting her, her chest ached. (Could it be her heart?) He looked old and haggard, a shadow where he hadn't shaved, circles under his eyes. Yet at the same time he looked young, bewildered, like a child separated from his mother. She remembered Hal looking like that the first time she came to pick him up at nursery school. But Gerald was not her child. It was not Gerald who was lost....

Then he spotted her and waved, a smile flickered, then guttered out. She supposed her face had done the same. When he reached her, he embraced her awkwardly with one arm, while he held onto his suitcase with the other.

"Bob's waiting out front with the car," said Anne.

They walked a few steps, and then Gerald put the suitcase down and turned to Anne, though he didn't try to touch her again.

"Has it been awful?" he asked.

"Awful," she said, and then she forced the words out, hard to speak but true, "I'm glad you're here."

Chapter Twenty-Eight

The light in Detective Smith-Jones' office was not bright, the same dreary grey inside as the weather outside. Yet Gerald felt as though he were sweating under stage lights or searchlights, the kind that would pursue a fugitive.

Maybe it was jetlag; maybe he was ill.

"Your wife said your daughter's behavior changed rather suddenly," the detective was saying.

Why wasn't Anne with him, Gerald wondered? Was he being interviewed separately to see if their stories matched up? Was the detective trying to catch him out in a lie?

"In fact, Mrs. Bradley believes the change coincided with the death of the civil rights leader Martin Luther King Jr. She says your work has something to do with the rights of Negroes?"

A bead of sweat began to roll from Gerald's brow and came to rest damply on his cheek, like a tear. Would the detective notice it? That night, that night. Driving into Riverton to help hold it down with Jeremiah, their community. Coming home late. Only Katherine waiting up for him, only Katherine. Watching the television. A lot to drink. A lot.

"I understand your daughter did some volunteer work for your organization last summer."

"Yes," said Gerald, not sure what else to say.

"But she refused to go back to the job this summer," continued the detective. "Do you have any idea why?"

Gerald's mouth felt so dry. *My tongue cleaveth to my jaws; and thou hast brought me into the dust of death.* A verse from Psalm 22 went through his mind. The psalm Jesus had quoted from the cross. He had preached on it so many times to prove that Jesus hadn't really despaired, because the Psalm ended in triumph. Stupid, Gerald thought now. Of course Jesus had despaired.

"Mr. Bradley? Are you quite well?"

The detective looked concerned, but Gerald thought he could detect suspicion underneath. What did he suspect? What had Gerald done? What had he done?

"I'm fine. If I could just have a glass of water...."

"Of course."

Maybe he was having a heart attack, like his father before him. For a moment he almost envied his father. Everything would be so simple if he could just drop dead. No more questions. Gerald put his hands up to loosen his tie when he remembered he was wearing his dog collar, as his mother insisted he should. To prove what? That Katherine came from a good family, a respectable family. It was not her family's fault; it was not his fault.

"Here you are." The detective handed him the glass. "I do apologize for not offering before."

These English. So damned polite. Suddenly Gerald felt homesick, not for his country but for Riverton, the streets, the Lunch Counter. People calling out to him, Hey, Rev, how you be this morning? And Jeremiah, waiting for him at the office, halfway through the morning papers, ready for a good-natured debate. Jeremiah. Gerald took a sip, and then he drained the whole glass. He hadn't known he was so thirsty. *I am poured out like water....*

"I understand it was your idea to have Katherine stay with your sister and brother-in-law?"

What was the detective implying? That he had wanted to get rid of Katherine, because...because she made him so uncomfortable. Those eyes in that picture of her as a little girl, the one he had put away....

"No," he said abruptly, taking himself by surprise. "Actually it was her," what to call Lucy Way, "her sort of unofficial Godmother's idea."

"Older woman, brought up in England. Read Shakespeare and Dickens with your daughter."

Gerald stared at the detective.

"Pardon the parlor trick." Detective Smith-Jones managed a wan smile. "I'm not a psychic. Your wife described the lady to me."

"Lucy," said Gerald, "Lucy Way." Tell Anne, Lucy had said. And all at once Gerald remembered what it was. "It just came back to me. Lucy Way called me before I left. She believes that Katherine might be using a name other than her own."

The detective waited, pen poised ready to make a note.

"Oh yes?" he encouraged. "Did she say what the name might be?"

Gerald tried to go back to the moment, the telephone in his hand as he barely listened. He had woken up in a man's arms. Where he'd slept. All night. You bet, Lucy, he had said, and he'd hung up the phone.

"No." That wasn't true. He should at least tell the truth. "I mean she might have. I think she did, but I don't remember. Everything, everything's been so...."

Why didn't the detective say something comforting and British like, I quite understand. But he just waited.

"Did Miss Way say why she believes Katherine might use another name?" the detective asked at length.

Gerald felt an odd sensation of relief. Now he knew why he hadn't paid attention or why it didn't matter that he hadn't.

"I remember now," he said. "I'm afraid it was only a dream she'd had. She...thought it might help."

The detective scribbled something on his notepad.

"Indeed, it might," said the detective. "We believe in following every lead. Is Miss Way by any chance on the telephone?"

Gerald felt confused and glanced at the telephone on Detective Smith-Jones' desk.

"I'm sorry," said the Detective. "I meant, does she have a telephone?"

"Oh yes," said Gerald. "I don't know her number offhand, but I am sure my wife does."

"Splendid." He made another note. "Now can you tell me anything, anything at all about your daughter's character, the changes you've observed. Any letters she might have written about how she was getting on here."

"I think she wrote to her mother," he almost mumbled. Say something more, he told himself, or he'll know…what?

"Katherine has always, well, she's always been a bit of a dreamer, imaginative, I guess you might say. I had hoped working in the day-care center with people who have very little might help her be more in touch with the real world. Maybe when Dr. King died…." Gerald trailed off.

Katherine waiting for him, late at night.

"Many people lost their dreams, didn't they?" the detective said at length. "Wasn't that one of his most famous speeches?"

What kind of a detective was he? Probing at all these sore spots, acting as if he knew—he couldn't know—what they were going through.

"Yes," said Gerald. "His dream speech. I have a dream that one day…." Gerald found himself choking up. he passed a hand over his eyes to make sure no tears joined the sweat.

"I am sorry, Mr. Bradley. This must be a terribly trying time for you."

The detective paused for a moment; then he went on.

"Your wife said Katherine may have had a romantic view of England from all the books she'd read. That perhaps she was disappointed when she found herself in a dull little suburb with relatives who are, forgive me for saying so, perhaps not quite congenial."

He left a small silence that Gerald did not know how to fill. He did it deliberately, Gerald was sure. It was how they got criminals to break down and sob a confession.

"Mr. Bradley, do you suppose it is possible that your daughter ran away?"

Gerald looked up at the detective.

"But who would she be running from?" he asked.

His sister was not the most sensitive person in the world, and Bob was a bit of a boor and a bore, but surely he was harmless—

"That's a question," said Detective Smith-Jones, "isn't it?"

Chapter Twenty-Nine

Katherine or Liza Jane or whoever she was—or wasn't—stood by the window that she could not open, that in fact had metal bars on the outside, into the little bit of the world she could see, an elbow (armpit) of a much larger building where the dumpsters were kept. Wheelie bins, they called them here. She reckoned she was about on the third floor. The walls she could see had no windows, though one wall had a bit of sickly-looking ivy making a half-hearted attempt to climb it. She could hear pigeons cooing from where they must perch on the fire escape that went down her side of the building, which she could not actually reach in case of fire (the window being barred). There was a rat perched on its hind legs on the edge of a wheelie bin. Her initial repulsion changed to mild interest. He looked clean, at least, cleaner than she felt, and alert and intelligent. She closed her eyes and tried to see him as a mouse with a plumed hat and a rapier sword in its belt, a Narnian mouse like Reepicheep, someone she could talk to. But when she opened her eyes, she saw only his hind-quarters as he disappeared into the bin.

At least he was free to come and go at will.

She was alone in her room as she had been since a silent breakfast with the others. No one talked when the Angel of Death was there. She had attempted to pretend they were all nuns in some strict religious order who had taken a vow of silence. (But there were no religious images anywhere. They wore loose day shifts instead of habits, and their mother superior reeked of gin.) Really they were all too tired to speak after the long, long seemingly unending night with its strange costumes and sinister comings and goings.

Katherine's Little Girl in Knickers outfit, which must have been washed and pressed while she was at breakfast, had been put on a velvet hanger and hung on a hook on the back of her door. If she had had scissors or her old Swiss Army Knife (the knife she had bought long ago with the savings from her piggy bank at Frankie's insistence) she would have slashed the hideous pinafore and knickers to ribbons.

They had come to her, at her, the men, old enough to be her uncle, old enough to be her grandfather. Ugly. The kind of men you were not supposed to accept candy from or a ride in a car. They had dandled her on their knee (one took her over his knee and spanked her before she knew what was happening). They had done things to her with their horrible fingers she didn't know men did. (All of it even worse, because the Angel of Death had shaved her down there. "Don't see the appeal of it myself, looks like a plucked chicken, but some gentlemen requires it.") The men had shown the part of themselves she knew about from anatomy books, from dirty jokes, but did not want to see. Even when that man Tom had raped her, she hadn't seen his penis. (She had always hated the word penis, and now she knew why.) Not the way she saw theirs, some purple, some red, some white as worms, some hooded like cobras, some slimy. Some had made her touch them, some had touched themselves, jiggering them up and down till they spurted.

She had wanted to scream, but she knew if she started screaming she would never stop. (*Last Little Girl in Knickers didn't last long. Screamed 'er bloody 'ead off. We didn't 'ear no more from 'er after that.*) So she kept holding her breath until she had to gasp for air. Then she'd hold it again.

One of the men wanted to do more than finger her. He had his ugly naked thing pointed at her. He tore her knickers off and tried to lift her onto it. She struggled then, soundlessly, twisting and writhing. Then, as if he had been waiting just outside the curtain (maybe he had) Mister Tobias had appeared.

"Now, now, now, my dear sir. I thought I had made the rules of etiquette in this delicate situation perfectly clear."

The man had huffed and snorted. "Good God, Tobias. You don't seriously mean to pass off this little baggage as unspoiled goods!"

"I beg you to remember yourself, sir!" said Mister Tobias. "And may I humbly suggest that you endeavor to recall that you are on probation in this privileged society."

Society? These awful men were part of a society?

"One more infraction and your membership can, and I daresay will, be revoked," Mister Tobias went on. "As it stands now your session with Miss Liza Jane has drawn to a lamentable close. You will excuse yourself, sir."

And the horrible man (who had a mottled bald head that made him look like a walking penis) zipped up his pants, angrily thrust aside the curtains and exited her diorama. She was left alone with the enormous Mister Tobias who looked as though he had wandered into the wrong set or eaten one of Alice's enlarging mushrooms.

"There, there now Liza Jane. Don't be frightened. Uncle Toby is here and he is very, very pleased with his little girl."

Word is Uncle Toby's quite taken wiv you. Lucky you while it lasts.

"Come then, let's get your knickers back on, shall we?" He picked them up and held them for her to step into. "We wouldn't want anyone to think we were a naughty girl who takes her knickers down for the asking, now would we?"

Katherine felt frozen as if she were playing a game of statues. Maybe if she'd stayed still long enough, she really would turn into a statue, like the ones in the White Witch's house, frozen where they were till Aslan came and breathed them back to life.

"Now don't be frightened of your Uncle Toby, there's a good girl. Here. I'll help you."

And he pushed her back into the chair and proceeded to kneel down in front of her and put her legs into the knickers. She looked around. If she had a paperweight or if she could get hold of the lamp, she could smash it down on top of his head. Maybe she should just kick his face. She began to lift one of her legs, but before she could aim, he had grasped both her ankles with one of his hands, and with the other, he probed between her legs. He found a spot and tickled and tickled till she thought she would wet herself. Then something strange and awful happened, a spasm that started where his finger was and then shook her whole body. She could not control her breathing.

"That's Uncle Toby's good little girl."

He let go of her legs and she saw him doing what the other men had done with his hideous thing, so enormous it would surely shatter anything it went inside.

Her legs free, she tried to get to her feet to make a dash for it. But her knees gave under her, and before she knew it, he yanked her knickers up the rest of the way and scooped her up as if she were a child. He had an awful smell, sickly-sweet but with something underneath it that wasn't. She pulled away.

"Now, now, little Liza Jane. There's no call for that, no call at all. I'll tell you what, my dear. Since you've been such a good girl, how about, as a special treat, I let you have an ice cream and then you can sing a song for all the gentlemen."

He started to carry her down the hall, past the other curtained dioramas. She could hear moans and giggles, grunts, slaps and shrieks.

"Please, Uncle Toby, let me walk." In character she added. "I'm a big girl, I am. I want to walk by myself."

"Oh, what a cunning little thing you are," he said. But he set her down, keeping a tight hold on her hand.

Leaning against the window pane, Katherine saw a couple of feathers drop down, followed by a huge splat of pigeon goo. Her mother had told her that when she was a girl visiting New York City a pigeon poop had landed right on her head. It was as big as an egg, her mother would exclaim, when she told the story.

Katherine felt tears starting. Her mother did not know where she was. Her mother would never believe the things that were happening to her.

And it was her fault. Her mother would never forgive her. And Lucy. She could hardly bear to think of Lucy. There was no place for what Katherine had become in Lucy's life.

Sshh, Aramantha whispered in her head; or maybe it was just the wind on the hollow of the alley. *Sshh. You still you.*

She had no idea if that was true, and besides, what did Aramantha know? She was just a voice in her head. The real Aramantha was as far away as everyone else. She would think Katherine was an idiot for letting herself get drunk and kidnapped. Aramantha would never have been so stupid.

The place where all the gentlemen sat drinking drinks and smoking cigars had a stage in the middle, with no scenery but lights that followed you and changed color.

"Can you sing 'The Good Ship Lollipop,' little Liza Jane?" Uncle Toby asked. "I am sure the gentlemen would love to hear a sweet song like that."

She just shook her head. He had forgotten about the ice cream. She wished she had an ice cream cone so she could shove it his face, no, on his pants, his crotch.

"What can you sing then?"

"I can sing all of *My Fair Lady*."

He went to speak to the piano player, who promptly played the opening bars of "Wouldn't it be Loverly." She came in on cue with her best Julie Andrews voice. Before the thunderous applause had died down, without waiting for accompaniment, she launched into "Just you wait, 'enry 'iggins." All the while, picturing Uncle Toby, drowning or facing the firing squad. She threw herself into it. She did not care anymore what he might do to her. She did not care. If she had to go back to that room, she *would* scream her head off.

There was a short, shocked silence when she finished. Then one slender gentleman standing in the back (one of the only young ones she'd seen) started to clap till all of them were on their feet applauding.

Except Mister Tobias. He sat, toad-like, considering her, while he carefully licked a fat cigar (just like her father did) preparatory to lighting it. She hadn't seen him after that. The Angel of Death (in a dress that rattled with black jet beads) escorted her off the stage and yanked her through the curtained corridors back to the dingy part of the building where they ate and slept.

"That's enough out of you for one night," she said and before she locked her in. "Don't be 'owling for the loo. Remember you got a chamber pot."

Except for breakfast, where she at least caught a glimpse of her fellow prisoners, (surely they were prisoners; no one could want to be here), Katherine was still under lock and key. She had hoped lunch might have been in company, but instead another dry meat-paste sandwich was shoved into her room. So much for finding favor with Mister Tobias. (The thought made her gag.) Perhaps she was out of favor already. She didn't know which would be worse. All those men pawing at her, and Mister Tobias had only rescued her so that he could paw at her himself.

And he had made her have, what was it called, an organism. Organisms were supposed to be with someone you loved or at least liked, someone your own age, a boyfriend, not a dirty old man. Why had her body done that to her?

Because you are dirty, some voice inside her said; she didn't know whose it was, but it hated her. *You are dirty. You did it with your own father. No wonder you ended up here. It's no more than you deserve.*

Katherine ran to the sink. She wished she could be sick again. She wished she could throw it all up, turn her insides out, get away from herself, get away. But she didn't seem to have control over her body at all anymore. All her dry heaves had done was bring tears to her eyes. She lay down on the bed and closed her eyes. She tried to think of Frankie, Frankie touching her breast, soft as sunlight. Frankie holding her. "Who hurt you, Katherine, who hurt you?" But if Frankie knew what those men had done to her, if he knew that she'd had an organism for Mister Tobias, he wouldn't want her. He didn't want her anyway. Not like that. He never had.

Hush now, Aramantha's voice again. *He touched your thing, he didn't touch you.*

How could Aramantha know that? She couldn't know, she didn't know, no one knew.

A sob rose up from Katherine's gut, but she pushed it back down. She didn't want anyone to hear her. Then, outside her door, she heard whispering and tittering.

"Warbler?" one of them finally spoke. "Warbler, is you alive in there? You been awful quiet."

"I'm alive," she said tentatively. Then she remembered her cockney accent. "If you calls this 'ere a life."

"'ow come you ain't singin' today?" asked someone else. She thought she recognized the voice of the knicker-less French maid.

"Wot I got to sing about, then, eh?" said Katherine.

She was Eliza now—not plaguing little Liza Jane. But Eliza Doolittle who gave as good as she got.

"Us. You could sing for us."

More titters and giggles and whispers. Maybe they were just making fun of her, trying to get her into trouble.

"Why should I do that?" she wanted to know.

"Cor blimey, Warbler, cos we the only friends you got in this 'ere 'ell 'ole."

Friends?

"Wot about the Angel of Death? Wot if she 'ears?"

"Snoring her ugly 'ead off, she is."

"Wot you want to 'ear then?" she said after a moment.

"Dusty Springfield, Marianne Faithful."

"No, no, Lulu! No, Petula Clark."

Her unseen friends argued and interrupted each other, giving her a moment to collect her wits. She knew Marianne Faithful's "When Tears Go By," but she might break down if she sang it, and she didn't know the other singers' songs well enough to sing one through.

"'ave any of you ever 'eard of soul music?" she ventured.

"Course we 'ave. The Temptations, Four Tops. The Supremes. Yeah, that's right, Dianer Ross! Sing something by 'er!"

Diana Ross could not hold a candle to Aretha Franklin, but Katherine thought it might be best to oblige her...friends? Summoning up Diana's slightly nasal plaintive tone, she sang out,

"*Stop! In the name of love, before you break my heart—*"
Then her friends joined in, "*Think it o-o-ver.*"

(*He made his way down the stairs from his eyrie as he sometimes thought of it. He usually preferred to wait till evening, to see them lined up in their places, dressed in their costumes, suspended, perfect, but he couldn't wait till tonight to see his little girl, so innocent yet so naughty. She might need some special attention from her fond uncle. She might need...hmm, yes, indeed...some discipline. Now was a good time. The wardress would be resting. He trusted they would all be resting. Perhaps he would find his little girl splayed out on her bed, a forlorn rag doll, just waiting for him to bring her to life.*

He walked the passageway over the street that connected the main building to the one where he kept his dolls. He unlocked a heavy door and locked it again, walked down another corridor. As soon as he pushed open the door to the girls' wing, he stopped, frozen.

What was that? What was that horrible caterwauling?

They were singing, howling, off key.

Just like his nightmare. Just like his nightmare.

He took a few steps down the hall, turned a corner, and then he saw them.

Gyrating like savages, howling. In front of her door, his favorite. He could hear her singing loudest of all.

How dare she, how dare she.

He broke out into a clammy sweat, his vision turned blotching and dark.

He was going to die, he was going to die. Unless....

On his great soundless feet, he turned and fled.)

Chapter Thirty

Lucy was in her garden, staking tomato plants, which already promised a good yield. Usually she enjoyed garden tasks. They brought back pleasant memories of her uncle and mother, seasonal feasts, the ritual of walking out to the flat rock to see the Perseid meteor showers. She did not have to worry about her mother or uncle, or any of those she lost in the war or even dear old, awful old Charlotte Crowley. It was the living who pulled at your heart strings, sometimes past the breaking point.

She tied a plant in place and stood up, easing her knees and back. Then she sat down for a moment on her shady bench and blurred her eyes, hoping for some vision that she knew could not be willed. (Who *was* it that had wrung her hands in another world beyond Lucy's garden?) But she saw nothing, sheer nothing but the shifting light as the breeze moved the branches of the old maple.

Then she heard the phone ring.

She turned and ran for the house as fast as she could, barely catching herself as she tripped on an uneven stone in the terrace, hurtling towards the French doors. A lot of use she'd be if she fell and broke her hip. Five rings now. I'm coming, she called silently to whoever it was. Gerald! Anne! Don't hang up, please don't hang up. She lifted the receiver on the seventh ring.

"Hello? Hello?" she almost pleaded, breathless.

"Miss Way?"

A British voice, a man's, one she did not know.

"Speaking."

"Detective Smith-Jones here of Scotland Yard. I wonder if I might have a few moments of your time, Miss Way."

He was calling about Katherine. He must be.

"Of course, Detective."

She was still standing by the wall phone in the kitchen, one hand on her heart that seemed to jump into her palm. He had not asked her if she was sitting down, but perhaps she ought to.

"I understand that you are a close friend, a sort of a Godmother to Katherine Bradley who, as I am sure you know, has been reported missing."

"That is correct, Detective."

Lucy pulled out a chair from the kitchen table and sat, perched at the edge, ready spring again.

"I have been assigned to Miss Bradley's case and have now spoken with both her parents as well as her uncle. In the course of our interview, Mr. Bradley mentioned that you believe Miss Bradley may be using a name that is not her own."

Thank heavens, Gerald had remembered, and he had told the proper authorities.

"He was unable to remember the name you believed she might be using, so I thought it best to go to the source."

Lucy was aware of breathing again, breath as something steady, with a clear course.

"I am happy to tell you anything I know. Well, know may not be the exact word. Did Mr. Bradley tell you, tell you how I...."

"That the information came to you in a dream?"

Information. The detective regarded dreams as capable of imparting information?

"He did," confirmed the detective. "Now Miss Way would you be so kind as to tell me the dream in as much detail as you can remember."

She closed her eyes again as she spoke, describing the room she'd seen, the huge bulk of the man, his manner of speech, her strong impression of Katherine's fear, the man's examination of the damage that had been done to her.

"But you did not see Miss Bradley in the dream?" the detective verified.

"I did not," Lucy confirmed. "It was her voice I recognized. She said her name was Eliza Doolittle, a favorite character of Katherine's. She tried out for the part of Eliza Doolittle in her school's production of *My Fair Lady*."

There was a pause. She imagined him taking notes.

"And why do you suppose she might be posing as a character in a play?"

Lucy hesitated. How to explain Katherine, who did not just read but lived stories.

"Her father has suggested that she perhaps has an overactive imagination," the detective prompted, "that she is not in touch with, shall we say, the real world? Do you find that to be the case?"

"No, no I don't," said Lucy, deciding that if she must contradict Gerald, she must. "She is sensitive and imaginative, yes. But she is perfectly sane."

Or at least she was, Lucy did not say.

"And if my dream has any veracity," Lucy continued, "I don't believe she was merely posing."

Her eyes still closed, Lucy heard again for the odious voice of the big man.

And you are perhaps not quite what you seem, what?

"Oh no?" the detective encouraged. "Please give me your interpretation, Miss Way."

"I think…." Lucy felt herself slipping into a dream-like state. It was hard to form words, but she must. "I think that she is afraid of what would happen if the man knew who she really was."

She tried to get clearer, she felt as though she was not making sense.

"Miss Way, do you think it possible that Miss Bradley might have run away, perhaps from a family problem, either with her aunt and uncle, or…at home? Both her parents say her behavior changed abruptly in the spring."

What was he trying to get at, and how could she speak to him about Anne and Gerald, all she did and didn't know of their unhappiness. And yet how could she withhold anything that might help? Anne wouldn't want her to, and Gerald...something murky surrounded the thought of him, like the old London fogs thick with coal dust.

"It's true," she said at length. "Katherine changed this spring. No, not changed," she amended. "More as if some, some part of her disappeared, went into hiding."

The detective allowed a silence before he spoke again.

"Is it possible that she might use a false name because she does not wish to be found?"

Lucy rubbed her forehead between her eyes, darkness churned there, and color. A flash of Katherine's hat, the green of a London park, a man's leer, a gold-capped tooth.

"No," she said abruptly. "No, you've got the wrong end of the stick, Detective."

"How so, Miss Way?"

"I had another dream. I can't be certain that it's related but—"

"Please proceed, Miss Way."

She told him about the well-dressed men walking through a slum to a what looked like an old warehouse where one of the men appeared to give a password to gain admission. There was a silence when she finished, and she thought she could hear the sound of a pen—a fountain pen—scratching on paper.

"And you think the location might have been somewhere in London or the outskirts?"

"I did not recognize the place, but the men were definitely English."

"And unknown to you?"

"Quite."

"Miss Way, supposing these dreams are clairvoyant...."

He was taking her seriously, deadly seriously.

"What might be the connection between the two dreams?"

Lucy opened her eyes. There was a tiny patch of light on the floor from the window in the Dutch door, the summer sun still so high overhead. She closed them again and saw the man's bulk, taking up the entire doorway.

"I believe that wherever and whatever the place may be, the one in the second dream, Katherine is being held prisoner there. And...."

What was the source of this intuition? Should she trust it?

"Yes, Miss Way?"

"If she is, if what I saw is real, and I make no claims, Katherine might not be the only one."

There was a long pause. She thought she could hear him not saying something, something he knew or suspected.

"You've been very helpful, Miss Way. Do you have pen and paper handy?"

"Yes." She got up and fetched the pad where she wrote shopping lists.

"Good. I am going to give you the number for my direct line. Please call me if you have any more dreams or if you think of anything else at all."

Chapter Thirty-One

Anne gestured angrily for Gerald not to follow her and stormed out into the storm, which is to say she slammed the door on purpose for the first time in her life. Of course, outside the storm wasn't a storm, just more perpetual English drizzle. Gerald ran after her down the front walk, looking as miserable as the weather, and handed her an umbrella before he turned around and slunk back into the house, where his sister was holding forth to Detective Smith-Jones.

Closed doors meant nothing. Not with the volume of Pat's voice. Anne could barely hear the detective's discreet murmur, but her sister-in-law's answers were plainer that the murky daylight.

"Uncooperative, self-absorbed, eccentric, to the point of, well, I don't like to say it, but my niece appeared to me to be mentally unstable. We had no idea the extent of her problems when we agreed to have her for a visit. Of course, I am not qualified to say, but I think she might hear voices, talk to people who aren't there. That's called schizophrenia, isn't it, detective? I am sure you come across cases like this all the time. Yes, I know she's an adolescent, but my own children never...."

That was when Anne left. Now she walked down the suburban streets blessedly deserted in the middle of the day, these rows and rows of predictable brick houses, their famous English gardens just as predictable. She hated this country, hated it. She hated Bob and Pat, she hated Gerald. She walked on and on, past a shopping district, past more streets and houses, until she came to the surprise of a hill, a park surrounding a dull ruin of a castle, so generic looking no tourists bothered to visit. She walked on, up the grassy rise, until she found herself alone with stone and rain and sky and suddenly, finally, she began to howl. As soon as she let loose, she knew why she'd been holding it in and holding it in—this scream that would never stop.

Gerald had made another mistake. He had thought Anne just needed a moment to herself. But she'd been gone for an hour now. He paced while his sister talked—and talked!—to the detective, who had already searched Katherine's room for anything that might give a clue as to her whereabouts or state of mind.

Worn out with doing nothing, Gerald busied himself with making tea, the proper English way that he learned when briefly stationed here in the war. He took a tray up and offered his efforts to the detective and his sister, hoping to be invited to stay. But after a polite thank you from the detective, he was dismissed. Under the circumstances, he thought he could be pardoned for adding a shot of whiskey to his own mug of tea. He took the bottle with him and settled in the living room where he tried to read the local paper without success. The pages wouldn't fold back correctly, and the print refused to cohere. When he heard the detective coming downstairs, he leapt to his feet, wobbled a bit, but managed to right himself in time.

"Please don't get up," the detective said from the front hall. "I'll see myself out."

"My wife," he started to say.

"I'll be in touch with you and Mrs. Bradley the moment I know anything. And if you think of anything more, you know where to reach me. Good day."

"My wife is missing," he said to the closed door.

Gerald hurried to the closet and grabbed the first thing he saw that resembled a raincoat. (It turned out to be his sister's). By the time he got outside the detective's car had pulled away.

"Anne?" he called out. "Anne!"

And then, without telling his sister where he was going, he set out to look for his wife, rain on his face mixing with tears. It was a miracle, the kind he didn't believe in, that they bumped into each other, literally, crossing a busy street, her umbrella (the one he'd gotten for her) nearly poking out his eye.

"Pardon me," she said, not even seeing him at first.

"Anne!" he grabbed her arm.

"For God's sake, Gerald. Let's get out of the street."

And he turned and crossed the rest of the way with her. Back. She had been on her way back. To him?

"I don't want to go back to your sister's house," she said, over the sound of rain and traffic.

"Let's get in out of the rain."

She let him lead her to a tea shop where she ordered what the waitress called Nescafé and he had more tea.

"Did the detective say anything?" she asked after a silence he didn't have the courage to break.

"Just that he would call us when they find out anything. And that we can call him if we do. If he found anything in her room, he didn't tell me."

Because he thinks I'm to blame, Gerald did not say out loud. He did not want to burden Anne with his own sense of guilt and unease. But maybe she blamed him, too. Maybe that was why she wouldn't look at him. Or maybe she was exhausted. Anne rested her forehead against her fingertips, her face hidden from him.

"I'm going to get my things and go to a hotel in London," she said. "I want to start out from Bob's office and walk where she might have walked. I have to do something, and I can't think of what else to do."

Gerald waited, waited for her to turn to him, to need him. But she never would. In the end, he was the one, always the one, who needed her.

"Please, Anne. Let me go with you."

Without moving her hands from her forehead, she nodded.

At least he thought she had.

Chapter Thirty-Two

She could not go through another night like last night. Then she had not known what was going to happen to her. Now she did. Really, she didn't know which was worse. The Angel of Death came to her room with two dour assistants who barely spoke and might have been aged twins. Both of them strangely resembled clothespins, stiff and unbending. It was almost surprising that they had animate arms and hands that they put to work dressing her in the freshly washed and pressed pinafore, then sausage-rolled her hideous curls (why had she ever lamented having straight hair). Katherine suspected they yanked her hair on purpose when they tied and knotted the over-sized bows.

"I'll not!" Katherine heard herself saying, almost from a distance, watching herself be whoever she had become, hardly even Eliza Doolittle anymore. Ghastly Liza Jane.

Madame Angelique, who had gone out ahead leaving the clothes pins standing sentinel, turned on her heel.

"You'll not! Did I 'ear you right? You'll *not*? You'll not what?"

Madame Angelique looked more excited than angry, and Katherine felt what she'd managed to swallow of dinner (unidentified fish and mashed peas) congeal in her stomach.

"It's wrong." Katherine tried again. "What you're making us do is wrong. It's...it's against the law."

It must be. She was being held prisoner; she was being pawed and fingered against her will. She had been kidnapped, raped. But as the Angel of Death began to advance on her, she lost all certainty of anything.

"The law, the *law*? What does a nasty, stupid little girl like you know about the law? Now you listen to me. The only law around 'ere you need worry about is Mister Tobias'."

"So you've said," Katherine shot back at her.

The blow to her face came so fast, she heard it rather than saw it. The dingy room turned red with the stinging of her cheek.

"Don't push your luck, is my advice. Now come along, you silly little baggage."

She gave a nod to the clothespin twins, who took an arm each. Katherine leaned back and dug in with her heels. The Angel of Death stood with her hands on her hips and regarded her through narrowed eyes. Then all at once, she shrugged.

"'ave it your way then. Why should I give a pig's arse what 'appens to you. It's your funeral, if you get my meaning."

The clothespins let go so abruptly that Katherine almost fell down. Madame Angelique rattled her keys and began to close the door. Suddenly anything seemed better than being locked in alone with no hope of escape and no knowing what Mister Tobias might do to her. She lunged for the door.

"Well, aren't you the contrary one. Per'aps we should call you Mary, Mary. I'll 'ave a little word with Uncle Toby about that, shall I?"

Katherine didn't answer this time, just walked silently, head slightly bent to hide the attention she paid to every turn and flight of stairs, every door locked and unlocked as they made their way through dingy warrens towards the other place that Katherine recalled as huge. From the way her footsteps echoed and from the sounds of traffic below, she thought the two places might be in separate buildings, connected by an elevated passage over a street, but she couldn't be certain. When they reached the other place, barred by extra bolts and locks, the Angel of Death disappeared through a door that sounded as though it might open into the room where she had sung on stage. She could hear men's voices calling out and laughing, the chink of glasses. The sound vanished as the door closed and the clothespins bore her on through the immense space with all the little stage sets.

As they passed by, each girl froze into place, looking as still and lifeless as any mannequin in a store window. The clothespins proceeded too quickly for her to take in much detail, but she saw again the dark girl who appeared to be part of a sculpture and a plump girl with a pitchfork of what might be real hay in a fake barn scene. In the diorama made to look like a chapel, a nun knelt before an altar but instead of a crucifix over the altar there was a satyr with a huge horrible penis protruding. Each figure stood so still, she could have mistaken them for life-sized dolls, except she recognized some of them from having seen them hunched around the breakfast table. And surely some of them must be the same girls who had crowded outside her door that very afternoon demanding that she sing. But it was hard to know. The row the clothespins were forcing her down was only one of the rows in a hall as huge as an airplane hangar.

Then Katherine caught sight of someone wearing ornate-looking jewels, like Queen Elizabeth I might have worn—but very little else. She had red hair like Queen Elizabeth too, frizzed and pushed back from her whitened face. She looked as lifeless as all the others until her eyes met Katherine's, just for a moment. She didn't wink or smile; her face remained immobile, but some kind of light flashed out from her eyes, a spark, a blue flame. It made Katherine think of seeing a rainbow, and then it wavered and vanished as if it had never been there. But as she walked on, Katherine found she felt less alone—and braver.

"We're the only friends you got in this 'ere 'ell 'ole," one of them had said to her, maybe that naked bejeweled girl.

Friends. She reckoned that was something Mister Tobias and Madame Angelique of Death hadn't reckoned on. She resolved to survive the night and find out more from her friends about what the 'ell was going on in this 'ell 'ole.

That's right, agreed Aramantha. *They don't know about friends, and you better make sure they don't find out.*

Chapter Thirty-Three

You can't will these things, her friend Rowena used to tell her when they were girls at school dabbling, well, Lucy was only dabbling, in all things occult. (Lucy wished she could consult Rowena now, but there had been something so intrusive and abrasive about Rowena that Lucy had uncharacteristically let the acquaintance lapse after the war.) "You can only make yourself a vessel," she'd said in that theatrical voice of hers, "and a clairvoyant dream may come as the gods will—or not. You must be pure, Lucy, as spotless as a new-washed windowpane." Well, Lucy didn't know about all that, she was certainly as spotted and warped as anyone. But she had taken to having a little lie-down when she came home from Elsa's before she fixed her supper. She was tired, honestly tired....

She is in what appears to be an Edwardian gentlemen's club. Tables and chairs made for large sprawling sizes, a sumptuous bar with low, glowing lighting, a sense of heavy elegance and exclusivity. There is a small, currently empty cabaret stage and below to one side a trio of musicians, pianist, cellist and percussionist, play variations on show tunes. Most men are in formal dress, including, Lucy is surprised to see, herself. Or maybe not herself. She looks down at her arms and sees an elegant smoking jacket, a silk shirt with costly cufflinks. Her hands don't quite look masculine enough for the heavy ring she wears—

(She is filled with alarm. She has seen this ring before, a college ring bearing the insignia of Balliol. Where? *When you see your hands,* Rowena's voice instructs, *then you are having a lucid dream. You are in some sense, conscious. Pay close attention.*)

Whoever she is in the dream reaches into a breast pocket for a cigar, which—ugh—(he?) wets with his tongue before clamping beneath his teeth.

"Allow me."

Another man, older, more portly, offers a light. He looks vaguely familiar, as though she might have seen him in a news photograph, but she can't place him.

"Don't think I've seen you here before. New member, are you?"

"Ra-*ther*." The man she is inhabiting answers in an affected upper class drawl. "Gift from my Uncle Archie, for my majority, don't you know. Pater doesn't know about it," the young man confides. "Wouldn't approve. Old Archie's always been a bit of a black sheep, I'm afraid."

The older man seems to consider.

"Archie...yes, I don't seem to...."

It is important, Lucy understands, for the older man to establish the younger one's pedigree. And the younger one knows it.

"Sorry. I suppose he doesn't go by his family nickname here."

And the younger man (who is also herself) trots out a long titled name that includes Archibald somewhere in the middle. Then he introduces himself by an equally cumbersome one. Lucy is so lost in trying to remember the endless monikers that she doesn't catch the older man's introduction, but he appears to be some sort of aristocrat, an earl perhaps.

"Been back inside the Doll House yet?" the older man asks.

"Not yet," confesses the lad (as she decides to think of him/herself). "Thought I might need a little Dutch courage. I hear it's pretty over the top back there."

"That's putting it mildly." The man laughs a little too heartily. "Another?"

The earl indicates the lad's glass which glows with what Lucy suspects is a single malt Scotch.

In response to a mere nod, a waiter appears, looking as elegant as the patrons. With barely an exchange of words the lad's glass and his benefactor's are refilled.

"I won't say there's nothing to fear in the Doll House," says the earl, touching his glass to the lad's. "Fear can add a certain frisson, don't you find? But the thing to remember is that even if you're tied up by your ankles, hanging from the ceiling, not that I go in for that sort of thing myself, mind you, well, our inestimable host knows what he's about, doesn't he? First class all the way. Knew him at Eton. Nothing to worry about. One of us," he pauses for a moment. "More or less. In any event, he knows how things are done. Knows what's what and who's who. You can rely on his discretion."

The lad draws on his cigar. Thank goodness he doesn't inhale it all the way into his lungs or Lucy might cough. Then he takes a sip of his drink. Yes, a single malt from somewhere in the Hebrides, Lucy guesses. Lucy can taste the peat smoke as he breathes out.

"Come here often, do you?" The lad makes pleasant conversation but Lucy can tell he is not focused on the earl. Without moving his head, he is taking in the whole room, the other patrons. He is listening to the musicians as if waiting for some cue.

"When I'm in town. Not often these days, alas."

And the earl begins to ramble about the cares of landholding, the demanding wife, feckless sons and difficult daughters. The young shirking responsibility, ruining themselves with drugs, flaunting their sex lives, girls dressed like boys and boys looking like girls. "Twiggy, I ask you?" He blames it on the pill. The man is revealing himself as a pompous bore, and the lad nods and murmurs without listening.

"But you seem like a steady young chap, Balliol man, I see. Cambridge man myself, King's College. What do you think of your generation's antics?"

Lucy feels one eyebrow going up as the lad raises his. She feels his youthful contempt for the older man's mindless hypocrisy. Before he is obliged to answer, the music shifts and a sense of expectation circles the room like a light breeze.

From the wings comes a little girl who appears bewildered as if she has lost her way and wandered into the club by mistake from the nursery. She wears a short pinafore that barely covers her lacy bloomers. She has huge polka-dotted bows in her tightly curled hair. She looks all of about five years old. As she steps up to the stage, Lucy (and the lad) register that her legs are too long and shapely to belong to a child. It is a costume.

"Haven't seen this one before," murmurs the bore. "They have some first class burlesque here, you know. They raise it to an art form. Don't know if you were here earlier to see the slave girl act. What she did with that whip.... Now let's see what this naughty little miss gets up to."

The girl still stands looking dazed in the spotlight. The musician cues her and she begins almost lisping Liesl's song from *The Sound of Music* as if she is six rather than sixteen.

Then in the middle of the song she stops. She fixes the audience with what can only be described as a glare. The musicians attempt to keep playing but the tune peters out. Lucy can't tell if the interruption is planned or is some sort of a rebellion. Suddenly the girl points her finger at the audience and starts to sing in an entirely different voice, as if some other being had taken possession of her body.

"*What you want, baby I got it, what you need, you know I got it. All I'm asking is for a little respect.*"

The musicians are forced to follow, stumbling at first, then catching the rhythm as the girl begins to, well, dance seems hardly the word. She is advancing on her audience with a sensuality and command that makes her little girl costume utterly incongruous. Lucy feels a smile tugging at the lad's lip, which she resists, because she is frankly horrified, all the more so because, oh dear God, dear God, this voice, she's heard it before—and felt mystified by it even then in her living room, when Katherine, raised to sing in the church choir, transformed before her eyes into...what was the singer's name...Wreathe something? Despite the ludicrous costume, the blonde curls, the raw, powerful voice, Lucy cannot help but know her. This is Katherine singing suggestively, angrily, and somehow truthfully, in this terrible place. This is Katherine, her own Katherine, the child of her heart.

Then over his left shoulder, the lad senses a presence, a watchful presence, a menacing presence, attention entirely fixed on the figure

on the stage. The lad keeps his eyes straight ahead. He does not want
to turn. He knows who is behind him. But Lucy feels an urgent need
to see. Whoever is watching the stage with such malevolent intensity
is a threat to Katherine. The lad picks up the scotch, downs it, and
then, on the pretext of looking toward the bar, Lucy gets him to turn.
At eye level is a vast bulk in a silk waistcoat draped with a gold watch
chain. Swiftly she casts her gaze up and up to the top hat.

It is the man, she is sure of it. The man who took up the whole
doorway of the room where Katherine was a prisoner. The lad turns
away before the other man can notice him. Lucy puts up no resistance. There is danger here. Both she and the lad know it. He holds
still. His hands tensed, so that his ring presses through flesh against
bone.

(That ring, those hands, around someone's neck, smashing someone's head against pavement.)

Watch, she hears the lad think, *wait*.

The pain in Lucy's hands woke her, she was clutching them so
hard. Her own hands. She stared at them, disoriented. An old woman's hands. No rings. She never wore rings in the summer.

Balliol man, I see.

Who was that young man. Who was he?

And what did he want with Katherine?

*(He retired earlier than usual, but he did not go to bed. He was
not tired, and he did not want to sleep, he especially did not want to
dream.*

*He sat in his chair in his dressing gown and drank brandy. God
knows he needed it after that shock. He dimmed the lights in the
room, even though no one could see him. The first two tears had
to be forced out through a duct almost too small to accommodate
them—for surely his tears were huge, oceanic, a whale's tears. The
others followed more easily and he let them roll silently, majestically.*

*She had betrayed him, his favorite. He could no longer deny it:
her innocence was false.)*

Chapter Thirty-Four

Over Gerald's persistent snoring, Anne heard some clock, maybe Big Ben—she didn't know; she didn't care—strike four in the morning. If she were at home, she would go downstairs for peanut butter on a slice of bread and a glass of milk. She would let the dog out early or in if he was out and smoke a cigarette in the dark. Now she lay as far as she could get from Gerald on the too-small bed in the nondescript room of a hotel that had nothing to recommend it except its central location.

She had walked all afternoon and evening, through park after park, to the Tower of London, across the Thames to Shakespeare's Globe theatre, anywhere she thought Katherine might have wanted to go. She carried a photo of Katherine and asked tube station attendants and people waiting at bus stops if they might have seen her. She even went up to vagrants who looked as though they might sit in the same spot every day. No one remembered seeing her, though one old woman on a bench, surrounded by pigeons that, from the look of her soiled coat used her as a perch, spoke to Anne kindly, "Lovely girl. Is she yours, dear? Have you lost her?" Anne had to fight back tears. And she kept fighting till she constructed a dam that nothing could breach. Her heart itself felt walled off, deserted, a desert waste.

Gerald on the other hand, seemed to be constantly leaking, at the eyes and nose, sweat streaming down his forehead, dampening his shirt as he followed after her, always seeming to be a pace or two behind. Was he lagging or was she trying to shake him off? If he had not insisted, she would never have stopped to eat or drink and, no doubt, would have become dehydrated and likely collapsed. And maybe she wished she could collapse. She couldn't drink herself into a stupor, like Gerald. There was no easy oblivion for her.

They had finally stopped at a pub near the hotel. She had forced herself to drink some water and to eat a few bites of some awful meat pie, while Gerald had fish and chips and drinks she told herself not to count. They had fallen into bed exhausted and should have plummeted straight down into sleep, but Gerald had reached for her and begun to weep. What could she do? She held him and withheld herself. She knew he wanted to comfort her, but she could not, would not be comforted.

"We need to be together in this, Anne," he had pleaded. "Let me love you, please."

She had acquiesced, because it was easier than saying no, and because maybe he was right. She needed for something to break through her isolation, but when he tried to enter her, he was entirely limp. He wept some more and then he went, thank God, to sleep, although his snoring pursued her into the jumbled dreams she had before she woke again to the dark room with its sharp angles of streetlight.

Anne got out of bed, felt for her cigarettes and lighter on the bedside table and went into the cramped bathroom, described by the desk manager as *en suite*—which cost extra. But at least she could count on being undisturbed. She closed the door, locked it and sat on the toilet in complete darkness, Gerald's snores still audible but more a background noise, like traffic or surf. Nothing seemed real, not her body on the horrible, soft plastic toilet seat, not Gerald in the next room, not being in London, where somewhere Katherine was, too—or wasn't.

Anne fumbled with her lighter, striking three times before managing to summon a flame to her cigarette. Then she snapped it shut, the familiar orange glow the only light. She closed her eyes and felt the smoke flood her lungs, a deeper breath than she'd taken all day.

"Is she yours, dear, have you lost her?"

The old woman's voice came back to her and with it another, a dull thrumming voice.

Two children now, that's two children now you've lost, two children now.

In the silence and the dark, she realized these words had been saying themselves over and over all day.

Two children now, that's two children now you've lost, two children now.

The words sounded to the rhythm of her heartbeat; they were just as involuntary. They wouldn't stop. They wouldn't stop, unless... she did.

You have two children at home, a stern voice sounded over the drone, *two children who need you.*

But they didn't, Anne knew. The twins had never needed her, not the way Hal had, not the way Katherine....

Two children now, that's two children now you've lost, two children now.

"*She's alive, Anne.*" The memory of Lucy's voice cut in.

Lucy had dreamed that Katherine was alive. Why couldn't Anne reach Katherine that way? Why couldn't she reach her? What kind of a mother was she?

Two children now, that's two children now you've lost, two children now.

Anne stubbed out her cigarette on the edge of the sink and buried her face in her hands. There were cracks in the dam, and tears seeped through.

Let me see her, she prayed to the God she had never forgiven for Hal's death. Just let me know she's alive. All she saw was Katherine, not quite three years old, asking for Hal, crying for Hal, and then one day not asking anymore. Katherine hadn't smiled for a year after Hal's death. There weren't many pictures from that time but the ones there were showed a solemn child, with eyes that looked somewhere Anne could not see. Katherine still had those eyes, looking out from under her too-long bangs as she said goodbye to Anne at the airport....

Two children now, that's two children now you've lost, two children now.

Easy now, take it easy.

Whose voice was that? Not Lucy's, a man's voice, deep, reassuring. Could her prayer have been heard?

All right back there, Mrs. Bradley? Need some more air?

It was not Jesus' voice, it was Joe Petrone's.

"I can't breathe," she whispered out loud. "I can't breathe."

Easy now, take it easy. Everything is going to be all right.

How could he say that, how could he say that when he had lost his own wife and child.

Easy now.

Anne took a deep ragged breath, and then she wept.

Chapter Thirty-Five

"Mommy, Mommy!"

Katherine tries to scream but no sound will come out. She tries to fly, but her legs turn rubbery. The man chasing her is catching up. When he does, he will kill her—

"Mommy!"

Her own voice woke her. She lay still, her heart pounding.

She wanted her mother, she wanted her mother.

"Mommy," she called, her voice hoarse and scratchy.

From crying herself to sleep. From singing. For those men. In the club. Until Mister Tobias came and marched her off stage into a dressing room.

"I'm disappointed in you, Liza Jane, terribly, bitterly, grievously disappointed."

What did I do? she had tried to ask but no sound would come out.

"I can't think what I shall do with you now. No indeed, it doesn't bear thinking about."

And he had turned and left the room nearly crushing the girl who huddled in the doorway clutching a feather boa around what looked like green scales pasted all over her body.

"Cor, luv," she said, shaking her head. "You're for it now, I reckon."

"But what did I do?" Katherine managed to speak.

"Doesn't matter what you did, luv. It's what 'e'll do you got to worry about."

Katherine wanted to ask more questions, but the girl hastily checked her makeup and hurried back out.

"Got me own neck to watch out for, 'aven't I?" was all she said.

Katherine had spent the rest of the night huddled in the dressing room, watching other girls, who mostly ignored her, come and go. At last she dozed off in a corner and was wakened by a blow to her face. She opened her eyes to find the Angel of Death standing over her.

"Get up. I 'aven't got all night."

The Angel of Death dragged her through empty dark corridors back to her room, grumbling as she went.

"I seen 'em come, I seen 'em go. 'ow bloody stupid can you be, falling out of favor in less than forty-eight hours. I ask you. No more sense as God gave a bleedin' bedbug."

"Mommy," Katherine whispered again, huddled in her bed.

But she knew her mother would never come. And if she ever got away—(*Cor, luv, you're for it now, I reckon*)—she would never be able to go home. Not after what had been done to her and what she had done.

Chapter Thirty-Six

"I've got to call the office today," Gerald said as he and Anne sat together at breakfast in the basement cafeteria of their hotel.

And then at once he knew that it was the wrong thing to say.

"Of course," said Anne, which made him feel worse than if she'd lashed out at him. "I've got calls to make, too. We should both call home."

She looked as washed out as the weak coffee. By the time he'd woken up that morning, she was already dressed, frowning at a London guidebook, he supposed mapping out a course for the day. He wondered if she had slept at all. How long could she go on like this? How long did she intend to?

"Anne," he began, and found he didn't know what more to say.

She looked at him vaguely, as if she had forgotten he was there. Why was he here?

You got to be over there with Anne. You got to look for your daughter. Jeremiah's voice sounded in his head.

Well, here he was, and as far as he could tell he was useless, impotent.... He vaguely remembered weeping in Anne's arms last night. What a baby he was! And then trying to, what had he been thinking, to make a demand on her like that at a time like this? How selfish was he? Well, it hadn't mattered, because he couldn't get it up. He was impotent, literally. And Anne, Anne had probably been relieved.

(Jeremiah had held him all night long. Why was he thinking about that now? What was wrong with him?)

"What are your plans for the day?" he asked Anne, as if he weren't part of them. Maybe he wasn't. "I mean, should we split up, each take a route? Or should we go together?"

"I don't know," she said. Her hands pulled at each other, first one then the other. "I don't know what to do, Gerald. I don't know what to do."

He took out his cigarettes and gave her one to give her poor hands—(even, thin with bones and veins standing out, they were beautiful)—something to do.

"Thanks."

He lit a cigarette, and they smoked in silence.

"I can't go home, Gerald," she said after a time. "Not until I know."

Gerald felt as though he were looking at Anne from far away, the table between them, a chasm, a canyon. If he shouted to her across it, all he would hear would be the echo of his own voice.

Anne might never come back, she might never.

"But *you* must go home."

She spoke softly, but so clearly, as if she were sitting closer than she was. As if she were inside his head.

"Thank you for coming," she said formally, as if to a guest. "Thank you for coming to be with me."

"Anne," his voice broke. Damn it, what was wrong with him? Why couldn't he be strong for her? Why couldn't he be strong? "She's my daughter, too."

Anne looked thoughtful, as if he'd made a point she hadn't considered.

"Yes," she said. "Yes. And Peter is your son. And Janie is your daughter. You have another chance, Gerald. You have another *chance*."

Meaning he'd failed, failed with Hal. Failed with Katherine.

"*You* have another chance," she said again.

Meaning she did not?

"Anne," he said. He put out his cigarette and took hold of her free hand, her left, cold, dry, and so thin her engagement ring and her wedding ring had slipped to her knuckle. "Oh, Anne."

Chapter Thirty-Seven

Lucy was not happy about her last conversation with Detective Smith-Jones, and she didn't know exactly why. She had called him as soon as she rose, not quite five in the morning, because it was five hours later in London, nearly ten. She hadn't bothered to make coffee and only fed the cats, because they mewed and wove around her legs so insistently she could not do anything else. Perhaps that had been her mistake, perhaps she should have taken time to collect herself first, order her thoughts.

Or perhaps Detective Smith-Jones was simply losing faith in her dreams or had only ever been polite in the first place. But the source of her uneasiness didn't seem that simple.

Lucy took her delayed breakfast of coffee and toast into the living room. She opened the French doors just enough so that she could hear the summer rain, soaking into her gardens, in hopes that it might soothe her. She'd had the dream at such an odd time, waking disoriented at dusk, when it would have been after midnight in London, which meant, she'd tried to explain to Detective Smith-Jones, that it could have been happening in real time, if the place she'd seen was some sort of nightclub. Really, it hadn't seemed like a dream at all. It seemed as though she had been there, in the body of that young man. Perhaps that was where she had lost Detective Smith-Jones.

"I'm sorry, Miss Way," he had said. "Who did you say was wearing this Balliol insignia ring?"

She tried to explain to him again, that she herself was wearing it or rather the young man she appeared to be in the dream.

"I see," he said, in a wary tone that made her suspect he did not see at all. "And the older man, you say he looked familiar to you."

"Yes," said Lucy. "I thought I might have seen his photograph in a newspaper article or even a newsreel on television. He is titled, so he would be a member of the House of Lords, wouldn't he? And he told the young man that he had known the host, I suppose he meant the proprietor of the place, at Eton."

The detective didn't answer for a moment. She hoped he was writing down this detail.

"A gentleman's club," he said at last, with an almost audible sigh. "Yes, they all know each other, these old boys."

Lucy gathered Detective Smith-Jones did not count himself among their number.

"Am I to understand that you believe this gentleman's club is inside the warehouse that you saw in your previous dream. Is that correct, Miss Way?"

"It seems likely," she said carefully.

"And you still believe that Miss Bradley is somehow connected with this establishment?"

"I do," said Lucy. "This time I saw her."

And Lucy had proceeded to describe Katherine's musical performance, her drastically altered appearance, her shifting from the childish voice of the one song to the defiant sensuality of the other.

"As in your earlier dream, it was her voice that you recognized," said the detective.

At least he was paying attention.

"Yes, but in the earlier dream, I only heard her voice. I did not see her. This time I did."

Again a silence. Perhaps he was reading over his notes.

"If you had not heard her sing, would you have known her by sight?"

Now Lucy hesitated. "Her appearance was greatly altered. The curls, the hair color, the makeup changed the shape of her face. But...."

"So she was, in fact, unrecognizable to you? By face and figure, that is."

Lucy closed her eyes and saw again the long legs that had outgrown the rest of her—for she was not overly tall—the childlike hesitance, followed by a womanly authority that Lucy sensed Katherine did not really understand, was only imitating.

"No, not at all," Lucy said more sharply than she intended. "It's just that I knew her voice first. There is no doubt it was Katherine I saw in the dream. Do you want to hear the rest of the dream, detective?"

"Certainly, Miss Way. Please proceed."

And she told him about the man standing just behind her, how she had turned against the wishes of the young man whose perspective she shared. (She could not blame the detective for finding her dual dream persona bizarre.) She described the mammoth man, so huge, so distinctively dressed, that she was almost certain it was the man who had stood in the doorway of Katherine's room in the earlier dream.

"And so you believe that the exceptionally large man in formal dress that you saw in both dreams is one and the same and may be, in fact, the proprietor of the gentlemen's," he paused for a beat, "club?"

Lucy did believe the enormous man might be the proprietor, but she did not recall saying so. The detective was the one who had made that leap.

Lucy put down her cup and looked out at her garden, the cosmos and coneflowers bowed to the rain, the roses in their second bloom, dropped petals. That was it, she realized, that's what was troubling her. The detective knew something that he couldn't—or wouldn't—reveal.

"If my dream is accurate, detective," she had said. "I believe 'club' may be a polite word for something far less benign."

He had not asked her what she meant, so she decided to overcome her reticence.

"I mean a prostitution ring, detective."

"Yes, of course, Miss Way. I understood what you meant."

It was the first time that bland and correct Detective Smith-Jones had assumed anything other than a pleasant tone.

"As is standard procedure in cases like this one, we are searching for any trace of Miss Bradley in the red light districts of the city. I'm afraid prostitution is not an uncommon plight for runaway youth."

Katherine is not a runaway, Lucy had wanted to object. But of course she did not know that for certain. And whether she had run away or been abducted, she was a prisoner. If Lucy's dreams had any reality.

"Pardon me, Detective," Lucy had said. "I am sure you know how to do your job."

But in fact, Lucy realized, she wasn't sure. What if his job description did not include exposing his betters, the old boys, who, in his words, all knew each other.

Lucy stood up, rattled, and carried her plate and cup to the kitchen. They rattled, too, she noticed, in hands that shook not with fear but what with an emotion far less familiar, one that frightened her with its intensity. Rage, it was rage, not at Detective Smith-Jones, rage at her powerlessness to act, to confront people who thought they could get away with...murder.

Murder.

It was more than a figure of speech, the phrase that had come into her mind.

Those hands, her hands, and not her hands, around someone's neck, those hands committing....

Murder.

Whose rage filled her?

Somehow she managed to set down the plate and cup in the sink. Then she gripped the counter to still her hands....

Her hands, the gentle worn hands of an older woman, shocking in their strength.

Chapter Thirty-Eight

"Warbler?"

Katherine sat bolt upright in bed where she had managed to doze away some of her misery. She had no idea what time it was, she'd been in solitary confinement since last night, not let out for breakfast or a trip to the showers. Her unemptied chamber pot was beginning to stink even with the lid on.

"Warbler, is you still living, then?" someone said in a whisper.

"Who is it?" she called out, then remember her accent. 'oo's there?"

"Don't make such a ruckus," whispered her visitor. "Come close to the door. We can talk through the key 'ole."

Katherine slipped out of bed and tiptoed to the door where she knelt and peered through the keyhole. She saw an eye looking back at her, but couldn't see whose it was, not that she knew anyone by name.

"'oo are you?" Katherine asked.

"Don't matter," said the other girl.

She was a girl, not a clothespin or Madame Diabolique, as Katherine had renamed her in an attempt to divert herself by practicing French. And not a rapist or a madman.

"None of us 'as our own names 'ere. You can call me Bess if you like."

Bess, thought Katherine. Good Queen Bess.

"Or Bessie. Most of the others do. Makes me sound like a cow. Nor I wouldn't put it past 'im to dress me up as one, if the idea took 'is fancy. I should count me blessins', I s'pose."

"You're the one dressed up in the Queen Elizabeth jewels," Katherine guessed. The one who had flashed her a look last night.

Good Queen Bess snorted.

"I don't reckon they's real or Tom Cat would 'ave made off wiv 'em by now, but they's cold as 'ell on me bare skin, I can tell you that. It's a wonder I 'aven't died of consumptivitis or summat like that. And they do dig into me skin when a gentleman's riding me. Sometimes I even bleeds, and I got bruises all over. If I was the real Queen Bess, I'd say off with their 'eads. And I wouldn't stop there. Few other parts I'd like to see go missin'."

Despite her loneliness and misery or maybe because of it, Katherine felt excited. This was the most conversation she'd had with anyone since she woke to this nightmare. (She *wished* it was a nightmare). A conversation with someone who couldn't (and maybe didn't even want to) slap her or maul her or stick things into her.

"Bess," she said the girl's name. "Bess?"

"All right then, Warbler?"

She thought of telling Bess her real name, but she'd been warned not to reveal it, and she thought she'd be sick if anyone called her Liza Jane again. The name Eliza, which she'd once loved, was ruined now. She liked Warbler; it felt like Bess was making fun of her, but in a friendly way.

"Bess, what is this place?"

"You 'aven't figure it out by now?"

Katherine did not want to sound stupid. She had found some books about Victorian era sex on a high shelf in her father's study. They pretended to be novels, but there was very little plot. Lots of descriptions of quivering quims. It seemed as though the women in those books wanted to do what she'd been forced to do the last two nights.

"We've been made into 'ores," she tried it out.

"Wot?"

Maybe she hadn't said it right. "Trollops, 'arlots?" she tried again. "Ladies of the evening? You know, prostitutes?"

For a moment there was no sound, and then she heard a smothered snort, and the door started to shake as Bess leaned against it.

"Lord love a duck! Wotever gave you that idea? Prostitutes do it for money. We ain't never gonna see so much as a brass farthin'. Why do you think they keep us under lock an' key, give us just enough slop to keep us alive?"

There was a word for someone who was used and abused without pay. Katherine knew it well from history, only it wasn't supposed to exist anymore, and she had never guessed it existed, like...like this.

That's right, Aramantha prompted. *Slavery*.

"We're slaves then."

Bess was so quiet, Katherine wondered if she was still there. She pressed her ear to the keyhole; she could just hear Bess breathing.

"Yeah, I reckon," Bess said. "I reckon you could call it that, same thing as being a doll, something wot 'as to do whatever it's made to do—or its 'ead and legs get pulled off, and it's thrown in a rubbish bin."

The image of a Barbie doll pulled to pieces filled Katherine's head and made her feel queasy.

"'ow did you come to be 'ere, Bess?"

There was a sigh that came through the keyhole like a small storm.

"Picked off the same rubbish 'eap. Nowhere to go, no one looking for me. They don't want no trouble. First whiff of that...."

She made a sound, the kind of sounds kids make when they pretend to cut their throats.

"But why doesn't anyone stop it?" whispered Katherine. "Why don't the police come? You can't make people into slaves, or, or dolls." Not in America, she stopped herself from saying. At least, not anymore.

Was Bess laughing or choking? She couldn't tell.

"They do come 'ere. Along with all sorts of other 'igh muckety mucks. 'oo did you think you was singing to? If 'e wanted to, old

Uncle Toby could likely bring down the 'ole 'ouse of Lords. 'e's got 'em by the short 'airs right enough."

Katherine could hardly take it in. She had grown up admiring the leaders of her country. The Kennedys, Martin Luther King.

And they had been shot; they had all been shot.

"Listen, Warbler. I don't know why I'm bothering wiv you cuz there's no 'ope. But you ain't 'oo you say you is. We all know it. Sometimes you talk like us, then you don't. There's things you don't know wot you would if you was one of us. We fink, we fink you might be...somebody...."

Who? Katherine wanted to ask her, who? Sometimes she could hardly remember who she was herself. She did not feel like Katherine. Katherine lived in a small town across the ocean. She'd had parents. She could open the door and go to the bathroom whenever she wanted. She could go for walks. She was not the person crouched by the keyhole.

"Somebody who 'ad someone, as wanted 'em."

Sudden tears pressed behind her eyes and caught in her throat, and she held her breath to keep from sobbing. Maybe her mother did want her, but she would never find her here. And if she did....

"Any road, don't matter what we fink. Mister Tobias, 'e's got the wind up. 'e won't be takin' no chances. Do you understand?"

Katherine shook her head, then remembered Bess couldn't see her. "No," she said. "Wot d'you mean?"

She wanted to talk like Bess, even if Bess knew she was a fake. Bess was all she had.

"You're marked, Warbler. You're marked."

Just then a door squeaked open.

"'ose there?" called an angry voice from down the hall. "'oo's disturbin' me beauty sleep? I'll 'ave your ears!"

Katherine felt, rather than heard, Bess creep away. Jesus, don't let her get caught, she prayed, yes, prayed. Don't let Good Queen Bess get caught.

And then whoever she had become tiptoed back to bed and pulled the covers over her head.

Chapter Thirty-Nine

They called it a bedsit. And Anne was doing just that, sitting on a single bed, looking out across a side street to another building where perhaps other women, as alone as she was, sat on their beds, wondering how they had come to be there and why they went on. Anne did not know what to do, now she was here. She could unpack her few belongings in the small chest of drawers. She could fill the kettle with water and boil it on the electric burner to make tea, except she didn't want tea. She could, and she supposed she eventually would, go out to the shops (once she found out where they were) to buy instant coffee and maybe a can of soup. There was one pot, presumably meant for heating such things, and there was crockery for one, a cup, a bowl, a plate, made of heavy white ceramic that would not break easily. There was a small sink where she could rinse dishes, brush her teeth, wash her face. Toilets and shower stalls were down the hall. There was one room with a full-sized bathtub, the landlady had pointed out with pride. But Anne didn't care about taking a bath—or doing anything else.

She had never been so alone in her life, so without points of reference to tell her who she was—wife, mother, keeper of the house, cooker of meals, friend of women who would meet her for coffee. How did you know who you were, without such markers and daily routines? How did you stay tethered to this earth?

She still had a purpose, only one, to find Katherine, and no idea how to go about it. An eternity seemed to gape between now and the appointment she had that afternoon with Detective Smith-Jones, the one she had insisted on. She had spent part of yesterday finding this cheap place to stay while Gerald arranged for his flight home.

He had left before dawn. She had pretended to be asleep while he bumbled around in the dark, getting dressed, making something of a racket in the bathroom while he shaved. If she had continued her fake slumber, would he have stood in the doorway, hesitating, wondering if he should wake her, in the end not daring? It seemed cruel to let him go so uncertainly, without a goodbye, wishes for safe trip. Part of her wanted to be cruel, and part of her could not bear to be. While he was still in the bathroom, she got up, put on her bathrobe, lit a cigarette and sat on the edge of the bed, waiting.

"Are you sure you'll be all right here alone?" he'd asked.

"I can always call Bob and Pat if I need anything," she reminded him.

They both knew she wouldn't.

"Call me," his voice wavered between a question and a plea. "Let me know what Detective Smith-Jones says."

"I will," she promised.

His grip when he embraced her at the door was so desperate she could not help but remember Hal, clinging to her when she had to leave his hospital room for any reason. She pushed away the memory and Gerald with it.

"You don't want to miss your flight," she said by way of apology.

Without another word, he turned and left.

She could not seem to stop herself from hurting him. It was better he was gone, she told herself. Better she was alone.

Anne kept sitting still. Had she ever been so still? The sun found her closed window, spilled onto the floor, onto her foot. The air heated up, grew stuffy. And still she did not move. It felt as if the room was uninhabited, she was as lifeless as the scratched bedside table with its worn doily and the small chintzy lamp. Dust would gather on her.

Then a pigeon landed on the window ledge, its soft, whirring coos penetrating the glass. Pigeons were dirty city birds. One had once made a dropping on her head. She did not think she liked pigeons, but now this one was sitting outside her window. In the sunlight, she could see glints of green and purple in its grey feathers. It made its sound again, so soft, so sad. Were pigeons sad?

Anne drew in a breath so abruptly she startled herself; she rubbed her eyes as if she had just woken from sleep. Then she stood up and opened her valise. She took out a photograph wrapped in a scarf to keep it safe. She wiped off the glass, though it was not dirty, and set the photograph on the bureau. Unsmiling, clear-eyed, Katherine looked at her from under bangs that Anne was always trying to get her to trim. Her cheeks were still round as a child's, but there was a defiant tilt to her chin.

How could she have let this child go so far from her sight, how could she?

Abruptly Anne got up and began to unpack.

Chapter Forty

Lulled by several gin and tonics, Gerald dozed on and off during the flight, now and then waking to look down at the flocks of clouds grazing over the wide field of ocean. *All we like sheep have gone astray; we have turned everyone to his own way*, the line from Isaiah repeated itself in his mind, as if it were some Mother Goose nursery rhyme and not a pronouncement of prophetic judgment. *And the Lord hath laid on him the iniquity of us all*. Of us all. How many times had he preached that sin was a corporate affair, that to get caught up in petty individual transgressions was self-indulgent?

Maybe he had been wrong.

Yet the sight of clouds was comforting. Far below, subject to air and ocean currents, they could not err; they need not repent even if they gathered into a devastating storm. They had no ill-intent. They drifted over the good and evil alike, over ocean and land mass. Their moisture fell as rain or snow; it rose again without ever dying or harrowing hell.

Gerald felt his head nodding—how strange to feel yourself falling into sleep, into dreams that weren't quite dreams. He could hear his seatmate, a businessman, who mercifully had not wanted to chat over the drinks they were served, rattle his paper as he turned a page. He sensed the stewardess passing by, hesitating over his littered tray, then passing on.

At the same time, he dreams of Katherine in some place just beyond his reach, a child swinging on a swing. Then she is older, a shy, awkward girl walking down a trash-strewn street. Arms reach out to her, reach after her, but she walks on. Then Hal is there, in a dim alley where the light shines only on him. He knows it's Hal, even though Hal is grown up, wearing an army uniform. Don't go, he wants to tell Hal. Don't go. You'll get killed. Vietnam is not a just war; there are no more just wars. Before he can speak, there is Anne standing next to Hal on the deck of a warship. Neither of them waves to him where he stands on the shore, holding tightly to a little girl's hand. Katherine. She isn't lost after all. Katherine. He wants to shout to Anne and Hal. She isn't lost! But the wind blows his words back in his face....

His seat mate adjusted the light over his head, his arm brushing Gerald as he reached up. Gerald kept his eyes closed, though he knew he was awake again. He didn't want to be awake. Where everything was irrevocable, where all that was awful had already happened. Hal had died a long time ago. Katherine was lost. And Anne....

I can't go home, Gerald. Not till I know.

If a man have an hundred sheep, and one of them be gone astray, doth he not leave the ninety and nine, and goeth into the mountains, and seeketh that which is gone astray?

Please God, please God, he found himself praying silently. *I am a lamb of thine own flock, a sinner of thine own redeeming.*

But he did not believe it. He was lost, and no one was looking for him. When he had said goodbye to her, Anne had pushed him away. Two children lost, two children he should have protected, two children he had harmed.... *Please God, please God, please God....*

Gerald jerked awake as the captain's voice came out of nowhere, informing them that they were beginning their initial descent into John F. Kennedy International Airport. Gerald still thought of it as Idlewild and of Kennedy as a young president. Nothing had been the same since Kennedy's death. Was that where Katherine's generation had started to go wrong?

She was only a ten-year-old kid, a voice inside him said. She didn't do anything wrong. She wanted to go with you the night Martin Luther King was shot, remember? She tried to comfort you....

Gerald stood up abruptly, startling his seat mate.

"Excuse me," Gerald mumbled.

The man rose and stepped into the aisle to let Gerald pass, and he made his way to the toilet at the back of the plane. On the way back he had to squeeze by a stewardess making her final rounds. When he got back to his seat, he found his mess of bottles and nut wrappers had been cleared, his tray folded away. He buckled his seat belt, feeling the pressure in his ears as the plane changed altitude. He dreaded arrival. It was so much easier being suspended in air where he could do nothing, where the ground seemed so far away, his own life as insubstantial and void of meaning as clouds. He still had a tedious journey ahead. A taxi to Grand Central. Then he'd call his mother to let her know which train to meet. She would be there, with the twins in the back seat. No Anne, no Katherine. No news. No ending. No end.

He did not know if he could bear it.

At least he did not have to wait at baggage claim. He had managed to fit everything into his old army knapsack, the one he carried on the march to Montgomery. The bag had become a sort of talisman, a holy relic. It didn't matter who he was, how he had failed. He would just shoulder the bag and trudge on. He walked with his eyes down, following all the other feet towards ground transportation. There was nothing else to do in this moment. He stepped out into the humid summer afternoon and looked around for a taxi stand.

"Gerald," someone called his name. "Hey, Ger, over here."

There, parked behind all the taxis and limos, Gerald caught sight of the Jesus Christ-ler and Jeremiah, leaning out the window, waving to him. Then Jeremiah got out of the car. Gerald walked towards him, legs shaking, tears welling. He did not care who saw. Jeremiah must not have cared either. He held out his arms, and Gerald walked straight into them.

Chapter Forty-One

"Get up! Get up at once, you lazy git!"

Katherine startled awake to find the Angel of Death standing over her bed.

"Look at you, lying there in your old, sweaty rags, bed full of crumbs. Why 'e wants you I don't know, I'm sure. But you appear to be back in favor. 'e wants you cleaned up an' brought to 'im right away."

Katherine got out of bed and stood in a daze. The light outside her window looked as uncertain as she felt, not clearly day or night. She did not know what to do about her appearance. And although Bess' vague warnings had frightened her, she shrank from the prospect of being back in Mister Tobias' good graces—or clutches. Before she could ask any questions or make a move toward the sink, Madame Diabolique grabbed her arm, nearly wrenching it from the socket (the image of a doll's dismembered limbs tossed in the rubbish flashed through her mind) and dragged her from the room, down the hall to the showers.

"'ere, put this shower cap on. No point in doing any more damage to that perm than you already done, lollin' around in bed all day and all night."

Katherine stood naked under the lukewarm shower and washed herself with a cracked sliver of old soap that had dirt in its creases, shivering under Madame Diabolique's cold scrutiny. Her pubic hair was beginning to grow back in, itchy and scratchy and horrible in how it resembled a man's beard. She cupped her hands over her public bone, hoping the Angel of Death would not notice.

"That's enough now," she decided, turning off the taps.

Then she toweled Katherine off roughly and invasively. Removing the cap, she ran a brush through Katherine's curls, no longer tidy sausages, more like yarn that a kitten has hopelessly tangled. Her reflection in the mirror over the sink did not resemble any self she had ever known, not even Liza Jane. She remembered a doll she had as a child, with hair that could be made longer or shorter. There was a booklet of hairstyles with outfits to match them, but Katherine liked best to make the hair as long and wild as she could and have her doll run around naked. She felt for a moment, she could do just that, slip Madame Angelique's grasp and make a dash into the streets.

As if her captor could read her mind, she took hold of her again and dragged her to a locker where she found a hooded red silk dressing gown.

"Silk! On you," she muttered as she pulled it on first one of Katherine's arms, then the other. "Bloody waste, I say. But orders is orders. Come on, then."

She led Katherine down the hall through the passage that must cross a street—Katherine could hear the screech of brakes and the grinding of gears, she got a whiff of diesel fumes. Once inside the other building, they did not go to the large room with the stage sets or to the club. Still keeping a grip on Katherine's arm, the Angel of Death took out her keys and unlocked a door that opened onto a staircase with cement steps and metal rails, the same as you would find in any public school. Katherine counted five flights and took some satisfaction in Madame Angelique's wheezing and cursing.

"Why can't 'e put in a lift? 'e's rich enough. Rich as Croesus."

At the top, she knocked at a door.

"You may enter!" called a male voice; Katherine thought it was Mister Tobias'.

Madame Diabolique opened the door onto what appeared to be a study or library. There was a large heavy desk, two high-backed easy chairs in front of a fireplace, a crystal decanter of some kind of amber liquid and two glasses half full stood on a table between the chairs. The wallpaper was made of green silk with darker velvet stripes. A heavy velvet curtain framed a window through which light came, but Katherine could see no sky.

"Ah, my dear, here you are." Mister Tobias towered from one of the chairs. "Come give your Uncle Toby a kiss."

She thought that if she had to smell the smell of him or feel that skin, which made her think of a frog's belly, she might throw up. On him. Then there was no telling what he would do to her, but maybe it didn't matter. She saw herself running, running down the stairs, finding some door that opened out, out to whatever world might still exist.

"Oh, and Madame Angelique, you can take the other one back to her quarters till further instruction. Bring me Daisy Mae next."

"Very good, Mister Tobias, sir." To Katherine she hissed, "I'll leave you to your fate then. Go on."

She let go of Katherine and shoved her hard enough that Katherine stumbled. As she righted herself, she got a look through the window. A girl wearing nothing but a black cloak stood in a spotlight, surrounded by darkness, holding in both hands a huge knife pointed downwards. As she raised the knife higher, Katherine got a glimpse of the girl's pale, frightened face. Bess. Good Queen Bess.

Then Mister Tobias was upon her, lifting her into his arms.

"There's my dear little girl. All is forgiven."

(She didn't want his forgiveness; it felt like a slimy film on her skin. Besides she still had no idea what she'd done, right or wrong.)

"Uncle Toby has a special treat for you. Uncle Toby is going to make you a star. Come meet my dear friend and colleague Mr. Ware. I've told him all about you."

He put her down again, stepped aside and there stood a man, also dressed in a three piece suit, though he was dwarfed by Mister Tobias. He had more hair on his face than any man she had ever seen. She hoped she would not be forced to kiss—or do other things—with him. She bet he had hair on his palms.

"My, my, my, you're not wrong, Toby. You're not wrong. What a delicious Little Red Riding Hood she would make. Let's see if the camera agrees."

Katherine glanced out the window again.

Good Queen Bess had vanished.

The empty spotlight and the knife waited for her.

Chapter Forty-Two

"Lucy, Lucy, Lucy," murmured Elsa.

Lucy did not know if her friend was talking in her sleep. Her eyes were closed. She lay in a reclining chair on the porch all bundled up. It was a hot, humid day but dark clouds had rolled in, and Elsa was hopeful of a thunderstorm. Clara did not in the least share Elsa's enthusiasm for dramatic weather, but she was out with Teresa Lomangino, who faithfully helped her with the shopping and the laundry since Elsa had gotten sick.

"Ah, Lucy."

"I am here, *cherie*," Lucy answered softly, placing her hand over her friend's hand.

"No, you are not," said Elsa.

So Elsa was awake, but perhaps not quite coherent. They had just found out that the cancer had metastasized to her lungs.

"*Verdammt!* No cigarettes, no drink. What is the point of all this torturing?" Elsa had summoned what strength she had to throw a small tantrum. She was being kept comfortable and more or less sedate with regular doses of morphine.

"You are not here. Not at all. Not all."

"Pardon me?" said Lucy lightly. "Who is sitting next to you then, a ghost?"

She regretted the use of the word ghost. Elsa was far too close to being one herself.

"Yah, a ghost. Or maybe it is your ghost that is gone. Your holy ghost, searching, always searching for her, the child, *liebes kind....*"

Her voice trailed off, and her head nodded to one side. Lucy hoped she had fallen asleep again. She had tried so hard not to worry Elsa about Katherine. But no doubt Elsa, in her altered state, sensed far more than anyone knew.

"I am fond of the child," Elsa spoke again, eyes still closed. "She can sing. Like an angel, like a Schwarze. Her father loves them, the Negroes, and she wants him to love her. Can't you see that, Gerald, my friend? Just love her a little bit like you love the Negroes."

Lucy had never guessed how clearly this prickly little woman had seen the pain in those she loved. She felt awed and a little ashamed.

The wind kicked up, the leaves turned over, showing their silvery undersides. Elsa let out a long sigh.

"That's better," Elsa murmured. "Not so tight now."

Thunder sounded in the distance, more like a purr than a roar. The first drops of rain spattered against the screen.

"We'd better get you inside, *cherie*."

"Not yet," Elsa said, stubborn as a child. "Don't want to go yet. You go, Lucy. You go."

"What? And leave you here on the porch to get soaked? Clara would have my head."

But maybe they could wait for just a few more moments, the wind was so soft, carrying the scent of moistening earth.

"No, *dummkopf!*" said Elsa rudely, opening her eyes and looking straight at Lucy. "Go find the child. Bring her back. I want her to sing for me."

I can't leave you, Lucy did not say aloud, you might.... She held Elsa's hand tighter and closed her own eyes. The rain fell in fat drops. It was warm on her cheeks and tasted of the sea.

"Of course I will die," Elsa answered Lucy's thought. "All men must die." She hummed the opening notes of the Bach chorale. "But not yet. Not yet. I have one or two tricks in my choir robe...."

As if for emphasis, a bolt of lightning lit the yard immediately followed by thunder so loud it shook the porch.

"Come," said Lucy, "let's get you inside."

By the time Teresa's car pulled into the driveway, Lucy had Elsa safely tucked up inside the house, resting peacefully while the thunder shook the little cottage. Lucy wondered if the vibration of thunderclaps reminded Elsa of the organ, which she'd been too weak to play since chemotherapy began. She went to open the door to help Clara with the groceries and saw Frankie Jr. looming behind Clara, carrying two grocery bags in each arm, his young muscles clearly not straining. Clara carried a basket of neatly folded laundry. As they passed by her into the house, Lucy looked out to see if Teresa was waiting in the car for Frankie—how nice of him to help—and then she realized the car was empty.

It was still hard for her to remember. Frankie, the brave, sullen little boy who had saved her life, was sixteen now. He had his driver's license and a summer job on a road crew. When at work he wore his long hair (which he refused to cut) pinned up under a hard hat. Apparently, a few fist fights had settled the matter of the haircut in Frankie's favor. According to Teresa (who had sighed and rolled her eyes) he had his reputation as a rising rock star to defend.

"Just leave the groceries on the counter, Frankie," whispered Clara, who never remembered that a loud whisper was more penetrating than a soft voice. "Thank you and tell your mother thank you again. I don't know what I would do without her."

"It's nothing," said Frankie gruffly and gallantly, easing the bags onto the counter. "Besides, my Moms always says she doesn't know what she would have done without you the night Joey was born."

Now almost six feet and wearing work boots, Frankie somehow managed to make his way out of the tiny kitchen almost soundlessly, casting a glance at Elsa on the daybed. Lucy waited for him by the door. She didn't see him often these days. She hadn't seen him, she realized, since Katherine had gone missing. They paused and looked at each other. Then, Lucy couldn't help herself, she reached up and hugged him, and he put his arms around her, part holding onto her like a child, part holding her like a grown man giving comfort and protection.

"Can I talk to you for a minute, Miss Way?"

"Since when do you call your fairy godmother Miss Way?" she murmured. "Come. Let's go out on the porch. The storm is passing."

They sat in old wicker chairs, not quite facing each other, listening to the rain drip from the leaves, the air pleasantly cool, but not chilly. Frankie leaned forward a little, his black hair, straighter than his father's, obscuring his face.

"No one's heard anything," he said after a moment, not quite a question.

"No, not yet. Not that I know of. Her father just got back late yesterday. Her mother is still in London."

Lucy noticed that neither of them had said Katherine's name. Why was that?

"It's my fault." Frankie turned to look at Lucy.

His eyes were so dark, she could not see the pupils. He sounded almost angry. But that was Frankie, he covered whatever he felt with anger. He always had.

"Why do you say so?" Lucy asked, knowing better than to contradict him.

He shook his head, and she noticed his hands tensing against his legs. He had long fingers, musician's fingers. She hoped he wouldn't risk them in too many more fights or working with machinery that might damage them.

"There was something wrong with her last spring," he began. "Something happened to her. She tried to tell me about it without exactly telling me. I didn't know what to do. She—"

He stopped himself. He was a gentleman, Lucy knew. However rough he seemed, however indifferent to school or adult authority, he would not say anything about Katherine that might put her in a questionable light. Lucy had some idea of what he might not be saying. Anne had hinted at her concerns about what could have turned into more than youthful indiscretion.

"We both got in trouble at school, let's put it that way," he went on. "I didn't talk to her much after that. I didn't talk to her much before that. I just, I just left her alone. And she was my, is my…."

He shook his head and looked away.

"I know," said Lucy. "Our language doesn't have words for all the things people can be to each other. Especially not," she hesitated, "when they are young men and women."

For they were not children anymore, her dear children.

"She is my blood sister," he said. "Did you know that, Lucy Way? When we were kids, she stood up for me to Rick Foster, because he was trying to blame me for something his son did. So I asked her to be my blood sister. We nicked each other's finger with a knife and mixed our blood together."

"Ah."

Lucy closed her eyes for a moment. She could see them as children so clearly. Katherine with her straight blunt cut hair held back in the barrette she wore before she won her battle to be allowed to have bangs. Frankie, even then his hair longer than the common crew cut. His eyes as fierce and secretly sad as they were now. Did he still kick at loose gravel, she wondered? But now was no time for nostalgia.

"You feel responsible for her," Lucy said.

"I feel like I let her down."

He looked at his hands again.

"You know," Lucy ventured, "we all knew something was wrong with Katherine last spring. I did, too. None of us knew what to do to help her."

He looked up at her again, solemn but not accusing.

"Not even you, Lucy Way."

They sat together in silence. The sun came out and the wet leaves shone. Lucy wondered if she should tell him about her dreams, that the detective took them seriously. Or had at first.

"I'm going to find her," Frankie said abruptly.

Lucy found she could not say the reasonable things she should have. Ever since she had told Frankie and Katherine that they had fairy blood and she did too, she had never been able to be an ordinary grownup. She hadn't wanted to disillusion them. That was her sin, her pride. And apparently her tongue was still tied by it.

"My Uncle Joe, he'll take me, I bet," said Frankie, getting to his feet. "He's on break from his classes right now. If I ask him, I bet he will."

Before Lucy could say another word, he bent, kissed her cheek. "You should come with us, Lucy Way."

And he left the porch, taking care not to slam the screen door behind him.

Chapter Forty-Three

Anne had eaten canned beans, (or tinned as they called them here) heated on the hotplate, then poured over toast. She believed English people did eat things like that. The beans hadn't had much taste, and they had made the dry unbuttered toast unpalatably soggy. Nevertheless, she had cleaned her plate, so that she wouldn't have to figure out how to dispose of the remains. Now another long evening, and the longer night, stretched out before her. There were no landmarks in this awful expanse, only cigarettes smoked, piling up in the ashtray, and the bells of London ringing their changes. Every time she heard the bells, she wondered, was Katherine hearing them, too? Did she remember the nursery rhyme she had loved to recite? *Oranges and lemons, say the bells of St Clement's.* There was some gruesome ending, Anne recalled, that Katherine would chant to the twins to their terror and delight till Anne put a stop to it, fearing nightmares. How did it go? *Here comes a candle to light you to bed/and here comes a chopper to chop off your head.* It had shocked Anne how many rhymes and fairytales invoked carnage and death, even the seemingly innocent Rock-a-Bye-Baby and Ring around the Rosy. And children, her children, with the occasional exception of Janie, seemed to enjoy being frightened.

Because they knew they were safe. But no one was safe. She had not kept them safe.

The bells rang for nine o' clock. *Oh where is my daughter, rang the bells by the water.* They never said anything else. It was still just light outside. She could go walking the streets. She did not care whether or not it was safe. She had asked Detective Smith-Jones where Katherine might be if she had been forced into prostitution. He had assured her that all the red light districts were being searched and all the ticket sellers at bus and rail stations were being questioned. He had spoken to her gently and kindly, as he had the first day, but he had seemed distracted. He hadn't looked at his watch or over his shoulder, but she felt as though he were.

"And of course we are investigating other possibilities."

Anne did not want to consider what those possibilities might be.

"We needn't assume that simply because she is a young girl—"

"Just tell me," she had said.

"I beg your pardon?" he had said.

"Tell me where I should look for her. What are they called? The red light districts?"

"I certainly cannot, in good conscience, advise you to walk, unaccompanied, in such places. I assure you, Mrs. Bradley, we are making thorough inquiries—"

"Please," she had pleaded.

Piccadilly Circus, Soho, King's Cross, the names sounded in her mind. Once I had a daughter, now she is lost, Piccadilly Circus, Soho, King's Cross.

"Most inadvisable," Detective Smith-Jones had stressed.

Anne got up, went to her tiny closet and put on her old beige raincoat. She would be as good as invisible in it, she knew, a middle-aged woman, walking in the drizzle, dull as dishwater, dull as beans over toast. She could walk all night and maybe she would. There was nothing else to do. As she stepped out on the damp pavement, other bells chimed in, the streetlights bright in the gathering night. Her footsteps caught the rhythm of the rhyme.

Here comes a candle to light you to bed
and here comes a chopper to chop off your head.

Chapter Forty-Four

Gerald paused at the outskirts of the park.

It was almost as he had envisioned the interracial memorial camp for his son. Now here was his dream at the end of Lower Main Street, in this rundown waterfront park. White people had their own access to the river, private clubs, state parks. This park wasn't considered safe for a white person. He and Jeremiah had succeeded in getting a grant for the community to restore the park. This evening, co-sponsored by the OEO office, the Baptist Church, and the Lunch Counter, was the kick-off celebration. He looked out at Black and white kids playing together. (Well, the white kids, to be honest, were Janie and Peter and a few other children of white staff.) Gerald's mother had been embraced by all the other grandmothers who had cooked and baked for days to spread out a feast on folding tables borrowed from the church. Now his mother sat at a picnic table with half a dozen Black women. They had cleared away their plates, and she was dealing out hands of gin rummy. (He did hope she wouldn't cheat, her one vice.) Peter was doing his best to keep up with a wild game of basketball, the neighborhood boys alternately taunting and coaching him. Janie was standing on the outskirts of a fast and furious skip rope game. She was chanting with the rest, some rhyme that ended each time with See-la or Sea-la.

It was his dream, *the* dream, in the midst of his own ongoing nightmare.

Gerald had eaten several plates of barbeque and then had gone back to use the office phone to see if he could reach Anne at the bed-sit. She didn't have a phone in her room, but the landlady answered, chiding him mildly for calling at ten o'clock in the evening. With some obligatory grumbling, she went to fetch Anne and returned to inform him that the lady wasn't in. It worried Gerald that Anne would be out alone, late by her standards, in a big city. Should he have stayed, should he have stayed? The question dogged his footsteps as he went back to the park, forcing himself to walk past a liquor store and a bar. They had agreed to keep the community picnic alcohol free. No doubt some of the men were ignoring the rules. He thought he saw a brown paper bag passed from hand to hand among a group of men standing by the water with fishing poles. He didn't know if it was safe to eat the fish from the river, but fishing was a peaceful pastime even with a contraband bottle making the rounds. He wished he could join them. He wished he could know some kind of peace.

You don't deserve to, a voice that was always there reminded him.

I know, he answered silently. *But at least there is this, this moment of…something.*

All right, sit down on the bench. Relax, pretend, for a moment, that everything is all right.

He felt as though he didn't have a choice, as though his body was the weight at the end of a fishing line. He sank down. How could he be so tired, how could sleep drag on him? He hadn't even had so much as a beer, but he felt woozy. He closed his eyes and the world became sound. Men's laughter, the bouncing of the basketball. "You *skunk!*" came his mother's voice, what she always cried when she was bested at cards. He hoped the grandmothers would understand. Bongos from the other side of the park began tapping out a hypnotic beat. The little girls chant got louder, inspired by or competing with the drums.

> *See that man-see la*
> *Blue shirt on-see la*
> *you better leave-see la*
> *that man alone-see la*

Gerald opened his eyes. At least he thought he did. He saw a white girl jump into a skip rope game without missing a beat. For a moment he thought it was Katherine, jumping with the Black girls. Katherine, her startlingly gritty voice, singing nonsense rhymes.

> *the house is black-see la*
> *and the buggy's blue-see la*

Then he saw it, not the park, but the blackness of night, the flickering blue of the television hissing with static. Someone coming to him.

"Are you all right?" she'd asked. "Are the people all right?"

"Come 'ere," he had said, and he had held onto her. He had fallen into her. He had—

Gerald stood up so abruptly, the blood plummeted from his head, the sounds spun around him. He had to go somewhere, he had to do something. He took a few staggering steps.

"Ger?" someone was beside him, steadying him, guiding him back to the bench. "Are you all right?"

He was not all right. He would never be all right.

"Sit for a minute," the man was saying.

And this man, this amazing man, this blazing angel with a golden-brown face, undid the top buttons of his shirt.

"Talk to me, Ger," he said. "Can you breathe, man? Come on now, deep breath."

He didn't want to tell him, if he told him, this man, this man he loved would hate him, but he had to tell him. He had to tell him the truth.

"I remember," he said at last. "I remember what I did."

Chapter Forty-Five

An alarm goes off. He must be discovered. Her pounding heart or the heart of whoever she is in the dream pounds even louder. He has been watching through a heating grate, some transaction, briefcase opening, the crisp swish of money. She—or he—feels so cramped; a large ring cuts into his chest. It's him, she's him, the lad. He is hardly breathing; there is no room to breathe.

The alarm sounds again. There are two men, whose shoes she can see, one shiny patent leather pair and one pair of velvet Prince Albert slippers. Don't they know he is here, overhearing them?

But they go on talking.

"The driver will be at the corner for the merchandise, five in the morning sharp, white unmarked van, alley door. Best to have them blindfolded. Will you be there yourself to oversee the delivery, sir?"

Another blare of the alarm, yet somehow he—or she—catches the reply.

"Tut, tut, my dear Mr. Ware. I think indeed you know by now how very tender are my sensibilities, how I care for these young creatures as dotingly as if I were a mother. No, no, I cannot see my lambs to slaughter." (Is that a sniffle?) "My man Tom is quite capable of, er, seeing them to their final destination."

She knows that voice. Though from the young man's hiding place, she can only see his slippers, she can picture the huge bulk entirely filling a doorway.

The alarm shrills again. Surely they can hear it—

Lucy woke drenched in sweat, unsure of where she was for a moment in dusky light. Then the phone on her desk rang again and she ran to pick it up.

"Lucy?"

Yes, she was Lucy. She looked down at the hand, its age spots visible even in the twilight. How long had she slept?

"It's Julia, Gerald's mother, I am sorry to disturb you."

"Not at all," Lucy said.

But her heart began to pound again as hard as in her dream. What now, what now?"

"Don't worry. Everything's all right."

People always said that before they told you what was wrong. Lucy braced herself.

"It's just that Gerald was taken ill at the community picnic in Riverton. He went to the emergency room. That lovely colored gentlemen went with him. I had to take the twins home. Ezekiel or Isaiah, whatever his name is, just called to say that Gerald is fine; all his tests came back negative. No stroke, no heart attack. But they're keeping him overnight for observation."

It was too much; it was all too much. Poor Gerald. No wonder he had collapsed.

"I am so sorry, Mrs....Julia. Is there anything I can do? Would you like me to come over?"

"No, no thank you, Lucy. The twins have just settled down in front of the television. After that picnic we won't be hungry again for a week. And I'm so relieved that Gerald is all right. But there is something you can do for me," she paused. "I can't reach Anne, although it's awfully late there. I wonder if you would mind setting your alarm and trying her again, first thing in the morning London time. I hate to call my daughter and have her rush into London when she's not in the best of health herself. I would stay up but with the twins' schedule and Gerald not here...."

Poor woman. She had the weight of the world on her shoulders.

"Certainly, Julia. Just give me the number."

She wrote it down.

"And Lucy? Lucy, if you reach her, well, maybe you can talk to her. I hate to say it, I feel just awful, but I think it might be time for her to come home. Good night, dear, and thank you."

Gerald's mother put the phone down before Lucy could say anything more. She got up and switched on the desk lamp so that she would not trip over Lennon and McCartney who had begun to rub around her legs. The old grandfather clock struck seven. It was past time to feed them—and to feed herself. *And don't tell me to keep my strength up,* she remembered Anne saying. But Lucy knew she had to do just that.

It would be past midnight in London. If she set her alarm for two, she'd reach the boarding house at seven. Surely someone would answer then and be able to rouse Anne. Maybe she should just stay up. She'd only just woken from a nap—

Lucy stopped suddenly on her way to the kitchen. Her dream. She'd had a dream. The phone had woken her. She'd been disoriented. What had she dreamed? A ring cutting into her chest. She put her hand where she'd felt it as if she could feel the impression it left. Two men had been talking, but an alarm kept sounding. She'd been afraid of being caught watching.

What had they been saying? That awful unctuous voice, the well-oiled, flowery flow of his speech. What had he been saying? She closed her eyes and willed the words to come back to her.

(Really, it was better this way, he thought as he stood gazing out his window. He was doing them a favor, performing an act of mercy. Look what his mother's life had been after his father despoiled her. All these aristocratic snobs, they took what they wanted, used people as if they were handkerchiefs—or bog roll. They didn't care what happened afterwards. Well, his father had cared about him and all the others, for his own purposes, his own perversions. He'd taken him away from his mother and sent him to school to be brutalized by these bastards until he learned to best them. He'd never seen her again. He heard she'd died of liver failure in a charity hospital, no better than the poorhouse.

Yes, truly, it was better this way.

He watched the repulsive little man make his way out of the alley. The man who had paid him so handsomely to do exactly what he wanted done.

Genius, pure genius—

Then he stiffened. What was that? That shadow. It didn't belong there. It boded no good.

That fool, someone had killed that fool, dumped him in a wheelie bin.

And he would be a fool if he didn't find out who it was.)

Chapter Forty-Six

"I have to tell someone."

Gerald did not look at Jeremiah, but he was aware of him sitting next to the hospital bed where Gerald would be spending the night under observation. The venetian blinds had been closed earlier against the blare of late afternoon light; now it was twilight inside and out. He hadn't had a heart attack or a stroke, thank goodness. That's all anyone needed. Anne, his mother, the twins. Jeremiah. They all had enough on their plates. He supposed his death would have been burdensome, too, but it would have gotten him off the hook.

"You have to rest," Jeremiah countered. "That's what the doctor said. You're suffering from nervous exhaustion. You shouldn't have come back to work so soon."

Jeremiah sounded uncharacteristically terse, almost as if he were angry. With Gerald? Sure, why not with him?

"Maybe," conceded Gerald, though he could not imagine not coming to work; work was his solace, his refuge. It always had been, but he couldn't hide there anymore. "But that's not why I collapsed."

He waited for a prompt from Jeremiah. Why was he so quiet, so deadly quiet? Could it be that he had guessed what Gerald had done and just didn't want to know?

"Be careful, man, be careful."

"What do you mean?" Gerald asked.

"Be careful who you tell your secrets."

"It's a lot to ask, I guess." Gerald felt ashamed, and then, to his dismay, hurt.

"It's not just that," Jeremiah said. Gerald could sense Jeremiah's discomfort, hear him shifting in his chair. "The one you tell, the one who knows things about you, sometimes you regret it, you end up resenting that person."

Jeremiah was saying something without saying it. Had it happened to him? Had someone confided something and then turned on him? Or had it been the other way around? Was that why Jeremiah was so closed-mouth about his own life? It was true, now that Gerald thought about it, Jeremiah seldom talked about himself. He kept the focus on the other person, other people, and no one noticed, because they loved his attention, his kindness or what sure felt like kindness.

"I'm not a saint, Ger," he said, as if he could hear Gerald's thoughts. Jesus, maybe he could. How terrifying.

"I never said you were," Gerald protested.

"You didn't have to."

"What do you mean?" Gerald asked, alarmed.

Was it because of that night? That night he had spent in Jeremiah's arms. Did Jeremiah think Gerald had a…a thing for him? Oh, God what was he saying? What was he thinking?

"It's not uncommon," Jeremiah went on. "When a Black person and a white person manage to become friends, well, the Black person is still guarded, but he doesn't want his friend to know that, so he pretends to be more open than he really is. And that white person, maybe to make up for all the mess of history, slavery, Jim Crow, the white person idealizes the Black person."

"Oh," said Gerald, taken aback, but at least distracted, momentarily, from his other fears. "You mean it's a kind of reverse racism? Oh, geez. Do I do that to you?"

It was probably true, Gerald realized, he was practically in love with….

"I'm sorry, Jer," said Gerald. "Tell me anything you want to tell me, I mean, about the real you. That is, if you want to. I wouldn't blame you if you didn't."

He wouldn't blame Jeremiah, but he would feel, what would he feel? Lost, bereft.

"All right then," said Jeremiah after a long moment. "You asked for it."

He had, and whatever Jeremiah told him, he could take it. Even if Jeremiah had killed someone, was a fugitive from the law, Gerald had done worse.

"Ever wonder why I'm here in the backwater of the movement, organizing picnics and what not? Not that there's anything wrong with that."

"You know I do, Jer. I've asked you that before, someone with your talents. I'm not idealizing you now. Just stating the facts."

"Thanks, Ger."

It was almost night now, the room was dark, except for the light coming in from the hall. The darkness made everything seem strange, like they were kids hiding out, staying up late.

"I'll tell you why," said Jeremiah. "I am a homosexual."

For a moment the words hovered in the darkness, not quite real, as if they could disappear again, and then Gerald felt them land, with a soft thud, on his chest, his gut, all the places he could no longer protect.

"Okay," he said.

Gerald didn't know what to say, but he knew had to say something.

"Okay," he tried again. "But that doesn't let you off being a saint."

There was a moment's silence. Gerald glanced at Jeremiah, worried that he'd said the wrong thing. He must have. Against the light in the hall, he could see Jeremiah shaking his head.

"Gerald Bradley, Mr. Reverend Gerald Bradley, of all the things you could have said, Good God Almighty!"

Suddenly Jeremiah exploded into laughter. Gerald didn't know why, but there was no resisting the force of that laughter, so he laughed, too. They laughed, wildly hysterically until they couldn't anymore. Until maybe they were both crying, but who could tell in the dark.

Then Jeremiah told him, what it was like growing up a preacher's son, knowing he was queer. How he'd had to hide it, even or especially from other people in the movement, what happened when he didn't hide it. He talked for a long time, then, abruptly, he stopped himself.

"You better get some rest now," he said gruffly.

And Gerald found himself praying. Don't let him regret telling me, don't let him resent me.

"Jer," said Gerald as Jeremiah began to get up. "I had sex. With my own daughter. I didn't mean to, I didn't even remember what happened until—"

He stopped. How could Gerald dare to justify himself when it was all his fault. Everything.

"Tell me," Jeremiah said softly, sitting back down again. "It's all right, Gerald, you can tell me."

And Gerald did.

Chapter Forty-Seven

She could have had a baby, a pretty little baby all her own. Katherine lay curled around herself, around cramps so painful it felt as though someone had a fist inside her, squeezing tight. The cramps were so bad they had a color, not red like blood, grey and cold as steel. She could have had a baby, a pretty little baby, all her own. Now she was alone, all alone. And she started to cry.

Girl, you're crazier than the bugs this nasty old bed infested with. Aramantha sounded disgusted with her. *You better be glad you're bleeding all over yourself like a baby with no diapers.*

Nappies, Katherine told her. *They say nappies here.*

It was crazy to talk to Aramantha in her mind, but who cared. She'd stopped crying and her cramps had eased a little.

All I know is, you do not want to have some rapist pervert's child! Bad as having your own daddy's baby.

I never told you, she said to Aramantha in her mind, *I never told you about my father. You can't know about my father. No one knows about my father.*

But everyone knew, everyone could see. That's how she got to this place, because that horrible man could see what she was. Now no one would ever find her here. No one would ever know what had happened to her.

You don't need to tell me, Aramantha spoke again. *You out your mind. I am a voice in your head. So of course I know everything.*

You always did know everything or you acted like you did anyway, Katherine retorted.

If she had to be crazy, she was glad it was Aramantha in her head. She did not want Lucy Way to see her the way she was. Or Frankie.

Well, I know one thing, you better get up and clean yourself up, stuff some toilet paper in your panties till you can get Madam Devilish to bring you some lady things.

Katherine got up and went to the sink where she found her damp wash cloth that smelled of mildew. No matter how long she ran the water, it never got more than lukewarm. There wasn't much point in calling for anyone. She had heard them all getting dressed and ready to go to what she knew now was the Doll House, and she had been left behind, even though she was supposedly back in favor with Mister Tobias. You're going to be a star, he had said. A star of what?

How can you still be so nai-eeve, Katherine, Aramantha drew the word out. *You heard of dirty movies, what your daddy and the firemen watch after the clambake. Porn-o-graph-y, it's called.*

Katherine shrugged. She wasn't naïve anymore. She knew more than Aramantha about all sorts of horrible things Aramantha probably didn't know existed. She bet Aramantha was still a virgin.

That's right, I am, said Aramantha. *And I'm going stay that way. I know you wish you were still a virgin, too, waiting for true love or some mess like that.*

And suddenly a big sob rose up. She wasn't supposed to be here, bleeding, with no baby, no mother. No one to ever love her and touch her the way Frankie had, and he hadn't even wanted to....

Hush, child, said Aramantha, *someone's coming.*

Katherine held her breath and heard footsteps in the hall. Then a key turning in her door.

"Madame Angelique?" she said. "Mister...Uncle Toby?"

The door opened.

"It's only me, luv."

Tom Cat strode into the room, looking even more sinister in the streetlight coming through the window.

"I fo't you might be lonely, f'ot you might want a little company on your last night in this 'ere fine establishment."

He took a step toward her.

"Last night?" she repeated, doubtful, hopeful. "Wot you mean? Where am I going then?"

"That would be tellin', wouldn't it?" He took another step toward her. "You'll find out soon enough, all too soon, I daresay. If you're lucky you won't never know what 'it you."

He took another step forward and started to undo his belt.

I taught you how to fight, lil sis, whispered Aramantha, *I want you to fight now. Fight dirty, understand? You got the curse? Curse him good.*

She had the wet rag in her hand, but he couldn't see it in the dark. She wiped it between her legs and threw it in his face. As he reeled back, she dipped her hands inside herself, then she pulled the light string and flooded the room with the harsh light of the naked bulb.

"Wot the 'ell?" he peeled the rag off his face, "Why you filfy little cunt, you—"

As he started for her, she raised two bloody hands and went straight for him. He backed away and then turned and bolted out the door.

In the back of her lost mind, she heard Aramantha clapping.

She also heard the key turn in the lock.

Chapter Forty-Eight

Piccadilly Circus, Soho, King's Cross.

Anne walked and walked in the bright lights (not red as far as she could tell) that caught the rain in their glare, reflecting off the damp streets, the disorienting blare of traffic on every side. She walked around and around in circles, watching girls who were all leg get into cars with men or lead them into shadowy side streets. Some might not have been any older than Katherine, but they looked older, their faces carapaces of make-up. Some may have been almost as old as Anne was, but they made themselves up to look younger. It took her awhile to be able to pick them out from the flood of tourists and pub crawlers, theatre goers out for a late supper after the show. But after a few times around—and around—the circus or square or wherever she was, she could see the ones leaning or sauntering, the ones with no destination, the ones who were someone else's destination, the ones who were preying or being preyed upon. Schools of fish swimming backward in the current. She did not know why that image came to her mind. Shimmering little minnows swallowed by the huge glittering mouth of night.

And none of them was Katherine.

She had walked so many times around the circus, she began to recognize some of the women she'd passed before. She thought one or two of them might have noticed her.

"'oy, lady in the raincoat," a voice called out.

Anne looked and saw a woman in something resembling a Victorian corset, incongruous with velvet hot pants that were looking somewhat the worse for wear in the damp. Her thin orange hair was frizzed and teased and deep lines around her mouth showed through caked make-up. She carried what looked like a stage prop parasol to protect her from the rain. And she looked tired, as tired and listless as Anne felt.

"You wouldn't 'appen to 'ave a spare fag, would you?"

Anne must have looked as blank as she felt. The woman snapped her fingers and then mimed smoking.

"Oh, sure," said Anne.

Anne got her cigarettes out of her pocketbook and handed one to the woman, who reached into her cleavage for a lighter shaped like, well, a penis and testicles.

"Ta, luv."

The woman exhaled smoke and waved her away, but Anne did not move.

"Would it be all right if I asked you some questions?"

The woman looked at her skeptically and raised an eyebrow.

"Wot for? I'm not doing noffink wrong. I got a right to be on this pavement same as you. 'oo are you then? Some kind of kinky tourist? I say, you're a Yank, ain't you?"

"American, yes," said Anne. "Not a tourist."

Not kinky, Anne added silently, because she could not bring herself to say the word.

"Wot you want then, eh?"

"My daughter," Anne blurted out, "she was visiting relatives in England. She disappeared in London, a week ago."

The woman was quiet for a moment, considering.

"Missing person. Police matter, innit?"

"It was reported to the police," said Anne. Not as soon as it should have been; she ground her teeth just thinking of her brother-in-law waiting till the next day to call. "They don't have any leads. Not one."

The woman took another long drag of the cigarette and looked over her shoulder.

"Well listen, sweet'eart, I'm sorry for your trouble, I'm sure. But you can't keep standing 'ere. You're driving off me trade."

"Oh, sorry."

Anne turned away, tears blinding her, feeling desperate and stupid. How was it just one remark, not even an unkind one, could put her over the edge.

"'old on," said the woman. "It's a bit out of the ordinary, but sometimes I will do a female. We can go somewhere out of the way for a cuppa. I'll 'ave to charge you, though. Got me quota to make, 'aven't I?"

Anne turned back, feeling absurdly grateful, considering she might be about to get fleeced.

"Do you take travelers' checks?"

"Lord love a duck!" the woman stubbed out her cigarette with the pointy tip of her boot. "Now I've 'eard everything. Come on, then, follow me. There's a little place just down this street 'ere where they don't mind a girl coming in out of the rain."

Somewhat to Anne's surprise, the spot was the London version of an all-night Greek diner, brightly lit. She realized that she had assumed all prostitutes were alcoholics or drug addicts. The frizzy-haired woman ordered a cup of tea, which she doctored with milk and lots of sugar, and a lemon cake. Anne ordered Nescafé and stared into its tasteless depths, not knowing how to begin.

"Right then, tell me all about it, luv. I 'aven't got all night. Name's Margaret by the way, Margarita on the street."

Despite the impatient words, the woman's tone was kind.

"My name is Anne," she said.

She looked up at the woman's face. There was something about the mildness of her eyes, the slope of her cheek that reminded Anne of her best friend Rosalie. She fought back a fresh spate of tears and began, telling far more than she had intended to.

"She's a lucky girl, that's all I can say," said Margaret, stubbing out another of Anne's cigarettes.

"Lucky?" Anne repeated, looking at her blankly.

"If I'd 'ad a mum like you come lookin' for me instead of throwin' me out when I was fifteen and me stepdad come after me, I wouldn't be where I am now. And if I'da been a mum like you, maybe them social workers wouldn't have taken me daughter into care."

"Oh," said Anne. "I'm so sorry."

"'sall right," said Margaret, looking away. "Better off, maybe. Wouldn't want 'er to end up...." Margaret trailed off, no doubt remembering where Anne's daughter might be.

She might not have thrown Katherine out of the house, Anne considered, but she had sent her child across an ocean to stay with people she didn't even like. Still, there was no point in wasting time in mutual self-recrimination with a stranger.

"Is there anything you can tell me, Margaret? Anywhere I might look?"

Margaret was quiet for a moment.

"You say the police 'as searched all the corners like mine? All the known 'ouses?"

"They say they have," said Anne. "But there must be so many...."

"Yeah, the old needle in the 'aystack, I'm afraid. Look, I don't know if I should even mention a rumor I've 'eard on the street. If it was me, I'm not sure I'd want to know."

She looked at Anne.

"Tell me," Anne pleaded. "Anything is better than not knowing anything."

"I wouldn't bet on that, but all right then. You be the judge."

"Go on."

And Margaret told her a tale of a legendary place. No one knew exactly where it was. On the outskirts of East London, disguised on the outside as a warehouse or an abandoned factory.

"Top secret, it is," said Margaret. "A secret society, like, 'toffs only. MPs, landed gentry, foreign royalty, that sort. You'd think we'd all be fightin' to work there. But the rumor is they don't want no professionals wot knows the score. They don't pay their girls tuppence. Keep 'em as prisoners, slaves, like. They take raw girls off the street, on the lam, no 'omes, no people, which is 'ow a lot of us get caught in the Life. But wot we 'ear is none of these girls is ever seen again.

There's some other sort of trade going on there...beyond rough. No one knows for sure. I don't like to even fink of it."

Anne felt cold all over. What was she saying? What was the woman saying?

"Look, time's up, luv. I got to get back to work."

"No, wait," Anne reached for her arm, stalling her. She needed to know more, she needed to know the worst. "I haven't even paid you yet."

Margaret shook her off.

"You don't owe me noffink, Anne. And don't worry about wot I said. If the rumors is even true, they wouldn't want a girl with a mum like you, out searchin' every nook and cranny."

Unless that girl was pretending to be someone she wasn't, someone out of a Broadway musical wearing her mother's old skirt and a hat from the rummage sale.

"Margaret!" Anne called after her. "Just tell me. Just tell me which way to start."

The woman paused in the doorway, putting up her flimsy parasol.

"East, luv, though you 'aven't got a chance of finding it. Just keep 'eadin' east."

Anne laid down much too large a note and did not wait for change.

Chapter Forty-Nine

Lucy sat up on the horsehair sofa in the living room. She'd brought her alarm clock downstairs and set it for two in the morning. She tried to distract herself, first with a Dorothy Sayers novel and then when that failed with the psalms in her *Book of Common Prayer*. Nothing worked. At last, still sitting upright, she closed her eyes and willed herself to go back into the dream, to retrieve the lost words that might hold the key to everything. She strained to hear. Then....

She is in an alley—or the lad is—in a fight. That insignia ring is grinding into someone's cheek bone. The assailant grabs both his wrists. She—or he—uses the man's hold against him, fanning out her arms to open him for a groin kick, which sends the man into the wall, his head cracking against the brick, knocking him out. A lucky shot, the lad thinks. Now quick. He crouches over him and reaches into his pockets and finds what he wants, keys to a car. Is it her nurse's training? He—or she—feels for a pulse in the man's neck. He might have killed him. Oh well, to her shock she feels herself shrug, no time to fret about it, not a second to lose.

The scene changes.

There's another fight. Inside a small, drab room. But she can only witness. A girl is struggling to wrench herself from the grip of a tall, muscular man with white-blond hair, a flash of a gold tooth. She catches a glimpse of the girl's tangled blonde curls coming undone before the man overpowers her and puts a black hood over her head. She reels, disoriented, and he seizes her arms. Twisting her arms behind her with one huge, deft hand, with the other he reaches into his pocket for hand cuffs. Then he throws the girl face down on the floor, pins her with his knee and cuffs her.

Before she can find out what happens, she's in another room. The huge man stands in front of a window, blocking grey rain-washed dawn light. He is wearing Prince Albert slippers.

Prince Albert slippers! She remembers. She remembers.

"The driver will be at the corner for the merchandise, five in the morning sharp, white unmarked van, alley door. Best to 'ave 'em blindfolded."

Now, as if she is the light itself, or a pigeon roosting high above the street, she sees from above, a white van, and six figures, cuffed and hooded, being forced into it by the blond-haired man and a stout woman in a white dressing gown who is making liberal use of a rolling pin. The last girl has streaks of blood on her bare legs. She struggles to the end.

Katherine. Lucy's heart falls off the ledge, out of the sky. Katherine.

She hears a wail. Thank God! The police must be coming.

The wailing goes on and on....

Lucy woke up wailing. McCartney and Lennon leapt from the couch, their fur on end. She had to do something quickly. All the pieces of all the dreams came together. *No, no, I cannot see my lambs to slaughter,* the huge man had said, the man in the Prince Albert slippers. Something terrible, something evil was about to happen. She had to stop it.

She got up and hurried to the hall phone where she kept the number Detective Smith-Jones' direct line. What time was it? Just after midnight here, five in the morning in London. She prayed to God that this number was connected to his home phone. The overseas operator put through the call.

The phone rang. And rang. And rang.

She couldn't wait. She got the operator back on the line and managed to get through to the Metropolitan Police.

"This is Lucy Way. Detective Smith-Jones gave me his direct number, but I am unable to reach him. I need to report a crime right away."

She spoke as calmly and clearly as she could, describing everything she could remember. But of course she could give no location. And she had failed—how could she have failed—to get the license number of the van.

"I am very sorry, Miss Way. If you witnessed the crime, as you say, where were you at the time? Where are you now?"

"I am," she fought through a sob. "I am in White Hart, New York."

Another pause.

"New York? The United States of America?"

"That's right."

"Pardon me, Miss Way, I don't understand. You said you witnessed a crime in London?"

"In a dream," she barely managed to speak. "I saw it in a clairvoyant dream. Ask Detective Smith-Jones. He takes the dreams seriously. He told me to call night or day. He gave me his direct line."

There was an odd pause.

"Detective Smith-Jones is on sick leave, Miss Way."

She started to shake so badly she could hardly hold the phone. She forced herself to sit down.

"I am sorry to hear that," she managed to say. "When do you expect him back?"

"I'm afraid I can't say. He's in hospital. I'm sorry. Miss Way. I am not at liberty to say more at this time."

"I understand," said Lucy, although she didn't. Not really. "Who has been assigned to his cases in his absence?"

"I am afraid I don't have that information available at the moment, Miss Way. Try ringing back after nine and ask to speak to Chief Inspector Hollingsworth."

"But what are you going to do? About the crime. If you wait, it will be too late."

"I will send a description of the van to all our officers on the street. And now, may I suggest you get some rest, Miss Way."

"You may not," she said as the receiver went dead.

She called the operator again and put through a call to Anne's boarding house.

"Calling hours are between nine in the morning and eight o'clock at night," the irate landlady snapped.

"But it's an emergency," pleaded Lucy. "I must speak with Anne Bradley at once."

The landlady grudgingly agreed to fetch her. After an excruciating wait, she came on the line again.

"It appears the lady is not at home. I suggest you call back at a decent hour."

"Please. Can you tell her to call—"

The landlady slammed down the receiver.

Lucy found herself doubled over on the floor sobbing. She must, she *must* get hold of herself. Before she knew what she was doing, she dialed the number of the rectory.

In three rings a sleepy voice answered, "Ralph James here."

Lucy opened her mouth, formed words but as in a nightmare, they did not come out.

"Hello, who's there?" he demanded.

"It's Lucy," she finally managed. "Lucy Way."

"Lucy!" He sounded alarmed. "Are you all right? Do you need an ambulance?"

She must calm down. She must let him know she was all right. But she was not all right.

"I'm not ill," she said. "It's Katherine. I dreamed…Katherine. I can't reach anybody. No one who will listen. Katherine—"

"Hang on, Lucy. I'll be right there. Sit tight and pray."

"Oh, but you mustn't trouble your—" He hung up before she could finish.

Still on the floor, she prayed, silently at first, and then out loud.

"Defend, O Lord, this thy child. Defend, O Lord, this thy child from all the perils of this night, from all the perils of this day. Defend, O Lord, this thy child…."

(Sorrow is a beautiful, elegant garment, a dignified covering for naked relief.

How he will miss what she might have been. But was not.

Yes, it's better this way, yes. It's all for the best.

Now only one loose end remained to be tied up....)

Chapter Fifty

All she could hear was the roar of the van. She thought there were other people near her, but the hood made her feel trapped and alone, mute. That's how birds were silenced, she remembered. You put a hood over their head or covered their cage, and they thought it was night and went to sleep. Well, she was not going to go to sleep. And she was not going to be quiet.

She was going to sing. The first thing that came into her head.

"*Yea, though I pass through shadowed vales, yet will I fear no ill,*" she sang the descant she learned as a child in Miss Ebersbach's choir, softly at first, then louder and louder, "*for thou art with me and thy rod and staff me comfort still, thy rod and staff me comfort still.*"

Kinky, the thought stopped her. How ruined she was, forever, to think that the Twenty-third Psalm had anything to do with sex.

"Warbler?" someone spoke. "Is that you?"

"Bess?" Katherine answered. "Good Queen Bess?"

"I'm 'ere."

"Warbler?" someone else said. "You mean the little girl in knickers?"

"I prefer Warbler."

"'oo else is here? Is that you? Fifi the French Maid?"

"Oui! 'oo else?"

"Daisy Mae," called a voice. "Barnyard."

"Devidasi. Fake temple of Khajurho."

"Bernadette. Feckin' Satan-worshipping nun."

Then they fell silent again, each in her own darkness.

Katherine could picture them all. They were all from her aisle. Maybe they were the ones who had huddled outside her door. Maybe they'd all been marked for whatever was happening, because of her.

"Warbler, sing something more," said Bess. "Sing something we all know."

Katherine thought of the day they crowded around her door and sang with her, raucously, almost happily.

We're the only friends you got in this 'ere 'ell 'ole. It was the least she could do.

"*Stop in the name of love!*" Katherine belted out.

"*Before you break my heart,*" they all joined in.

"*Think it o-o-ver.*"

As she sang, Katherine heard another voice join them. From the driver's seat.

"*Haven't I been good to you, haven't I been sweet to you?*"

It was a woman's voice, low, rich, but definitely, a woman's.

Chapter Fifty-One

She had walked all night, straight into the sunrise, so at least she had been going the right direction. She had passed through dreary neighborhoods, clothesline jungles, trash uncollected, now she was in a wasteland of warehouses, near what she supposed was some part of the Thames. She had no idea where she was, no idea what to do beyond get a cup of coffee. But there were no shops around here, no taxis, nothing but pigeons cooing on the ledges of derelict buildings. Should she just randomly pound on doors? If Katherine was being kept prisoner in such a place, who would open the door? Could she offer ransom when none had ever been asked?

Anne stood in the middle of the street that was empty except for loose plastic trash the breeze picked up and dropped now and then. She was so tired and lost and defeated, she thought she might just lie down in the street and go to sleep, maybe be run over and never wake up. Then she heard the roar of an engine. A white van going much too fast rounded the corner. She jumped out of the way, but the van passed so close to her she could heard a sound, an extraordinary sound.

Girls singing. Not a radio. Girls, live girls singing. Loudly.

License. A voice spoke in her head. Get the license plate number. And before the van careened out of sight, she had it by heart.

part three

Liberation

(It must have been the shadow he had seen flickering against the wall twice before. He should have hunted it down then.

He should have known there was a breach. He had known.

That stupid man, who had been found dead. Someone had killed him.

The shadow. It must have been the shadow.

And something else he should have known, but he had been blinded by his own tenderness toward the little thing....

Who was not who she had pretended to be.

He had known, all along he had known.

Now she had disappeared. It must have been the shadow who had stolen her, stolen them all.

And that woman in the ugly raincoat, he'd lay odds that woman was searching. He had spotted her in the street below that very morning. He knew she didn't belong there. He'd had his man follow her. All the way to New Scotland Yard. She had seen the van. She must have seen the van. Now the police were searching, too.

But whatever the police discovered, he would be the first to know. H. would see to that....

He would find them before anyone else did, his precious, stolen lambs. He would hunt the shadow down.)

Chapter Fifty-Two

"You are not prisoners anymore," said the woman with the low voice.

After what seemed like an endless ride, hooded, so that they could not see where they were going, and cuffed, so that they could not sit back and get comfortable, the vehicle they'd been loaded into came to a stop. The driver had gotten out, opened the back door and climbed in.

"So sorry I couldn't stop sooner," she went on.

She had a genteel voice, not the least bit cockney. Eliza Doolittle at the ball.

"I thought it best to get straight away."

Katherine could hear the cuffs being unlocked, the rustle of hoods being lifted off. So far none of her friends had said a word.

When it came to her turn, Katherine sat still and held her breath. Her hands released, she lifted the hood herself, her hands brushing against the woman's, who was...not a woman?

She found herself looking into a face that could have been a young man's—or a boy's, short gold, brown hair (the color of a lion's mane) brushed back from a lean face. Wait! She'd seen him before! Standing in the back of the gentleman's club, clapping his hands after she sang "Just you wait 'enry 'iggins."

"It's all right," the low, beautiful voice reassured her.

She was a girl, Katherine decided, a few years older than herself. Or maybe a dryad, tall and slender, her figure disguised by a loose workman's jumpsuit.

"You are no longer prisoners."

They all stared at her mutely, like cattle, Katherine thought, scared but belligerent.

"Wot are we then?" said Bess at last, with a lift of her chin, "and 'oo the 'ell are you, pardon my French."

"Excellent questions," the girl said, "and you shall have answers. If you'll bear with me a little longer, it will be the better part of valor to ditch this van. I've a well-victualed picnic basket nearby, and thermoses of coffee and tea that I hope are still warm against all odds. Now then, shall we?"

She led the way out of the van. With her back turned to them, Katherine and the others exchanged wordless glances that translated, should we follow her? jump her? make a run for it?

"I don't know about you, but I'm 'ungry," Daisy Mae made her decision.

"Not to mention," added Fifi. "We 'aven't a clue where we are."

And so they followed the boyish girl, ducking through a gap in a chain link fence, wading through a vacant lot full of weeds and broken bottles, through a thicket, to a small clearing where the promised picnic basket sat on a blanket just large enough to accommodate them all. They sat down at the edges of it warily. The girl who claimed they were no longer prisoners opened the basket and served them thick cheese and chutney sandwiches on brown bread, all the while asking, coffee or tea, sugar, milk? As if she were a waitress or an airline stewardess.

Katherine found she was ravenous, and so, apparently, was everyone else. For a time there was no sound but chewing and swallowing and birds singing in the thickets. A breeze rose and stirred the leaves in the brush. The sound of traffic seemed far away. Everything seemed far away. The girl, whoever she was, had brought them here. Away. The grey sky, the cool breeze, the greenery, the taste of delicious food, all of it came from this girl. Katherine wished they could go on sitting here for a long time till everything that happened before disappeared as if it had never been.

"Let me ask all of you a question."

The girl did not so much break the silence as stir it, causing little swirls and ripples. She was sitting cross-legged and looked comfortable, as if she was used to sitting on the bare ground. Yet, Katherine noticed, when she picked up her tea cup, her hand shook.

"Do you know where you were to be taken in that van?"

No one answered for a moment. Katherine wondered if they were all as reluctant to remember as she was.

"Begging your pardon, miss," said Fifi with a mix of deference and sarcasm. "Since you was drivin' 'ow 'bout you tell us."

"Quite right," the girl said. "I forgot. You're missing a vital piece of information. I wasn't supposed to be driving. I intercepted the van."

"You wot?" asked Daisy Mae.

"She nicked it," explained Bernadette.

"That's right, I stole it."

Everyone looked at the woman with new interest. Spines straightened, heads turned.

"But why?" ventured Bess.

"Because I knew what they meant to do with you. I wanted to stop it."

There was a wary silence. Katherine sensed they didn't dare trust the girl yet, even though they wanted to.

"Wot?" whispered Daisy Mae. "Wot was they going to do?"

"But we know," said Bess, before the girl could answer. "Don't we? Didn't you all 'ave to stand naked in front of the camera. 'e were going to put us in porno movies, 'e was."

There was nodding and murmuring.

"But so what?" Bernadette said; with her Irish accent, sounding every h. "What's so bad about dirty pictures compared to what we already done? Why'd they have to blindfold us and cuff us. I'd've jumped at a chance to get out of that place."

"Except," put in Bess, "we all know that anybody 'as ever disappeared wasn't never seen again. Remember all those nasty 'ints the Angel of Death kept dropping whenever she opened 'er ugly pie 'ole."

The girl said nothing for a moment. She stared at the ground and tore at bits of grass. At last she looked up, her eyes traveling from one face to another.

"Have any of you ever heard of snuff films?"

Katherine had not. Maybe none of them had. But somehow, suddenly, they all understood.

"You mean where they—"

"Kill people, girls usually. Kill them, live on camera."

Kill them live. It didn't make sense. But Katherine's stomach, so happy a few minutes ago, understood before the rest of her did. She felt sick.

"Wait just a minute," challenged Fifi, "'ow do we know any of this is true? And if it is, 'ow do you come to know where they was taking us?"

"Let's just say I had reasons for wanting to find out what was going on in that place. I've been investigating the operation for some time."

Now Katherine understood at least one piece of the puzzle.

"You infiltrated it!" Katherine spoke up.

"She wot?" said Daisy Mae.

"She disguised herself," Katherine went on, "as a man. I recognize her."

The girl nodded.

"Oh! So you're a copper then." Bernadette accused. "Undercover. You're not as young as you look, neither, I bet. What do yer want with us?"

"Don't you see?" Katherine was excited. "We know what was going on. We can testify! Testify against Mister Tobias."

No one seemed pleased or convinced. Katherine remembered none of them had any reason to trust police. Bess had implied the police knew what was going on and didn't want it found out.

"I'm afraid I'm not with the police," said their rescuer. "Far from it."

"'oo are you then?" said Fifi. "You said you'd answer."

"Call me Robin."

A perfect name for a girl who looked like a boy. A girl who had stolen a van, stolen them away.

"Like Robin Hood," Katherine said. "I mean 'ood."

Bess rolled her eyes at Katherine.

"Robin Hoodlum, more like," muttered Bernadette.

"Hood, hoodlum. Either one will do," said Robin. "And believe it or not, I do live in the greenwood. It's a rough life in the open air, but anyone who'd like is welcome to come with me."

The wind lifted again. The tension in Katherine's stomach eased. It felt like there was suddenly more room inside.

"And anyone 'oo would not?" demanded Fifi.

"Then I give you fare for the train to London and enough left over for a few nights' food and lodging." Robin reached into a deep pocket. "There's a railway station not ten minutes' walk from here."

Everyone stared at Robin; Daisy Mae's mouth hung open.

"What's the catch then?" Fifi spoke for them all.

"No catch," said Robin.

"Why do you do this for us, Miss Robin?" Devi spoke for the first time. "Why you steal van, take risk of being caught. Give money. Why? No one does anything for girl like us, unless they want something."

Robin looked at each of them and beyond them.

"Did any of you ever know a girl named Pippa? When you were in that place?"

All of them shook their heads.

"But none us goes by our real names," put in Bess. "Wot did she look like?"

"She…" Robin began, and looked down again, her fingers digging into the dirt. "Perhaps I'll tell you another time. All you need to know right now is…I'm doing it for her. In memory of her."

There was another silence as they guessed what Robin was not saying.

"I hate to rush your decision," said Robin, beginning to gather up the empty cups, "but very likely someone will be trying to trace that van. We don't have the luxury of time."

"Right then," Fifi spoke gruffly, getting to her feet. "Thanks very much. I for one will accept your offer of train fare. 'oo's coming with me?"

Everyone stirred, some started to get up, others just looked dazed, even panicked.

"Wot I want to know is does anyone 'ere 'ave a place to go? Does anyone 'ave an 'ome?" wondered Bess.

Katherine stared down and like Robin began to pull at bits of faded grass. What should she say to Bess? Katherine had a home. She'd had a home. But it was far away. Long ago.

"Robin 'ood 'ere says she'll give us enough for a few nights lodging," pointed out Fifi. "I reckon after that I can make it on me own."

She took the money Robin handed her, and as she made to pocket it, Fifi noticed that she was wearing nothing but a tattered robe.

"Bloody 'ell."

Then they all looked at each other, all of them were in nightshirts or bathrobes. Some had slippers; some were barefoot. Katherine looked down at her blood-smeared legs. She tried to imagine herself going back to London in her rags and bare feet. Looking for her uncle's office, making a collect call home. Things her friends could not do. Really, she wasn't sure she could either. Wasn't she one of them now?

No you are not, Katherine Bradley, Aramantha tried to argue, but Katherine could barely hear her. There was too much happening.

"We look like a bunch of escaped loonies!" Bernadette concurred.

"Oh dear! I'm terribly sorry," Robin was visibly flustered. "I should have thought of that. Listen, darlings...."

Darlings?

"I've got at least one change of clothes in the lorry and some blankets, if you care to—"

"The lorry?" interrupted Bernadette. "Wait. You stole a lorry, too?"

"Actually, the lorry is borrowed, more or less. It's concealed in the next field. I took the train to London last night. It's a farm vehicle, no plates. We'll be taking back roads, not the most comfortable conveyance. I quite understand if you'd prefer not to trust me. Anyone who wants the train station, just retrace your steps to the vacant lot and turn right at the street. I do apologize for not being more thoroughly prepared—"

Katherine wanted to reassure her, defend her against all reproach.

"Do you fink," Daisy Mae gulped and her eyes bugged out, "do you fink they'll be on the lookout for us. Mister Tobias and them?"

It was too easy to picture it. Tom Cat waiting around every corner.

"London's a big place," argued Fifi, but she sounded less sure of herself.

"They wants us dead," said Bernadette bluntly. "They're not going to risk us going to the police, not that the police would believe us. Lock us up for vagrancy more like."

Just then, as if the mere mention of the police had the power to summon them, they heard the sound of a siren, faint and distant but under the circumstances, discomfiting. Robin reminded Katherine of a deer, perfectly still but poised for instant flight.

"I'm afraid the moment of decision has come, my dears." She handed them each a packet of bills. "This money is yours, whether you come with me or take the train. Before you decide, there's something else you should know."

"A lot else, if we 'ad the bleedin' time," said Bess. "You don't add up, you don't. Talking like a 'toff, dressed like a grease monkey."

"I'm a fugitive."

"A wot?" asked Daisy Mae.

"An outlaw," Robin said. "Just like my namesake, who also happened to be a toff. I'm not going to say more than that. I don't want to risk your becoming accessories after the fact."

Daisy opened her mouth, but before she could say "wot," Robin went on.

"I don't want any of you accused of aiding and abetting me. If you do come with me, and if anyone ever should ever find us, you are to say I kidnapped you, which is more or less true."

"No argument there," said Bernadette.

The sound of the siren was growing closer.

"I've got to hoof it now, girls. Best of luck to you all, whichever way you choose."

Robin gave them each a quick smile, picked up the basket and blanket and took off at run. Katherine looked at her friends and looked at Robin, the dryad, the outlaw, the open air they'd been breathing.

"I don't know about you," she said. "I'm going with her."

Barefoot, she began to run as fast as she could. Everyone followed.

"Oh, bloody 'ell."

Even Fifi.

Chapter Fifty-Three

The silence of the cross, the words kept sounding in Lucy's mind, as the plane roared over the Atlantic through the night toward the dawn. Most people were sleeping now, or trying to. Frankie's head leaned against the window, as if, even dreaming, he did not want to miss any of his first flight, not the dark ocean, or the drift clouds, lit for a time by the setting quarter moon, or the stars shining in the clear sky above all the turbulence below. On the other side of her, Joe Petrone slept neatly, hands folded in his lap, head bowed, as if he were praying. Maybe he was, but now and then his head righted itself, to stop him tilting one way or another. Uncle and nephew had both offered her a choice of the aisle or window, but she was the smallest, the one who had traveled most often, so she insisted on the middle and had even managed to doze a bit after a glass of wine with dinner. (Two glasses would have meant too many trips to the tiny plane toilet, with Joe having to get up for her each time.)

She closed her eyes again, hoping to sleep a little more, tonight being her second almost sleepless night. She did not want to be useless when she arrived, though what use she could be was not clear to her now. What use could any of them be, except to keep Anne company? Joe, as someone who had worked in law enforcement, might be able to find out more about the investigation or what was holding it up. And Frankie, well, Frankie was not going to be allowed to wander unsupervised to look for Katherine no matter how much he might want to.

Everything had seemed clearer to her last night when she sat with Father James in her living room. He had made a fire in the fireplace, even though it was the end of July, and had wrapped her in blankets. He had poured her brandy he had brought himself.

"Like a Saint Bernard," she had murmured.

"Yes, exactly like a Saint Bernard," he agreed. "You are in shock. Now drink up and get warm so that I don't have to take you to the emergency room."

She did as she was told. Then, almost as if she was still in a dream state, she described everything she had seen in her last dream. And then the dream she'd had at dusk, before the phone woke her, returned in more detail.

"Lambs to the slaughter," she repeated. "The awful man I've seen in dreams before, he said he did not want to see his lambs to the slaughter. Not that he was going to stop it. He just didn't want to see. Where they were going, what was going to happen to them. But he sold them, he sold them to be...."

She could not bring herself to say it. But Father James knew. He came and sat next to her on the couch and held both her hands in both of his. Neither of them spoke. That's when she heard the words in her mind, the silence of the cross. Where they came from she did not know. Was the cross really silent? Maybe when the darkness fell and the birds ceased their song and people were too frightened even to cry out. She thought of the silence of hospital wards at night and of people whose screams had ceased with death. As she sat with Father James, she went into that silence, that terrible silence, its heart. Her heart.

Then she heard the first birds singing in the grey light.

"I have to go to England," she said to Father James. "I have to look for her."

"Yes," he said simply.

"But Elsa...if I leave her...."

She didn't want to finish that sentence either. She didn't need to.

"Elsa would be the first one to tell you to go," said Father James.

Lucy almost smiled.

"She was the first one."

"Of course you must go," Clara had said when Lucy went to say goodbye a couple of hours later. "Elsa will never forgive me if you don't."

Which didn't quite make sense, but Lucy knew what Clara meant. Clara did not want Lucy to stay because she thought Clara couldn't cope.

"Teresa and Frank Lomangino will make sure we're all right," Clara added.

Lucy knew it was true. Teresa and little Joey were also going to come to Lucy's house to care for the cats and the garden. Sally James, who as a school teacher had the summer off, was going to spell Teresa. And Rosalie Brown had taken on cooking for Elsa and Clara. Everyone wanted to help. Desperately.

Still it was hard for Lucy to say goodbye to Elsa. She had that stretched-thin, translucent look that Lucy knew so well, in the midst of illness something shining through, so that you could almost see the child Elsa must once have been.

"I am tougher than you think, Lucy," Elsa insisted. "So is little Katherine. I am praying, praying you will be so surprised, so surprised you won't know who hit you."

Lucy smiled at Elsa's characteristic misuse of American idiom.

"I hope no one will hit me," Lucy teased.

"You know perfectly well what I mean, Lucy," Elsa scolded. "You will see that I am right."

Lucy had already been surprised that very day when Joe Petrone, whom she'd hired to drive her to the airport, announced that he and Frankie were going with her.

"I'm sorry to butt in when nobody asked me to," he apologized. "But I think you and Mrs. Bradley could use some backup. Sounds to me like something fishy is going on with that investigation. As for Frankie, he won't take no. What can I say? He insisted on paying for our tickets out of his summer wages."

"Does Anne know you're coming?"

"I don't know," he said. "I talked to Mr. Bradley, of course. Poor guy. He's beside himself, but the doctors say he shouldn't travel."

Lucy had talked to Anne early in the morning before she went to see Elsa. Both of them had been awed that her dream and Anne's sighting of a white van matched. And Anne, dear sensible, quick-thinking Anne, had gotten the plate number.

"And they were singing, Lucy," Anne kept saying. "Singing at the top of their lungs."

Lucy leaned back her seat and closed her eyes. She saw a pattern of leaves against a brightening sky and over the roar of the plane, beyond the silence of the cross, she heard a chorus of birds singing with the mad joy they reserved especially for dawn.

Chapter Fifty-Four

She must be in Narnia!

That was Katherine's first thought—or first sense—when she woke at dawn to the sound of birds singing in a canopy of trees, more birds than she had ever heard in her life, so close, practically singing into her ears. She was lying on something fragrant but a little scratchy. A heather bed, she thought, covered with a light, warm blanket. She was comfortable and strangely happy. If this was a dream, she didn't want to wake up. But the birds were so loud, Narnian birds....

She opened her eyes and sat up. Everywhere she looked she saw boughs, dense with summer leaves, going on for as far as she could see. She was in the trees. She was...in a treehouse! She swung her legs over what seemed to be her own little raised bunk. There was a wooden roof overhead; the wooden floor was built around a massive trunk and several branches almost as thick. A railing, also made of wood, surrounded the platform but otherwise it was open. Katherine tiptoed over to it and looked down, a long dizzying way down. But of course there was a ladder. She and the others, all asleep still in bunks like hers, had climbed it half asleep late last night.

She was not a prisoner anymore. She had made the right choice.

"Crikey!" Bess came to stand beside Katherine at the railing. "Now we're for it. Living in the bleedin' woods. That's a long way down to go to the loo."

Some of her friends had probably never been out of the city, Katherine realized. She had grown up next to a wood where she had always wanted to live.

"Or swing our arses over the side, I don't think," put in Bernadette.

Daisy Mae sat up and began to moan.

"I'm scared of 'eights. 'ow'd I get up 'ere. I'll never get down, I tell you."

"Don't worry Daisy," said Fifi, "We'll bring you a piss pot."

"I stay with you, Daisy," Devi sat down next to her. "I am scared, too. I am no monkey to live in tree."

"All right up there?" Robin called.

"Yes!" Katherine answered for all of them.

It was true, whether they knew it yet or not. They were in Narnia with Robin Hood.

"Come down when you're ready," Robin encouraged. "Eggs for breakfast."

"Fresh stolen?" called Bernadette.

"I shan't answer that."

"Shan't," repeated Bess. "I do love to 'ear 'er talk. Come on then, last one down is a rotten nicked egg."

Chapter Fifty-Five

Gerald woke with his heart pounding. He did not need to look at his watch to know it was probably three in the morning, which is to say the dead of night. He'd woken every couple of hours, as if he were a newborn needing to be fed. But even though his mother was asleep in another wing of the house, there was no one to get up with him, and there was no comfort for his torment. No bottle of milk or alcohol that could soothe him.

It had been easier last night in the hospital, a time out of time, in a place that was intentionally sterile, impersonal. Jeremiah had stayed with him well past the end of visiting hours till a nurse, who came to check his vitals, told Jeremiah he had to go. He had told Jeremiah everything he could remember about that night, what he was afraid had happened. No, he knew it had happened. His body remembered and would never again let him forget.

Why hadn't his body killed him? Why couldn't he die of shame?

Jeremiah had said nothing at first. The silence was awful. That's what hell was, Gerald thought, not fire or brimstone, nothing so fevered or frantic. Just silence, that held everything and nothing, a silence as awful and limitless and cold as space, silence loud with his own self-loathing.

He had to fill it, so he kept talking. He accused himself of everything. He was the one who had sent Katherine away to England, who had wanted her out of his sight, never mind if it was Lucy's Way's suggestion. He seized on it; he'd made it happen. He couldn't wait for her to be gone. And now she was gone, maybe forever. She had probably run away, because of him. And what if she was dead? If she was alive, wouldn't the police have found her? If she was dead...he had killed her.

That's when Jeremiah had finally spoken up.

"It's harder to find someone who's alive," he said. "A live person can keep running and hiding. A dead person stays dead."

Gerald had been speechless for a time, but Jeremiah did not elaborate. He just stayed right there in the chair next to the bed, not looking at Gerald but not looking away, not leaving.

"You think she's still alive?" Gerald asked after a moment.

"I do," said Jeremiah. "I don't know why, but I do. And Gerald," he hesitated.

(Would he and Jeremiah ever call each other Jer and Ger again? How could they be friends now?)

"I believe you are going to have to face her, and I think part of you would rather die. This might sound harsh, but I got to be real with you. I think part of you would rather she was dead."

Gerald could hardly breathe. His heart wanted to jump out of his chest. But Jeremiah's words, his presence, held Gerald there, fixed... nailed.

"I only know one thing for sure. You're going to have to face yourself first. You got nowhere else to go." He paused again. "Believe me, I know. I've been there."

Gerald's heart had beaten so hard, it seemed to flare like a light behind his eyes. It was happening again now, but now he didn't have to stay in bed and sweat it out. Now he was alone, which was a different kind of agony. Who would want to be alone with someone so despicable?

"Don't trip too much," Jeremiah had cautioned him that morning as he drove him home. "Hating yourself can be a cop out. You got things to do. Rest up, so you can come back to work, and be there for your kids, all of them."

He hadn't been able to speak when he got out of the car, but he reached out and hugged Jeremiah's arm, and Jeremiah had let him, he hadn't pulled away. Gerald had to pull himself away to stop from turning to Jeremiah and burying his head in his chest.

He didn't deserve Jeremiah's love.

Or Anne's, which he might have already lost and would certainly lose when she knew the truth.

Face yourself first, Gerald.

He didn't know how. He couldn't even stand to look in the mirror to shave. He was glad he had missed Anne's call. He had tried to call her, to let her know Joe Petrone was coming with Lucy, but he hadn't gotten through. He hoped she wouldn't mind.

(*Of course she won't mind*, a voice in his head insinuated.)

No, it was good that Anne wasn't coming back yet. Anne had a lead, his mother said. Maybe Joe Petrone could help. He could at least be decent enough to hope so. (Was there a decent bone in his body?) For a moment, Gerald had let himself believe that it would be all right, everything would be all right.

Maybe it would, dear Lord and Savior Jesus Christ, maybe it would be all right, for Anne, for Katherine.

But not for him. Never for him.

He couldn't stand lying in bed awake, but turning the light on to read seemed like cheating. He wasn't hungry, and he had poured out all the alcohol in the house. An impulsive penance.

Penance. What penance would ever be enough? He deserved punishment. He had committed a crime.

He sat up in bed and swung his legs to the floor. There was nowhere to go. (*You could turn yourself in*, a voice whispered, *you could turn yourself in to the police.*) He would just get up and go downstairs. Maybe he'd go for a walk in the dark. He didn't know what to do, he didn't think he would ever know what to do.

As he opened the bedroom door and stepped out into the hall, he heard a sound. Someone else was awake. Someone was crying and trying not to make a sound. He could hear the short gasps of breath and the sob that couldn't quite be held back. He stood still and listened. This crying had been going on a long time, and it wasn't about to stop.

Janie.

Peter is your son. And Janie is your daughter. You have another chance, Gerald. You have another chance.

Anne wouldn't have said that if she knew what he had done.

Janie went on weeping. Gerald thought it was the saddest sound he had ever heard. This child did not expect comfort. She was alone. They shouldn't have put Peter in the downstairs room, so far away. They should have given the twins the separate wing with two rooms, Katherine's and a guest room where his mother slept. But they had thought Katherine needed privacy, and it was time for Peter to be his own boy. They thought Janie, who seemed like the youngest even though she was Peter's twin, would be all right in the room next to theirs.

Janie's sobs went on and on. He should wake his mother or Peter. They would know what to do to comfort her.

"Mommy, Mommy, Mommy," he heard her whisper, like an incantation.

Janie's mommy was an ocean away.

Her father was right here. He realized he barely knew this child, this second daughter, born after the obliterating grief of Hal's death. A sweet child, he thought, so much less complex and challenging than Katherine. She had a mother, a sister, a twin brother. She hadn't needed him.

"Daddy?" Her voice changed. She must sense that he was there.

How could he go near her? How could he, after what he had done to Katherine...to Hal.

"Daddy?" she said again.

How could he not?

"It's all right, Janie," he answered. "I'm here."

And he opened the door to her room and went in.

Chapter Fifty-Six

Anne stood in the lobby outside baggage claim, waiting for Lucy, surrounded by eager or anxious people, some drivers holding signs with their passengers' names displayed. All except one woman, who perched on the edge of a window ledge (there were no chairs) knitting placidly as a cow might chew cud. Anne could not help but notice her, because she wore a ridiculous hat festooned with fake cherries and complete with a veil. She was draped in more scarves and shawls than Anne could count.

Anne glanced at her watch. Lucy's plane should be landing now, but of course she would have to go through customs and then wait for her bag, unless she had only a carry-on suitcase. Anne did not know how long Lucy intended to stay or what they would—or could—do. But it would be good to have a friend with her, a friend who loved Katherine and knew her as more than the strange, distant adolescent she had become. (They would find Katherine, they must. Anne could not bear to think that her last glimpse of Katherine would be her walking away at the airport, wearing her own eccentric hat, not turning even once to look back at her parents.)

Maybe in Lucy's company, Anne would recognize herself again. Or at least make some connection between the self she had been and the lone woman who perched in a bedsit, eating out of tins, who had gotten on the wrong side of her landlady. Who had stayed out all night, talked to a prostitute, who braved New Scotland Yard on her own.

After Anne had seen the van and heard the singing voices of girls, she had turned away from the rising sun and walked west till she could find a cab to take her to New Scotland Yard where she found to her dismay Detective Smith-Jones was absent on sick-leave. No one would tell her the nature of his illness, and who was taking over his cases was not yet clear. Still, she had been treated courteously by the short, bald officer on duty, who brought her a cup of fresh-brewed coffee instead of instant. (Who was she, that this small courtesy made her want to weep?)

She had rehearsed the whole story from the beginning, though the officer had the file open in front of him. Then she added the new information, her conversation with Margaret aka Margarita the street walker, the rumor about a secret, illicit sex club somewhere in East London. Her long walk to a district of old warehouses, and then the white van, the license number so indelible in her mind that it might as well have been tattooed on her skin.

"Tell me again, Mrs. Bradley, if you would be so kind, why you believe your daughter was in the van."

"I heard her voice," Anne said, wondering, as soon as she spoke, if she really had.

Had she recognized Katherine's voice as distinct from all the others? She probed the memory as you might probe a sore or missing tooth, while the detective watched her.

"She was in that van," stated Anne with a certainty that surprised her. "Those girls were being taken somewhere, somewhere dangerous. I expect you to find them."

The interview was over. She had ended it. (Who was this person, issuing orders to a policeman, behaving as if she were sure of being obeyed?)

When she got back to her bedsit, the glowering landlady handed her a message from a Miss Way, who had called at an indecent hour. And speaking of decency, the landlady would have her know, she ran a respectable establishment, and she could not tolerate tenants who came and went at all hours and expected her to answer the phone for them. It would not do, it would not do at all.

And who was this person who stared coldly back at this prim, bullying stick of a woman, and felt no compunction, no need to apologize or placate, no compulsion to explain herself.

"I will keep that in mind," Anne had heard herself saying. "And if you are too inconvenienced by my search for my daughter, who has disappeared into your cesspit of a city, and by calls from my friends and relations, I will be glad to find myself more congenial lodgings after I place a collect call to my husband and to Miss Way."

And she turned and walked down the hall to the residents' phone.

"Well," she heard the landlady saying, "seeing as you paid in advance till the end of the week...."

Anne called Gerald first, hoping to catch him before he went to the office. It was still only seven in the morning at home. Her mother in-law had answered.

"Anne, thank God," Julia said. "I've been trying and trying to reach you. I asked Lily or Lucy, whatever her name is, to call, too. He's all right. Gerald's all right. They only kept him overnight for observation. But you really must, you really ought to come home. The children...."

It took some time for her to get a coherent story out of Julia about Gerald's collapse in the park, the tests for stroke and heart attack.

"But he's all right?" she kept asking. "He will be all right?"

"He's supposed to be released from the hospital this morning. That wonderful colored friend of his Joshua, Jonah?

"Jeremiah," put in Anne.

"He'll be driving him home. I don't know what we'd do without him. He's been so kind. But Anne, listen to me, I don't know what good it can do for you to stay in London. Surely the police—"

"Listen, Julia," Anne cut her off. "Tell Gerald I'll call him later. I can't come back home. Not yet. There's a lead. Tell Gerald I've got a lead, and the police are pursuing it. Put the twins on, would you?"

"They're still asleep," her mother-in-law said. "I'll see if I can wake them. They miss you, Anne—"

"No, never mind. I'll call later. I've got to call Lucy Way now."

And she had hung up on her mother-in-law without the slightest qualm.

"Anne, thank God!" Lucy had greeted her with the same words.

Lucy listened attentively while Anne told her about the van and the all points (or ports, as the British called it) bulletin that the police had put out to find it.

"Thank God," Lucy said again. "Thank God you got the plate number, because I didn't."

"What do mean?" Anne asked.

And Lucy described her dream and referred to other dreams.

"What other dreams?" asked Anne.

"Didn't Gerald tell you?" Lucy seemed surprised. "I thought sure he had. He told Detective Smith-Jones. That's why the detective called me. He took my dreams seriously, and oh dear, now it seems he's left his post."

"Or been removed," Anne said.

There was a long transatlantic silence. Why hadn't Gerald told her about Lucy's dreams? Why the detective and not his wife? Had he not wanted to get her hopes up or had he simply forgotten?

"Anne, I'm coming to England," Lucy broke the silence. "I've booked a flight and hotel. I hope you don't mind. After the last dream, I felt I just had to."

"I'm glad, Lucy," Anne had said. And silently she added, and I am glad Gerald can't come.

Gerald had collapsed. He would have to stay home now.

She didn't want him to die. Of course, she didn't. She just didn't… want him with her. The very thought of him made her tired. Who was this person she had become? This person who had found her way to Heathrow on the Underground, who was waiting alone for a woman who dreamed clairvoyant dreams.

Now passengers from Lucy's flight began to make their way into the lobby, scanning the crowd for friends, family, or drivers, and people stood on tiptoe, waving and calling as they spotted their passenger. People began to rush toward each other, laughing, embracing, shouldering baggage. Anne moved to the front of the crowd and there, at last, was Lucy, slight, almost frail, white-haired, carrying no luggage at all.

Because she was flanked by two men.

Who on earth?

Joe Petrone, Frankie.

What were they doing here? How could whoever she had become make any sense of them?

"Lucy!" Anne waved, not knowing how to greet Lucy's companions, though they waved, too, Joe not sure whether to smile and Frankie, frowning.

Lucy held out her arms and began almost to run.

But before they could reach each other, the woman with the hat and the shawls stepped between them.

"So," she said. "It's you I was to meet. I thought it might be, but I wasn't sure."

Anne stood back, exchanging glances with Joe Petrone, shrugging to let him know she hadn't a clue. Lucy looked as though she hadn't either.

"Surely you know me," said the woman. "I know it's been too long time, but I haven't changed that much. Nor have you. I must say the white hair becomes you. Most people couldn't carry it off so well."

And Anne noticed the woman's hair under the hat, a most unnatural shade of orange overlaid with just a hint of magenta.

"Why thank you, Rowena," said Lucy recovering herself. "Anne, Joe, Frankie, may I introduce you to my old school friend Rowena. Rowena Trebilcock. Rowena, please meet my friends Anne Bradley, Joe Petrone, and Frankie Lomangino."

"A pleasure, I'm sure," the strange woman extended a hand that was both gloved and be-ringed. Joe recovered himself first.

"Likewise, Miss...uh."

"Trebilcock. I am sure we shall know each other better. Come along then. I didn't expect quite so many, but I can manage tea and breakfast. You must be hungry."

Chapter Fifty-Seven

Everyone was so quiet, you could hear forks scraping the tin plates. In the canopy, the birds had resumed singing after the girls' noisy descent from the treehouse. The breakfast fire crackled and hissed, keeping a large tea kettle warm and heating water for washing up. There were stumps for sitting on, but Katherine's friends had favored sitting on the ground and huddling together as if it were still cold, which it wasn't with the sun now risen over a hill and pouring down into the glade.

Robin sat a little apart from them, quick to refill a cup or a plate but otherwise, not ignoring them exactly, but not looking at them too directly. Katherine would have liked to go nearer to Robin, but she did not want to break from the herd yet. Yes, that's what it felt like, that they were herd animals, cows or maybe deer. Prey. And they did not yet feel safe in this strange place, with this person who appeared to be a protector but might pose a threat. All of them had been lured to that other place (as Katherine thought of it now) by false appearances and promises. Yesterday they'd run in Robin's direction, instinctively. She seemed the lesser danger. Now they were not so sure. They instinctively mistrusted their instincts.

Katherine studied Robin with sidelong glances. Her eyes were golden with flecks of green, like the light in the glade. She seemed to understand that the girls were afraid. She made no sudden moves. She waited, patiently. Here in the greenwood, Robin's hands did not shake, Katherine noticed. She seemed alert as if she sensed every shifting breeze, understood the language of the birds and trusted them to warn her of any danger. The more time passed, the more Katherine felt Robin's calm flowing, lapping at the edge of their huddle. The others must have, too. A leg relaxed here, a clenched hand unfurled there.

Then, without quite knowing what she meant to do, Katherine got to her feet and stretched her legs and arms, such a long stretch, she felt as though she were growing toward the light that grazed the treetops. Then she sat down on one of the stumps partway between Robin and her friends. In response, others stretched and unfolded. The cluster of girls stirred till each one found a stump, and they sat in a loose circle.

"Are there bears in these 'ere woods?" Bess broke the silence first.

"I've never seen one," said Robin. "It could be there are no more bears in England at all, no more wolves either. All hunted to extinction. But if there were bears, they might live here. This is the wildest, vastest forest left. That's why we can be safe here."

A skeptical silence followed. Katherine guessed she was the only one who felt safe in the woods. The only one but Robin.

"But 'ow long can we 'ide out 'ere?" said Fifi. "Stealing food, sleeping in trees. And wot about winter? I bet it gets bloody cold out 'ere, wherever the 'ell we are, which none of us knows, thank you very much."

Robin listened, with her head cocked to one side, the way Katherine's dog did when you spoke to him, as if he could understand English, which he could. Her dog. She'd had a dog in another life. For a moment Katherine felt lost.

"No, you don't know where you are," Robin acknowledged. "But whenever anyone wants to leave, I promise you, I will see you safe to a train. There are towns and trains beyond this forest. As to winter, I've already started to frame a wattle and daub hut that will be big enough for everyone who wants to stay here."

"A waddle and wot?" asked Daisy. "Wot's daub?"

"Wattle is willow or some other supple tree like hazel," explained Robin. "Daub is soil or clay mixed with animal dung and straw," Robin began.

"Animal wot?" persisted Daisy.

"Shite," translated Bernadette.

"Shit," clarified Bess.

"You mean manure, like," said Daisy, who had maybe been a real farm girl once. "From cows."

Robin nodded. "Or pigs or horses."

"But shit," said Fifi. "An 'ouse made of shit! What 'appens when it rains?"

"Well, when the dung is dried properly and mixed with straw, it's as watertight as anything," said Robin. "Sometimes the material is called marl. Our ancestors built round houses with it—"

"Not just ancestor," Devi spoke up. "In India, we use dung to make house floor. Dry yes, Dry enough also to burn, to make cook fires."

"Ah," said Bernadette, "that would be hot shite then."

And suddenly they were all laughing and talking at once. Merrily, the word came to Katherine. We are merry maids living with Robin Hoodlum in the greenwood.

If Frankie could see her now, he would envy her.

Frankie. Her own laughter ebbed away. Tears rose. Lucy. Bear. Her mother. Aramantha, who had stopped talking in her head ever since Katherine ran after Robin.

Does anyone 'ere 'ave an 'ome? Bess had asked.

Well, they had one now. Katherine swallowed her tears and joined the laughter again though she had lost track of the jokes. They had a home now.

Chapter Fifty-Eight

"Now then, dears, shall you tell me what has brought you here?" Rowena ventured. "Or shall I tell you?"

Lucy didn't know quite how, but Rowena had managed to seat them all at what had at first appeared to be a small table for two but had somehow accommodated all five of them, along with a large teapot, a platter heaped with eggs and another with bangers and mash. There was also a basket of fresh bread that renewed itself regularly and an old-fashioned crock of butter. Frankie's appetite was making a favorable impression on Rowena. She beamed as she heaped seconds of everything on his plate.

"Rowena is a sensitive," Lucy explained to Anne and Joe who were looking to her in some perplexity.

None of them had spoken en route to Rowena's Bloomsbury flat. They'd all sat, more or less stunned, crammed into a London cab, Frankie and Joe sitting on the foldout seats usually reserved for children. Anne kept stealing glances at Joe, then looking at Lucy over the small bulk of Rowena between them. Lucy had felt unequal to answer the questions Anne could not quite bring herself to ask.

"That's the old-fashioned, polite word for it," agreed Rowena. "So of course that is the term our Lucy would use. To put it more plainly, I am a clairvoyant, a psychic, if you prefer."

Frankie was now staring around the room. It would not disappoint, Lucy thought, as a stage setting for séances and other parlor tricks. Although perhaps that was unfair. The room was not unpleasing, cozy yet airy, the general impression green with hints of gold, perhaps the effect of the gilt-edged frames of the paintings, portraits and landscapes. With the morning light coming in through an alcove window, the place had the feel of a woodland glade. There were trailing plants everywhere and pots of ferns. In one of two alcoves, a table draped in a green brocade cloth was topped with a crystal ball. Fanned out was a deck of large cards, their backs a field of black with a colorful Rose Cross, gilded with many symbols.

However strange Rowena was, however self-important, whatever else she believed, Lucy reminded herself, Rowena had put herself into the service of the Rose Cross. She hadn't just served in the women's army, she had been one of another army that met each week to meditate and pray under the guidance of a woman some thought a witch, others, an esoteric saint. Lucy had gone with Rowena to some of the meetings. The leader had given Lucy a nod and a look of recognition, then accepted her into the hidden ranks that were fighting the magical battle of Britain. Lucy had seen things on that other plane, the cavern beneath the Tor, the Rose Cross, the shadowy figures of the Guardian spirits or angels, that Lucy could not deny then or now. So, however reluctantly, she did believe in Rowena's powers. That didn't mean they should all be bullied into following her lead.

"You mean you have ESP?" Frankie asked with his usual bluntness. "Mrs., uh, Troublecock," he added after a nudge under the table from his Uncle's foot.

"Miss," she corrected, "Trebilcock. Old Cornish name. Extrasensory perception. That's another way to look at it, yes. Though, really, if we pay proper attention, we can all develop more powers of perception. We all have a sixth sense, don't we?"

Joe nodded, politely or warily or both. Lucy saw him casting anxious glances at Anne, who was so pale her skin took on a green cast from the drapes.

"Lucy has dreams," said Anne, not adding, so why do we need you, but Lucy could sense Anne's resistance.

Before she could say anything, Lucy was distracted by claws digging into her leg as a large cat came out of hiding from under the table and leaped into her lap, all black except for a small white star on his forehead. At Lucy's touch, he began to purr so loudly that everyone laughed, and some of the tension dispersed.

"My familiar," said Rowena. "Such a naughty Sootykins. That's what I call him. His fancy name is Sir Night, but we don't stand on formalities here. Oh, dear. I do hope he didn't put a run in your stocking, Lucy."

"Not to worry," said Lucy. "I have two kittens at home. I'm used to it."

"Lennon and McCartney," Frankie spoke up. "I found the kittens for her. I mean, we found them, Katherine and me."

As Katherine's name was spoken, a stillness fell, so heavy, so charged, you would have to be utterly sixth senseless not to feel it. A sudden breeze came through the windows, lifting the heavy drapes and stirring the plants to life so that they sounded like leaves of trees.

Then Anne began to weep. Joe hesitated for a moment, glanced at Lucy, as if for permission, then got up from his place and went to put an arm around her.

"Katherine," said Rowena, in a soft voice, a different voice than she'd used before.

She was putting them into trance, Lucy could feel it. She immediately put up her guard and wished she could warn the others without being rude or alarming. Rowena's revenge, Lucy used to call it. Rowena had been such an odd, picked-upon girl at school, short and wall-eyed with shocking hair as orange as a young carrot. She only wanted to be liked, but she didn't know how to go about it. So instead she learned that she could frighten people or at least make them very uncomfortable, which of course made her more of a pariah, but a somewhat more mysterious one. Lucy had once come upon Rowena sobbing her heart out behind the school's garden shed.

"Go away," the miserable girl had shouted. "Leave me alone or I'll turn you into a toad, I swear I will."

Lucy was well-liked at school, but she was lonely, too, and homesick for France. She and Rowena were some of the few girls who didn't come from London's upper crust. Lucy's mother was American, and Rowena's mother was dead. She lived with an aunt on her mother's side. A peculiar old woman who claimed descent from Morgan Le Fey.

"I've always been rather fond of toads," remarked Lucy.

And she sat down next to Rowena and offered her a handkerchief. They became friends of a sort—given the vast difference in their degree of popularity. Lucy's championship gave Rowena some measure of protection. Rowena's devotion to Lucy kept in check, more or less, her desire to abuse what she called her powers.

"Tell me about Katherine, all of you," said Rowena in that soothing voice that sounded at once as though it came from far away and from inside your head. "Tell me all about Katherine."

And they did, for what seemed like hours. Even Lucy lost track of time as she listened to Anne talk about Katherine from before birth through an early childhood tragically disrupted by the death of her older brother. She talked and talked, Katherine's favorite food, favorite books, how she had changed from a sweet, solemn child to a sullen teenager. How Katherine loved to sing and could make her voice sound like anyone's from Julie Andrews to who was that vulgar, ugly woman who screamed all the time?

"Janis Joplin," Frankie supplied.

And Frankie, Frankie must have been in trance. Lucy had never heard him be so forthcoming. He talked about the games he and Katherine played as children, how they had become blood brother and sister. How they had plotted to catch the man who murdered Charlotte Crowley and was about to kill Lucy. A story known in great detail to everyone but Rowena. Lucy was almost soothed by its repetition. She began to succumb to the half-waking dreamlike state she had been resisting. Then all at once she snapped awake.

"She took her shirt off," Frankie was saying.

Joe Petrone, still standing next to Anne, tensed.

"Frankie," he warned.

"Let him go on," said Anne. "I want to know. I have to know."

"It was never like that with Katherine and me," Frankie said. "I thought of her like my sister, even though I think she might of started to think different about me. She wanted me to touch her, I mean all over, and…and I did. Then she started to cry and I just held her. Who hurt you, I asked her, who hurt you? But she never told me."

Lucy could see it so clearly. The wood they had loved as children, that they had sprinkled with Lucy's holy water after the capture of the murderer. These young almost grown ones, still so soft, Katherine's skin, Frankie's touch….

"I should have tried harder to find out. I didn't see her much after that day. I should have…."

Then someone else was speaking.

"She is the child of my heart. She is the child I never had. I thought the child I lost so long ago was a son. Maybe he was. But Katherine is the child who came to me, who called to me, or maybe I called to her. I promised, I promised to defend her from all the perils of this night, I promised…."

The voice stopped, and Lucy saw that everyone was looking at her. What had she just said?

The child, the child she lost, the child she found, the child she lost. Defend, O Lord, this thy child.

They were all looking at her, Anne, Joe, Frankie. They all had tears in their eyes. All except Rowena who sat calmly, her good eye and her wall eye gazing into a distance far beyond the room or the London streets outside her window.

"I see," said Rowena. "I see."

(Now he saw. The substance of things once unseen. A phrase he remembered from mandatory chapel attendance drifted though his mind. The shadow was no longer a shadow.

A slim young man in workman's clothes, the driver of the van had regained consciousness after a bad concussion and had described his assailant to the police.

A slim young man in evening dress, who passed himself off as the nephew of one of the longtime members, a doddering old fool inbred to the point of idiocy as so many of the aristocracy were. He hadn't had the mental or physical capacity to visit the Doll House in a decade. Then this membership for a nephew, a slight young man with long fingers.

He began to pack his valise. He could have had a servant do it, but he didn't like anyone touching his things. It was a horrifying intimacy he never allowed.

No need for undue haste. H. had called him immediately when the van was found. They had not reached the woman in the raincoat yet. She had left her boarding house. She was sure to call with her new address, and when she did, H. would relay the information. The dowdy, ill-dressed American woman would be misled by the driver's description of his attacker. They all would, even his contact at New Scotland Yard.

Only he knew the shadow for who she was.

Only he had any idea where to look for her.)

Chapter Fifty-Nine

Anne looked around the small, comfortable hotel room with its view of a quiet street in Bloomsbury. Quaint was the word that came to mind to describe the faded floral patterns everywhere, the bed-spread, the seat of a small chair at a fold-up desk. The wallpaper had raised green stripes that looked like ribbons. A dreamy shepherdess decorated the curve of a water pitcher set on a lacy doily on a stand by a porcelain sink. Though it must be noon, the room was heavi-ly-shaded, restful and dim. The four-poster, three-quarter bed, made for the comfort of one respectable body, beckoned primly.

To say that she did not know how she got here would be inac-curate, but she felt a dream-like disorientation. It was still the same day that she had gotten up before dawn to set out for the airport. It had rained in the night and the wet pavement had reflected the street-lights. Out of the corner of her eye she had caught the motion of her landlady parting the drapes and peering out at her, keeping count of one more of Anne's untoward comings and goings.

Then there was the shock of seeing Lucy coming from baggage claim flanked by Joe and Frankie. Before she could fully take in their unexpected presence the Troublecock woman (Frankie's misnomer seemed apt) had accosted them, rounded them up into a huge black London taxi cab, with fold-down stools for Frankie and Joe, and wafted them off to her flat, which couldn't have been much more than a bedsit, but which seemed to have an expanding table and walls that could be mistaken for a jungle.

Such things happened in the kind of children's books that Katherine used to read, but they did not happen in real life, not to Anne. Nor did she cry in front of strangers or allow herself to be held and comforted. By a man who wasn't her husband. Come to that, she'd rarely allowed herself to be so held even by the man who *was* her husband.

Gerald. Far away in another world she could scarcely believe she had once inhabited, taken for granted. But theoretically it still existed, Gerald existed, as precariously as she did or more so. He'd been in the hospital for tests. When was it? So confusing with the time difference. The night before last? If she called him now, she could reach him before he left for work, if his health permitted a return to the job. She ought to find out how he was, and she ought to let him know the number of this hotel. Rowena Trebilcock had invited Lucy to stay with her. Telephone communication had been so difficult through Anne's landlady, Lucy came up with the idea that Anne should vacate the bedsit and take Lucy's hotel room.

Just down the hall from Joe Petrone's and Frankie's room.

In fact, they would all be using the same WC, which was separate from the room with the bathtub. No shower anywhere. Anne felt shy about such intimacy, yet it also seemed comforting to have the people down the hall be familiar to her. Familiar. Like family. Almost.

On the way to check in at the hotel, they had given the grim-faced landlady notice and picked up Anne's few belongings. The plan was for everyone to settle in and then reconvene at Rowena's flat for high tea. Possibly more bangers, beans, and mash with some cakes and scones thrown in. Not that it mattered to Anne what she ate. What mattered was what they were to do next, and why, suddenly and inexplicably, Rowena Trebilcock seemed to be first in command. The self-professed clairvoyant had not yet told them what she had "seen." Maybe it was all nothing but the self-importance of a lonely old woman. For all Anne knew, Miss Trebilcock might go to the airport every day in hopes of making a psychic pronouncement to some old acquaintance met by chance. She couldn't quite get a read on

Lucy's attitude towards her old schoolmate, yet she did not appear to question Miss Trebilcock's abilities.

If the woman didn't have anything of substance to offer at tea, Anne would...Anne would what? Make an alliance with Joe, get him to help her get the official investigation back on track. She would do that anyway. Why else would Joe have come all this way? Which reminded her, after she called Gerald, she must call New Scotland Yard, to let them know her new address and phone and to find out if they had traced the white van. The first solid lead in the case. Well, maybe not as solid as she'd insisted. But more solid than a dream or a vision. And evidence, as far as Anne was concerned, that if anyone had psychic gifts, it was Lucy.

Anne stepped out into the hall where she remembered seeing a phone on a table next to a comfortable chair. As soon as she picked up the receiver, a man at the front desk responded. Kindly and efficiently he put through her transatlantic collect call.

"Gerald Bradley speaking," Gerald answered as if his home were still the rectory where he was always on call.

"Gerald?" she said. "It's Anne."

How odd to identify herself, as if her voice wouldn't have been enough. Maybe Gerald thought it was odd, too. He didn't say anything for a moment. She couldn't even hear him breathing.

"Gerald?"

"I'm here."

And then she understood, he was struggling not to cry.

"It's all right, Gerald." Stupid thing to say, she realized. Of course it wasn't. "I mean, I don't have any more news. About Katherine. I just called to say I've moved to Lucy's hotel."

She decided not to explain that Lucy wasn't here and that Joe was down the hall. She just gave him the name, number, and address of the hotel.

"I'm going to call New Scotland Yard as soon as we hang up," she added. "I haven't heard anything more. But they are searching for the van I saw. Did your mother tell you?"

She realized how muddled everything seemed. They hadn't talked since his collapse.

"Are you all right, Gerald? I'm sorry, I should have asked right away. All the tests came back negative?"

"I'm fine." Gerald took a gulp of air, as if he'd surfaced from being too long underwater. "Are you all right?"

"Yes," she said.

Any other answer seemed too contentious or too complicated.

"My sister's been phoning," Gerald said. "She wants to help. She said she could never reach you at the other place."

"I don't want her help," Anne snapped. "Sorry, Gerald. I just, I just can't deal with Pat and Bob. It may not be their fault, but I can't help blaming them. I know they blame me. Everyone in your family always has."

Anne stopped herself. What did it matter? She needed to get off the phone.

"Anne," Gerald said.

Anne waited but nothing more came out. Was he holding his breath again?

"Listen, Gerald. I ought to call Scotland Yard to let them know how to reach me. Are Peter and Janie all right?"

"Janie was crying last night." How strange. Suddenly he almost sounded normal. "She misses you. And Katherine."

Anne felt her own throat tightening with tears.

"Peter does, too, but he doesn't talk about it. He just acts goofy; that's his way of covering up how scared he is."

Anne felt a prickle of rage. Now after years of ignoring them, he was explaining her children to *her*? But she said nothing.

"You were right, Anne."

"About what?" She knew she sounded abrupt. She wanted not to cry. She wanted to get off the phone.

"About having another chance. With the twins. Anne," he said again. "There's something I have to tell you. When you know, you might not want me to—"

Maybe she was psychic. In a flash, she knew. She did not want to hear it; she could not hear it. Whatever he wanted or needed to say.

"Not now, Gerald. Please not now. Tell Janie and Peter I love them. Tell them I am going to find Katherine. I have to go now."

"But Anne, this is about Kath—"

Anne put down the receiver so softly, she imagined Gerald hadn't heard and was going on speaking to a dead connection.

A door opened just as softly, and Joe stepped out into the hall. He must have been waiting for her to finish her phone conversation before he went to the WC. It was almost unbearable that a man should be so considerate.

"Everything all right?"

Don't cry, don't you dare cry, she told herself. If he held her again....

"Yeah, fine," she said, forcing herself to sound calm. "I'm going to call Scotland Yard now, give them the number here. Find out what I can."

"Sure thing," he said.

"Then maybe this afternoon, unless they have something. Well, I've gotten to know London awfully well." Awfully. "I could show you and Frankie some of the sights."

"Sure thing," he said again and went down the hall to the WC.

Chapter Sixty

"I 'ave somefink to tell everyone," Bess announced.

After spending the morning getting the lay of the land, as Robin said, and gathering firewood and kindling, they were having lunch, some kind of soup made of wild plants and, Katherine suspected, bits of wild game. They were also downing dark bitter ale. Fifi had called for gin. "To calm me nerves, medicinal like." Robin had apologized for the lack of strong spirits but had disappeared into the wood and returned rolling a keg.

"Fell off a lorry, did it?" guessed Fifi. "Cor if I'd 'ad your talent for thievery, I never would 'ave given in to the temptation to sell meself."

Katherine had not had any kind of beer since she'd tried it long ago at a church workday where the men kept beer on ice in tubs. She'd choked on it and it had run out her nose. She was managing to keep it down now. She wasn't sure she liked the taste, but she liked the effect. Her belly felt warm and glowing as the campfire and she was quite sure she loved everyone around her, and the trees and the breeze and the light falling in dappled patterns on the ground.

"Get on with it then," said Bernadette. "This better be good."

Bess took a deep breath.

"My name," she said," is not Bess. Nor Elizabeth neither."

"Not even Queenie," put in Fifi, a bit sarcastically.

"Or Regina," added Robin, more kindly.

Bess, who was not Bess, kept shaking her head.

"What is then? This better be good," Bernadette warned again.

She leaned into the circle, looked over her shoulder as if to make sure no one else outside of it could hear.

"It's…Doreen."

This solemn announcement was met with silence followed by a burst of laughter.

"It's not funny," protested Doreen, but she was laughing, too. "Wot's your names then? I bet they're worse than mine. Go on then. Tell! I dare you!"

"You know what's worse," said Bernadette, when the laughter subsided, "my name really is Bernadette, as in "The Song of Bernadette." Try to live that one down. Or try to live up to it. Everyone else gets a stage name, but not me. I'm cast as a feckin' nun. And after running away from when they tried to lock me up in a laundry with the nuns."

"Wot?" asked Daisy. "Wot d'you mean, locked in a laundry with nuns!"

"Your scene could 'ave been a whole lot worse if Mister Tobias ever 'eard about laundering nuns," said Bess who was Doreen.

"You mean you never heard of Magdalen Houses! All over Ireland, they are. If you get up the pole or even look at a fella sideways, they lock you up. Most girls don't get away till they're carried out in a coffin. So before they could get me, I ran. Much good it did me. Straight from the frying pan into the fire."

In fact, Bernadette looked cold. She wrapped her arms around her, even though the sun was nearing its height and the fire still burned.

"Wot you done?" said Daisy Mae. "Why did they want to lock you up?"

"I did nothing," growled Bernadette. "I didn't take me own knickers down, I tell you. The eegits that did ran away and the nuns that found me lying there in the dirt said I was to blame."

No one spoke for a moment.

"It's always the girl's fault," said Fifi. "We all know that, don't we? And by the by, my name is Vicky. Short for Victoria. Right," she gave a bitter laugh. "Victorious, that's me, innit?"

"You are victorious," said Robin quietly. "We are all victorious."

Robin's words eddied into a small silence.

"You're quite mad, you know," Vicky told Robin "You don't come from where we come from. But I reckon you mean well."

Katherine didn't either, but no one knew where she'd come from. She'd been lying all along.

"Our Robin's a bit of all right, I say," said Doreen, "stealing a van, saving our arses. Talk about frying pans and fires. Go on then. The rest of you. Give us your names. Oh, except poor old Bernadette."

Suddenly they all began to talk at once, all except Katherine. She felt a bit woozy as names and snatches of stories swirled around her. Daisy Mae was Maggie, and her mother really had been a dairy maid. She never knew who her father was. Maggie hated life on the farm and vowed not to end up like her mother. So when a fine gentleman offered her a lift to London in his motor car, she took it.

"Promised me a good time, he did. He had a good time, I reckon. Left me in a hotel with the bill unpaid and never come back for me."

Devi's real name was Sarita.

"It means river," she told them.

"So pretty!" everyone exclaimed.

But what happened to her wasn't. Her family was very poor. She had been sold as a child bride to a man from London who kept her locked in the basement kitchen of his restaurant. One day she managed to persuade a delivery boy to let her out and ran off with nothing but the clothes on her back.

Vicky was tricked out, as she put it, by her stepmother. Doreen was thrown out by her mother who accused her of seducing her stepfather.

"But I never. I used to put the dresser by the door to try to stop him coming in."

Once the girls started, they couldn't stop talking. Their stories were like hideous fairytales. They were all lost but in a city instead of a forest. No crumbs or clues could lead them home, because they had no homes. In all the stories, Tom Cat appeared first as a rescuer, paying Maggie's bill, offering to get Vicky away from her stepmother's clutches and set her up on her own. Persuading Bernadette that nuns would set the Vatican police on her. He'd seen it before, but he could get her to a safe house. Assuring Doreen he would go with her to report her stepfather to the police. Promising Sarita he'd buy her passage back to India. Then later he revealed himself for who he was, the big bad wolf, no, worse, someone who tricked them and led them to Mister Tobias' lair, the evil sorcerer.

Katherine listened, as if watching a game of skip rope that never stopped, wondering how to jump in and but always missing the beat. They were telling her story, too, except they weren't. They couldn't. Hers was different.

Maybe it was being in the wood, a real wood, a fairy wood. *You must have fairy blood*, Lucy Way had said to her long ago and far away. In that other life, she'd had a sleigh bed in a room with sloping eaves at Lucy's house. She'd had a mother who might have loved her once, a sister and a brother. She'd had a dog with white fluffy fur who herded black cows, got covered in mud and burrs. She'd had a brother who had died. And a blood brother who was alive but might not love her. He had touched her once when she'd asked him to, then held her, just held her.

She'd had a father, who wept late one night and held her too tight.

She could hardly breathe.

She had a wet place between her legs.

Her father, not a stepfather, her *father*. That was worse than what anyone else had said about their lives, even though they were poor. (Her father loved poor people.) And she had not been poor.

"Warbler, are you still wiv us?" Doreen called her back from what seemed like a long way off, as if she'd been looking at them from the wrong end of a telescope. "Tell us 'oo you are then. You was never Little Liza Jane."

Who she was. Who she *was*?

Katherine opened her mouth but no name came out. Eliza Doolittle, she had called herself, and the next thing she knew she was naked and alone in a locked room. But who was Katherine? A girl from America who had pretended to be from a London slum.

"She doesn't have to speak," said Robin. "Not until she's ready and not then unless she chooses."

Katherine felt her eyes filling.

"All right, Warbler?" Doreen put her arm around Katherine. "I'm the one as named her Warbler. Not that 'orror of a man. It'll do for now. She can sing then, can't she? Wot's that song you sung, got you in so much trouble? Put you on the snuff list, it did. And very like the rest of us too."

"Respect," Katherine managed to say. "Aretha Franklin sings it."

"Sing for us now, Warbler," urged Doreen. "Loud as you please."

"Yeah. Sing, Warbler, sing!" urged the others.

Doreen, Vicky, Sarita, Maggie and Bernadette born Bernadette.

"Sing!"

Katherine wanted to sing Aretha or Diana Ross or Janis Joplin. She wanted to be someone else. She wanted to show off. But when she opened her mouth she was a child again in Miss Ebersbach's choir. A child again singing for Crazy McCready who would not let her buy a knife at the rummage sale unless she could recite a psalm, a lost child, blind-folded in the back of a van.

"*Yea though I walk through shadowed vale.*"

Her voice high and clear on the descant. Then someone was singing with her, singing the tune.

"*For thou art with me, and thy rod and staff....*"

She couldn't bear it, she couldn't bear it. She was going to be sick.

She stood up and ran as fast as she could away from the clearing, away from the others, deeper into the wood.

"Warbler!" Doreen shouted after her.

"Let her be," Robin said, loud enough so that Katherine could hear, was meant to hear. "She won't get lost. She has fairy blood."

Chapter Sixty-One

Lucy was trying to stay awake so that she could go to bed (albeit early) on London time and be ready for a full day tomorrow, whatever they were going to do. Which was not at all clear. She sat as upright as she could in Rowena's old-fashioned horsehair chair, but she felt herself nodding off, though she could still hear Rowena bustling about making yet more tea.

In her dream, the light and colors were also green and there was the sound of a stream rushing over rock. And just audible, the sound of someone giving way to sorrow.

Katherine, Katherine.

"Here you are then, dear," Rowena set down a cup on the rickety old table next to Lucy's chair. "Or would you rather go on dreaming."

Lucy snapped awake, more awake than she had been all day. Rowena fetched a chair from the table and sat down next to Lucy, balancing her own cup and saucer in her lap. For a moment neither of them spoke or even looked at each other directly. Lucy was reminded of two cats, ignoring each other till one of them either hissed or made a friendly offer of grooming.

"I suppose I ought to tell you about the dreams," Lucy began. "Unless you already know."

"Are you testing me, Lucy?" asked Rowena. "By the by, your friend, Anne Bradley, thinks I am a fraud."

Rowena did not seem offended, and yet Lucy felt tempted to take offense on Anne's behalf.

"You haven't done anything yet to prove otherwise," Lucy pointed out. "Apart from casting us into trance so that we told you more than we've ever told anyone else."

Rowena took a sip of tea, then turned her wandering eye on Lucy.

"You hold that against me. You think I was playing a cheap parlor trick," stated Rowena.

Lucy searched for a diplomatic answer and decided to be direct.

"You know you and I have always had differences of opinion. I don't believe it's right to trick people into confidences. You have to gain their trust."

It was hard to tell if Rowena was pondering or pouting.

"It will not be easy to gain Anne Bradley's trust," pronounced Rowena.

"Nonsense," said Lucy. "Help her to find her daughter. That is the only thing that matters to her. She will follow any lead."

"Yes," agreed Rowena. "And I will do all I can to help find the child, for the sake of our friendship, Lucy, and for the sake of the girl. No, I don't doubt her mother will go to the ends of the earth to find her. But she does not want to know about the source."

"The source of what?" Lucy felt impatient.

"Katherine's trouble."

"The source of Katherine's trouble?" Lucy said. "Whatever do you mean? Speak plainly."

Rowena's only answer was to stare straight ahead of her, eyes blank, her head slightly tilted as if she were listening. The medium in a trance, how stagey. Lucy felt a surge of annoyance, and then the next minute she felt uneasy, almost frightened.

"I think," said Rowena at length, "it is for the girl to reveal—or not—when we find her."

If we find her, Lucy almost snapped. But how could she say it, even think it. They must find her.

Now then," said Rowena, all business again, "about your dreams, I suspect you know that the child is no longer in London."

"I keep dreaming of a forest," Lucy acknowledged.

"And that person, the slender young man with the Oxford ring...."

If Rowena was showing off, she was doing a good job. Lucy had not told her any of those details.

"Go on," said Lucy.

"She was driving that white van."

(The American woman had phoned Scotland Yard with her new address, as he'd known she would. He'd sent his man round at once. Now he knew more. The woman was not alone. She had a man with her and an adolescent boy. Her husband and son, family of his treacherous, lying little girl? They'd gone to New Scotland Yard and then had wondered around London playing at being tourists, visiting the Tower, Buckingham Palace, Hyde Park. Why hadn't they gone to search the dull little suburb where the van had been abandoned?

He would have to wait, watch until he knew what their next move would be.)

Chapter Sixty-Two

Robin was right about her. Katherine did know how not to get lost, at least in the woods. She had found a stream and followed it, sometimes stepping on stones, sometimes walking in the stream itself. It wouldn't matter if the old pair of sneakers someone gave her, trainers they called them here, got wet. After a time, the stream narrowed to a torrent and the banks rose steeply above it. She scrambled up and up, the climb steep enough that she had to breathe hard. Short breath and streaming sweat loosed her tears. At the top of the bank, she crumpled to hands and knees and gave way to weeping. As long as the tears flowed, she didn't have to think. She didn't have to remember. There was only dappled light, breeze weaving in and out of leaves, the sound of water, the softness of earth. Here she was alone. Here she was finally safe. When her tears stopped, she looked up at the sheltering branches of an ancient beech tree. Its roots made a lap. She curled herself into the tree, leaned against it, and closed her eyes.

She did not know whether or not she dreamed. Brightness and darkness came and went. Someone had turned the world upside down, all the colored pieces shifted, drifted, flurried, fell. She never had to wake again. She did not want to wake.

And then her eyes opened.

A slender tree she had not noticed before was standing over her, as if guarding her sleep. Light had caught in the tree's hair, fine-edged gold and rays fanning out around her head.

"May I sit with you for a bit?" the tree asked.

Katherine sat up straight, rubbing her eyes. The tree turned into Robin sitting down beside her. Robin wore shorts and work boots. Katherine could see blonde leg hair glinting in the light. Katherine's own legs used to be like that before she made the mistake of shaving them and turning the hair to ugly black stubble.

Katherine looked up at Robin, who sat quietly gazing across to the stream's other bank as if she could sit there, not just for a bit but forever if she chose.

"Robin?" Katherine finally spoke, and Robin turned that gaze on her. Katherine felt as though she was looking into a forest, a forest that looked back at her.

"My name is Katherine," she said so softly she could hardly hear herself. "I'm from America."

Robin leaned closer to Katherine, her head inclined, the better to hear her. Katherine found herself distracted by the warmth of Robin's body.

"I pretended," Katherine made herself go on, "I pretended to be Eliza Doolittle, and then, then I couldn't stop when that man, Tom Cat we call him, took me to a pub."

Slowly at first, then in a tumbling rush, the rest of the story poured out.

"And I never let on to Mister Tobias," she concluded. "I thought if he knew who I was, knew that I wasn't a girl from the streets, like the rest of them, he would kill me. And then, well I guess he decided to kill me anyway. Not just me, but the others, too. And it was my fault, because…because they were, they are my friends. If it hadn't been for you…."

"Shh," Robin put her hand over Katherine's lightly, the way a shaft of sun might rest on you for a moment before it had to ebb away. "Katherine, listen to me. It's not your fault, any more than it was Pippa's fault, what happened to her and the ones who were taken with her."

Robin fell silent again, and though her hand still rested on Katherine's, it felt heavy now, as if Robin had forgotten it was there, as if she had forgotten Katherine was there.

I'm doing it for her, Robin had told them, *In memory of her.*
Pippa.

"Will you tell me about her?" Katherine spoke just above a whisper, so that Robin did not need to hear if she did not want to.

Robin took her hand away and put it in her own lap. She shouldn't have said anything, Katherine reproached herself. Now Robin would be angry with her.

"Pippa was my beloved," Robin said. "My true love."

She didn't sound angry. Only sad, so sad, Katherine felt the ache of the sadness in her own chest.

"She came from the streets herself. And I came from, well, as she put it, the castle. 'You're forgetting to crook your little finger, Lady Jane,' she'd tease me when we'd toss back a pint at the corner pub."

"How did you meet her?" Katherine asked. Maybe Robin wanted to talk about her.

Robin did. She talked in gulps as if words were water and she was parched with thirst. She told Katherine about quitting Oxford to enroll in the Anti-University in Shoreditch.

"Working class women started organizing in Shoreditch for the vote. Organizing is putting it mildly. There were riots in the streets, women were beaten, jailed. They lost their jobs, their families...."

For a moment, Robin reminded Katherine of her father, as she launched into a history of women's suffrage. Except that when her father spoke, Katherine resented being lectured to, as if she weren't there or it didn't matter who she was. But she felt she could listen to Robin forever; Robin was somehow including her in the cause.

"And it seemed to me that after all of that struggle, women were being excluded again, relegated to making the coffee and tea, running off copies of pamphlets, that sort of thing. I felt we needed our own meetings, our own space."

Robin wrote a grant (Katherine wasn't quite sure what that meant, but it was the sort of thing her father did, too) and opened a center where women could meet, or just stop by, eat a meal, take and give classes.

"That's how I met Pippa," Robin said at last. "She was so tough and smart. She knew everything I didn't—and everyone. I hired her to help me run the center. We called it Jane's Place for Jane Shore, Edward the IV's mistress, who was supposed to have been buried there in a ditch, 'the merriest, the wiliest, and the holiest harlot in his realm,' he called Jane. Much good it did her in the end, Pippa would always say."

Robin paused, staring into the distance again. Katherine sensed she was not seeing the wood now, but the chaotic streets, the crowded center, the rooms loud with women's talk and raucous laughter.

"Of course, I fell in love with her. Pippa was small and dark, beautiful and ferocious, full of fine withering scorn that covered her fire that would never stay tamped down for long. I tried to keep my love a secret. I thought she resented me, well, she probably did. She didn't trust people of my class. Still, we found we worked well together, picked up each other's cues, took up each other's slack. Late one night, as we were cleaning up the endless ashtrays and tea mugs, she...she took hold of me and...she kissed me."

Katherine closed her eyes. Despite the cooling air, the shift in the wind, she could imagine that moment, the heat of it, how their arms around each other made one close, dark space.

"And after that we were just together. We made a little flat for ourselves in the backroom of the center, just a hot plate and a kettle, two cots pushed together. 'Not what you're used to, I'll warrant, Lady Jane,' Pippa would say. But to me it was paradise.

"It was Pippa who suspected something was going on. She'd been a prostitute herself before she came to work at Jane's Place. She always had her ear to the ground. Women came and went all the time. At first I thought nothing of it, the girls who stopped coming round, girls no one would think to look for. Except Pippa. There was a pattern, she was convinced of it, and she finally convinced me. I told her we had to go to the police, report the girls as missing. We had a huge row then.

"'The police!' she shouted. 'The police! You don't get it, do you? Even after all you've been through. Even after that balls-up of an inquest.'" What inquest? What *was* an inquest? Katherine didn't know, but she did not want to interrupt.

"'Don't you see, my fine Lady Jane!'" Robin went on in Pippa's voice, "'Ten to one, the police are in on it. You tip them off, and they'll cover their arses so fast, no one will ever find those girls. Me, I 'ave me own ways. I'm not asking you for 'elp. Just keep clear of the coppers till I 'ave a chance to do me own investigation.'"

Robin stopped for breath, and when she spoke again, she was herself, alone.

"And she did, took to walking the streets at all hours. It became an obsession with her. Then one night, when I was on my way home from an Anti-U meeting, I happened on it. Not quite by accident. I spotted someone I knew, someone who didn't belong in that part of town. I followed him, shadowed him. He was walking with someone else, another man. I overheard things, dreadful things. They knocked on the door of what looked like an empty warehouse, gave a password, and went inside. I was sure I had found the place where the girls must be disappearing. I raced home to tell Pippa."

Robin stopped speaking. The silence lengthened. Katherine felt her own hands shaking, her own throat thickening.

"I never saw her again. She had disappeared, too. I waited a couple of days, asked everyone I knew if they had seen her, searched everywhere, and then I panicked. I went to the police and reported her missing. I told them about the man I had followed and what I had overheard."

Robin fell silent again. Katherine held her breath.

"It was the exact wrong thing to do. The police did nothing. Or worse than nothing. No one was going to help. It was up to me. I did my own investigation. By the time I infiltrated that place it was too late. She was gone. But I kept going back. That's how I found out that it was going to happen. Again."

Katherine took a breath and gathered up her courage.

"But how do you *know*? How can you be sure Pippa was there? How do you know, she was...?"

"Murdered."

The wind hushed all at once. The stream went on and on below.

"I can't tell you how I know; I can't tell anyone," Robin said. "But I do, and I wish I didn't, I wish...."

It's not your fault, Katherine wanted to say. It's not your fault. Instead she reached out for her hand. Robin took it, and they sat silently for what seemed like a long time. Katherine would sit forever if Robin wanted her to.

"Forgive me, Katherine," said Robin at length, "I don't mean to intrude, but there is something I must ask you."

Katherine could feel her heart beating faster. Anything, ask me anything.

"Do you think your people are looking for you?"

"My people?" she repeated. *My people Israel*, the phrase went through her mind. *Let my people go.*

"Your family," Robin clarified. "Do you have parents, Katherine?"

Katherine looked at her, puzzled. Of course she did, and if she did....

"I'm only asking, because not everyone does. I don't, for example."

Maybe she had sprung from the forest, Katherine thought wildly. With Robin anything was possible. Maybe she really was a dryad.

"They're dead," she said, almost lightly, but the word was so heavy. Dead parents, dead. "If your parents are living," Robin went on, "surely they are trying to find you."

Living, her parents, living. She had almost forgotten them; or forgotten they had anything to do with her. Katherine felt confused, even panicky, almost the way she had when she woke in that room and didn't know where she was.

"They're in America," Katherine began uncertainly. "I was staying with my aunt and uncle...."

She trailed off. She did not know how to connect one thing to the other. When she was in that other place, with those things being done to her, she couldn't. Her hair had been dyed, she'd worn knickers so that men could take them off and do things to her. All that had nothing to do with her life before.

"Your aunt and uncle would have told your parents when you went missing," Robin said gently. "They would have filed a police report."

Ten to one the police are in on it, Pippa had said. Bess, who was Doreen, had said so, too. A new horror dawned on her. What if—

"But they can't come here." Katherine turned to Robin, resisting the urge to fling her arms around her. "I don't want the police to come here and find you. You're an outlaw. You can't get caught!"

"Oh, you sweet child." Robin reached for her and Katherine was encircled, her head against Robin's heart. "You darling girl."

Robin's heart was so loud, so strong.

"Now listen to me."

Robin held Katherine away from her, hands still on her shoulders.

"I am an outlaw. I take my chances. You have a place here as long as you need it. But I am thinking your parents might want to know you are alive."

Katherine hadn't let herself feel it before, what her parents might feel, or anyway her mother. She still couldn't think about her father. But now she imagined her mother, how sad her mother must be. Her mother still missed Hal. Katherine did not think she was as good as Hal. Her mother could not love her as much. But still, she didn't want her mother to think she was dead, too.

"My mother," she said, and then she began to weep.

And Robin held her again and rocked her.

"We can get you home," Robin said. "Don't you worry about me. Not a bit of it. I am a very clever outlaw. I'll be all right. Not to worry, my dear, not to worry. We'll get you home again."

Katherine tore herself away from Robin and looked at her. Robin was beautiful, the most beautiful human being Katherine had ever seen.

"But I don't want to go home, Robin. I want to stay with you here in the forest."

Chapter Sixty-Three

"Spotted dick!" announced Rowena with a flourish.

And she set down on the table something that unfortunately, in Lucy's opinion, resembled its regrettable name. Lucy was about to reassure her friends of its harmlessness when Frankie spoke up.

"Whose was it?"

"Frankie!" said his uncle. "Don't be—"

Rowena's chortling, yes, that was the word for it, drowned him out.

"Aren't you the cheeky one!" she said with obvious approval. "Well, whoever it was, he's better off without it, isn't he?"

Lucy bit back her impulse to admonishment. It would only encourage Rowena.

"Now who'll have some?" she inquired. "Not to worry, loves, it's only a bit of suet."

"Suet!" repeated Frankie. "You mean what you put out for birds to eat?"

"That's right, dearie. Mutton fat. Of course there are lots of other ingredients, currants, lemon and what not. It's very sweet, altogether delish, especially with a bit of custardy cream on top, eh Lucy?"

Lucy blanched and hoped Frankie would not think the unseemly thought that she was shocked to find had come to her mind.

"We used to have spotted dick at school, Lucy. Remember?"

"I do," said Lucy grimly.

She had never particularly cared for it but decided not to say so.

"Right then. Young man?" Rowena appealed to Frankie.

Frankie paused to consider, put off perhaps by the suet. Then he girded his loins.

"Yes," said Frankie. "Yes, I will try some spotted *dick*!"

"That's enough now, Frankie," said Joe again.

But Lucy could see he was having a hard time keeping a straight face. And so, to Lucy's surprise, was Anne. Especially when she caught Joe's eye, which, Lucy noted with alarm, was happening with some frequency.

"Yes, *please*, Frankie," Anne admonished, as if he were her own much younger child.

She attempted severity, but Lucy could see Anne was barely repressing giggles. Really, Lucy told herself, she shouldn't begrudge Anne a moment of diversion from her grief, but to her shame, she found she did.

"Yes, *please*, Miss Troublecock."

"Frankie," Joe admonished weakly, and then he coughed into his napkin.

"You're a little devil," said Rowena, giving Frankie a heaping serving. "But handsome enough to get away with it, I daresay."

Lucy sighed. She felt like the lone grownup among a group of naughty schoolchildren. She suddenly found herself wishing Father James could keep her company. As it was, she took comfort from Sir Night, who had jumped into her lap. She resolved to share her spotted dick.

"Please feel free to smoke, Mrs. Bradley, Mr. Petrone," said Rowena, placing an ashtray between them. For somehow after sitting across from each other at supper, they had ended up side by side.

Lucy had helped Rowena clear and had rinsed and stacked the dishes while Rowena made coffee and filled a decanter of brandy, setting out five snifters.

"Frankie is only sixteen," Lucy informed her.

"I'll just give him a wee drop," Rowena promised. "And I'll thank you to remember, I set the rules in my own house."

Frankie's request for a cigar to go with his drink fell on deaf ears. Nor was he offered a cigarette. He sulked for a moment, then made the best of a drink that had been rather more generously poured than Rowena had promised. Lucy took a healthy sip of her own drink and felt the weight she'd taken on her shoulders ease a bit. Frankie was not just a school boy but something of a knight. The ordinary rules did not apply. Katherine was in peril. They were united in their quest to find her. At least, that's how it felt to Lucy in this moment, despite her annoyance with Rowena. As anyone who'd been in a war knew, you didn't pick your comrades, you didn't always like them, but you would die for them.

"Let's start with the information we already have before we lift the veil," began Rowena.

Lucy saw Anne cast a glance at Joe, just short of eye rolling. Without turning towards her, Joe appeared to catch her look. He nodded slightly and smiled, as if to reassure her. Then they all got down to business, reviewing what they knew from the day of Katherine's disappearance to the present.

"The police found the van," Anne concluded, reporting on the meeting at New Scotland Yard. "It was apparently abandoned in a vacant lot twenty miles to the north of London. They found some blood in the van that matches Katherine's blood type. But they think," she blanched but forced herself to go on, "that it may be menstrual blood rather than blood from a wound."

Frankie stared into his empty brandy snifter, and Rowena got up and poured him some more, which he upended.

"How can they tell?" Frankie asked.

A brave knight, indeed.

"Mucus," said his uncle, a medic, a former policeman, and nurse-in-training, unfazed by bodily fluids.

Unlike poor Anne. Never a drinker, she held out her empty cup to Rowena and took a medicinal dose of brandy.

"Will you tell them the rest?" Anne appealed to Joe.

"The presumed driver of the van, the one who was intercepted, was sent to emergency, and treated for a concussion. The police questioned him later that same day."

She hadn't killed the driver, *she hadn't killed him.* Lucy felt weak with relief. If she'd been standing, her knees might have given way. As it was, she nearly dropped her snifter, catching it just in time with her free hand.

"All right then, Lucy?" asked Rowena. She hardly needed second sight; her sharp little eyes missed nothing. "You look as though you've taken a turn."

"Perfectly all right," Lucy said, but she did not refuse when Rowena added another splash to her glass. "Do continue, Joe."

"The driver is a Caucasian male, average height and build, commercial driver's license. He was paid cash for the delivery of girls to what he was told was the address of some sort of film studio."

"Does the driver recall anything of the attack?" Lucy asked. "Sometimes concussions interfere with memory. Did he describe the...person who attacked him?"

Did he suspect, do police know, she did not ask, that a woman stole the van?

"When the driver first regained consciousness," Joe went on, "he didn't know how he came to be in the hospital. Later he recalled that he'd left the van and gone into an alley to relieve himself. The attack was very sudden. Someone, or something, coming out of nowhere. Apparently, he told the police it felt more like a lightning bolt, than a person."

"How very poetic," murmured Rowena.

"He remembers grabbing the attacker's wrists, slender for a man's. That's the one detail that stuck with him. He doesn't remember anything after that—"

"I kicked him in the groin."

Who was speaking? Lucy felt confused.

"He fell backwards, hit his head and went unconscious. I didn't waste any time, I rifled through his pockets and found the keys."

The silence felt like death. Like a weight pressing down on her chest. She was about to faint. Then Rowena and Joe sprang into action, one on either side of her.

"Put your head between your knees, dear," Rowena said.

Joe was busy taking her pulse. Frankie made himself useful retrieving the snifter that had rolled onto the floor. She heard him uncorking the bottle and pouring more brandy.

"It's all right, Lucy," Anne said, her voice strong, reassuring, a mother's voice, used to comforting frightened children. "It was a dream, the dream you told me about. Like the other dreams where you saw things through the young man's eyes. It's all right."

"Woman," Lucy took a breath and sat up, taking the brandy from Frankie. "She was, is a young woman. Rowena guessed it."

"Guessed?" huffed Rowena.

Lucy ignored her and went on. "Now the other dreams make more sense. She must have disguised herself as a young man, so that she could go into that…club unrecognized."

"So she was spying on the operation," said Frankie.

"Do you have any idea who this young woman might be, Lucy?" Joe asked.

"No, I'm sorry, no. Well-educated, I would say, a member of, or at least able to pass as, aristocracy."

"That's something to go on," said Joe. "We need to have another meeting tomorrow at the Yard."

"Do you think so?" said Rowena slowly. "Do you really think so?"

Joe frowned. "What do you mean, Miss Trebilcock? Why wouldn't we share any relevant information with the police? Do you mean because the information has an unusual source?"

"No, not all," said Rowena. "The police sometimes consult psychics, as you no doubt know. I believe the detective originally assigned to the case showed an interest in Lucy's dreams."

But then Detective Smith-Jones' manner had changed, Lucy remembered. Abruptly.

"Let me ask you this," Rowena went on, "how much information have the police shared with you?"

No one answered for a moment. Joe and Anne exchanged a worried look. Rowena took out her knitting and filled the silence with the click of her needles. Somehow it was not a reassuring sound.

"The officers we spoke with today told us the alleged film studio has been searched," said Joe. "They found it abandoned. No equipment, no office, no paperwork. I'd like to take a look myself, but I believe they would regard any initiative on my part as interference in the official investigation."

Not that he'd never interfered with an investigation before, Lucy considered. "I asked if they had searched the area where the girls were to be picked up in the van," Joe went on. "It's a warehouse district. Lots of places to hide an illegal operation."

"'We'll keep you apprised,'" put in Anne. "That's all the officers would say."

"Of course, it is not unusual for professional law enforcement to keep the details of an investigation out of the public eye," said Joe, his voice trailing off.

"But what you're saying is, something stinks," Frankie cut to the chase. "I bet Miss Troublecock thinks so, too."

"What I think is it might be best if you simply called me Rowena, my lad."

Knit one, purl two, Lucy tried to soothe herself. She wished she had some handwork of her own.

"Mrs. Bradley," said Rowena, "when you were at New Scotland Yard, did you think to inquire for the health of Detective Smith-Jones?"

For a moment, Anne looked stricken, as if accused of a breach of manners.

"No, I didn't," Anne called up her irritation. "Perhaps I should have. It didn't occur to me at the time. I was told that Chief Inspector Hollingsworth is overseeing the case himself. Listen, Miss Troub... Trebilcock, if you think something suspicious is going on, get to the point. Please!"

By way of answer, Rowena laid aside her knitting, stood up and went to the alcove where she kept her tarot cards with Rose Cross backs. Lucy wondered if Rowena intended to draw a card and return to them brandishing The Hanged Man or Death. Instead she opened a drawer of a filing cabinet that seemed prosaic and out of place among her other furnishings. As she rifled through some files, Sir

Night jumped down from the windowsill and stalked the ball of yarn Rowena had carelessly let roll across the floor.

"Ah, here's what I was looking for," said Rowena, and she returned, holding some scraps of newspaper. "I clip things. At the time I don't know why. I get a sort of tingling feeling. It's like pulling a card or being guided to letters on a Ouija board. Sometimes I never find out the significance of a clipping; sometimes I do."

She handed two clippings to Lucy. The first, dated three days ago, described a hit and run accident. The victim, one Richard Smith-Jones, was in a coma at The Royal London Hospital, not far, Lucy knew, from where the white van had been stolen. The police were investigating and welcomed all leads. The second, dated yesterday, was a very short obituary for one Detective Richard Smith-Jones, late of New Scotland Yard.

"Read them aloud, Lucy."

Hands and voice trembling, Lucy complied. Rowena meanwhile went back to her desk and returned with two more clippings, the first with a large headline, dated from last March:

"Renegade Heiress Missing.

Poor Little Rich Girl Roberta Loveridge disappears."

Under the headline was a photograph of a tall, slender girl with blond hair swept carelessly back. She looked pale, perhaps because she wore no make-up. Though she was dressed in drab clothes that might have suited a charwoman, she had the bearing of someone accustomed to striding through the world. Someone who would have an excellent seat on a horse....

The image blurred, and Lucy clutched the table. Eyes closed, she saw the hands of a young man wearing an Oxford ring, so heavy on those slender fingers. She had been inside that slight, strong body. She had looked out through those eyes. All at once, Lucy knew, knew who she'd seen in that waking dream in her garden last autumn, before the nightmares began—the lone figure among the headstones, so full of rage....

"No fainting, Lucy," said Rowena sharply. "There's more."

She handed Lucy another clipping, dated two weeks later, the lurid headline:

"What's one Lawyer at the Bottom of a Wheelie Bin?

No joke: Dustman finds celebrity solicitor George Adcock dead."

Lucy knew this face, too. With her own eyes—no, with Roberta's eyes—she had seen those bland, good looks fall away to reveal something hideous beneath.

"Brace yourself, Lucy. Have another drink. Before we lift the veil, or perhaps I mean *as* we lift the veil, you will tell us all you know about the homicide, I don't call it murder, not yet. And I don't mean the questionable demise of Detective Smith-Jones, poor chap. I mean the killing you dreamed. Last spring, I believe."

"Last spring?" said Anne. "Katherine hadn't even gone to England then!"

"But she started acting weird before she left," put in Frankie, "before the end of school."

"What Lucy dreamed last spring may have had nothing to do with Katherine then," Rowena indulged in another dramatic pause, "but I believe it does now."

"That makes no sense," protested Anne.

"Ah, my dear, surely you know that time doesn't run in a straight line. Much more like a tangled skein of wool. Naughty Sootykins!"

The cat had rolled onto his back, all four claws stuck in the skein.

"And speaking of time, it's just coming twilight. I'll just draw the curtains, shall I?"

No one spoke as Rowena pulled the heavy green curtains together, making the room feel close and secretive. Then she sat down, shooed away her cat, who promptly jumped into Lucy's lap, and picked up her knitting again.

"Now then, Lucy. Sir Night will protect you. Please proceed."

With effort, as if she were still in the dream, Lucy began to speak.

(*He was the shadow now. When the streetlight came on, he stepped outside of the pool of light and kept his vigil.*

It had been so long since he'd left his lair. The ordinary world was so drab compared to the world he'd created, the world no one could guess at from the outside. But something had compelled him to come see for himself, the now-shabby little square in Bloomsbury where his man had followed the American woman and her entourage. The man was not her husband, H. informed him, but a self-styled ex-detective type. That criminally unstylish woman was no better than she should be; the rotten little apple had not fallen from the tree....

What were they playing at?

And why did the lights from the dingy little flat glow so warmly? Why had the big black cat stared at him so intently? Why did he suddenly want his mother, her sloppy comfort? Why had his father taken him away from her?

That woman, the woman swaddled in loose shawls, her head haloed with a turban. Who was she? Had she seen him before she closed the curtains?

Why was he always shut out?)

Chapter Sixty-Four

It had been his mother's idea to invite Jeremiah to dinner. But Gerald had to admit he was glad she had. Sitting alone on the shady terrace, ostensibly tending to the charcoal grill, but really just catching his breath, Gerald wondered why he didn't feel guilty, having a friend over for dinner while his daughter was still missing and his wife still searching. But he didn't. Jeremiah's easygoing presence made them all feel less abandoned and marooned, uselessly waiting for news from Anne.

Anne had called that morning, only to tell him that she'd moved to a hotel. She wouldn't stay on the line long enough to talk to the twins, she was in such a hurry to call New Scotland Yard. (Really, she had hung up on him. Because he had tried to talk to her. About what he had done. Did she know? Deep down, did she know?) She had promised to call back when she knew anything about the van she'd reported to the police, but he hadn't heard from her yet. What time was it in London now? Almost eleven o'clock in the evening. He probably wouldn't hear from her again today.

Gerald took a swig of his beer—he was still eschewing gin—and got up from his lawn chair to check on the charcoal. Soon he could put on the steaks. He'd wanted to make something special for Jeremiah, as a thank you for, well, everything. His mother approved; she doted on Jeremiah. She was inside making home-fried potatoes instead of heating up frozen ones from a package, the way Anne did.

She was also making coleslaw from scratch—which she would insist the twins try, although most vegetables (apart from potatoes) were distasteful to them.

Jeremiah was playing frisbee with Peter, Janie and the dog, who was a fairly good catch but had a tendency to change the game to keep-away. Jeremiah was a game-changer too. Instead of giving chase, as Janie and Peter always did, which only encouraged the dog to run, Jeremiah let out a Bronx whistle. Bear, comically, skidded to a stop, then bounded towards Jeremiah and dropped the frisbee at his feet.

"How did you do that?" Peter wanted to know. "Show me! Show me!"

"Me, too!" said Janie.

Bear frisked and jumped as Jeremiah began a whistling lesson. Gerald stayed with his beer and the grill, content to watch, for a moment having no one who needed attention he wasn't sure how to give, no one to fail. But he was paying attention from a distance, not hiding behind a newspaper or his work. For a moment there was only this. His friend, his children, their fingers crooked in their mouths as they tried to imitate Jeremiah. Maybe for a moment they had forgotten to miss their mother, their sister.

When the phone began to ring, he didn't get up at first, figuring his mother would answer it. But it kept ringing. Anne, he suddenly remembered, Anne. He couldn't miss it, oh God, what if he missed it. He sprinted for the door, almost losing his balance on an uneven flagstone.

"Have you got it, Gerald?" his mother called from somewhere in the yard.

Gerald picked up the phone.

"This is the transatlantic operator," said a British voice. "I have a reverse charge call from—"

"Yes, I'll accept the charges, yes!" he cut her off.

"Very good. You are connected."

"Anne?"

There was a silence on the other end of the line.

"Anne, are you there?"

No answer.

"Operator, Operator? We seem to have been disconnected."

Again, no answer. Maybe he should hang up and call Anne back.

"Who is it, Gerald?" his mother came in the backdoor with a bouquet of black-eyed-susans.

He waved her away, then said, "Go find Anne's hotel number. It's in my office."

There was something about the silence at the other end of the line that seemed strange. He thought he heard the sound of a passing car. Someone was on the other end.

"Anne?" he said again. "Anne, what's wrong?"

"It's me," came a voice almost too soft to hear. "Katherine."

Gerald couldn't speak, couldn't breathe. His mother, coming back into the kitchen, grabbed a chair and made him sit down.

"Katherine?" he managed to croak. "Katherine, where are you?"

Another silence.

"Where are you!" he said again, desperation making him sound angry. "Your mother, I, we—"

"I can't tell you where I am," she said in a stronger voice. "Because I don't know. But you don't need to worry. Tell my mother not to worry about me. I'm all right, I'm...happy."

"Katherine, your mother is in London looking for you. Lucy Way is there, too, with—"

He heard the click of the receiver. The line was dead.

But Katherine, Katherine was alive.

Chapter Sixty-Five

Katherine stood in the telephone booth at the edge of some tiny village with street lamps few and far between, and darkness thick on every side. Robin had helped her place the call, then left her alone with the door open so that the light in the booth went out.

Robin was somewhere out there, waiting for her, but for a moment Katherine could not move. If they hadn't been shaking so hard, she could not have felt her legs. Her hands shook too, still holding on to the receiver she had hung up. She had thought, without thinking, that her mother would answer. She had not thought any further than that. She had only made the call, because Robin wanted her to. Because Robin could never again call her own parents.

Where was Robin? Katherine peered into the darkness beyond the deserted petrol station. A horrible thought struck her. What if Robin had left her? Left her here, lost, to be found by her parents or the police, because Robin knew Katherine would never leave her willingly.

Katherine took a blind step out the booth and almost stumbled. Her legs did not know where to go. Her eyes did not know where to look. She wanted to cry out for Robin, but she knew she must not. Robin was an outlaw. She had taken a risk driving Katherine on the motor scooter she kept hidden ("for emergencies," she'd explained) away from the safety of the deep forest to this sleeping town.

"I am sorry to have to blindfold you," Robin had said gently before they'd set out. "It's for your own protection and for mine."

"Of course," Katherine had said. "I understand."

But she didn't really understand anything. Even less now than she had before. Why her father was at home and her mother and Lucy here—in England!—looking for her. (Did she want to be found?) Why she had hung up on her father. He'd sounded angry with her. That was nothing new. And of course, it was her fault, all her fault that she'd caused her mother worry. And Lucy. Lucy. And they were looking for her.

"Robin," Katherine whispered, beginning to panic, "Robin!"

And Robin, a tall shadow stepping out of the shadows, was right there.

"All right then?" She slipped her arm around Katherine's waist, as if she knew Katherine needed help to stand. "Did you reach someone at home?"

And they began walking towards a clump of shrubbery where Robin had hidden the motor scooter.

"My father," said Katherine. "I...I didn't want to talk to him."

She hoped Robin would ask her why. Then maybe Katherine could tell what she had never told anyone. (Except the Aramantha in her head who knew everything. But Aramantha hadn't spoken to her, not since Katherine had defied her and run after Robin.)

"And your mother?" was all Robin said.

"She's in London," Katherine forced down the lump in her throat, "looking for me, and so is..." she paused, not sure how to describe Lucy Way, but knowing she had to somehow, "so is my fairy godmother, Lucy, Lucy Way."

"Ah," said Robin, as if that explained everything. "But of course you have a fairy godmother."

Robin took hold of the motor scooter, turned it towards the road, then stopped.

"Of course," Robin said again. "Lucy, Lucy Way."

A shiver went through Katherine. Robin spoke Lucy Way's name as if she knew Lucy. Knew her better than Katherine did. Maybe

Katherine didn't know Lucy at all anymore. Or Lucy didn't know her, couldn't know her. After what had happened, what she had done.

"Oh, Katherine, Katherine," said Robin. "I didn't think, how could I not have thought!"

"Thought what?" asked Katherine, thoroughly alarmed.

"Your mother, Lucy Way, if they're looking for you, they could be in danger."

Katherine's stomach turned over. More harm, more harm she had done, more harm she was doing.

"It's my fault, not yours," Robin insisted, wheeling the bike to the road. "Not to worry. I shall talk to my fairy godfather. He'll help."

"You have a fairy godfather?"

"So to speak!" she laughed out loud, but did not share the joke with Katherine. "Hop on. We daren't linger here."

"Shouldn't you blindfold me?" Katherine reminded her.

"It's so dark," said Robin. "Let's not bother. Just close your eyes but mind you don't fall asleep. Hold on tight."

Katherine climbed onto the small uncomfortable seat and put her arms around Robin. The engine masked her trembling. As the scooter tore off down the dark road, she rested her head on Robin's back, between her shoulder blades where her fairy wings lay furled.

Chapter Sixty-Six

"What say all of you," said Rowena, "do we go to the police about Katherine's call? Or do we keep matters in our own hands? I, for one, agree with our young friend that there is something rotten in the state of New Scotland Yard."

The five of them were sitting in Rowena's tiny parlor, cups of tea or coffee (surprisingly good coffee, Anne thought) in hand. It was the middle of the night. Anne had decided the news of Katherine's call to Gerald could not wait till morning. She, Joe and Frankie had thrown on raincoats over the pajamas. Lucy and Rowena had on bathrobes over their nightgowns.

"I'm afraid that particular matter is out of our hands," Anne said. "Gerald tried to trace the call right away. He called a transatlantic operator, who told him to report it to New Scotland Yard. Then he called me. He thought he had to report it immediately. Who is to say he was wrong?"

Anne was surprised at her calm and the absence of her age-old impulse to blame Gerald. Even inside Rowena's flat, with the heavy curtains drawn, Anne could hear a midnight bell ring its changes. *Your daughter is living,* Anne sang along silently. Her daughter was alive, Katherine was alive. Really alive, not just in Lucy's dreams or Rowena's vision. Alive on the other end of a transatlantic phone call.

"Any of us would have done it," said Joe. "He probably thought if he acted quickly enough, someone could find her. Maybe the police could have, if they had been able to pinpoint her location and rouse the local police. Somewhere in the Midlands was as close as they could get. I think we can assume that the police have issued an all-points bulletin with Katherine's description."

"The Midlands. Clever," remarked Rowena. "From there, you could go anywhere. North, South, East, West. That's why it's called the Midlands."

"So, you think her kidnapper chose the location for that reason?" said Joe.

"Very likely," said Rowena. "But why do you persist in believing she's been kidnapped. instead of rescued?"

"I'm sorry," said Joe. "I don't want to upset anyone. I don't think we can rule out the possibility. If this young woman did in fact kill someone and is in hiding, why would she lumber herself with Katherine and the others? That's a huge risk to take, unless she's at least considering using them as hostages. Also, Katherine said she didn't know where she was. That's common in kidnapping."

"Or maybe," said Frankie, "maybe Katherine doesn't want to be found."

There was a moment's perturbed silence.

"Tell us again, Anne," said Lucy. "What exactly did Katherine say to Gerald."

"Not much," said Anne. "She hung up abruptly."

She hadn't told them the most important part. She was still clutching it to herself.

"She probably didn't want the call traced," said Frankie. "Don't the police always keep the bad guy on the line as long as they can so they can find out where he is. But he knows what they're doing, so he hangs up."

"That's just in the movies, Frankie," said his uncle.

"But Katherine might have thought it was true, same as me," said Frankie. "She's the one who hung up."

Anne hesitated, hoping and fearing that Frankie might be right.

"Katherine did say one more thing to Gerald," Anne decided the others had to know. "She said...she said she was happy."

No one spoke for a moment. Anne, in a strangely heightened state, could almost hear what they weren't saying. Joe didn't want to tell her how captives sometimes admired, even fell in love with their captors. Frankie was like a puppy, pulling at a leash, ready to follow any scent. Lucy was standing on some fine edge, gazing into the unseen, a glimmer of dawn along a far ridge. As for Rowena, she was a dark mass at the edge of Anne's awareness.

"But why?" Anne could not hold back anymore. "Why doesn't she want to come home?"

"Do you really want to know?" Rowena asked. "Are you ready to know?"

Anne could not look at the woman. It took all her will not to get up and bolt from the room.

"That's easy," Frankie suddenly spoke up. "I can tell you, Mrs. Bradley."

Had he ever addressed her by name before?

"She's living in the woods. Didn't you say you saw a treehouse, Miss...Rowena? Katherine's always wanted to live in the woods. Me and Katherine both. Lucy, you've known that about Katherine and me ever since you found us in the woods when we were kids. Of course Katherine doesn't want to go back to boring, old home. She's afraid if you find her, you'll make her go."

"Frankie!" cautioned his uncle.

"It's all right," said Anne, feeling fonder of Frankie than she ever had before. "Frankie probably understands her better than the rest of us."

The menace of Rowena receded like a wave that would inevitably rise again.

"Yes," agreed Lucy. "But I would wager all of us can remember being young, making blind choices, getting into trouble, not sure of the way out."

What was happening to her, Anne wondered? Suddenly she could see a young Lucy, curled into a self-protective ball on a narrow bed in a shabby room.

"Did you dream last night, Lucy?" asked Anne. "Is there any more you can tell us?"

"I've had nothing more since arriving in England other than glimpses of a forest. Perhaps it's proximity. I'm too...close to whoever, whatever this...young woman is."

"But where is this forest?" demanded Frankie. "Can't you look into your crystal ball or something, Miss Rowena?"

"I could," acknowledged Rowena, "but in this case, I don't need to. I agree with your uncle. If our renegade heiress, one Roberta Loveridge, a good old Herefordshire name, by the way, is the woman of Lucy's dreams, then she's on the lam. The police must have made the connection between her disappearance and the body in the wheelie bin. The estate where she spent or misspent her youth borders one of the last wild forests in Britain. Someone who knows the terrain well could disappear there."

Beyond the quiet square, ambulance or police sirens sounded, trucks shifted gears, cars honked. A mouse stirred in the wainscoting and Sir Night went on the prowl. The bells chimed the half hour, half past midnight. *Your daughter is living.*

"I'm sorry, Miss Trebilcock," said Joe, "but from the point of view of law enforcement, that's the first place the police would look for her. With dogs and helicopters, it's hard to see how she could hide for long."

"Unless," put in Frankie, "there are reasons why someone doesn't want her found. Or not found alive. Like she might have the goods on someone."

Katherine is alive, Anne clung to the thought. *She spoke to Gerald not quite two hours ago. She is happy, happy with a...killer.*

"What we don't know," said Rowena, "is whether the police—or anyone else—have made the connection between the apparent young man who stole the van and the young woman who went missing some four months ago and very likely killed a man."

"Look into your crystal ball!" demanded Frankie.

Anne surprised herself by nodding agreement.

Rowena made no answer except to stand and pile the cups and plates on a tray.

"You three," she indicated Anne, Joe, and Frankie, "go back to your hotel and get a couple of hours' sleep if you can while I get in touch with an old friend. Then pack what you need, but don't check out of the hotel. Don't tell anyone where you're going."

That much was easy, Anne considered. She wouldn't know how.

"And Mrs. Bradley. You had better tell your husband not to ring you for the next few days."

"Is all this subterfuge necessary?" Anne felt that things were suddenly moving way too fast. "Do you really think we are in danger from the police?"

Then she thought of Detective Smith-Jones, how kind he had been to her, how thorough.

"Not. Only. The. Police."

Rowena stopped on her way to the kitchen and turned to look, not at them, but through them. Suddenly the cups began to rattle. Lucy rose and took the tray from Rowena and set it next to the sink. Joe helped Rowena sit down, and then went to stand beside Anne, so close she could feel his warmth.

"We have to find her first," Rowena said in a low voice, as if talking to herself. Then she looked at them all. "We have to get there first."

Chapter Sixty-Seven

He is looking for her. Even though she is pressed up against the wall where the door will hide her when it swings open, she can see him padding through the halls of that horrible place. She can see his top hat and his slithering slippers. She is all alone in the building. No one will hear her if she screams.

He comes to her door. He scrabbles at it like a rat. He is a rat, dressed in a tux and tails that do not hide his long scaly tail. The door creaks open, slowly. She can't see him anymore, but she hears him breathing. Then he starts to whimper.

I love you, I love you so much.

It is her father's voice. He is her father in disguise.

She tiptoes out from behind the door and he whirls around and grabs her, crushing her into himself, crushing and whimpering and pressing himself onto her and into her.

She has a knife. She bought it with her own money at the rummage sale.

He is pressing himself into her knife. He is falling on her. She can't breathe.

Get off me! She tries to scream. *Get off me!*

"Warbler, wake up, Warbler, it's all right!"

It was dark, but she could breathe, even though she was shaking all over. Someone was blocking her view of branches and stars.

Branches and stars, branches and stars. She was outside in the tree-house. She was safe, safe as treehouses.

"Bess?" Katherine said. "I mean Doreen?"

"'ush now," she whispered. "You was just 'aving a bad dream, I reckon. I 'ave 'em, too. I'll 'old your 'and for a bit, if you like."

She and Doreen lay on their sides, facing each other, Doreen's hands cradling hers. Katherine did like it.

"I dreamed about him, about Mister Tobias," Katherine said after a moment.

She spoke in her own American voice, without dropping h's, though she hadn't yet told anyone but Robin where she was from. If Doreen noticed, she didn't say.

"That's a nightmare, that is," Doreen agreed.

"Do you think he's trying to find us?" Katherine asked.

It had alarmed Katherine to see Robin so alarmed. When they'd gotten back to the forest, Robin had said a quick goodnight, told Katherine to get some sleep, and then disappeared into the wood before Katherine could say a word. Was she going to the Fairy God-father? In her mind Katherine pictured him as a bear living in a hollow tree, wearing a dressing gown. He would gather Robin into a bear hug and make her a cup of tea. He would keep them all safe.

Her mother and Lucy, too.

"Dunno. But why else would our Robin go to such trouble to make sure nobody knows where this place is. Not even us."

Our Robin. How comforting and comfortable it sounded. Our Robin. It was true, none of them knew where they were. The ride to and from the payphone had taken at least an hour and lots of twists and turns along country lanes. When she had climbed into the treehouse and found her way back to her cot, all the others had been asleep, worn out by a long day outdoors. Most of the others were not used to so much time in the open air.

"Do you like being here, Doreen?" she asked.

Doreen was so quiet, Katherine wondered if she had fallen asleep again.

"Didn't think I would at first," she said at length. "It's a bit of all right, innit? Like going to bloody girls' guide camp, which I never 'ad the chance. Me, I'm going to learn archery. Then if Mister Tobias and 'is lot should chance to find us, we'll see wot's wot. Like to see 'im wiv a feather stickin' out 'is arse."

Katherine started to laugh silently, and Doreen did, too.

"Stop," said Doreen. "We're shakin' the 'ole treehouse. Everyone'll think we're 'avin it off."

That sobered Katherine up.

"But I'm not..." Katherine didn't know what word to use. "Are you?"

"Not what? Not a lezzie, not a muff muncher?" Doreen paused for a moment. "Like our Robin."

Suddenly the endearment sounded insinuating instead of comforting. Katherine rolled onto her back, letting go of Doreen's hands as she did.

Pippa was my beloved, Robin had said, *my true love.* They had loved each other.

"Maybe you knows more about it than I do." Doreen rolled onto her own back. "Riding off into the night with our fearless leader on a motor scooter."

"No!" protested Katherine. "I mean maybe Robin is a...a lesbian." That was the correct term; it didn't mean anything bad. She had heard her mother refer to Elsa Ebersbach and Clara Barker as lesbians. "But she didn't, she never—"

But what if she had? Katherine loved Robin. Could she love her that way? Did she?

"Don't get your knickers in a twist, Warbler. So wot if you wasn't sneaking off to 'ave it off—not that I care, mind, after all we been through wiv blokes could make for a nice change. Might give it a try meself one of these day—then where did you go?"

Katherine debated for a moment whether she wanted to tell Doreen anything. But if her mother and Lucy were in danger because they were looking for her, her friends might be in danger, too. And it would be her fault. Again.

"I called my parents in America."

"Cor! I knew it!"

Doreen rolled towards her again, then sat up. Katherine couldn't see her eyes in the dark, but she could feel her staring. Or glaring.

"I knew you was a bloody Yank. And you 'ave *parents*! Crikey. Wotever was you doin' in that place then? Come to that, wot are you doin' 'ere?"

Doreen was angry, and why shouldn't she be? Katherine had deceived everyone. Or tried to.

"If you 'ave folks in America, folks as you can ring up, why don't you bloody go 'ome?"

It wasn't that easy! Katherine sat up, too.

"Just because I'm American—"

"And rich!" Doreen interrupted. "I bet you're rich. That's why you and Robin is thick as thieves, know all the same churchy 'ymns and that."

"I'm not rich!" protested Katherine.

Being rich was almost as bad as being selfish. You couldn't get into heaven or get your camel through the needle's eye or whatever that parable was. But, she could almost hear her father expounding, compared to Doreen, she *was* rich or anyway privileged.

"And wot if I am?" Katherine slipped back into cockney; she didn't know how to defend herself in her own voice. "You don't know wot 'appened to me before I come 'ere to your bloody, pervy country." No one does, she did not say, not even Robin. "You don't know noffink about me, except I been through the same 'ell as you 'ave in that place. And if Robin 'adn't rescued us, I'd be just as dead!"

Doreen surprised her by reaching out and patting her arm.

"True enough, Warbler, true enough. Except your name ain't Warbler."

"It is," insisted Katherine. "You gave me the name yourself."

"All right then," acknowledged Doreen, "but it's a nickname, see? Wot's your real name then? You're the only one as 'asn't told. Can't be worse than mine."

She took a deep breath. It was time.

"My name is Katherine," she said. "Like three out of Henry the Eighth's six wives, only I think they spelled their names with a C."

Doreen blew a raspberry and some of her spittle landed on Katherine's cheek.

"You don't need to give me a bleedin' 'istory lesson, Yank. I know 'oo 'enry the Eighth is and wot 'e done, the ugly old wanker. I seen pictures of 'im. Come to think of it, 'e looks just like Mister Tobias, don't 'e?"

"You're right!" Katherine said, and they both started to shake with laughter again.

"You don't want to be named after none of 'is wives," said Doreen when she caught her breath. "'ow 'bout we call you Kat?"

"Kat," she repeated. No one had ever abbreviated her name, not her mother, Lucy, Frankie, or Aramantha. Maybe that was who she was now. Kat, who lived in the greenwood with Robin Hoodlum and the merry maids.

"Right then, Kat," said Doreen, "let's get some sleep before the bloody birds start their racketing."

They lay down again facing each other again. She was glad Doreen had not asked anything more about her parents. Or whether they were trying to find her. What if her mother and Lucy found her? What if they didn't? What if Mister Tobias....

"I killed him," Katherine whispered. "In my dream, I killed him."

Mister Tobias, her father.

"If he ever comes here, I will. I won't let him hurt us. Or Robin. Or anyone."

"Go to sleep now, Kat," murmured Doreen. "No more nightmares."

They fell asleep holding hands.

Chapter Sixty-Eight

Gerald sat on the couch in the living room, the only light coming from the muted TV where the late night news flickered and flared. He was shaking all over. Jeremiah had gotten up to turn the television off, but Gerald told him to leave it. He wanted blue light, the blurred serious faces, just not the voices, the relentless noise of ongoing crisis.

Jeremiah sat back down on the couch next to him, placing his hand lightly on Gerald's back. (Light as sunlight on a spring morning a long time ago, when he was still a child. He wished he could be a child again with everything in his life undone. *Except ye…become as little children, ye shall not enter into the kingdom of heaven….*)

Gerald did not know how he would have gotten through the evening without Jeremiah. He had kept the children occupied while Gerald frantically tried to trace Katherine's call. He had taken over grilling the steaks while Gerald called Anne.

(Had he and Anne ever been closer than in that moment? *Katherine called, she's alive.* Or more far away, far more than an ocean separating them.)

They hadn't talked long. Just long enough for him to tell her that the police had traced the call to the Midlands. And one other thing.

"Anne, I don't know what to think, but Katherine said she is happy."

Happy.

"Oh, Gerald" was all Anne said.

He could not hear any reproach in her voice. Only sorrow and something else he did not know how to name. They had never been closer.

"I've got to go," she'd said. "I've got to tell the others."

Or more far away.

"Me, too," he'd said, but she was already gone.

When he told the twins, during dinner, that Katherine was alive, Janie had put down her fork and started to sob. He had gotten up and gone to hold her and she had clung to him. Then, to his surprise, Peter had gotten up from his place, wrapped his arms around Gerald and buried his face in Gerald's side. Out of the corner of his eye, he saw Jeremiah attempting to get up, no doubt to slip away discreetly, but his mother grabbed hold of Jeremiah's wrist and made him sit. She'd kept a tight hold on his friend's arm and buried her face in her other hand. He did not know how long the five of them had stayed like that, wordless, holding on to each other or how long they might have gone on if Bear hadn't started jumping and whining at the window.

"He wants Katherine back, too," said Peter, and he went to let the dog in.

Bear promptly scrambled under the table and sat at Janie's feet. Neither Gerald nor his mother had the heart to scold Janie for feeding the dog tidbits of steak.

At last the twins and his mother had gone to bed after endless rounds of gin rummy that Jeremiah had cheerfully endured. Gerald knew he should have let the long-suffering Jeremiah take his leave. But before he could grab his hat, so to speak, because he hadn't been wearing one in the summer heat, Gerald had pressed a beer on him.

"Stay and watch the news?" more a plea than an invitation.

Now here they were, not watching the news, sitting close together on the couch, Jeremiah's hand rubbing circles of comfort into Gerald's back. The same couch where he wrecked his daughter's life— and everyone else's. He thought of saying something, but Jeremiah was not impressed with breast beating.

"You got to face yourself," Jeremiah had said.

What did that mean, if he hadn't even had the guts to tell Anne? How would he ever make amends to Katherine?

I'm happy, she had said.

What did that mean?

Happy she'd gotten away. From him.

The phone rang. Gerald sprang from the couch, stumbling over the coffee table as he sprinted for his office.

"Hello?"

"Gerald, it's Anne. No, no news. Listen, Gerald. Don't call me at the hotel for the next few days."

"What?" He couldn't form a more coherent question.

She was quiet for a moment. He could almost hear her carefully choosing words and phrases.

She didn't trust him, it dawned on him. He was not to be trusted.

"We are going to look for Katherine."

We. Lucy, Anne, Frankie. And Joe. Joe Petrone.

"Lucy has a friend. I don't know if I've told you much about her." Or anything at all.

"She's an old school friend of Lucy's, Rowena Trebilcock. She's a...she has some idea where Katherine is, who she's with. We think Katherine might have been rescued."

"Rescued?"

"From someone or something much worse than where she is now."

"Do the police know?" Gerald asked.

There was another silence that held all Anne didn't want to tell him.

"That's just it, Gerald. We think...we think it's better we follow up on our own. So please, please don't say anything to the police. We...."

He was starting to hate that pronoun.

"I don't like the sounds of this, Anne. Not telling the police. No one knowing where you are."

Him not knowing, her husband.

"Trust me, Gerald. Please just trust me."

He owed her one, even if it killed him...or left him out, left him powerless.

"All right, Anne." His throat was too thick to say more.

"I'll call you, Gerald, as often as I can. Are the twins, did you tell the twins...?"

"Yes, they're, well, they want her to come home, of course. They're...."

He wished he could tell Anne: I held them, we cried together.

"Jeremiah came over for dinner this evening," he said instead. "He's been a big help."

"Oh, good," said Anne. "Listen Gerald, I've got to go. We're leaving before dawn."

We.

And she was gone.

Gerald replaced the receiver and slowly walked back to the living room.

Jeremiah, thank God, Jeremiah was still here.

Chapter Sixty-Nine

Lucy leaned back her head and closed her eyes, attempting to get comfortable in the Land Rover (circa 1944). Rowena had borrowed (or commandeered it, Lucy wasn't sure which) from a mechanic she'd known (rather well, she implied) when she served in the Auxiliary Territorial Service in the war. He had a collection of antique vehicles. Rowena hinted that this wartime flame might still carry a torch for her. (It must be true, for apparently, he had also agreed to feed Sir Night and water the plants.) Lucy only hoped he had preserved his mechanical skills. The slightest bump in the road felt like an explosion, with the frame ready to unhinge and fly out in all directions. Surely the engine, which Rowena's erstwhile swain swore had a working muffler, announced their approach for miles in advance.

Joe, with as much tact as possible, had inquired if they couldn't find something more up-to-date and nondescript and suggested that maybe he could rent a car, as a tourist, without rousing suspicion.

"No, no," said Rowena. "This is just the ticket. We may need to drive off-road."

Frankie, in contrast to his uncle, had pronounced the Land Rover "cool." Rowena had rewarded him by designating him her navigator and installing him in the passenger seat beside her. It was Lucy's own fault that she had waved away Joe's gallant insistence that she should have the slightly more capacious front seat. Anne also declined the front, preferring, Lucy suspected, Joe's proximity to Rowena's.

Joe sat in back in the middle, straddling the seats (it couldn't have been comfortable) Lucy on his left and Anne on his right. He had a better view of the road than they did and could also peer over Frankie's shoulder at the map and backseat navigate. Rowena had been equally insistent on plotting a circuitous course. Joe and Anne had wanted to retrace the van's route as far as possible, stopping where it had been found abandoned to see if they could find any clues about what route the kidnapped/rescued crew had taken and in what sort of conveyance.

"No, no, no!" Rowena had insisted, as she'd loaded a wicker picnic hamper with sandwiches, fruit, thermoses of tea, and a bottle of brandy. "That place will be crawling with police and reporters scavenging for their scandal sheets. We don't want to be seen anywhere near there. We'd be sure to be followed. Besides we don't need to trace Miss Loveridge's exact route. We know where she went. Well, roughly," she'd conceded. "Not to worry, my dears, we shall be guided."

And with that they had all clambered into the antique vehicle and racketed off through drizzly dawn.

Lucy was just as glad conversation in the car was impossible. However loud and uncomfortable the drive, it gave Lucy time to retreat into herself. Since she had gotten into Joe's limo, she had not been alone except for a couple of hours of exhausted sleep in Rowena's tiny guestroom. They had left the outskirts of London some time ago, departing the highway for smaller and smaller roads, winding deeper into the countryside on lanes not wide enough for two vehicles. Fortunately, it was still very early and a Sunday, Lucy believed. It was hard to keep track of time. Despite the jolting ride and the loud engine, she settled into silence and gazed at the countryside, fields of ripening grain, lone trees rising up out of the mist, muddy foot paths, flocks of equally muddy sheep. She remembered her brief excursions into the country used to comfort her during the war. Despite rationing, children billeted out with strangers, the English landscape had its own timeless pull. She could believe then that all time was concurrent, flowing, eddying, sometimes almost still, bearing all its sons and daughters away....

Lucy felt her head fall to her chin and forced herself awake again. She wanted to think. Last night after the others had gone back to their hotel, she had read the news clippings. The headline had been deceptive. Roberta Loveridge was in fact not the heir to the estate where she'd grown up, not after a much younger brother was born to her stepmother, a socialite née Priscilla Benton-Burton. Here was where the story went beyond the bounds of even the saddest fairy-tales: Roberta's father had died, too, in a hunting accident. Her step-mother had remarried, a prominent solicitor, one George Adcock, the man Lucy had recognized in the other clipping. And yet there was no mention in that story of his connection to the missing erstwhile heiress, nor any speculation that Roberta Loveridge might be a sus-pect in his death. Odd, unless Frankie was right. No one wanted her found. Alive.

Lucy shuddered. She could still feel her fingers closing around his neck, hear the sound of his head smashing against the pavement. If she had killed him (she had killed him) it wasn't over an inheritance.

It was your bullet!

Where's Pippa! Where are all the others?

Others, like Katherine. Others Roberta Loveridge had come back to London to spirit away. Were they hiding in a place you could find with a map or had they gone through some gap in a hedgerow to another world...? Lucy gazed out the window, trying to keep her eyes open, but her head felt heavy as a fieldstone and she was suddenly chilled. She let herself lean ever so slightly into the warmth. Oh, that was Joe, with Anne on his other side....

The warmth grows stronger, it makes a cheerful crackling sound, a little campfire in a wood. Katherine sits there with some other girls, all of them huddled together. They are laughing. They sound like a gabble of geese, a gaggle of girls. And somehow Lucy is there with them, not seeing from inside that tall, lean body so easily mistaken for a boy's. This time she is sitting beside the young woman. Only no one can see Lucy. Perhaps she is a ghost....

"Come on, Lucy Way," someone speaks her name in a low, sweet voice.

Then she and another little girl, (they are both little girls) are walking hand in hand through an old forest full of trees with faces, some kind, some frightening. With their free hands they are dropping breadcrumbs to mark their way.

"But the birds will eat them," some old woman in a rattling car strains to make herself heard.

The other girl laughs, a rich, happy laugh, light splashing on a stream.

"Good. Then that man will never find us...we will be safe, safe forever and ever...."

All at once, Lucy's body slammed against the side door. She woke in a panic to the car bobbing and pitching as if it were a boat. It looked as if they were going to drive right into a hedge and then Rowena swerved at the last minute and cut the engine. The shock of silence made Lucy's heart pound.

"Have we broken down?" Lucy whispered.

"It's possible that we are being followed," said Joe. "Not certain but possible."

"Ford Cortina," said Frankie. "1966."

"They wouldn't have been able to drive through that mud. You were right to choose a vehicle that can drive off road, Rowena," Joe conceded gallantly.

"But what if they follow on foot?" Anne sounded scared.

"Then they will find some day trippers having a country picnic," said Rowena.

"In the fog and drizzle?" asked Joe. "Wouldn't that seem odd?"

"Not in the British Isles," said Rowena. "We do it all the time. Which brings up a point. You are all Americans. And I'll lay odds whoever is following us—"

"If they are," Joe put in.

"Well, very likely they know Katherine is American. Lucy can pass as a Brit, but if you don't mind, I'll do the talking. Now who would like a sandwich?"

Lucy suddenly realized she was famished. There was a thermos of coffee in the hamper, she believed, and she wouldn't mind a cup with a drop of brandy.

"I don't think we should stop for a picnic," Frankie objected.

"Afraid of a little rain?" Rowena teased.

"No, I'm afraid they'll get ahead of us."

Rowena shook her head. "They're following us for a reason. They don't know where she is. And they think we do."

Lucy found herself feeling a little light-headed. She knew there was something faulty in the reasoning, but she couldn't pinpoint what it was.

"Hey, wait a minute," said Frankie. "What if they saw that newspaper clipping, too? The bad guys, I mean. What if they figured out that he was a she in disguise? What if they know as much as we do? What if they're following us to try to stop *us* getting there first?"

There was a moment of appalled silence.

"Bugger," said Rowena at last. "Bugger all."

Under the circumstances, Lucy decided, foul language might be excused.

"Right then, troops," said Rowena firing up the engine again. "Grab a sandwich if you're hungry and hold onto your hats. We're pressing on."

(External reality was so clumsy, so crude. He cursed himself for ever allowing it to penetrate the walls of his citadel. He could have disposed of his own problems much more elegantly and efficiently. Then they wouldn't have been problems at all. Did one consider it a problem to pour away cream that had gone off or to replace wilted flowers with fresh ones? Now here he was in a cramped car—modern conveyances were not made for men of his majesty—with its wheels spinning in the mud till he told that hairy jackal to desist. The other one, the bleached blond gorilla, had wanted to give chase on foot. He'd had to extricate himself from the tiny contraption to call the vicious brute to heel. At least the gorilla, with his dumb strength re-directed, was able to push the kiddy car out of the mud.

He knew where they were going, the American woman and her bizarre entourage, with their pathetic attempt at subterfuge. Once they knew they were being followed, they'd panicked. They were bound to get lost or stymied by some impassable sty. It would take them one or two eternities to cross the country. Meanwhile, he would direct the half-dwarf to turn the car back to the highway.

He would win this race.

The spoiled spoils would be his.

His alone.

They would be dead, and he would be gone.

He patted his waistcoat. It was there, too small for anyone to notice, precise, elegant, lethal.)

Chapter Seventy

Sometimes being awake seemed like a dream to Katherine, a good dream, the kind you wanted to go on dreaming. The afternoon had turned warm after a damp, chilly morning. After breakfast they'd gone to cut hazel saplings in a swampy part of the forest and now they wove them in and out of the uprights Robin already had in place. Their girl chatter and the birds' chatter all blended together.

"Sort of like basket-weaving, innit?" one of them said.

"Wot you know about basket-weaving then?"

"Juvie. Occupational therapy. 'oo knew it would come in so 'andy?"

Then a silence might fall, broken by laughter or good-natured cursing. Katherine taught them silly songs she'd learned at summer camp (long ago now it seemed), some of them British to begin with, "*I'm 'enery the eighth, I am.*" and "*I've got sixpence, jolly, jolly sixpence.*" Doreen was right. Living in the greenwood was like being at camp, being kids again. Except it wasn't. They weren't going home at the end of the summer. They had no other homes.

You do so have a home, Katherine Bradley, said Aramantha-in-her-head, the first time she'd spoken in the greenwood.

Katherine did her best to ignore her.

If only this afternoon could go on forever, warm and green and golden as they wove their own nest, cheerful and certain as birds.

Then Robin, who had been weaving inside the hut, stepped outside and stretched.

"Righty-ho," she said. "It's coming along splendidly. We'll be ready to start mixing daub tomorrow."

"You mean the shite?" said Bernadette. "I forgot about that bit."

"Not just shit," said Robin, "mud and straw as well. If you can carry on with the wattle, I'll fetch a load of straw and manure."

"Where you going to get manure?" asked Maggie (who still seemed like a Daisy Mae to Katherine). "I ain't seen no cows around here. Nor pigs come to that."

"She's going to steal it, wot else?" said Vicky, formerly known as Fifi (she liked to be addressed that way). "That's our Robin 'oodlum."

"Whoever heard of stealing shite?"

"There's people as pays good money for manure," said Maggie. "Ladies as wants to win prizes for their roses, don't yer know. So stands to reason you can steal it."

"Gold," put in Sarita. "Black gold."

No one seemed to notice that Robin hadn't answered their questions.

"Back in a trice," she said, and began to walk out of the clearing where they were building the hut, into the deeper wood.

"Wait," called Katherine. "I'll go with you! I can help shovel."

"Hark at her," said Maggie. "Me, I never had to ask. Where I comes from, they just hands me the shovel."

There were titters and teasing, but Katherine ignored the others, keeping her attention on Robin, who had turned her back but seemed to hesitate.

"All right then. Come along, Kat."

Katherine ran to catch up with her.

"The name Kat suits you," said Robin as they followed the stream away from the encampment. "You're rather like a cat. The way you leap from rock to rock. You've got good balance, you know how to land on your feet. I daresay you were a tomboy, like me."

Katherine was glad they were walking. Silence was less awkward that way, and she didn't know what to say. She felt too shy and happy. She had been told she was bright, and she knew she got good grades, or used to before she refused to study. She knew she could sing. But she'd never liked gym or team sports. No one had ever noticed the way she moved. And that Robin should say so, Robin who was so strong and graceful.

"Have you always been called Robin?" she asked after a moment.

"Someone gave it to me as a nickname when I was very small. My christened name," she grimaced, "is Roberta. Such a clumsy name, don't you agree?

Katherine nodded, earnestly.

"I mean, look here, if you want to name a girl after her pater—"

They paused for breath at the top of the steep hill, looking down at the encampment, just visible under the canopy.

"Probably best," Robin said after a moment, "that you not know too much about me, my full name, that sort of thing."

"I would never tell anyone," Katherine said. Then she wondered if she might break down under torture. She hoped not or that she would have the wit to lie.

"It's not that I don't trust you," Robin assured her. "But you must remember, if anything happens, I kidnapped you."

"But that doesn't even make sense!" Katherine protested. "Why would you kidnap us? For ransom? Who on earth would pay to have us back?"

Your parents would, Katherine Bradley, Aramantha told her.

But Robin hasn't asked, argued Katherine. *She never asked to speak to my father on the phone.*

"Well," said Robin slowly, "has it never occurred to you that I could use you as hostages in a standoff with the law?"

"No," said Katherine. "It hasn't."

It should have, said Aramantha. Katherine's stomach gave a lurch.

"You can be sure, if the police find out that you lot are with me, it will occur to them," said Robin. "After all, they would never guess the actual reason."

"You mean rescuing us from almost certain death?"

"No," Robin said solemnly. "Shite!"

"Shite!" Katherine burst out laughing. "Shite!"

"Too right," said Robin. "I need someone to help me shovel it. Hi, ho, off we go!"

They turned away from the stream into the deepening silence of the darker forest. The birds and the squirrels liked the glades where sun and shelter met. They weren't following any path that Katherine could see. Because of the heavy shade, there was very little undergrowth, so it wasn't like bushwhacking. Every so often, Robin would stop still, then place one hand on Katherine's arm, pointing with the other.

"Do you see that cleft rock there with the ferns growing out of it? When you come to that, you bear right. Then keep on straight till you come to an oak with a double trunk."

Each time they stopped, Robin would ask her to repeat the descriptions of the landmarks in order. Clearly, she wanted Katherine to know how to find her way on her own. What Katherine didn't know was why.

After walking what seemed like miles from landmark to landmark, they came at last to the edge of the wood where they stopped. Wide fields and huge sky spread out before them. Katherine had always loved open fields at home, but now she felt herself shrinking back into the shelter of the trees. In the empty sky, a hawk screamed and circled. Their presence had been detected. How could they risk the exposure of the treeless expanse?

"If we walk along the stone wall over there," Robin pointed, "we'll come to a byre just over the rise. But first tell me all you can remember about how we got here."

Katherine gave all her attention to the task, determined to be the "A" student she'd always been, at least till last spring. With minimal prompting from Robin, she remembered each landmark.

"Jolly good!" Robin clapped her on the back.

Then she had her repeat the directions from their camp to this field twice more until she had it perfectly.

"Robin," she ventured at last, "am I going to have to find my way without you?"

"I don't know," Robin said as they began to walk along the edge of the field towards the wall. "But when you asked to come with me, it dawned on me that one of you should know how to get to safety."

Safety? Without Robin?

"But I thought we *were* safe in the greenwood!" said Katherine. "I thought that was the whole idea. That no one can find us in there."

No one. Not Mister Tobias or Tom Cat.

Not her mother or Lucy.

(Who might be in danger, because they were looking for her.)

"That was the idea," agreed Robin. "But perhaps I…didn't think it through very clearly."

She got that right, said Aramantha.

Katherine wanted to protest. Everything Robin did was good, right. After all, no matter what she wanted them to say to the police, she hadn't forced them to come with her. Or to stay.

"I mean it was all very well when it was just me in the forest. It didn't, it doesn't really matter what happens to me—"

"Yes, it does!" Katherine almost shouted.

"Hush, darling," said Robin and she put her arm around her.

Did Robin love her, did Robin love her *that* way? She only knew that when Robin touched her she felt safe.

"We're getting nearer the farm."

So Robin had just wanted her to be quiet, not to give them away.

But you love her…that way!

Shut up, Aramantha!

"I wanted to save you all," Robin said in a low voice.

The way she couldn't save Pippa.

"You did!" Katherine whispered. "You did."

"But what if I can't keep you safe?"

Robin moved her arm from Katherine's shoulder and grabbed one of her own hands with the other, holding them tightly, as if stopping herself from wringing them.

"That's what Little—I mean my Fairy Godfather asked me when I went to him."

Was the fairy godfather one of the little people? She had liked thinking of him as a bear. But he was probably just a person, a grownup. Like Lucy Way. Outside of the greenwood it was harder to believe in magic.

There is no such a thing, inside or outside any wood, huffed Aramantha.

"Where does he live?" she asked.

But Robin put her finger to her lips and motioned for quiet as they reached the rise and saw the byre on the other side. In the muddy yard was a heap of manure and not far away a stack of hay. Cows standing in a field close by stopped grazing and lifted their heads as one to look at Katherine and Robin. Then from the other side of the barn an enormous animal lumbered into view.

No, it was a man, with two gigantic beasts at his side.

There was only one man that large.

Katherine stuffed one hand into her mouth to keep from screaming and clutched Robin's arm with the other.

"It's all right," Robin whispered. "It's all right.

The beasts, whose fearsomeness was undermined by wagging tails and plaintive whines, stilled at the man's command. But surely Robin and Katherine had been seen. Then the man with an almost imperceptible nod, turned away, calling his hounds to heel as he shambled in the opposite direction. The cows went back to grazing.

"Right then," said Robin. "The coast is cleared."

Not clear, cleared.

Chapter Seventy-One

Anne remembered hearing that no point in Britain was farther than seventy miles from the sea. The whole island was no bigger than New England. So how could it be taking so long for them to be getting anywhere? If indeed they were not just going in circles, round and round the same muddy farm lanes. At least so far there were no signs of that car, what make had Frankie said it was? They were too far off road to see any traffic but the odd farm vehicle, mostly standing idle on a Sunday afternoon. But whenever they did see a farmer driving a tractor or once pulling a load of hay in a horse drawn cart, Rowena would wave cheerily and accelerate slightly so that no one (but Anne) would think she had lost her way and needed direction.

Anne's arms and legs ached from bracing herself to keep from sliding into Joe Petrone. She was leaning on him enough already without doing it literally. Now and then a collision was unavoidable, and then they would both murmur an apology they could barely hear above the noise. Once Anne fell practically across his lap and he caught her in his arms, helping her to right herself.

Had he kept his arms around her a moment longer than necessary? Did he, too, wish they could just let go of their propriety and hold on to each other?

There was something about being torn from the life you knew, flung into circumstances you never could have imagined. Here she was driving across a foreign country in an antique heap, searching for a daughter who had vanished (by choice or force or now, it seemed, both) whom she had only a prayer (if she believed in prayer) of finding. The police, who might be corrupt, didn't know where they were. They might, or might not, have been followed by men who might intend to murder them, or worse, murder her daughter. They might all die before they knew what had really happened.

Maybe this was what it was like being in a war, not knowing if you would live another day. All the ordinary rules were suspended, who you could love, where to find comfort. What comfort? Could there be any? No, not really, no. Yet the next time she found herself in Joe's arms, maybe she would stay there. Lucy had been in a war, she should understand and not judge.

All at once, the car stopped. The sudden silence was louder than the noise had been. Anne felt it crash over her, a huge soundless wave taking her under. Maybe everyone felt it. They all sat still for a moment, stunned. Even Rowena.

"What's the matter?" Frankie spoke first. "Don't tell me the engine died!"

Anne was afraid there might be a simpler explanation. No gas. Or rather, petrol. And from what she could see around the back of Rowena's head, they were miles from anywhere.

"No cause for alarm, my little chickadees," said Rowena, reaching for her door handle. "Time to get out and stretch and take our bearings. Perhaps some of you need to spend a penny. We've got lots of cover up here, as you can see."

As much as Anne needed to stretch and, yes, to find a discreet place to squat—she was not particularly outdoorsy and hoped she could manage it without leaking on her shoes or underwear—any delay made her anxious. Those men might catch up with them, or more likely, be far ahead of them. If Frankie was right, they knew where they were going and had decided to get there first or to wait till the Land Rover caught up with them to finish whatever they had intended to do before. Take them hostage? Execute them?

All of them were a bit wobbly when they got out of the Land Rover. Joe had gotten out and gone around to Lucy's side and offered his arm, so she could steady herself, which was only right. Anne was relatively young and strong. How could she feel so well, she wondered? They had stopped on top of a wooded hill with a fresh cool breeze blowing in their faces, all trace of London fog and damp clean gone. Through the trees, she could glimpse a valley, a snaking gleam of silver that must be a small river or creek. Once they'd found their feet, all five of them wandered off to find a discreet tree. Hers might have been an oak, but she did not know trees well. Lucy would know, of course. She found herself wondering about Joe. Did he notice things like that?

Anne could not bring herself to use a dry leaf as toilet paper. Thank heavens she had thought to put tissues in the pockets of the slacks she had only recently started wearing. They were so comfortable and convenient, she thought she might never wear dresses again. Never having littered in her life, Anne carefully buried the tissue under loose leaves.

When she returned to the car, Anne found that Rowena had spread the picnic blanket on the ground, but there was no food set out. Instead, Rowena sat on the blanket, cross-legged, what the children used to call Indian style. Her hands rested on her knees, palms up, and her eyes were closed, or half-closed. Joe and Frankie stood to one side, Frankie looking curious and Joe—Joe caught Anne's eye and then shook his head while throwing up his hands. Lucy returned from her patch of woods. Taking in the scene, she sighed and sat down on the blanket, though not with her legs crossed but folded in front of her.

"Come on then, the rest of you, sit!" Rowena commanded, as if they were a pack of unruly dogs. "It will help me, if we all quiet and entrain our minds."

"What's that s'posed ta mean?" asked Frankie as he dropped down beside her easily assuming her cross-legged position.

"It's like looking into the crystal ball. You see, you don't really need an actual crystal ball; it's just a tool. But I am rather partial to mine, and I didn't want to risk breaking it on the trip."

"Will we get to see, too?" Frankie wanted to know.

"Close your eyes—and your mouth—and you might find out."

Now only Anne and Joe remained standing. They looked at each other and a wild idea flashed through Anne's mind. Take the keys, take the keys and go, just herself and Joe.

"We're losing time!" Anne snapped.

"They might be way ahead of us by now," agreed Joe.

Rowena sat for a moment, slit-eyed.

"You may not believe it," she said, "but we have, in fact, taken a short cut. We are very close to our destination. More or less within sight of it, if you look across that valley to the mountains beyond."

Anne felt a shiver go through her. All that vastness, wildness. Even if Rowena was right and Katherine and her rescuer were hiding out there, how would they ever find them?

"That is exactly the point of this exercise," Rowena answered Anne's thought directly. "Now will you please sit. Your agitation is interfering with the frequencies."

"Come on, Uncle Joe, sit down," said Frankie.

Joe looked at Anne again. Anne felt rather than saw Lucy intercept the glance.

"Best to do as she says, Anne," said Lucy. "We are rather at her mercy, and she may just know what she's talking about."

Anne and Joe moved toward the blanket and Joe helped Anne down, and then sat beside her, their knees touching.

"Ah, that's better already," Rowena said. "Oh, steady on, lads. This just in. They're about ten miles behind us. In their haste to overtake us, or arrive ahead of us, they forgot to stop for petrol."

"What about us?" said Anne. "Won't we run out, too?"

"Bigger tank," murmured Joe, lightly touching Anne's hand.

"Also, that second picnic basket, strapped to the rack on the roof of the rover. Not food, extra petrol. A trick I learned in the war."

"But isn't that dangerous?" Anne asked.

"Not so dangerous outside the car. It's the fumes that cause the problems."

Joe's hand stayed where it was, and Anne subsided. No, she gave up. Gave in.

"Now," said Rowena. "Don't do anything for a moment but breathe. Breathe in to a count of eight, pause for a count of eight, out for a count of eight, pause for a count of eight, repeat."

To Anne's surprise, the breathing and the counting took all her concentration. She could not think of anything else. (Well, except the warmth of Joe's hand.) He was breathing, too. They were all breathing together. It got quieter and quieter inside and out. There was just the wind, soughing over them and the occasional cry of a hawk or raven.

"Now I want you all to see the rose cross. Yes, like the one on the back of my cards. No need to see anything elaborate. A simple five petal rose in the center of the cross and the circle."

Anne had never attempted such an exercise before. In church she'd always said the prayers by rote, week after week, like everyone else. They had no meaning for her. The only thing that had ever moved her was music. She had never tried to see anything, unless she was reading a novel. She found that, like the breathing, forming the image took all her concentration. She could not get the cross to become clear, but the rose was there, a blown open beach rose that she remembered from her childhood on the Jersey shore. The golden center, the sweet scent on the salt wind.

Rowena was intoning something now, calling in angels from the four quarters. Uriel, Michael, Raphael, Gabriel. Anne knew nothing about angels. Gerald's understanding of the social Gospel had no room for otherworldly beings. But she bet Lucy knew all about them. She wondered what Joe thought, and then she stopped wondering as she listened to Rowena praying for help, for help finding Anne's daughter, praying as if Katherine mattered to her as much as she did to Anne.

Then there was silence again. Anne did not know what she was supposed to do or see. With her eyes closed, she found she was seeing hands, Joe's hand on her own, Lucy's hand on her heart, Frankie's hand holding onto the earth, Rowena's hands upraised. And then she saw Katherine running across a muddy field, her hand reaching out to another hand, a strong, slender hand. At last, without understanding why, she saw a Black man's hand resting on a white one.

We are in God's hands, the words came into her mind.

She did not believe in God, she remembered.

But she believed in hands.

"Now, friends," said Rowena, after what seemed like a long time or no time at all. "Let your breath bring you back. From where you have been walking to and fro, up and down between the worlds."

She had not gone anywhere, Anne thought. Or maybe she had. But where?

"Come back and open your eyes and let us sit together in council."

Anne opened her eyes, everything seemed more vivid than usual and at the same time a little out of focus as if the worlds, as Rowena called them, had not fully cohered. Joe shifted, adjusting his posture. Before he let go of her hand, he squeezed it.

"Does the name John Little mean anything to any of you?" Rowena asked.

No one answered for a moment.

"Sure," said Frankie. "Little John, you know, in Robin Hood. They fought on a bridge with quarterstaffs. He beat Robin, but then they became best friends."

Rowena smiled on her protégé.

"That's it! That's it exactly!"

"What is?" asked Joe. "I'm afraid I'm not following."

What would they have done without Joe on this journey, Anne wondered. What would she have done?

"John Little, Little John," answered Rowena, as if it made sense of everything. "Roberta Loveridge, Robin Hood. She has to have had someone helping her with vehicles, supplies, with keeping her hide-out secret. John Little. I remember now. He was mentioned in the article I clipped. He is the gamekeeper on the estate where Roberta Loveridge grew up. If we find him, we can find her. That is, if we can persuade him that she is in danger, and we must warn her. Now then, do the rest of you have anything to report before we push on?"

"Wait," said Joe, "is that something you, uh, saw, or something you pieced together? Meaning no disrespect, but for some reason it seems important."

Rowena considered for a moment.

"Right you are, Joe. It was both. I kept hearing the name. Did I mention I am clairaudient, as well? It came with an image of a countryman, not young but still robust. But I didn't put it all together till Frankie mentioned Little John. Then I saw, if you will, that he must be an ally."

"You're sure of it?" Joe pressed.

"Why?" Rowena paused for a beat. "What did you see, Joe?"

"A constable, an old-fashioned constable with a billy stick. Not some fancy detective or policeman, more like what I used to be." He paused for a moment. "Call for backup, that's what I kept hearing. Call for backup."

Rowena closed her eyes again for a moment.

"You may be on to something, Joe," she allowed. "And if we can find John Little, he'll be the one who will know the local constabulary. Anyone else?"

"Weapons, we need weapons," said Frankie. "I keep seeing bows and arrows."

Anne looked at Frankie, Katherine's best childhood friend. He'd whittled javelins for them and egged her on to buy her own knife. She didn't want to sell Frankie short. He and Katherine had caught a murderer and saved Lucy's life. But those men, those men who were hunting Roberta Loveridge, she'd lay odds they had guns.

"Lucy?" said Rowena.

Everyone turned to look at Lucy. Her face was almost as white as her hair. Her eyes still looked unfocused as if she hadn't returned when Rowena called—or could not. Her lips were moving as if she recited something silently.

"Lucy!" said Rowena sharply. "Come back at once."

Lucy appeared to obey and looked around at all of them, blinking a little.

"What were you saying just now?" asked Rowena. "Can you remember?"

Lucy closed her eyes again, and then she spoke clearly enough for everyone to hear.

"I am the one you are looking for."

She was quoting something, something from the Gospel. Anne wished she had paid more attention in church.

"A sacrifice," nodded Rowena. "A saving sacrifice."

Anne did not know what they were talking about and it frightened her, more than that. It made her angry.

"Does no one want to know what I saw or heard? Do you all think I am so unimaginative and uninteresting that I can't see!"

"Go on, then," said Rowena. It sounded like a challenge.

She felt Joe's hand on hers again.

"Hands!" Anne heard her voice getting louder, stronger. "We are in God's hands!"

Chapter Seventy-Two

Gerald gazed down at his cupped hands as he knelt by the communion rail, waiting for the host. But he was remembering Elsa's hands, so powerful once, crashing down on the organ keys, now thin, spotted with liver blotches, as if she were much older than she was.

"It is you I am worried about, my friend," Elsa had said.

She had reached over the railing of the hospital bed to hold his hand, as if he were the one in need of comfort. He had stopped to see Elsa on his way to church. He had taken his own car. His mother and the twins had been invited to a picnic after the service. He had begged off going, pleading work to catch up on as well as not wanting to be far from the phone in case Anne called. He had thought visiting Elsa was one thing he could do, when there was so much he couldn't. One thing he knew how to do.

"No need to worry about me," he mumbled, then stopped, aware that he should not go on to say, I don't know where Anne is. They've struck out on their own to find Katherine. I can't even call the police.

"I am not worried about Lucy Way and her little gang." Elsa spoke to his thoughts. "Wherever Lucy Way is, there are angels and archangels hoovering about."

"Not to mention bright seraphs, cherubim and thrones," Gerald quipped quoting "Ye Watchers and Ye Holy Ones," a triumphant hymn Elsa favored because of its musical complexity.

"Them too," she let out a sigh, "*die ganza Bagage.*"

Anne, the German major, would probably be able to give an exact translation, but he got the gist. A whole bunch of angels, following Lucy wherever she went, ready to do her bidding. He had never had much truck with angelology (it boggled his mind that there was such a field of study). Elsa's eyes had closed again. He hoped she was drifting into a pain free sleep. He had to get going if he was to be on time for church. Slowly he began to let go of her hand. Then she gripped his tighter.

"You, Gerald," she said in a rasping whisper, "something is troubling you. I feel this for a long time, even before Katherine is lost. I wish I could help you as you have helped me. Get help, Gerald. For my sake, if not for yours."

He wanted to make a bad joke. No dying requests when you're not dying (except maybe she was. Poor Lucy. She would want to be here. What an awful choice she'd had to make) but he found himself too choked up.

"You bet," he said instead, squeezing her hand in return.

Now at the communion rail, Ralph James moved along dispensing the host, murmuring "the Bread of Heaven, the Body of Christ." Out of the corner of his eye, Gerald could see Janie's bent head and upraised hands. The twins had been confirmed last spring, Janie excited to have a formal white dress. There wasn't much in it for Peter, he supposed. A new suit didn't hold the same thrill, and having to memorize the Ten Commandments could only, at his age, be considered a drag. But Peter was kneeling at the rail, too, on the other side of Gerald's mother.

"The Body of Christ, the Bread of Heaven."

"Amen," he heard Janie whisper, what he would have scorned as a high church affectation in anyone else. But Janie was sincere. There wasn't a mean or cynical bone in her body. She had never hurt anyone in her life.

Whereas Gerald....

I am not worthy so much as to gather the crumbs from beneath thy table. He found himself silently praying the prayer of humble access. The prayer went on, *But thou art the same Lord whose property is always to have mercy.* But he couldn't get there. God might be merciful, he might even want to bestow mercy on Gerald. He knew he was supposed to believe in divine mercy, take it on faith. But he didn't, he couldn't.

You need help, Gerald. You need a priest.

Gerald could not believe he was making such a stagey, dramatic gesture. But he couldn't help it. Just before it was his turn to receive the wafer, his arms, seemingly of their own volition, folded themselves across their chest. Without breaking his rhythm, Ralph James made the sign of the cross over Gerald's head. Not that Gerald could see it, but he could feel it. Possibly breaking a liturgical rule, the priest murmured, "Defend, O Lord, this thy child from all the perils of this night."

"Bless me, for I have sinned."

Gerald and Ralph James sat in the study in the rectory, the study that had once been Gerald's. He could have knelt at the altar rail in the church and would have if Father James (yes, he actually thought of him that way at the moment) had preferred a more formal setting. Or they could have met in the office at the parish house. But the priest had said, "Let's meet in my study. We'll be more comfortable there."

Comfort. Was that what Gerald was seeking? To want such a thing for himself seemed weak and craven. Well, it was not comfortable to sit facing Father James, both of them holding open *The Book of Common Prayer*, following the form for "The Reconciliation of a Penitent." Gerald had taken the priest's role (in this very study) on rare occasions. Personal confession was not something he had encouraged in his parishioners. The General Confession ought to suffice. But for Gerald, it no longer did, and he wasn't sure this rite would work either. But he had promised Elsa he would get help, and he didn't know what else to do.

"The Lord be in your heart," Father James read the response, *"and upon your lips that you may truly and humbly confess your sins: In the Name of the Father, and of the Son, and of the Holy Spirit. Amen."*

Gerald took a gulp of air as if a wave were about to take him under and he would have to hold his breath, and then he read his part.

"*I confess to Almighty God, to his Church, that I have sinned in thought word, and deed, in things done and left undone; especially_____.*"

Gerald stared at the small blank line that indicated he should specify his sin, the one that was not general, the reason he was here. He put the book down. To his utter shame, he began to weep. No, it was more than weeping. It was blubbering. He was wailing. Thank God everyone, including Father James' wife, had gone to a picnic on Marge Van Wagner's farm.

Father James just sat in silence. He didn't offer a tissue, he didn't put a comforting hand on Gerald's shoulder. He just sat, so quietly, so...peacefully. And all at once some of the peace stole over Gerald. By God, the man must have been praying. For him. Which made him weep again, but this without sound this time, without struggling for breath.

Gerald picked up the prayer book again to find his place.

"Especially for what I did to my daughter Katherine."

He put the book in his lap and looked up at the priest. If he was going to face himself, he had to look at the priest's face. Jeremiah, sitting beside him in the dim hospital room, had spared him that much.

"I had intercourse, sexual intercourse with my daughter."

It took all Gerald's will not to look away or down. Father James' face did not change. No repulsion, no sympathy, just....

"I am not sure how it happened," Gerald went on. "No, that's not true. It was the night Martin Luther King was killed. I'd been drinking. A lot. So much I couldn't remember anything later, or I didn't let myself remember. Not for a long time. I do remember holding her and crying, telling her I loved her, I loved her so much. I doubt she knew what was happening. I don't think I did, either. Not then. But I know now. I know now, it was rape. I raped her."

Still, Father James did not flinch. Just nodded, almost imperceptibly, to show that he had heard.

Inadvertently, Gerald closed his eyes. All at once, he saw, as vividly as if he had been there, Katherine waiting, and waiting, for him to pick her up after her first day at the daycare center. He remembered her defying her mother to get him the car keys, that night. That night....

Gerald opened his eyes again. There was Father James, waiting patiently, without judgment, waiting to grant him absolution. *He is a priest, you need a priest*. But he was not Katherine. He could not understand or forgive on Katherine's behalf. He must not.

"I see now that all Katherine's trouble at school began then, and she started shutting herself away in her room, her," he paused, but forced himself to go on, "her acting out with Frankie Lomangino.... Maybe it's not fair to call it acting out. It's not Katherine whose, whose desires are disordered."

Gerald stopped again. Disordered desires. Did he have any desires that weren't? He didn't have to close his eyes to feel Jeremiah's hand on his back, to remember the comfort of sleeping in his arms.

"There's something more."

He looked at Father James again, who looked steadily back at Gerald, his eyes never leaving his face, as if only Gerald existed in this moment. Existed not to be judged but to be known.

For now we see through a glass, darkly; but then face to face, the lines from Corinthians sounded in his mind, *now I know in part; but then shall I know even as also I am known.*

"I think, no, I know, I am in love. Not with another woman," he said, speaking in his mind to Anne. "I'm, I'm in love with a man. Someone I work with. He's, he's the only other person who knows what I've done."

Gerald covered his face again and wept.

When he was quiet, Ralph James spoke for the first time.

"This man knows what you did, and he did not turn away from you."

Gerald rested his hands in his lap again and looked at the priest.

"He did not turn away from me."

Father James waited a beat.

"And neither has God, Gerald, neither has God. Shall we go on?"

Gerald picked up the prayer book and saw that he had stopped halfway through the part of the penitent.

"For these and all other sins which I cannot now remember, I am truly sorry. I pray God to have mercy on me. I firmly intend amendment of my life, and I humbly beg forgiveness of God and his Church, and ask for your counsel, direction, and absolution."

Gerald looked up again.

"But I'm not ready for absolution. I don't even know if I believe in it anymore. Can you give me a penance? I need help. Help me. Please help me."

Chapter Seventy-Three

Lucy was having déjà vu. It was not just that the landscape was familiar, the stately beeches and oaks along the long winding approach, the park-like land rolling away into forest and mountain, which gave her an odd sense of homecoming. It was also the back of Frankie's head, Joe's profile, and Anne's just beyond, as she leaned forward. Rowena's grinding shift of the gears. Most of all, was the mix of dread and hope, the sense that they had all been here before on the verge of some unknown that they already knew.

"Stop!" Lucy said abruptly before she quite knew why. "We've got to turn here."

"Into a cow field?" asked Joe.

For, in fact, as Lucy now saw, there were red-brown cows dotting the fields. Herefords, she thought, and here they were in Herefordshire.

"We've been through rougher fields than this one," Frankie pointed out. He turned and craned his head to look backwards. "Are the bad guys catching up with us?"

Everyone else looked back also, everyone but Lucy.

"Do you see that lane?" Lucy pointed. "On the other side of the field? I just...have a feeling that it leads somewhere."

"Get out and open the gate, Frankie, there's a good lad," said Rowena. "Then close it behind us. We don't want to be accused of cattle rustling."

Frankie unlatched the gate. The cows lifted their heads, a few of them trotting forward, then thinking better of it as the Land Rover lumbered through. They backed away, some them giving a nervous little leap. The herd advanced again while Frankie secured the gate and got into the car. On the other side of the field was another gate, and beyond, the small shadowed lane Lucy had seen. Frankie clambered out, opened and secured the second gate.

Before Frankie got in again, Rowena turned away from the lane and parked the behemoth behind a yew hedge where you might not see it—if you were blind or oblivious.

"I say we go by foot from here," said Rowena, opening her door.

They all got out. Joe, as usual climbing after Anne, then hurrying around the car to hand Lucy out. She didn't really need the help, but she appreciated the old-fashioned gallantry.

Although it had been Lucy's idea to turn from the drive to follow this lane, Rowena firmly took the lead, with Frankie beside her. Lucy observed Anne hanging back until Joe caught up with her. Following a pace or two behind the pair, Lucy observed their heads slightly inclined towards each other, as if listening, though neither of them spoke. Ahead, Frankie dragged his feet, to slow his pace to Rowena's. All at once, Lucy had a dizzying sense of déjà vu in reverse. How had she come to be here, walking alone, falling further and further behind….

Stop it! Lucy silently rebuked herself. Katherine was in danger. They were all in danger. She picked up her pace, shoes squishing in the muddy ruts of the farm road.

"All right, Lucy?" Joe stopped, turning to look.

And Anne paused, too, stepping aside so that Lucy now walked between them.

"Quite all right," she said.

They walked on together through a copse of mixed beech, hickory and oak. Ahead Lucy could see the trees thinning towards what appeared to be a farmyard. Late light touched the thatched peak of a stone barn or croft.

Then they heard the baying, for the ferocious sounds went beyond barking, and the creatures capable of it sounded far worse than dogs.

Rowena and Frankie froze. In a moment, two huge hounds, easily the size of small horses, stopped just feet away, their fangs bared and, yes, frothing.

"Nice doggies," Rowena pleaded, clearly terrified. "Lucy, do something!"

She clutched Lucy's arm as Lucy came to stand beside her, Anne stood on Lucy's other side while Joe and Frankie flanked the small group, Joe holding a stick he had picked up, preparing to advance on the dogs.

"Stay back," Lucy warned. "Don't threaten them."

"Do as she says," Rowena commanded over a sound that had becoming a deep growling, even more menacing. "We used to call her St Francesca at school."

"You mean like Saint Francis?" said Frankie. "Hey, I'm named for that cat. Let me try."

Frankie held out his hand, then jumped back as one of the hounds lunged for him.

Lucy waited for a moment, willing her heartbeat to slow, taking long even breaths. Then she smiled at the dogs, whose growls turned to yips and finally high whines before they subsided. Only then did Lucy bend forward and hold out her hand to the creatures, who began to wag their tails. The larger, blacker one, dropped to his belly and wriggled toward her.

"Holy shit!" breathed Frankie.

No one bothered to admonish his language.

"Cerberus, Mauthe Dhoog!" a man's voice called.

The Latin and Celtic names for his hell hounds, Lucy guessed. And the two dogs sprang to attention, as a huge man, built on the same scale as his beasts, rounded the corner of the barn, brandishing a pitch fork.

Lucy stood up and the others flanked her. Then Rowena stepped forward, extending a hand that was still visibly trembling.

"John Little, I presume?"

The man stared at them, his eyebrows bristling, then he opened his mouth.

"Arrr!" was all he said.

"We're looking for Roberta Loveridge," Rowena informed him. She might be psychic, Lucy thought, but clearly that didn't mean she was sensitive in the ordinary sense.

"Can't help you," he said without elaboration, and whistling for his dogs, he turned to walk away.

"I quite understand, Mr. Little," said Lucy. "But in fact, we are not looking for Roberta Loveridge."

At the sound of her voice, the dogs turned around and looked towards Lucy with loving expectation. Slowly their master turned, too.

"We are looking for this lady's daughter." Lucy pressed her advantage and gestured toward Anne. "The child's name is Katherine Bradley."

"Arrr?" he said with a hint of inquiry.

"She is a young American girl. We have reason to believe that Roberta Loveridge rescued her, and several others, from dire circumstances and brought them somewhere near here to be safe."

John Little kept his face as still as rock. You could have climbed it with a rope and pickaxe. Then the mountain moved.

"Happen I was about to put the kettle on."

He turned, indicating with his head that they should follow. The dogs bounded ahead leading the way to the stone cottage.

(Finally, they were moving again. But due to this utterly avoidable delay, they wouldn't reach Loveridge Hall till midnight, and he had no way to ring Lady Loveridge to say they'd be late. Running out of petrol, how utterly imbecilic. He himself did not drive and took for granted that his useless companions would have seen to such basic essentials as sufficient fuel. It had taken the thug hours to walk to a petrol station and back, for of course no one wanted to risk giving a lift to such a disreputable character.

He'd not met Lady Loveridge, but of course he knew her late husband, the second one, that is, who had come to such an undignified end in the bottom of a wheelie bin. And really it was all that fool's fault that he'd gotten lumbered with the hairy pornographer. Making the widow's acquaintance was a perquisite to this tedious trip. *Rumor had it that the lady was no better than she should be, and very likely a great deal worse. It might be time to seriously consider dedicating a corridor of the Doll House to the appetites of depraved wealthy women, to find men (or women) to service them. Of course, the project carried risks that must be carefully assessed. He would have to talk to H. about it....*

But first he had to dispose of those wretched little girls, and the shadowy abductor who had stolen them for her own perverted purposes....)

Chapter Seventy-Four

There was a lull in the laughter and talk. The waxing moon lifted over the tree tops and its light pooled in their clearing where the campfire burned low. Maybe they were all tired from being outdoors all day, their stomachs full of a stew made of fresh dug potatoes from Robin's small garden and bits of smoked venison from a root cellar Robin had dug last spring, all washed down with ale from the (nicked) keg. The fire made its soft whispering sounds. An owl woke up and made the night even more beautiful and wild with its cry.

Katherine looked at Robin across the fire, her head bent and her hair golden in the firelight, the moonlight, as if she had a halo. Robin seemed distracted, even sad. They'd all had a good day, weaving the wattle together. Once Katherine and Robin had gotten clear of the farm, they'd laughed as they careened back through the wood with their unwieldly cartload of straw and manure. Though now that she thought of it, Robin had stopped laughing when she noticed the tracks they were leaving. Katherine wished she could go to her, lay her head on Robin's shoulder.

You mean like in that picture of the Last Supper? Aramantha interrupted.

No, she answered crossly. *Not like that. Besides there's only six of us, not twelve. We're merry maids in the greenwood. Not disciples.*

You're the one seeing halos! pointed out Aramantha.

"Sing something, Warbler," said Doreen, forgetting to call her Kat, "that bleedin' owl is making me 'air stand on end."

The night, the subdued mood called forth a ballad.

"The water is wide," she began, "I cannot cross o'er...."

Robin glanced up at her, and Katherine's throat thickened. She could not cross the circle, or the water that separated one part of her life from another.

"No more have I," she tried to go on, "the wings to—"

Then in one silent motion Robin rose to her feet and motioned for them all to be quiet. They could hear something crashing through the woods, something large and heavy.

"A bear," whispered Doreen, "a bloody bear. I knew there was bears."

They all got up and drew closer together as a large figure stepped into the clearing.

It was not a bear. It wore a jacket and trousers and carried something that looked like a baseball bat.

"Good evening, Constable Albutt," said Robin.

"Did someone speak?"

It was not till she heard her voice that Katherine realized the intruder was a woman! She cupped a hand to her ear as if straining to hear and stared into the distance as if she could not see them either.

"I didn't think so," the woman said. "Because happen someone spoke and happen I were to look at her and recognize her as Roberta Loveridge alias Robin or Robin Hood as some calls her, happen I would have to arrest her on charges of kidnapping as well as suspected manslaughter—"

"Cor, I knew it," breathed one of them.

"A dangerous criminal."

"That's our Robin 'oodlum."

The constable waited till the murmurs subsided.

"But happen I didn't see her and happen one Katherine Bradley was to come along with me, peaceful like, then happen I would not have no need to investigate further."

No one answered, but Katherine began shaking. Doreen, standing next to her, took her hand and squeezed it tight.

"Happen there were anyone by that name loitering, malingering, not to say trespassing in this here wood, she'd best make herself known to me."

"I'd say you're out of luck altogether, Cunstable Allbutt," Doreen spoke up, mispronouncing her title and name. On purpose? "We don't know no Katherine Bradley, do we, girls?"

"Never 'eard of her. No, not us."

Katherine knew she needed to speak, but her throat constricted as she kept swallowing her breath.

"Wot's this Katherine done then?" she finally asked, automatically falling back into Cockney.

"Nothing as I know of. She's not wanted for a crime. She's wanted as a person as is missing."

But they were all missing. Except, Katherine remembered, they weren't all missed. Picked off the garbage heap, Doreen had said. If Mister Tobias had sent the constable, would he single her out because he knew her mother and Lucy Way were searching for her?

"Happen any of you was to know the whereabouts of said person and happen you didn't say nothing, you can all be charged as accessories after the fact to the crime of kidnapping."

Before she could think, Katherine took a step forward.

"But I wasn't kidnapped!"

"Eegit!" hissed Bernadette. "Now you're for it!"

The constable turned to Katherine, careful not to look at anyone else.

"Katherine Bradley, you will come with me."

"Wait, Jen!" Robin addressed the constable; clearly she knew her, not just as a constable. "Please just tell me one thing, did Little—did your brother send you?"

"Noisy owls tonight," remarked the constable. "Come along, Miss Bradley."

"I needs to ask you a question, Constable," Vicky formerly known as Fifi stepped forward. "*Did* your brother send you and by the way 'oo the 'ell is 'e?"

The constable still looked at no one but Katherine.

"He's my fairy godfather," Robin whispered, leaning towards her.

"As to whether my brother sent me, I will tell you this much, 'a sent *for* me. For don't I know these woods as well as he does? Happen we built the treehouses some trespassers might take advantage of, which if I cared to take notice of illegal occupancy I could. But happen I bring back one Katherine Bradley, the rest of you is free to do as you please. Though if I was you, I'd make myself scarce. Any trouble and—"

"It's all right," said Katherine. "I'll go."

"I'll go with you, Kat," said Robin.

"No!" Katherine almost shouted to keep back tears. "You can't! I don't hear you, either."

And she put her hands over her ears.

"There's a good lass," said the constable taking Katherine firmly by the arm and marching her away.

Katherine looked back once. Through her tears, she thought she saw the others holding onto Robin, holding her back from following.

Chapter Seventy-Five

Anne huddled by the fire in John Little's kitchen, not sure if she was dreaming or awake.

Had a giantess just burst into the cottage wearing a constable's uniform?

"Constable Albutt, my sister," he had introduced her, "If your lass be near, Fat Jen'll find 'un."

And after questioning Anne about Katherine's age and appearance, the blue clad, brass-buttoned giantess had turned to go.

"Let me go with you! She's my daughter."

"I could go, too," said Joe. "I used to be in law enforcement—"

"Bide here," the woman ordered, shaking her billy stick at them for emphasis. "You'd only hinder me."

And she was gone.

Rowena and Lucy finished washing up the tea things (if the hearty meal Anne hadn't been able to eat could be called tea), then sat down at the table. Frankie stood and gazed at a wall of bows and other weapons Anne could not identify. Joe took a chair from the table and sat near Anne. John Little sat by the door, motionless, attentive, his rifle on his knee, his hounds beside him. None of them spoke. Anne wondered if they even could anymore. She felt as though they were suspended in suspense, frozen in amber light. Fossils in stone. She remembered being in labor, not crying out or panting, as she'd heard women were supposed to do, but holding herself perfectly still, her breath barely coming and going. That stillness, the only safe place.

The dogs heard first, scrambling to their feet and staring at the door, their ears cocked. John Little rose too, his head also tilted, rifle not aimed but at the ready.

Anne tried to stand but couldn't get her legs to work. Her heart beat so fast, it flew to the rafters and perched there.

Then they heard footsteps.

"Arr," came the voice of the giantess. "I got 'un."

John Little opened the door.

Anne's heart plummeted to her feet.

A strange, thin girl Anne did not recognize stood in the doorway, tangled blonde hair, curls unraveling.

Katherine?

The girl stood and stared straight ahead.

Katherine.

How could she ever not have known even for one moment?

"Katherine!" Anne's voice broke.

The girl's eyes widened, but she held still, her arms crossed over her chest. She was wearing an over-sized man's shirt over some kind of leggings.

"Katherine!"

Someone was helping Anne to stand. She shook whoever was holding her and she crossed the room. Katherine still didn't move. Anne flung her arms around her daughter and held her tightly, too tightly. Katherine stood so stiffly, she lost her balance in the weight of Anne's embrace and had to reach for her mother to stop her fall.

Chapter Seventy-Six

Now that it was ringing at last, the phone made Gerald jump out of his chair, so that he tripped over his desk and landed on the floor, breaking his fall with his hands as the phone came crashing down beside him.

"Hello, hello!" he shouted, afraid he'd lost the connection.

"This is the overseas operator with a reverse charge call from Anne Bradley. Will you accept?"

"Yes, thank you, operator, yes!"

The line went silent.

"Anne, Anne?"

"We've, she's...." She let go held breath and began to sob.

"You found her? Is she...?" All right, he did not say. What if she wasn't, what if—

"She's alive, Gerald." Anne answered his fear. "Katherine's alive, but she...."

And the sobs started again.

Gerald listened. And waited. This is your penance, he heard Father James saying. Listen and wait. Set your own needs aside. Listen, wait until you know it is time to speak. Pray.

"Gerald?" she said when she could speak again.

"I'm here, Anne, I'm here."

Where are you? What is happening? he did not say.

"Katherine is here. In this cottage where we're staying the night. I think, I hope, I don't know if she's asleep. Lucy's with her, watching over her. But I don't know if she'll even talk to Lucy. All she says is she wants to go back, she has to go back. I think she might try to run away again if it weren't for Fat Jen, sitting guard at the door."

Why aren't you on your way to the nearest airport, he wanted to shout.

"Go on," was all he said.

"Fat Jen, she's a constable, Constable Albutt."

Thank God, they'd called the police at last.

"She's the one who found Katherine. She knew where she, they were hiding."

Gerald sensed that Anne was almost as confused as he was.

"I don't know why she didn't bring the others back or why she didn't arrest Roberta Loveridge."

"The kidnapper?"

"No, no! She didn't kidnap them, Katherine swears it. But Roberta Loveridge is a fugitive. She's suspected of killing a man. I don't know what to think, Gerald, I don't know what to do. But Katherine won't talk to me, she doesn't want to come with me. I just need to take her away, away from all this madness. Gerald, I don't know what to do!"

He needed to speak now, he knew it. Anne needed him. He didn't want to barrage her with questions like who in the hell is Roberta Loveridge, but he had so little to go on.

"Katherine wants to protect this Roberta," he began tentatively, neither a question or a statement.

"She calls her Robin. Robin is the one who rescued her, from, oh, Gerald, I don't even know yet what happened to her, what she's been through. She's, she's changed. It's like she doesn't know me anymore."

She broke down again.

"Oh, Anne." What could he say? "I am so sorry. After what she's been through, it will take some time—"

"But Gerald, we don't have time. There's…we think someone is following us here. Someone else is looking for, not just Katherine, but Roberta Loveridge. Dangerous people, people who, oh God, Gerald, might want to kill her."

He didn't know whether she meant Katherine or Roberta. But he was thoroughly alarmed. They needed help. And he didn't know what to do, he was far away, powerless, useless.

Put yourself aside, he heard Father James' voice again.

"You've got to get out of there, Anne. Find the nearest airport. Call me again and tell me what flight you'll be on."

There was another silence.

"I will, Gerald, when I can. I better go, now."

"Wait, Anne, what can I do to help? Tell me what to do. I could call Scotland Yard. Tell them you're in danger—"

"No, Gerald, no!" She sounded hysterical. "The men who are following us, we are almost sure they've paid someone off. Detective Smith-Jones, remember him, he might have been killed!"

"Anne, listen," he pleaded. "This doesn't make sense. Is the constable there, let me—"

"I've got to go, I've got to go check on Katherine. The constable is here, and so is her brother. He's the gamekeeper. They're both *huge*. Don't do anything yet, Gerald. Please, just wait."

And she hung up the phone.

Gerald found he was still on the floor, on his knees.

"Jesus," he didn't know if he was swearing or praying, it didn't matter. "Jesus."

Chapter Seventy-Seven

At dawn Katherine heard Lucy tiptoe out of the tiny room with the sloping eaves where she and Katherine's mother had taken turns dozing and keeping watch. Maybe Lucy thought Katherine was asleep. She had her eyes closed and she was lying perfectly still as she had all night, so that no one would ask her questions. Why should she answer questions, anyway? No one was listening to her.

She was a prisoner again. That constable, Fat Jen Albutt, was guarding the door. Katherine would have climbed out the window if she could, but it was too small, and her mother or Lucy or both were always with her.

Did they think she was a criminal? Did they think Robin was? She wanted to ask, but she didn't want to talk. It was better not to talk.

What could she say to her mother or Lucy? They didn't know what she had done. Or what had been done to her. They might feel sorry for her, but they wouldn't understand. And if they knew it had been her own fault, for pretending to be a cockney and going with that man, getting drunk in a pub, they would never forgive her. And they would never let her go anywhere again. She would be a prisoner for life.

Only Robin and her friends understood. Only Robin wanted them to be free. She had to get back to Robin somehow.

Katherine lay facing the wall, waiting for a step on the stair, for the changing of the guard, but for a moment at least she was alone. Cautiously she rolled over and looked at the window again where a little grey light crept through the ivy that overgrew the window. She could hear people moving about downstairs, stoking the fire, filling the kettle, murmuring as if she were still asleep or someone was. Maybe they were waiting for her to wake up and have to use the downstairs loo. They would ambush her with stares and questions.

Her mother. She had heard her mother crying last night. And Frankie's uncle—why on earth were he and Frankie here, and who was that strange woman in the shawls and turban sitting there looking smug?—had tried to comfort Katherine's mother.

She almost went down to her mother then, but she held back. Because she wouldn't have comforted her, she would have yelled at her. *I can't be who you want me to be. Leave me alone, go home.* She would have made her mother cry even more, and then she might have cried, too.

She couldn't do that. She had to keep her wits about her. She had to escape.

Lucy would hate her. No, it was worse. Lucy didn't hate people. She was disappointed in them. Katherine could feel it. Lucy didn't have to say anything. She just looked at Katherine, so sadly, so kindly. Katherine couldn't look at Lucy. She couldn't bear it. It was like being thrown out of Narnia.

But she hadn't been thrown out, she hadn't. She'd found Narnia with Robin and the others.

She needed to go back.

Katherine swung her feet out of the bed that was ridiculously high for a room with a ceiling so low she had to take care not to bang her head. She had refused to change into a nightgown, so she was still in her leggings and an over-sized man's shirt. Robin had had to supply them all with clothes and shoes. Katherine had the old pair of trainers that she had kicked under the bed to be sure no one took them from her, not that she couldn't run away barefoot. Her feet had toughened up again in the forest. She reached for the trainers now but did not put them on. If she crept silently down the stairs—really more a ladder to a loft—perhaps she'd find the door unguarded.

She turned around to climb down, but when she looked over her shoulder, she saw Frankie climbing up. Another step for either of them and he'd be face to face with her ass.

Kick him, she ordered herself, kick him in the face. As she lifted her foot, his hand closed around her ankle.

"Let go, you son of a bitch."

"Shh!" he said. "Lucy Way will hear, and my mother is not a bitch."

"I don't care. Let go, let go or—"

"Or what?"

"Or I'll kill you."

"Yeah, you just might. If you keep trying to kick, you're gonna lose your balance, then we'll both fall and break both our necks."

It sounded like a plan worth considering.

"What the fuck do you want, Frankie!"

Oh, that was a mistake, saying his name.

"I swear to God, Katherine, stop swearing!"

And that was worse, hearing him say her name. What had been her name? My name is Kat, she almost said. But no, that name was hers. Doreen had given it to her. Robin and the others called her that. Frankie didn't know Kat. She intended to keep it that way.

"I just want to talk to you," he said.

"Well, I have to piss," she shot back. "And if you don't move, I'll piss on your head."

That did it. He started backing down, literally. Good. There was a window in the loo she could climb out. She should have thought of that last night.

Even though he'd stepped aside, Katherine shoved Frankie out of the way at the bottom of the stairs. Another mistake. His body was too familiar.

She lowered her head as much as she could so that her hair veiled her face, and she stalked towards the bathroom, which was unfortunately near the kitchen. The kettle whistled, but all the clattering and whispering stopped. No one called out to her. Her pee sounded so loud (she'd held it all night). Were they all listening? She'd better be quick, or they might come to check on her. The door had no lock. She turned on the taps of the ancient half-sized bathtub. Let them think she was having a bath. As quietly as she could, she opened the window. No screen. Better and better. Still holding her trainers, she eased herself out the window, landing in some sort of shrubbery—at least there were no briars. She turned to run when Frankie popped up from behind a bush, grabbing her arms and blocking her way.

"God damn you to hell," she hissed. "Let me go. Leave me alone."

"No," said Frankie. "Not until you listen to me."

She stopped struggling. Let him think she was complying. As soon as he relaxed his guard, she'd be off.

"Why are you even here?" she demanded. "Why is your uncle here?"

"Boy, you are really dumb, Katherine. Your mother and Lucy and everyone have been worried sick about you. You *disappeared*, Katherine. No one knew if you were alive or dead."

"I said, why are *you* here."

Frankie looked down at his feet. She sensed he wanted to kick gravel, like he always used to do, but they were still in the bushes. His hold loosened a little, but Katherine didn't move.

"I thought it might be my fault," he mumbled. "That you ran away."

"I didn't run away," she began, and then she stopped.

How was it Frankie's fault?

"What happened to you, Katherine? Just tell me. I came all this way to find you, and I paid for my own ticket and Uncle Joe's with my own money from my job. What happened to you?"

Who hurt you? Frankie had asked her once, so long ago, in another world, when she was someone else. She had taken off her shirt and asked him to touch her and then he'd just held her while she wept. And they'd both gotten into trouble, because they'd run away from school to the woods, and she had been naked, half naked....

"I pretended I was Eliza Doolittle," she heard herself say. "I told this man that was my name, and I talked like I was from the East End of London and I made up a whole story and I couldn't stop. I couldn't get out of the story. He took me to a pub, and I got drunk and then somehow I got on the tube with him, and I didn't know where I was going or how to get back, and then he took me to an ugly room. I don't really remember much after that, but when I woke up I was sick and naked and the door was locked...."

She hardly registered when Frankie led her to a garden bench in the full sight of the kitchen windows. She just kept talking and talking while Frankie held onto her, and she didn't stop until she got to the end.

And then she remembered where she was.

"You can't tell anyone, Frankie. You can't tell Lucy or my mother. They wouldn't understand. Now do you see why I have to go back? Will you help me? Please!"

"Of course I'll help you," Frankie said. "But I'm not going to help you do more stupid stuff and get yourself and everyone else killed, including your girlfriend Robin—"

"She's not my girlfriend. She never—"

"Okay, okay. But if you care about her, don't be dumb, Katherine."

Years fell away, all the awkward years when they didn't speak in the hall at school. They were kids again, blood brother and sister. They'd caught a murderer together.

"Here's something you don't know," he went on, lowering his voice. "We've been followed. Probably by that creep Mister Tobias and the guy who was gonna snuff you and your pals. You gotta talk to everybody, tell everything. Rowena, too. She's cool. She's got ESP. We've got to make a plan. And cut Lucy and your mom some slack. They've got guts. And they've laid their life on the line for you. We all have."

"Oh," was all she said.

Oh shit, she was going to cry.

Chapter Seventy-Seven

Frankie had earned his spurs, the old-fashioned phrase kept repeating in Lucy's mind, perhaps because she was so tired from sitting up most of the night with Katherine and Anne. She could not think straight. She felt as if she were in two places or times at once, one the bustle of an English country kitchen where she was happy to note both Frankie and Katherine tucking into breakfast with good appetite. But another part of her saw though some mist. There Frankie did appear to have the gravitas of a knight, all his sullenness turned to determination; the boy who had kicked at gravel had become a rock, the planes of his face austere, almost ancient. Katherine was no distressed damsel to Frankie's knight, but something wild and canny, sturdy yet supple, like a tree in a gale, or a deer that knows the power of its leaps or maybe something fiercer, a cat that knows how to wait, then spring. These were the children of her heart. Whether they loved her or left her behind, she would be with them, a vein of underground water or rock, a wind at their backs. *I promise*, she spoke to them silently, *I promise*.

As if she had heard, Katherine looked up from her plate, and met Lucy's gaze for the first time. Katherine did not smile exactly, but something in her expression shifted, like the subtlest breeze skimming a pool, leaving in its wake a dark calm.

Then Constable Albutt rapped her teacup with a spoon, and Lucy snapped to, feeling as though she had been woken suddenly from a dream. The crowded kitchen table came into sharp focus and Lucy took a bracing sip of her tepid tea.

"If your mouths be full, by all means keep mastificating, but harken to me. It's time to see to what's what and make a plan before matters be out of our hands."

"Which may happen very soon," Rowena interrupted. "Our pursuers are close. Very close."

"Do tell," said the Constable, somewhat coolly.

In their short acquaintance Rowena and Constable Albutt had developed a rivalry.

"I just did," shot back Rowena. "And if you'll give me a moment to attune, I will tell you more."

The constable crossed her arms across her massive chest. Ignoring Rowena, she turned her attention to Katherine.

"Young lady, it's you we need to hear from first."

"Robin didn't kidnap us," Katherine said in a clear, strong voice. "She rescued us. We'd all be dead if it weren't for her."

"You've said as much before," observed the constable.

Katherine stared at her warily.

Rowena rearranged her shawls and leaned towards Katherine, clearly about to speak.

"I am not an enemy to Roberta Loveridge, her as we also call Robin," Constable Albutt went on before Rowena could get a word in. "Happen we have or had a common enemy. One George Adcock, late of Loveridge Hall. Nor I never set foot on this land while 'a desecrated it, not even to visit me brother. No, I am not blaming the lass for whatever she might have done. When a bounder marries your stepdame and adopts her whelp to gain control of the property what you've been disinherited and exiled from, then I say a girl might be driven to desperate if ill-considered actions. Actions, what if I weren't the law, I might cheer."

Lucy appreciated the much more succinct summary of Roberta's complicated plight than the muddled one she'd read in the newspaper.

"But that's not why!" Katherine began, then stopped herself.

"Go on, dearie," encouraged Rowena. "I know you don't believe it yet, but everyone here wants to help you—and your Robin."

Katherine cast her a dubious look, then turned back to the constable.

"That man, George Adcock, you say his name was," Katherine took a breath as if about to plunge into deep, cold water, "if Robin did kill him—and she never told us anything, because she didn't want us to get in trouble for being accessories—he must have been one of them, one of the men who sold girls to be killed. We weren't the first lot. Others disappeared before us. One of them...one of them was Robin's true love, Pippa. Robin told us that much. She rescued us so we wouldn't be killed, like Pippa."

Lucy's vision blurred. Once again, she was seeing double. No, not double. Now there was only the stoop in that London slum late at night. Her hands, her strong, slender hands, are around that man's neck again.

"I know what you are. And I know what you did."

He chokes and splutters.

"It was your bullet."

"Hunting accident," he wheezes. *"Inquest. Case closed—"*

She tightens her grip.

"I can get that case reopened, and I will if you don't tell me now. Where is Pippa! Where are all the others!"

Now Lucy knew who Pippa was, now she knew.

He killed them both! Lucy tried to speak, but she was still half-way in the nightmare. "He killed them both!"

Her voice woke her out of her trance, and she looked around the table as everyone stared at her, Katherine clearly shaken.

"That was no hunting accident. George Adcock killed Roberta's Loveridge's father," said Lucy. "And as Katherine has already deduced, he is, at the very least, responsible for arranging the sale of girls to be killed."

There was a silence broken by the sound of Constable Albutt heaving herself out of her chair and letting loose a wail that raised every hair on Lucy's neck and on the hounds, who stood and growled.

"Why didn't I kill 'un myself! Coward that I was! Coward! I should a killed 'un myself."

"Arr, Jen, easy now, lass!" murmured her brother. Lucy guessed he had spoken these words before, many times. The hounds quieted, though they remained standing, but Jen Albutt wailed on.

To Lucy's surprise, and everyone else's, Rowena rose and went to her, short round Rowena, looking like a corgi going to the aid of a Saint Bernard. Shedding one or two of her shawls, she wrapped them around the constable, as if swaddling her. Then as far as her arms could reach, she held the big woman and did her best to rock her in her arms.

"There, there, love," Rowena soothed. "There, there!"

The wails diminished to moans, though the constable remained standing and staring.

"'a has spells now and again," John Little told them. "'twill soon pass."

Rowena went on speaking in a soft, hypnotic voice.

"I know what he did to you, love."

Lucy, lulled by Rowena's voice, found that she knew, too. She could see this massive woman once a slip of a girl, cornered by a man, in what must have been servants' quarters, a closet where linens were kept in a remote part of a great house. He followed her there, and no one could hear her and no one could help.

"And I know he never paid for what he did," Rowena went on. "Not in life. Oh, the rotter, he thought *he* was the injured party. Disgraced, humiliated, made *persona non grata* on this estate, because the master believed your brother when he made an accusation. But justice wasn't done, was it? No, justice was never done. That's why you married Constable Albutt and took over his office when he died. To see justice done. And you will, love, you will."

Fat Jen Albutt let herself be rocked as she wept, more and more softly until she suddenly, almost violently, shook Rowena off, shawls flying and falling to the floor.

"Arrr, that's enough now. I don't need you to tell me my own story—nor to tell everyone else."

Appearing to take no offense, Rowena shrugged, gathered up the shawls and sat back down. The constable also resumed her seat and, for good measure, glared at everyone, except Katherine. She reached out and patted her hand.

"It's an old story, lass. Happen you thought it was a new one. Still and all it's your story we need now, lass. See, till last night, I made sure I didn't know where her we call Robin were hiding, not that I couldn't guess easily enough. If I didn't know, I couldn't arrest her. Dereliction of duty you might call it; I been treading a fine, wobbly line. How far I can go to help her depends a lot on you, young miss. I need to know all about what you and the others was rescued from. I need to know about those men Madame Blavatsky here says is pursuing. I need to know now. If you want to speak to me private-like," the constable cut her eyes at Rowena, "that can be arranged."

Katherine was silent for a moment, then she looked around the crowded table, for the first time taking in their presence as something other than a threat.

"Frankie said I should tell everyone. Everything," she said.

And Katherine began.

Sitting beside Anne, Lucy could sense her tension. Anne took small gulps of air whenever she ran out of the breath she'd kept holding. Lucy reached under the table for Anne's hand and found that Joe Petrone had already placed his hand over Anne's clasped ones. So Lucy withdrew hers and closed her eyes as she listened to Katherine's tale, one she half-knew from dreams. She saw all too clearly the huge and horrifying Mister Tobias, menacing and unctuous at once. But she had not known all the perverse horrors he and others had perpetrated on her child. Then Lucy slipped back into the body of the seeming young man, the one she now knew as the woman Robin. Once again Lucy witnessed Katherine's defiant performance of an American Negro woman's song, a performance that had marked her for death. Whatever Roberta Loveridge had done to rescue Katherine and others, Lucy felt, in her own clenched burning hands, she could do, too. God have mercy on her. God have mercy on them all.

Then Katherine fell silent and the whole room with her, except for the clock ticking, the kettle on the stove softly hissing, and Anne letting out a long, ragged breath. When the phone rang, everyone startled and looked at each other. They didn't need Rowena to warn them that the call was dire. Nobody spoke as John Little answered the phone with a growl, listened, growled again. He put the receiver down and came back to his seat at the table, sinking into it and resting his face in his hands.

"Well?" said his sister before Rowena beat her to it.

"Bide a moment, Jen. I have to ponder."

Tension mounted in the room, showing itself in different ways. Rowena's shawls all but flapped like the wings of some agitated bird. Frankie tapped his feet so that the table jiggled, and Katherine was half out of her chair, but she allowed herself to be stayed by her mother's hand reaching for her across the table. Lucy stilled the trembling of her own hands by folding them together so that they prayed for her without words.

"I'm called to the Hall," John Little finally spoke. "By Lady Loveridge, her that was Robin's stepdame till her father was killed...."

"Murdered," Rowena could not restrain herself.

John Little put his hands down heavily on the table.

"There's three men come to stay, two gentlemen and a valet. One says he is an old friend of George Adcock."

"That much we know," said Rowena. "They were all in cahoots."

"Hush," said the Constable Albutt. "Go on. What do they *say* they want?"

"To pay respects to the widow and do a bit of shooting. Grouse. She asks me to act as guide."

"What did you answer, brother?" asked Jen.

"I told her as how I've work to finish this morning. Happen I'll stop by this afternoon to meet the gentlemen and see to their needs."

There was a small silence, then Katherine was on her feet, pulling away from her mother.

"Let me go," she cried, "I've got to warn Robin and the others."

"Sit, lass," growled the constable.

Katherine would not sit, but at least she did not bolt.

"Can we be certain these men are the ones who followed us?" asked Joe.

"We can," stated Rowena. "If you will trust me for a moment, I have never seen these men, but I will describe them in detail."

Before anyone could assent or object, Rowena shut her eyes and went on.

"There is a very large man, tall and wide, in expensive clothes, the sort rich men wear in the country. He has a meandering way of speaking. The one dressed as a valet hardly looks the part, despite the uniform. He is younger, blonde hair, almost white, in his thirties perhaps, has a discolored tooth and a hole in his ear where he may have recently removed an earring. The other so-called gentleman is much shorter, has excessive sideburns and I suspect at the full moon sprouts hair on his palms."

"That's them," said Katherine. "Mister Tobias, Tom Cat, and the man who wanted to make a film of us being snuffed. I've got to go!"

"Wait, young lady," Constable Albutt commanded again. "We need a plan."

"What do you mean, a plan!" demanded Anne, getting up and putting her arms around Katherine. "If these are the men who run that terrible place where Katherine was prisoner, if these are the men who killed those girls, and plan to kill others, what are we waiting for? Go arrest them! Now!"

Constable Albutt didn't answer for a moment. She sat, stone-like, her chins held up by her finger.

"I need back up," she stated. "Happen these men be armed and dangerous. Even if the lass identifies them, how am I to get the cuffs on 'un. Better not to show our hand yet. That's why my brother concealed your automobile in the hay barn last night."

"Then get it out of there!" Anne was frantic. "Because we are leaving with Katherine, right now! For the nearest airport!"

"No!" Katherine wrenched herself away from her mother. "I've got to go. I can't leave Robin. I won't leave Robin!"

Lucy felt dizzy, her heart racing down the road with Anne and into the wood with Katherine.

"If we take the car, we will not get away undetected," Rowena stated. "They will follow us. We could all be killed."

Anne stared at her wildly.

"You don't know that! You don't *know* that. I promised Katherine's father I'd—"

"I'm going! Now!" Katherine twisted and ducked under her mother's arm.

Frankie managed to block her way to the door, grabbing both her arms.

"Wait, Katherine," said Frankie. "Just wait, till we all decide what to do."

Joe Petrone got up and stood next to Anne.

"I'm with you, Anne," he said, "whatever happens. Let's hear the constable out. Call for back up, remember? That's the message I got when we all sat together on the hill. Those same words."

Anne did not speak.

We are in God's hands. That had been Anne's message, Lucy remembered. She watched as Anne unclenched a fist and reached for Joe's hand, imploring Katherine with the other.

Lucy closed her eyes, remembering her own vision.

I am the one you are looking for.

Robin. Robin.

"Here's my idea, always respecting as you must do what you think best, ma'am." The constable acknowledged Anne. "We want to capture these men for good and all, not on hearsay, not in any way as they can deny what they've done, all that they've done. Right now they don't know you're here. Happen they think you broke down, got lost or mired in a bog. They don't know the law—which is to say me—has been called in. Happen they think they can do as they please, as they's always done. Katherine," the constable addressed her by name for the first time, "can you find your way back to Robin's camp?"

Katherine nodded, "Robin showed me."

"Good. Go now, and take your people with you. Warn Robin and the others, tell her to camouflage the tree houses best she can. I want Robin to meet me at noon sharp at the boundary oak. 'a'll know the one. Now go as quick as you can. All but you, constable," she said to Joe. "I'll want to swear you in. I'll need your help."

Joe stepped closer to Anne.

"I can't leave the women to go alone," he protested.

"I'll be with them," said Frankie. "Can I take the bow and arrows?" He appealed to John Little.

And Lucy remembered Frankie's vision. Weapons, specifically a bow.

"Does tha know how to handle 'un, lad?"

"I do, don't I, Uncle Joe?"

"He does, but—"

"Don't fret yourself," said the constable. "We'll all be in the wood soon enough. If everyone is agreed—"

Frankie took the bow down from the wall.

"Come with me," Katherine appealed to her mother. "Please come."

"Call, Gerald," Anne said to Joe, releasing his hand. "Tell him, tell him...tell him whatever you can. And for the love of God, get me some cigarettes."

And she hastened after Katherine.

"It's all right," said Rowena to no one in particular. "We are under the protection of the Rose Cross."

"Miss Way," said Little John, and Lucy turned back. "Take Cerberus and Mauthe Dhoog with you. I've kennel dogs to take with me on the shoot."

The dogs hardly needed telling, they sprang to their feet and flanked Lucy.

"You've a way with animals. Keep the beasts quiet till it's time to spring the trap. Tha'll know."

Lucy prayed with all her heart that she would.

(He had not enjoyed it. No, not at all. He fastened his cufflinks and covered the marks where the ropes had chafed his wrist. Older women were harpies, unnatural in their lusts. No, he would not be dedicating a corridor to their perversities, after all.

With any luck, he would not be further subjected to his hostess' appetites. His business would be concluded this same night. The gamekeeper Little—he almost felt sorry for the man, if his duties included servicing the lady of the manor—must be aiding and abetting the murdering thief and her stolen goods—which made him an accessory to her crimes and therefore subject to...persuasion.

He donned his jacket and regarded himself in the looking glass. There was no doubt he made an impressive sight in his summer-weight hunting tweeds. The understated elegance of the garments suited his height and girth. Indeed, he looked every considerable inch the gentleman he had not quite been born. A pity he would not appear in the film. But then, invisibility was the true measure of genius....)

Chapter Seventy-Nine

Anne had no choice but to keep running. There was only her daughter disappearing over a rise, then appearing again, as she paused by a rock or a tree, to wait for them to catch up, Frankie, tumbling to a stop a few feet ahead of Katherine. The rest, Lucy, Rowena, and Anne had to keep running to keep up, Lucy almost young in her gait, with the hell hounds bounding back and forth to urge her on, Rowena, shawls flapping, an earth-bound bird, too heavy to lift off, and Anne last. Was she the only one gasping for breath? Damn the cigarettes! Was she the only one who felt that she might die? She could not remember the last time she had run. Maybe she had never run, even as a child. It was easier to freeze. She'd been frozen, all her life she'd been frozen. Now her lungs squeezed and burned, sweat soaked her underwear, her blouse, even her slacks. The edges of her vision darkened.

She was going to die. She'd always been terrified of death. Now it didn't matter.

She had to keep running.

Then all at once, she stumbled to a halt. When the blood stopped roaring in her ears, she heard the sound of water and birds calling. Red gave way to green. And there was Katherine, hardly winded, standing next to her steadying her with a hand under Anne's elbow.

"All right, Mum?" Katherine asked.

Lucy and Rowena also stood still in milder states of recovery. Frankie stood a little apart, gazing around him.

Anne nodded, because she did not have enough breath to speak.

"Our camp is just down there," Katherine pointed to a place where the trees thinned. "All we have to do is follow the stream."

And she and Frankie bounded ahead.

Anne did not know how she managed to pick her way down the slope without tripping, Lucy and Rowena, just ahead of her, pausing now and then to make sure she was all right, she more than ten years younger than they were. (She still could barely breathe. It felt like, no, it was an asthma attack, like the ones she'd had as a child.) Then they were there in the clearing, surrounded by what sounded like a gabble of geese. Girls, girls of all shapes and sizes massing on Katherine, gathering her in. Anne stood still, her vision expanding and dimming with the pounding of her heart, her struggle for breath. Then a brief silence fell as the girls took in the newcomers.

"Oooo, a bloke!" one of them shrieked.

"'fot we didn't allow no blokes 'ere," said another.

"I don't care. I want that one!"

A bold redhead pointed to Frankie, who looked pleased but a bit unnerved.

"Constable Albutt said for them to come with me here," explained Katherine. "They're in danger. We all are. Mister Tobias and Tom Cat and that hairy man with the camera are after us. Where's Robin?"

Then, as if in answer, walking across the clearing, there she was. The girls turned towards her like plants towards light, and she even looked like a shaft of light, narrow, improbable, finding its way through dense canopy to the forest floor.

"Kat!" she called out. "You're back."

The young woman touched Katherine's arm lightly, then gestured towards Anne, Lucy, Rowena and Frankie who had backed away from the huddle of girls.

"These must be your people."

The girl approached them, grave and gracious as a head of state.

"Please make the introductions, Kat."

Kat, her daughter who'd never had a nickname, Kat. She stood next to Robin, shyly, proudly, her joy palpable.

"This is my mother, Anne Bradley. Mum, this is Robin. She drove me a long way so that I could call you, but you weren't home, you were...looking for me."

Robin took both Anne's hands in hers.

"I am so sorry. How terrible this must have been for you," she said.

As if this young boyish-looking girl had any idea what it was like to lose a child! And yet, suddenly, inexplicably, Anne felt that Robin did know all about it, all about the terror, the grief, the remorse. She had to fight back sudden tears.

"And this is Miss Troublecock," Katherine went on hurriedly, almost as if she wanted to prevent Anne from speaking.

"Miss Trebilcock," Frankie corrected. "She has ESP."

"At your service, Miss Loveridge." Rowena was uncharacteristically restrained.

They shook hands like gentlemen.

"And you," Robin turned to Frankie, "let me guess. You are Frankie, Katherine's blood brother."

"Katherine told you that?" Frankie seemed surprised.

"And I told her about how we caught a murderer—"

Katherine stopped abruptly, perhaps remembering that her precious Robin had likely killed someone herself.

"My uncle helped investigate," said Frankie. "He's here, too, working with Constable Albutt. We're going to trap them, the men who are trying to track you down."

Robin looked at Anne again, a questioning look. She understands, Anne thought, she understands that I want to take Katherine and run. And now Anne understood why Katherine wouldn't go.

"Constable Albutt wants you to meet her at the boundary oak," said Katherine, "at noon."

"We shall speak more of these matters presently," said Robin. "But first...."

Robin turned towards to Lucy.

"This is Lucy," said Katherine, "Miss Lucy Way. She's my—"

"Your fairy godmother," Robin said softly.

Lucy did not speak at all. Everyone else fell silent, too, riveted by the meeting of the tall girl with the short-cropped golden hair and the small older woman with the soft white curls. Both of them had eyes that looked like forest light, Anne noticed. An unmistakable current passed between them, so magnetic, so strong, Anne found herself feeling that one of them might be drawn into the other and disappear. The hounds seemed to sense it, too, whining softly and rolling on the ground between the two women.

At last Robin bowed her head, and Lucy answered with her own bow. A breeze stirred the leaves in the upper canopy as if the trees had let out a breath they'd been holding. Anne found herself able to breathe again, the sweet, fresh air flowing in, opening all the constricted passageways sure as a rising tide.

Chapter Eighty

Gerald stirred in his sleep and half woke. He had a crick in his neck; he needed the bathroom, but he didn't want to move. He and Jeremiah had fallen asleep together on the couch. The television blared static and snow. My God, what time was it?

Jeremiah had come over after work, not long after Anne's call, bringing Gerald some files he needed from the office, not that he could concentrate, but he was glad it gave Jeremiah a reason to see him. And of course, Gerald's mother and the twins had lobbied for Jeremiah to stay for dinner. Thank God. Gerald had told them Anne had found Katherine, and he was waiting to hear what flight they'd take. Which was true, as far as it went. But if Jeremiah hadn't been there to provide diversion, his mother would have worried more truth out of him. Jeremiah's tiny TV was broken, which gave him an excuse to stay and watch the second night of the Republican Convention—a mild horror compared to Gerald's life. They fell asleep together and now here he was, leaning back against Jeremiah, his head on his chest, Jeremiah—how had it happened?—holding him as if he were a child.

Jeremiah must have sensed his wakefulness, he stirred and half sat up, but not before he dropped a kiss on Gerald's head. Before he could think about it—he didn't want to think—Gerald turned and kissed Jeremiah on the lips, so quickly Jeremiah could not kiss him back.

"Ger—" Jeremiah began.

"I'm sorry," Gerald said. "It's not you. It's me. I love you, and I can't—"

"Ger," said Jeremiah gently, touching Gerald's cheek. "You're not even making sense. Don't sweat it. You're not yourself. Nothing happened."

"But I *am* myself," he realized. "I am this son of a bitch who's ruined the life of everyone I love. That's who I am—"

Then the phone rang.

Gerald bolted for the office.

"Yes, I'll accept the charges," he said before the overseas operator even asked.

It was four in the morning; it couldn't be anything else.

"Joe Petrone here."

"Joe? Where's Anne? Where's Katherine?"

"She's all right. Katherine's all right. Anne asked me to call and tell you. We're working with the police. We've called for backup."

Thank God for that!

"But where's Anne? Why can't she come the phone?" Why won't she, he did not say.

"Anne and Katherine, Frankie, Lucy and her friend Rowena, are in a safe place."

"A safe house? The police have them in a safe house?"

"A safe place," Joe repeated. "I'm going back there now. Anne said to tell you she'll call as soon as she can."

"But I don't even know where you are!" protested Gerald. "Anne insists that I shouldn't alert Scotland Yard. You were in law enforcement. Does that make any kind of sense to you?"

There was such a long pause. Had he lost the connection?

"I'm afraid it does, Rev, I mean Mr. Bradley."

Had Anne explained to him about not using the title as an address, he wondered inanely.

"We are working with the police here," Joe tried to reassure him.

"A constable," Gerald said. "A local cop. Anne said she was a woman."

"That's right," acknowledged Joe. "Constable Jen Albutt. We have a plan, Gerald."

We. Joe and the constable. Joe and Anne.

Then it better work, Gerald almost snapped. Stop, he told himself. He wasn't there. He had to trust Joe, trust Anne. Trust.

"God," he said out loud, "God."

"Anne will call you as soon as she can," said Joe again. "I better go."

"Thank you," said Gerald, not sure Joe had heard him.

Even after the line went dead, Gerald held onto the phone, until he started to shake so badly, he couldn't hold it.

When he came out of his office, Jeremiah was standing by the front door, shoes and jacket back on, ready to leave.

"Everything all right?" Jeremiah asked.

"No. I don't know. I just...feel so helpless."

Jeremiah stood quietly for a moment, waiting, Gerald didn't know for what.

"It's probably best I go," Jeremiah said at last.

It probably was, Gerald knew that. But he couldn't bear it. He was despicable, he was weak, and he didn't blame Jeremiah for wanting to go, but he couldn't bear it.

"Aw, Ger," Jeremiah sighed, and he gathered Gerald into his arms.

Chapter Eighty-One

As quietly as she could, Katherine set down the branches she'd gathered for camouflaging the tree house, turned around, and headed back into the forest.

She didn't want them to know that she had seen them, her mother and Frankie's uncle. Kissing. Her mother, who had never liked parishioners hugging her—or anyone hugging her—had thrown her arms around Joe Petrone's neck when he came back to camp with her cigarettes. And then she had kissed him. On the lips. She could not remember her mother ever kissing her father that way.

Katherine walked on deeper into the woods. If only she could just keep walking. But there was nowhere to go now. No place in the world that that was safe, not even the greenwood, now that her mother was there, kissing Frankie's uncle.

She heard footsteps coming up behind her. Maybe her mother figured out she had seen. Katherine didn't want to hear her mother apologize or explain. She picked up her pace, just short of breaking into a run.

"Hey, Katherine, wait up." Frankie caught up with her. "Where are you going?"

"Just getting more branches."

"You don't need to go very far to do that," Frankie gestured to the trees, "we're in the woods already."

"I wasn't running away, if that's what you're thinking," she said. "Not with everyone in danger from those men. I just wanted a little time to myself. Jeesh!"

Frankie did not take the hint to go away.

"You saw," he said.

"Saw what?" she turned toward him. Make him say it.

"Your mother, my uncle. In a lip-lock."

"Yeah," she admitted. "And I wish I hadn't."

"So? They have a crush on each other," Frankie shrugged. "It's life. These things happen."

He was trying to sound so cool, so grownup. It made her mad. What did he know? What had he ever been through compared to what she had? He was just a kid from a small town, even if he thought his rock and roll band would be the next Beatles or Rolling Stones.

"Not to your parents," she pointed out. "They like each other."

She had envied Frankie that. How his parents laughed together. Once she had seen Frankie's father pull Frankie's mother into his lap at the dinner table. She remembered being amazed.

"Yeah, I guess so." He seemed embarrassed. "Well, let's get some more branches, and then we'd better head back, find out what's going on."

They found an alder thicket not far away and cut branches for a while without speaking.

This is your chance, Little Sis, whispered Aramantha. *Ask, ask him what you've been wanting to ask him all this time. You might not get another chance, with all your girlfriends elbowing each other out of the way to get next to him. Not to mention, you all could die tonight.*

Her hands shook, and she fumbled with a branch.

"Stop torturing that sapling, Katherine. Here, watch me."

He cut the branches off neatly, leaving no jagged edges.

"Frankie?"

"What?" He sounded wary.

Go on, urged Aramantha.

"Why did you stop liking me?"

"Stop liking you?" he protested. "What do you mean?"

"You know what I mean," she insisted. "You stopped talking to me at school. You stopped going to Lucy Way's house with me. I know you mowed her lawn, but you didn't go there with me anymore, not the way we used to."

Frankie cut another branch.

"I didn't stop liking you, but, well, we weren't kids anymore. I couldn't keep playing like we were. You're like...my sister, Katherine. I mean you *are* my sister, my blood sister or I wouldn't be here."

She knew what he was saying. I like you, but not in that way.

"That day," she went on—it was like picking a scab, once you started you couldn't stop, "that day in the woods, when I took off my shirt and asked you to touch me, did you, I mean, did it gross you out, to touch me? Am I...repulsive?"

He whacked at a branch.

"Jesus, Katherine, what kind of question is that?"

"It's just a question," she said. Tears started to press behind her eyes, but she wasn't going to cry. "You don't have to answer if you don't want to."

She put away her knife and bent to gather up her pile of branches. Then Frankie pocketed his knife and lifted her by the shoulders, turning her towards him.

"You're pretty, Katherine. You're as pretty, prettier than any of the girls I go out with. You were my friend, my best friend when we were kids. And I just never thought of you...."

"That way," she finished for him.

"Yeah, no, I mean, but that day, well, I did touch you, remember? But you were so upset. You...you weren't yourself. I couldn't...I mean I knew something was wrong, really wrong."

Katherine couldn't help herself. The tears started to fall, but at least they were silent. Frankie wouldn't know. Then he reached out and touched her cheek.

"Who hurt you, Katherine?" he asked, as he had asked that day. "Who hurt you?"

She shook her head. She still couldn't tell him. She couldn't tell anyone, not even Robin. Even though she had told him, told everyone, about being raped and pawed by all those men. Even after she'd seen her mother kiss Joe Petrone. She couldn't.

"Katherine."

He took her face in both his hands and kissed her on the lips lightly, gently, his tongue just a flicker, sunlight, flame.

Well, at least if you die, you had one kiss from someone besides disgusting old men, sighed Aramantha, *even if it is only Frankie Lomangino Jr.*

"What's funny, Katherine?" demanded Frankie, letting her go.

"Nothing!" she laughed, and she threw her arms around his neck and kissed him, quickly, just once. "We better get back now."

And they gathered up their branches.

Chapter Eighty-Two

Dusk was falling. Yes, it felt like falling. Birdsong twittering into silence. Leaves shifting with the changing rivers of air. The girls were quieting, too, fading into the forest, finding their hiding places, the men the constable had called for backup, also taking their positions in the frontlines and in the camouflaged treehouses. Lucy sat on a stump just outside the half-built hut that had also been covered with branches, a hand on the hounds who lay beside her, both of them warm, relaxed, and completely alert.

Everyone was here but Robin. She and the constable had been gone all afternoon. Now Jen Albutt had returned and, of all things, commandeered Rowena. It struck Lucy that, in shifting configurations, there were couples, likely and unlikely, all around her, elephants and giraffes, moles and warthogs, preparing to escape catastrophe two by two. She had seen Joe and Anne embrace each other and Katherine and Frankie returning from the wood with armloads of branches, Katherine with a lightness about her Lucy had not seen in so long. Now in a huddle, not far from her, the constable and the medium.

Then the hounds rose, quivering with expectation, sensing just before Lucy saw a tall figure coming towards her, so tall and lithe it would be easy to take her for a dryad, the walking form of a young birch. Before Lucy could get to her feet, Robin sank to her knees, as graceful and silent as the falling light.

"Lucy Way."

Those eyes that Lucy had seen out of now gazed into hers.

"Why do I feel that I know you or perhaps I mean that you know me?"

"I am not sure I know the answer to your question, dear heart."

Lucy thought back to her first glimpse of Robin at the edge of her garden, the rage that had so frightened her, that she now recognized as her own.

"Perhaps," Lucy spoke tentatively, not sure what she wanted to say could be put into words, "perhaps we are not as separate as we seem, one from another. Perhaps sometimes God lends us each other's eyes, if there is something we need to see, to know."

"God," Robin repeated. "I'm afraid I am not well-acquainted with God, despite being christened in the C of E. More at home in the woods than in the church."

"Christ spent much of his time outdoors," Lucy noted. "Out on the water, in the mountains or the desert, riding a donkey in the streets of Jerusalem. One hardly pictures him indoors. Of course there was the time he was teaching in Peter's house and someone tore the roof off to bring him a paraplegic."

Robin laughed softly. "Sounds like a chap after my own heart."

"Yes," said Lucy.

Neither spoke for a time, the light fading, the distance between them a small darkness.

"I thought I could keep them safe here, the girls," said Robin at length. "I suppose because I felt safe here as a child. I didn't think very far, I'm afraid."

"Far enough," said Lucy. "Far enough."

"I've got to go now," said Robin, getting to her feet. "I've got to wait for those men by the fire. Pray, Lucy Way, please pray that all the others will be safe. Katherine and all the girls, Jen, your friends, Little John—"

Her voice broke and the dogs whimpered softly.

"Hush Cerberus, Hush Mauthe Dhoog," said Robin. "Stay quiet with Lucy Way till your master gives you the signal. Do you understand?"

Their silence answered. Then Robin knelt again, bowing her head next to Lucy's heart.

"Will you give me a blessing?" she asked.

Lucy put her hands on Robin's head. Whose fire did she feel, what fire? Dark, bright what was this invisible light between them?

"Defend, O Lord, this thy child from all the perils of this night."

Lucy lifted Robin's face to hers and kissed her forehead. Then the tall girl rose into the night.

(It had taken hours to break the wily gamekeeper, who led them in circles on the heath in pursuit of those stupid birds. He knew, he knew all along what they were after and he thought to deceive them by playing the ignorant country oaf. That was before they put a gun to his head, tied him up, beat him just shy of a pulp and made a call to H. at Scotland Yard.

Still bound and on a rope lead, the giant was guiding them into the forest now, surer-footed than his captors. How he hated what others simpered over as nature. It did not belong on his shoes, or brushing up against his jacket. But tonight it was necessary. The shadow had wrapped this shadowy forest around her when she infiltrated his world. Now they were here, invading her on her own ground. They'd picked up her scent, they would hunt her down, bait her, and she would take the bait.

They would leave her no other choice.)

Chapter Eighty-Three

Anne desperately wanted a cigarette, but of course she could not light up and give away their presence to the men they were waiting to ambush. She had a job to do: keep Katherine safe, Katherine and her motherless friends. She could almost feel her arms spread into wings, keeping them behind her, holding them back from their beloved Robin, who sat alone on one of the stumps beside a campfire that burned low enough so that every sound could be heard and bright enough to cast the surrounding woods into obscurity. A full moon was rising, too. Anne had fretted about that. Wouldn't it be that much easier for them to be seen? Joe said not. He said the moonlight created confusion, threw off depth perception, made it hard to tell what was substantial and what wasn't.

She hoped he was right. About the moonlight, about the crazy plan she had never really agreed to. She'd been too busy running after Katherine. (She really should give up cigarettes; maybe now was the time when she might not have long to live anyway. She would die before she would allow any more harm to come to her daughter.) Joe had been right before, she reminded herself. And she was not sorry that she had kissed him today. Not sorry at all.

"We'll have them surrounded," Joe had assured her.

He was positioned in the hidden treehouse with Frankie and another of Jen Albutt's men. Jen had also rounded up tenant farmers who'd been evicted or had the land sold out from under them by

George Adcock. They'd come armed with hunting rifles and pitchforks. They were stationed on the ground, ready to rush the pursuers at a signal from Jen. And Lucy had charge of the hounds who could take down a man and rip out his throat.

If they weren't shot first. Any of them, all of them could be shot, if those men suspected an ambush. They could fire randomly into the woods. Moonlight and shadow, substantial insubstantial, wouldn't matter....

Gerald, she found herself thinking, *Gerald I forgive you, please forgive me. If we meet again...*but she found she couldn't finish that thought. No vision of the future made any sense. There was only this moment, nowhere else to be and nothing else to do. *The twins will be all right, the twins will be all right,* those words repeated themselves in the back of Anne's mind, a kind of prayer. *The twins will be all right. Gerald will take care of them.* A surprising thought, but there it was. And she, she would take care of Katherine.

And then Anne heard the sound of twigs breaking under heavy footsteps. John Little, gagged and with his hands bound behind his back, stumbled into the clearing followed by his captors.

Chapter Eighty-Four

"Anne!"

Gerald's own voice woke him. He had fallen asleep on the couch after lunch. What time was it? The house was so quiet. His mother must have gone to pick up the kids from camp and taken the dog with her.

"Anne?" he said, as if she could hear.

In his half-dream, she had felt so close, closer than usual. When she had been here at home, he often couldn't talk to her. Or maybe he did talk, talked too much about news or politics, but she didn't listen. And why should she? Mostly he talked bullshit, utter crap. He never said what really mattered. He was a liar, or had become one.

"Anne," he said again, "when you come home, I am going to tell you the truth. You can leave me or turn me over to the police or stay with me and punish me the rest of my life. I will tell you the truth."

He sat up, swung his feet to the floor, and then found himself slipping to his knees.

"Let them be all right," he prayed. "Let Katherine and Anne be all right. In Christ's name I pray, let them be all right.

Chapter Eighty-Five

Katherine stood on tiptoes, straining to see over the shoulder of the burly farmer who stood in front of them, her mother and her friends. She could just see Robin in profile rising to her feet. She couldn't bear not knowing what was happening. Slowly Katherine lowered herself to the ground and crept forward just an inch, so that she could peer past the farmer's legs, her view unobstructed. She felt her mother bend and put a restraining hand on her back, but her mother knew not to make any sudden movements or to speak at all, even in a whisper.

Now she could just see Little John, his mouth gagged, his hands bound behind him. There was Tom Cat pressing a gun at his temple. Tom Cat looked just the same. He could be in a park or a pub, an alley or a room with a naked bulb, or here in the wood with a campfire. If his orders were to trick or bind or beat or rape someone, then he was in his element. The hairy little man had no care for anything but his camera, which was aimed at Robin.

Like Mister Tobias' gun.

Such a tiny gun compared to his huge body, his enormous shadow pooling out behind him as he stepped into the firelight. The gun was like his willy, she suddenly thought, a toy thing, a tadpole till it turned lethal.

"I am the one you are looking for."

Robin spoke in a low, clear voice. It was not loud; it had nothing to do with shouting. Yet Katherine was sure the birds in the highest branches, wings over their heads, could hear it in their dreams.

"Miss Loveridge, I am delighted to meet you again in your true, shall we say, guise, no longer falsely, though I must admit quite convincingly, posing as a young gentleman to gain admission where you had no right to intrude, or skulking about in alleyways of London slums, something someone of your breeding surely should have avoided. Here, yes, here you are in your natural habitat, as it were."

Mister Tobias' voice might give the birds nightmares, but it also carried.

"How this hapless gentleman fares is entirely up to you, as I am sure you have the mental and perhaps even the moral acuity to understand. By the bye, it took a modicum of, shall we say, persuasion. But in the end, as you see, he's betrayed you."

John Little hung his head, as if in shame, but Katherine knew he saw everything that his captors did not. He was waiting, like all of them, waiting. The breeze hushed and the fire dropped its hissing to a whisper, as if everything were listening, the moon inching higher for a better view. Katherine willed her hearing to sharpen and her mind to remember every word.

"The same applies to the fate of your erstwhile attendants, your gamboling nymphs, as it were."

"Gamboling nymphs?" Robin managed to sound mystified and contemptuous at the same time. "How fanciful you are, Mister Tobias. But I forget, you read classics at Oxford until you were sent down for...I believe the charge was pandering?"

Mister Tobias shrugged, and his shadow appeared even more grotesque, an oversized vampire.

"My past is of no import here, Miss Loveridge. Your present and your future, should you have one, and the future of the charges you have so ignominiously procured, is our only concern in this moment."

Just listening to him speak, as if he were fingering words for his own sick pleasure, made Katherine feel claustrophobic. Even in the open air of the forest, she could feel the walls of that dingy room closing in on her as Mister Tobias dwarfed the doorway.

"'e means those birds wot you nicked out from under our noses, you lezzie bitch."

Tom Cat's interruption was almost a relief.

"Now, Thomas, there is no need to be unnecessarily crude. But yes indeed, Miss Loveridge, there were some young ladies in my care whom I believe it would be fair to say you abducted, even kidnapped, a fact that, as I explained to Mr. Little here, would be of great interest to my friends at Scotland Yard. Call them forth, Miss Loveridge, do."

Robin appeared to be puzzled.

"I'm sorry, Mister Tobias, could you be a little more explicit? Which young ladies and how did they come to be in your care?"

With his free hand, Tom Cat reached into his back pocket, pulled out a flask and took a swig.

"'ow? you ask. Why I picked every one of 'em off the street like the filfy garbage they is. Gave 'em a fine 'ome."

Tom Cat was drunk, Katherine realized. Even with bound hands and hobbled ankles, Little John could probably knock him over if he needed to.

"I see," said Robin. "You took in girls without connections and gave them a chance to improve their lot through," she paused delicately, "sexual slavery."

It seemed to Katherine that Mister Tobias was swelling up, growing bigger. Like a toad puffing itself. But what they needed were words, incriminating words.

"Indeed, indeed. I endeavored to give them useful skills, artistry, acting, costume, makeup, that might serve them in later life. Dear miss or sir, if you prefer, apprenticeship is not be conflated with slavery. And what, in your wildest imaginings, do you suppose you have to offer these poor unfortunate children of the streets, a life as fugitives in a savage wasteland? Call them to you, I say, unless you've imprisoned them in wicker cages to be victims of sacrifice in some horrific rite to satisfy your own perverted lusts."

Katherine looked at the whiskered werewolf. He had his camera trained on Robin. He was filming.

"So that's the script," Robin stated.

"I beg your pardon?" said Mister Tobias.

"That's the plotline of the film your friend was going to make with the girls you sold to him."

"Is, miss, not was, *is*," muttered the whiskered man.

"Say again?" said Robin.

"I must say," the hairy man went on, panning the camera to the fire, then up to the full moon, "I couldn't ask for a better setting."

"Ah," said Robin. "But don't you think the storyline is a bit hackneyed? Wicker cages, virgin sacrifice? Hasn't it all been done to death?"

"To deaf!" Tom Cat took another swig. "Now you're talkin'!"

"No, no, no," protested Mister Tobias. "I would not call it hackneyed, oh, no my dear. I am surprised to hear someone of your intellectual training say so. I think we may safely say that we are in the realm of classical tragedy. We are talking about art—"

"We are talking about a snuff flick," said Robin calmly, "for wankers. Or rather a series of them."

She turned directly towards the filmmaker.

"This man," she gestured to Mister Tobias, "is your supplier. You were introduced to him by a mutual friend, one George Adcock, who would have taken a cut of the proceeds."

"Had he lived, Miss Loveridge," said Mister Tobias, taking a step closer to her. "Had he lived. For your own good, I beg you not to be so frivolous and precipitous in making such offensive, not to say presumptuous, accusations. You are, as the saying goes, treading on thin ice, very thin ice. For I suspect, and you have already intimated as much to interested parties at Scotland Yard, that you and you alone may have intimate and personal knowledge of how the late lamented George Adcock came to end his days in a wheelie bin not far from your domicile."

"The stupid git," put in Tom Cat, staggering a little. "Fancy getting' blowed by a muff-munching toff. Like to get 'er in a dark alley, I would. Show 'er a fing or—"

"Accuse me all you like," Robin cut him off. "You and your artistic associate here are responsible for the death of Pippa Worth and five of her friends."

"Alas, I'm afraid that film was my first effort in the genre," said the filmmaker almost apologetically. "I am eager to improve on it. This new film, you see, even in these primitive conditions, has the potential to become a classic. Fantasy meets cinéma vérité, shot in real time. The lighting is perfect right now. We don't have a moment to lose. Come, Tobias, you've been paid and paid handsomely. Round up the cast! I've got a film to shoot and a plane to catch."

"Call the girls," said Mister Tobias, his voice without the florid speech dropping to a different register.

"Supposing there were such girls and I had the power to call them, now that you've made it plain you intend to kill them, why would I do any such thing?"

"Because, my dear Miss Loveridge, if you don't, I will kill you and your accomplice slowly and painfully. Then we will hunt down every one those little trollops and kill them in a similarly excruciating fashion. Whereas if you give us your full co-operation, their inevitable deaths will be painless, elegant, and administered by your own hand. This is the last good office you can render your little—"

"Cunts!" shouted Tom, jubilantly, weaving and waving his gun about erratically.

"So which is it to be?"

With one huge step, Mister Tobias closed the gap between himself and Robin, grabbed her hair, wrenched back her head and jammed the gun into her mouth.

Oh god oh god oh god.

Katherine held her breath. If any of them moved, if the dogs rushed him, if the constable tried to arrest him, Mister Tobias would kill Robin. Something, someone had to distract him, turn him away from Robin. They had all promised they would not let themselves be seen but—*Stop!* Katherine tried to speak, but no sound came out. She took another breath.

"*Stop!*" she sang out. "*In the name of love.*"

And then all the other girls joined in.

"*Before you break my heart.*"

Mister Tobias let go of Robin and whirled around wildly, a strange look of terror on his face.

"*Stop! In the name of love*," they sang on together, on and off key, louder and louder. "*Before you break my heart.*"

"Mummy, mummy!" Mister Tobias whimpered, and then he shouted. "They're doing it again. Make them stop. Make them stop!"

"*Think it o-o-ver*," they caterwauled.

He started walking towards the sound of their voices, his gun pointed at their hiding place.

And then something whistled through the air. Mister Tobias let out a howl, dropped the gun, and turned in circles trying to grasp the arrow that had found its mark.

In his ass.

After that, everything happened very quickly. John Little tipped over Tom Cat who fell flat on his face, losing his grip on his gun just as the hounds charged into the circle, Mauthe Dhoog knocking over the filmmaker whose camera went flying. Cerberus leapt into the air and brought down Mister Tobias, who screamed again as he fell backwards, the arrow penetrating deeper into his massive flesh.

"Don't move!" bellowed Constable Albutt on a bullhorn. "You're surrounded, and you are all under arrest for abduction, rape, pandering, sex trafficking, human trafficking, murder and attempted murder and more as I think of it."

Constable Albutt's reinforcements swarmed the men and soon had them cuffed and shackled.

"Escort them out," ordered Jen. "There's a police van ready and waiting for them at the farm."

As the men disappeared into the surrounding darkness, Katherine and her friends ran to Robin and threw their arms around her and each other. Robin held them close.

"Darlings," she kept murmuring, "oh, my darlings."

Katherine did not know how long they stood, laughing and weeping together. As they quieted, she became aware of another circle standing silently around them, waiting.

"Darlings," Robin said one more time. And very gently Robin loosed herself from their arms.

Katherine turned and saw her mother, Lucy, Rowena, Frankie's uncle, Frankie, still holding the bow—it must have been his shot that saved them!—John Little, freed from his gag and ropes, and Jen Albutt, in her uniform, brass buttons gleaming in the firelight. The huge dogs lolled and panted near Lucy's feet. She thought she detected traces of blood on their jowls.

Then the constable stepped forward, parting the tight circle of girls and coming to stand face to face with Robin.

"Are you ready?"

"I am, Constable Albutt."

"Roberta Loveridge, it be my sad and solemn duty to arrest you on the charge of homicide in connection with the well-deserved death of George Adcock. May his foul soul rot in hell."

There was an awful silence. The fire hissed and an owl's cry rang out. And then Katherine and all the girls began an uproar, wailing and shouting as they rushed to Robin again.

"We won't let you take her! We won't!"

And Robin managed to encircle them all again, as if she were a goddess with infinite arms.

"Hush, darlings," Robin said in her low voice. "All shall be well."

"No, it won't. It isn't!" wailed Doreen. "What's to become of us! We was going to stay 'ere with you in the forest. Forever and ever. In our wattle and shit 'ut!"

Robin didn't answer for a moment. Katherine with her cheek pressed next to Robin's felt the escaped tear.

"Forgive me, all of you, please forgive me." Robin paused. "There has been a slight change of plan. But if you will stick by me, well, darlings, you will be protected, provided for and have a chance to take part in the trial of the century."

The girls began to murmur and question.

"Right then, time to move out," said the constable.

"Let's sing as we go," said Robin. "Kat, lead us. Something lively!"

Robin was asking the impossible. But she was asking it, and Katherine could deny her nothing. She swallowed a storm of tears and took a deep breath.

"*R-E-S-P-E-C-T*," she belted out, her voice filling night, big as the full moon, "*find out what it means to me. R-E-S-P-E-C-T, take care, TCB!*"

"*Re, re, re, re, re, re, respect!*" Robin and the girls came in on the chorus.

And they sang on stronger and surer till everyone, *everyone*, Frankie, Rowena, Joe, Jen, and even her mother and Lucy joined in. Robin started to clap a rhythm, and their walk out of the greenwood became a dance.

Chapter Eighty-Six

Lucy sat in the aisle seat this time, Katherine beside her in the middle and Frankie in the window seat Katherine insisted he take. Lucy could not tell if Frankie was asleep or just gazing out at sky, clouds and far, far below them the sea. Katherine had been reading a detective novel, an Agatha Christie whose plot Lucy had forgotten, nothing like what Katherine had gone through. That was the comfort of detective novels, she supposed, they brought order to human aberration. Really, they were the antithesis of mystery. Perhaps the novel failed to hold Katherine's interest, or just as likely she was simply exhausted. She had put the book down and closed her eyes, letting herself lean against Frankie's shoulder.

They were all in the air, in every sense, neither here nor there. It felt at the moment like mercy or anyway a small remission. "*His blood was shed for you and for many for the remission of sin*," the line from the Communion service went through her mind. So much sin. Maybe sin could not be cured, just go into remission as Elsa's cancer had. Father James had left a message for her at the hotel. No one knew how long it would last. Lucy hoped she would not have to leave Elsa again at a critical juncture, but she might.

Lucy had promised Katherine that she would return with her to England for Robin's trial and for the trials of the three men. Anne, Joe, and Frankie would also return, if called to testify. That was the only way Katherine would consent to return to the States. Rowena had extended hospitality to any girl who wanted to go back to London and Jen Albutt to those who wished to remain in the country. Robin had spent her last afternoon of freedom with a solicitor, transferring a trust she'd come into at her majority to John Little to be administered on behalf of the five girls who had no home, no family. They would have a chance, at least, at making a life for themselves. Lucy knew it had been wrenching for Katherine be parted from friends who had shared sufferings that no one else knew. And saying goodbye to Robin had been hardest of all.

They'd had a late supper at John Little's cottage. Then they'd all followed Robin outside to Jen Albutt's car. A head taller than most of the girls, her hair gleamed in the light of the setting moon as she embraced each girl one more time. Lucy and the others had stood back, but she would never forget the look that passed between Robin and herself just before Robin got into the car. There were no words for what it conveyed. But in its wake, she felt an inexplicable peace.

Lucy closed her eyes. Would she be able to see with Robin's eyes again? Share her prison cell? Because Robin had disappeared for so long, evading arrest as far as the law was concerned, she would not be released on her own recognizance and it was possible that she would be held without bail till her trial. Lucy wished she could keep Robin company or perhaps take her place. Had she not shared in her crime?

Lucy shifted from waking to dreaming so seamlessly she hardly knew it happened. She could still feel herself in the plane, but the sound of the engines faded. Clouds drifted under her eyes, turning her cheek bones to sky; faraway, and then so near, the sound of wind soughing over waves, the touch of its mightiness, soft, even warm. Then, quite distinctly, she heard someone speak. *Yes, yes, Lucy, let me see with your eyes now.*

(Everything was too small, the absurd striped uniform that did not cover his ankles or wrist and cut into his private parts. He overflowed the narrow bed—really hardly more than a shelf built into the wall. He filled the tiny cell so completely he might have been a crustacean outgrowing a shell. At least there was some dignity in being

alone, not sharing his quarters with common criminals. And it was better than those tedious, jolting hours crammed into the back of a van, chained next to his odious companions. Where they had been stashed he did not know or care. No, he did care; he hoped they were being buggered to death by insatiable thugs.

When he was allowed to make his one phone call, he had telephoned the woman. He had never liked her or the airs she gave herself, but she had been useful, efficient, tending to her charges with just the right degree of brutality. She served him well, not out of loyalty, but because she knew he had the power to send her back to prison. He told her to destroy all the records of membership, to turn the girls into the streets, and to make herself scarce, as in leave the country.

He could not help but feel noble, self-sacrificing, troubling to save his clients' reputations, such as they were, keeping the government itself from chaos and collapse. He had thought H. would commend him and in return do all in his considerable power to help the old school friend who had kept his secrets so discreetly, who had procured esoteric pleasures for him so readily and imaginatively....

In the end, H. was like all the others, like his father, all of that class who used and discarded whatever, whomever they pleased.

It wouldn't matter. Not for long. He knew how to do what he had to do, and H. had provided him with the means. Putting on gloves, H. had removed his very long belt from his trousers. But he had not unzipped his trousers, demanding one more sexual service, nor had he wielded the belt as an instrument of punishment and humiliation, all of which he might have expected as his due, as the price for whatever H. would do to help him out of this...scrape.

No, H. had made the belt into a simple noose, placed it under the naked pillow on the cot. Then he'd called for the guard and walked out without a word or a backward glance.

Was it a favor or an order?

He didn't know. He hardly cared.

The room was far too small, life was far too small.

He would just be going now.)

Chapter Eighty-Seven

Anne's and Joe's joined hands rested in her lap as he dozed. He had turned towards her so that his back shielded her from their seatmate, who was snoring now after several martinis, just as Gerald would have been. She did not think Gerald had ever tried—or at least he had not succeeded—in shielding her from anything.

Apples and oranges, she heard Joe's voice in her mind. He had said it before, when she had mentioned the differences between her husband and whoever Joe had become to her. And he was right. You could not compare a husband and a…lover? He wasn't, technically. There had been no time or place but the unspoken word tasted delicious, not like forbidden fruit but like something more homely and essential, cool water, warm bread.

They'd be landing in another couple of hours. Though Joe had left in his car in long term parking and could have driven them all home, Gerald was coming to meet Anne and Katherine. Of course he is! Joe had said. What man wouldn't? Though he didn't say it, she knew Joe was thinking of the wife and child he had never been able to find.

She lifted his hand to her heart, and he smiled in his sleep.

Anne was surprised that she wasn't more anxious about seeing Gerald again or more bereft about losing this sweet, brief what to call it—love?—with Joe. But neither the future nor the past seemed real to her right now.

"I'm not going to disappear from your life, Anne," Joe had said. "We don't have to do anything or decide anything. Not now."

And that felt true. The lack of urgency about anything felt luxurious. She had found Katherine. Katherine was safe. And, Anne was beginning to believe, whatever horror she had been through, she was going to be all right.

Because of Robin.

Anne closed her eyes and leaned her head against Joe's shoulder, not to sleep but to see again what she would always remember. Robin in the moonlight and firelight facing down those men. Robin holding the girls whose lives she had saved, then...letting them go. That was it. That was the saving grace. Katherine adoring this beautiful boyish girl who asked for nothing in return, didn't poke, prod, violate, or seduce. Though Robin was an avowed lesbian, had killed a man with her bare hands, she was, if not innocent herself, the protector of innocence, the restorer.

Joe woke and stirred, bending his head closer to Anne's.

"All right?" he asked softly.

"All right," she answered.

And maybe, for the first time since Hal died, she was.

Chapter Eighty-Eight

"It'll be all right, Ger!" Jeremiah said.

They were alone at the office. Gerald was leaving from work to drive to the airport and was now engaged in looking for his keys (why weren't they in his pocket where he always kept them, oh, here they were they were on the top of the toilet tank) and gathering scattered change for tolls. Now where had he put his cigarettes? He thought he had an unopened pack. It drove Anne crazy when he fumbled with his pipe while he was driving.

"Here, take mine." Jeremiah handed him a pack of Kools (how could anyone smoke mentholated cigarettes? It was better than nothing.) "It'll be all right," Jeremiah said again. "Your daughter is safe. Nothing else matters."

Gerald stopped and looked at Jeremiah, the smoothness and brownness of him, the kindness of him. Nothing would ever be all right without him. As if he heard what Gerald couldn't say, Jeremiah came and put his hands on Gerald's shoulders.

"I'm not going to disappear from your life, Ger. But you got business to take care of. You got to get your head back on right."

He had to face Anne, face Katherine. Face the music. Face himself, what he had done, everything that had happened because of it. The strangely peaceful hiatus was over, waiting at home, getting to know the twins, evenings on the couch with Jeremiah. How could he even think of that time as good, when Anne and Katherine had been facing dangers he did not yet fully comprehend?

"Now are you all set?" Jeremiah let go of him. "Got everything?"

Gerald patted the keys in his pants pocket and the cigarettes in his shirt pocket.

"Everything but a plan."

"Some things you can't plan ahead," said Jeremiah. "You'll know what to say when it's time."

Gerald reached for Jeremiah and pulled him close as if he could absorb his calm, his certainty. He would know what to say when it was time. He would know what to do. He hadn't told Jeremiah yet, but he was going to find a way to tell Anne that he loved this man.

Chapter Eighty-Nine

Katherine wished she did not have to have parents. Not a pair of
them, anyway, telling her they needed to talk to her. Oh, God, in her
father's office with the door shut. Her father sat at his desk with his
head bowed, as if he were reading or praying. She sat in the leather
easy chair (the uneasy chair it should be called) and her mother sat
in a straight-backed chair brought in from the kitchen. She had that
familiar look, closed and angry, that had always filled Katherine with
dread, since she was a kid. She could hear the twins outside playing
frisbee with Bear. She wished she could be with them. They'd hung
back from her at first, but when she was alone with them, they'd
asked questions and listened enthralled to her story of being rescued
and living in a treehouse. More than anything, Katherine wished she
could be back in the parentless world of the forest. It was a terrible
thing to be alone with her parents. Two against one.

And if they were going to talk to her, why didn't they talk already.
Maybe because there wasn't enough air in the dark book-lined room.
Maybe that's why she kept holding her breath. If she were lucky, she
might black out.

"Gerald, I think you should begin," her mother said at last.

Her father's throat needed a lot of clearing first. Katherine
couldn't stand to look at him. She looked at the shelves instead. D.
H. Lawrence. Her father's favorite author. It made a kind of horrible
sense.

"It wasn't your fault, Katherine." His voice sounded thick, like he hadn't cleared all the phlegm.

Here it was then. She supposed she would have to talk about it again. So different here from John Little's crowded kitchen.

"It *was* my fault," she said. "I went with that man to a pub. I got drunk, and then I went with him on the underground. I made everyone unhappy. I know. I'm sorry."

She didn't think she sounded very sorry. She sounded sullen and angry.

"Katherine!" her mother's voice broke.

Of course, her mother had suffered most of all, Katherine knew, nearly losing her daughter after losing Hal.

"I'm sorry," she said again more gently.

"I didn't mean your being kidnapped," said her father. "And I don't think that was your fault. You were too young to be wandering alone in a big city. And you were probably still upset by…well, you'd been upset for a long time. You didn't know what you were doing."

"I did," Katherine insisted. "I *did* know I was making up a story. I just didn't know how to stop. And I wasn't too young. I walked alone to work in the ghetto last summer when I was only fourteen!"

Katherine felt angry again, without knowing fully why.

"Gerald." Her mother sounded angry, too. "Say it."

There was a silence, a black pool of silence. Katherine wished she could dive into it and never surface, or surface in another world entirely.

"It wasn't your fault," her father said again. "What I did to you, the night Martin Luther King was shot. It wasn't your fault. You came to comfort me, and I did what no man should ever do to his daughter."

Her father was starting to cry, like he had that night. If she had a gun, she suddenly realized, she would shoot him.

"For a while I didn't remember what happened," he went on, "but I know now that's why you stopped studying and stayed in your room. And I know that's why I couldn't face you, and I, well, I was relieved when you went to England. And if it hadn't been for what I did, none of those awful things would have happened to you."

He had finally stopped talking. Did that mean she had to say something? She didn't want to. She didn't want to speak ever again.

"What your father did is called rape."

The metal of that gun was in her mother's voice, how cold it was.

"It is against law. He could go to jail. He has offered to turn himself in to the police."

Katherine looked up, startled. Her father's face was red and covered with sweat and tears. For Christ's sake, he had snot running from his nose. Without a word, she got up and went to get a tissue.

"Katherine!" her mother called after her.

Before either of them could follow her, she was back. Without looking at him, she handed her father a tissue. He blew his nose.

"Jesus Christ!" she said when he was done, still standing, not quite facing him. "Jesus Christ! Just leave me alone. And don't go to the goddamn police. I don't want to go to your fucking trial. I'm going back to England. To Robin's trial and the trials of those men who tried to snuff us, at least the two that are still alive."

Sick rose from her stomach into her throat as it always did when she thought of Mister Tobias hanging himself. It made him seem even more obscene. Feeling dizzy, she sat back down on the easy chair hard, so that it wheezed. Her parents were silent. She had silenced them.

"And by the way," she went on, "I know what rape is. I know a lot more about it than either of you do. And I know about people wanting to hurt other people on purpose. I guess what happened that night Martin Luther King died was rape. It was also a stupid, disgusting accident, and I don't ever want to talk about it again. Do you understand? Not. Ever. Again. What you did, it's your problem now. It has nothing to do with me."

She could breathe now. Breathing felt good. She thought she would just sit and do it for a while.

"Katherine," said her father.

Thank God he had stopped sniffling.

"I don't expect you to forgive me."

"Good," she said.

"But I still have to ask your forgiveness. I do ask your forgiveness."

She sat for another moment. There was a world outside, fields, trees, sun.

"Thank you," she heard herself saying. "I'm going to take Bear for a walk now."

And without rushing, she got up and went outside, closing the door quietly behind her.

Chapter Ninety

When she woke in the small hours of the morning, Lucy tiptoed down the hall to look in at Katherine, asleep in the sleigh bed with Lennon and McCartney who had shamelessly abandoned Lucy since Katherine had moved in a few weeks ago. Elsa, who never tired of teasing Lucy, now referred to Lucy's house as a home for wayward girl. She and Clara as well as Ralph and Sally James had come for supper that evening. Katherine's friend Aramantha had joined them after spending the afternoon drilling Katherine on Algebra II.

"So if you think X and Y are boring, use that wild imagination of yours, make up a story about them. Whatever you have to do to solve this equation!"

Aramantha had made it her personal mission to get Katherine back on the honor roll. In the late afternoon, Lucy had turned the girls outdoors to pick raspberries for a pie. Frankie had allowed himself to be served a large piece when he came to pick up Katherine for band rehearsal.

"He's not, well, not exactly my boyfriend," Katherine had told her. "But finally he admits I can sing. Bands with female vocalists are cool now. Because of Janis Joplin and Grace Slick."

(Who, with a host of other pop stars, were becoming household names in Lucy's own old-fashioned household.)

Frankie had fixed up an old jalopy. He never failed to have Katherine home by midnight (ten if it was a school night), the curfews everyone had agreed on. She was not really *in loco parentis*, Lucy told herself. Katherine's parents still made the decisions, some Lucy wouldn't have made herself. Of course Anne had to take Katherine to a gynecologist after all she'd been through, just to make sure she was all right. But Anne had decided it would be best for Katherine to take birth control pills, an idea Lucy could not get used to.

Katherine sleeping looked so young, her face softened to the child's face Lucy remembered so well. Having Katherine come to live with her instead of just staying a night or a weekend now and then was not something Lucy had undertaken lightly. She had been inclined to think that the Bradleys needed time to become a family again. She had said so the evening the Bradleys invited her over to discuss the idea. At Lucy's demurral, Katherine had gone very silent and then excused herself from the table. The twins had followed suit, and soon Gerald, too, found an excuse to leave the room.

Then Anne told Lucy what Gerald had done to Katherine, and everything made an awful kind of sense.

"Everything has changed, Lucy," Anne said. "Everything."

Lucy had wished Anne would not go on to put into words what Lucy had already guessed, but she did.

"You know, I think, how I feel about Joe. I don't expect you to approve. Well, that's not all. Gerald, Gerald has fallen in love, too."

"Perhaps you shouldn't tell me Gerald's secrets," Lucy protested.

"Oh, Lucy," Anne said. "I am so sick of secrets. I want to go shout everything from the rooftop. Besides, I don't think Gerald would care if I told you about Jeremiah."

"Jeremiah?" Lucy repeated confused.

"His co-worker in Riverton. That's who he loves. He wants to go with him to the Democratic Convention, and I told him go, just go."

Lucy sat trying to absorb what felt like an explosion. Nuclear family. She had always thought that was an absurd modern term. Now it felt more like an awful metaphor. This nuclear family was exploding. There would be nothing left.

"We're not going to separate, not yet," Anne went on, ignoring Lucy's silent distress. "This is a big house, room enough for us to lead semi-separate lives. I think it's better for the twins to have us both here. They got quite attached to Gerald while I was away. But Katherine, she can hardly stand to be in the same room with him."

It was too much, too much to take in all at once.

"If you don't mind, Anne," Lucy had said. "I need to take some time to think about it. You know I love Katherine, as if...."

"As if she were your own daughter," Anne finished. "I know. I've sometimes been a little jealous. You've always seemed to understand her better than I do. She's been through so much. I just want what's best for her. Anyway, it's what she wants."

Which might not, Lucy did not say, be the same thing.

Lucy had made an appointment with Father James the next day. She hadn't seen him except in passing since she had been back. And somewhat to her dismay, she found herself pouring out the whole story from the beginning, even though Father James already knew about the dreams. When she described meeting Robin face to face, attempting for the first time to put into words what it was like to look into those eyes she had looked out of, Lucy broke down and wept.

Father James just sat, quietly. His silence made her think of being alone in the church, with sun pouring in through the window of Jesus the good shepherd. Catching the dust motes, making the air seem like a living, substantial thing. His silence, she realized, reminded her of Robin.

"You know, Father James, Ralph," she amended when she could speak again, "I know we are supposed to see Christ in everyone, the least of these, but when I was with Robin, I felt as though he was really there, she...I'm sorry I am not making sense at all. She's, well, she's been arrested for homicide. And before that, she was pursuing this mad plan of living as a fugitive in the forest with all those girls, those lost girls...."

"Well," Father James spoke at last, his tone mild and light," it's not really so far-fetched. Jesus had a lot of somewhat clueless ex-fisherman following him. And then he was sentenced to death for sedition."

And suddenly they were both laughing, merrily, helplessly.

"And the girls are found now, more or less?" Father James asked when they subsided.

As found as they could be, Doreen and Maggie staying with Jen Albutt, Vicky, Bernadette, and Sarita camping out with Rowena. And Robin—hadn't she been a lost girl, too?—in HM Prison Holloway where she was awaiting trial.

"And you, Lucy" said Father James, "you've found your own lost girl."

"Yes," Lucy hesitated.

She did not feel it was right to tell him about what Gerald had done to Katherine.

"I understand," he said.

And she understood that he was under the seal of the confessional.

"It makes me sad," Lucy said, "to see that family breaking apart...." She mustn't say more. She didn't know what was going to happen. "It's just that, I never had a family of my own, I mean a husband, children. I always thought if I had...."

He waited a minute and then he finished her sentence.

"You would never be alone or lost or uncertain of your purpose."

"Yes," she acknowledged, "I suppose that's it. Really, I know better. Or maybe I mean I don't know. I don't know anything at all."

The silence fell around them again, a comfortable silence, like an old worn flannel shirt.

"Lucy," he said at length, "we can't know what is best for anyone else. We only know what the Bradleys are asking of you. Rather a lot, I'd say. The real question is whether you are game for it, taking on a teenaged girl, who's been through all kinds of horror, who has more horror to face when she attends those trials."

"I've already promised to go back with her for the trials," Lucy said.

"That is different from having her come and live with you in your home. Only you can know if you want to give up your peaceful life or if you are willing to risk whatever it might mean."

Risk? The word startled her. Risk?

And then she heard Katherine's brave voice, singing out to save Robin, risking death herself.

"Yes," she said. "Yes, I am willing."

Lucy watched now as Katherine stirred restlessly in her sleep. Then she cried out, sitting bolt upright looking blindly into the night, clearly not sure, for a moment, where she was. Startled, Lennon and McCartney sprang down from the bed and ran past Lucy as she came in and sat on Katherine's bed.

"Lucy?" said Katherine.

"I'm here," Lucy said. "You're here."

"Good," Katherine whispered.

As Katherine lay back down, Lucy sat and prayed silently, *Defend, O Lord, this thy child from all the perils of this night.*

When Katherine slept again, Lucy tiptoed back to her own room, pausing by the window to look out at her garden now just visible in the first dawn light.